PRAISE FOR BRIAN

T0013132

What Can't Be Seen

"The book's well-constructed plot matches its three-dimensional characters. Psychological-thriller fans will be eager for more."

—*Publishers Weekly*

A Familiar Sight

"A horrific brew for readers willing to immerse themselves in it."

—*Kirkus Reviews*

"A strong plot and unforgettable characters make this a winner. Labuskes is on a roll."

—*Publishers Weekly*

"*A Familiar Sight* has everything I crave in a thriller: a shocking, addictive female lead; unexpected twists that snapped off the page; and an ending that made me gasp out loud. I never saw it coming, but it was perfectly in sync with the razor-sharp balance between creepy and compelling that Labuskes carries throughout the novel. This is a one-sitting read."

—Jess Lourey, Amazon Charts bestselling author

Her Final Words

"Labuskes skillfully ratchets up the suspense. Readers will eagerly await her next."

—*Publishers Weekly*

"Labuskes offers an intense mystery with an excellent character in Lucy, who methodically uncovers layers of deceit while trusting no one."

—Library Journal

Girls of Glass

"Excellent . . . Readers who enjoy having their expectations upset will be richly rewarded."

—Publishers Weekly (starred review)

It Ends with Her

"Once in a while a character comes along who gets under your skin and refuses to let go. This is the case with Brianna Labuskes's Clarke Sinclair—a cantankerous, rebellious, and somehow endearingly likable FBI agent with a troubled past. I was immediately pulled into Clarke's broken, shadow-filled world and her quest for justice and redemption. A stunning thriller, *It Ends with Her* is not to be missed."

—Heather Gudenkauf, New York Times bestselling author

"*It Ends with Her* is a gritty, riveting roller-coaster ride of a book. Brianna Labuskes has created a layered, gripping story around a cast of characters that readers will cheer for. Her crisp prose and quick plot kept me reading with my heart in my throat. Highly recommended for fans of smart thrillers with captivating heroines."

—Nicole Baart, author of Little Broken Things

"An engrossing psychological thriller filled with twists and turns. I couldn't put it down! The characters were filled with emotional depth. An impressive debut!"

—Elizabeth Blackwell, author of In the Shadow of Lakecrest

SEE

IT

END

OTHER TITLES BY BRIANNA LABUSKES

Dr. Gretchen White Novels

What Can't Be Seen

A Familiar Sight

Stand-Alone Novels

Her Final Words

Black Rock Bay

Girls of Glass

It Ends with Her

SEE
IT
END

BRIANNA LABUSKES

THOMAS & MERCER

This is a work of fiction. Names, characters, organizations, places, events, and incidents are either products of the author's imagination or are used fictitiously. Otherwise, any resemblance to actual persons, living or dead, is purely coincidental.

Text copyright © 2023 by Brianna Labuskes
All rights reserved.

No part of this book may be reproduced, or stored in a retrieval system, or transmitted in any form or by any means, electronic, mechanical, photocopying, recording, or otherwise, without express written permission of the publisher.

Published by Thomas & Mercer, Seattle

www.apub.com

Amazon, the Amazon logo, and Thomas & Mercer are trademarks of Amazon.com, Inc., or its affiliates.

ISBN-13: 9781542035545 (paperback)
ISBN-13: 9781542035538 (digital)

Cover design by Rex Bonomelli
Cover image: © monkeybusinessimages / Getty Images

Printed in the United States of America

To Charlotte Herscher
For the many ways you've helped me grow as a writer.
And for loving Gretchen as much as I do.

CHAPTER ONE

GRETCHEN

Now

Dr. Gretchen White wondered if her steak knife was sharp enough to open up her date's carotid artery. She lovingly pictured the warm splash of blood that would follow, the flap of serrated skin, the goldfish gape of his mouth.

"So then you own the digital image . . ." The man went on, unaware that he was one more migraine-inducing story away from a violent end.

For most people, the threat was hyperbolic, but Gretchen knew she had to remove herself from the situation before her control truly slipped. She was often just a hairbreadth away from consigning that *nonviolent* part of her diagnosis as a sociopath to hell.

She had made it to thirty-eight years old without having murdered anyone, though, and this sad excuse for a dinner companion wasn't going to break her streak.

Gretchen stood while the man was midsentence, and walked away from the table, the quick click of her stilettos matching the pulse that had spiked with rage.

From a lifetime of experience, she knew the emotion was dispro-portionate, knew it would simmer into almost nothing if she gave it even a little bit of time. But while it burned bright, she decided she would aim it at the person who should really take the blame for tonight.

Detective Lauren Marconi, who tried to convince Gretchen she was normal, that she could sit in a trendy restaurant and pretend politeness for the length of an entire dinner.

Gretchen had to put up with things far worse than a dull date, both in her personal life and as a consultant for the Boston Police Department. But she had a finely tuned appreciation for the cost and the benefit of any given situation. The BPD cases helped scratch an itch that she would have had to turn to more dubious methods to satiate. They were worth the effort it took to rein in her impulses.

In tonight's cost-benefit ratio, the benefit of sitting through the rest of her current date would be a romp in bed that—given the way he'd talked about himself all night—would likely be disappointing. Walking away was the right choice for everyone involved.

Outside the restaurant, Gretchen stopped, leaned against the brick wall, dug her fingernails into her palms to give herself something to focus on beside the savage desire that still whispered sweet nothings in her ear.

When that didn't work, she dipped her hand into her purse for her phone and opened the text thread with Marconi. The latest message was just a string of knife emojis that Gretchen had sent while her date had been talking at her. He hadn't faltered one bit at her deliberate rudeness.

The message to Marconi was marked as read, but she hadn't responded.

Gretchen's finger hovered over the call icon. Marconi usually answered her texts when she saw them, even if it was just with an eye roll.

After a moment's debate, Gretchen put the phone to sleep. She wasn't in the mood to burn bridges, and that's what would happen if she talked to Marconi right now. Instead, she just rested her head against the brick wall.

The sky had deepened from burnished gold to velvet blue during the time Gretchen had been inside, and a light mist cooled her overheated skin as she turned her face toward the newborn moon.

"You're not as dangerous or mysterious as you like to think, Dr. White," Marconi had told her six months ago, after they'd cleared Gretchen's name from three-decades-old murder charges.

At the time, riding high on her own impeccable control, Gretchen had nearly agreed. She almost hated Marconi now for giving her that hope. This dinner was one in a line of Gretchen's stabs at normality since she'd learned she hadn't killed her aunt in cold blood as a child. Not all her attempts ended this way, but enough did that Gretchen wondered why she was chasing *normal* so hard.

Yet it was a hard habit to break once you started.

She pushed off the wall and then turned down the alley where she'd parked her Porsche. Despite the fact that she'd left it unlocked, it was still there, untouched.

Gretchen let herself enjoy the thrill of that. Everyone always walked around so scared, clutching purses and pearls, and installing every dead bolt on the market. It was so much more interesting to just see what would happen when she let fate take the wheel. She hadn't lost a car yet.

Except tonight there was someone waiting for her in the passenger seat. In the dim light of the alley, it was just a shadow, but as Gretchen moved forward, it shifted into a familiar shape.

"I'm sending you some kind of bill for emotional trauma for that date," Gretchen said, after she yanked open the door.

Marconi's dark bangs were plastered to her forehead, her eyes deep pools of an emotion Gretchen couldn't read. Her whole body sagged as if she'd been holding herself in perfect stillness, waiting for Gretchen.

"Or not," Gretchen murmured, scanning her for injuries.

There was dried blood in the beds of her fingernails, on her shirt.

"Who did you kill?" Gretchen asked. Because it wasn't a question of *if*.

Marconi stared at her, unblinking. "You have to promise me something."

Gretchen didn't say anything, but there was no way in hell she was going to promise Marconi anything, not when she looked like this— pushed to the very edge of sanity.

At her hesitation, Marconi's hand lashed out, gripped Gretchen's wrist, hard, so that there would be half crescents in Gretchen's flesh where her fingernails dug in. "Promise me. Don't investigate."

"Stop being melodramatic." Gretchen heard the edge in her own voice. "We'll get rid of the body. Easy."

The corner of Marconi's mouth twitched up, and something vulnerable and fond flickered across her expression. Then it went neutral once more. "It's too late for that."

That was stupid. "It's never too late."

"Gretchen, listen." Marconi was almost desperate now. "I did it, okay? I know you. You're going to think I was framed, or, or . . ." She shook her head. "But I wasn't. It was me."

She held out her hands as if the blood would prove a point.

Except it did the opposite.

Gretchen had no one to blame but herself for not realizing it sooner. Marconi wouldn't have come to her like this. She was a cop, and a damn good one at that. If she'd killed someone, she would have cleaned up the evidence.

And once Gretchen realized that, it struck her how odd this was. Marconi seeking her out to beg her not to get involved with whatever this was. But by doing so she was getting Gretchen involved. Marconi knew her too well to believe she'd just listen.

Gretchen's eyes narrowed. "You're lying."

Marconi huffed out a laugh that was stripped of any amusement. "I'm really, really not. I just wanted to say goodbye."

Then she was out of the car, on the street, gone in the next blink of an eye.

Gretchen wanted to chase after her but knew it would be fruitless. She cursed, soft at first.

The word didn't reverberate like she wanted it to, though.

She swore again, loud and hard and crude, and it bounced satisfactorily off the low roof, sinking back into Gretchen's chest, fluttering and then settling there.

For one glorious second, Gretchen let herself panic.

And then she pulled out her phone and called a number she'd never thought she'd willingly dial.

CHAPTER TWO

LAUREN

Then

Lauren Marconi pressed her forehead to the frosted glass of the back door of her shitty apartment.

She clutched the thick, handmade mug of coffee between both hands, breathing in the steam as she tried to wake up properly.

This was going to be a long day.

Vermont was no stranger to blizzards, but according to the local news Lauren had chattering on in the background, this one was already getting billed as the storm of the decade.

Lauren's phone rang, and she picked it up with a grunt of acknowledgment.

"Hey." Montpelier PD's Investigation Division Chief, Imani Abaza, didn't wait for Lauren to respond before continuing in her clipped, no-nonsense way. "The chief wants all hands on deck today doing patrols."

Though Abaza couldn't see her, Lauren nodded. She'd expected as much. Anytime there was a potentially catastrophic weather event, the lines between specific beats started to blend. "Partners?"

"No. One a car," Abaza said. "Don't bother coming in—the ice has already started. I'll text coordinates for your shift."

From where she was standing, Lauren could just make out the SUV that was already layered with snow. She took a deep swallow of coffee and tried to dredge up the will to go scrape through the powder that had settled over the black-and-white exterior. "'Kay."

"I don't have to remind you the hospitals are already at seventy-five percent capacity," Abaza said, mostly like she was trying to wake Lauren up fully.

Lauren dragged a hand over her face. "I hear you."

She pulled the phone away from her ear and ended the call. Abaza would text her where she needed to patrol, and Lauren was far from a rookie. She didn't need the lectures.

A blizzard meant power outages, which meant the city's most vulnerable caught without food, water, or in the most dire situations, oxygen. People couldn't evacuate because the storm was supposed to sit on top of New England, settling in nice and comfy for the next few days.

The rest of the coffee burned down Lauren's esophagus, and she spared a thought for the cold case she'd just started to dig into in her spare time the week before. She wanted to be promoted to detective within the next few years, and studying the old investigations helped sharpen her skills. The most recent one came from a friend of a friend up in Burlington, who'd gotten a little weepy at a bar over the case. Eight-year-old Peter Stone had been taken in broad daylight, and there had been no leads, no ransom note, no body.

She wished she had more time for him, but he'd spent eight years in a dusty archive box. A few more days wouldn't matter.

Lauren sighed and glanced at the clock.

Rafael should be getting to the fire station for his EMT shift within the next five minutes. She hadn't seen him in the past week, but his schedule was taped to the fridge.

She hit "Call" on his contact name without thinking too hard about it.

"Can't talk, babe," Rafi said, sounding for all the world like he was about to hang up on her.

"I know," Lauren rushed to say, feeling silly and foolish and all of twelve years old. "I just wanted to say be careful today."

A pause. Shuffling in the background and then a siren. "I should be saying that to you."

"You should be," she teased, closing her eyes, her forehead cold against the glass once more.

"You'd slit my throat if I told you that," Rafi said on a laugh, and then someone in the distance called his name. "I've got to go."

The line went dead before she could even reply.

Lauren sighed, tossed the phone on the cracked laminate kitchen table, and then stretched until her spine popped once, twice.

Movement in the doorway between the kitchen and the living room caught her attention, and she shifted, smiling.

"I've packed my bag for Aunt Sandy's," Elijah said with a gap-toothed smile that had her crossing the room to gather him in her arms. Lauren truly didn't know what she would do without Sandy. Even though they weren't technically family, her friend loved Elijah like he really was her nephew, and had a flexible-enough schedule to help out on days like these.

Lauren pressed a sloppy kiss to Elijah's temple. "You're going to be good for her, right? It might be a couple days."

Elijah wiped at the spot. At seven, he was getting too old for affection. "I'm not a baby."

Lauren pulled him tighter, rocking him to and fro until Elijah dissolved into giggles. "You'll always be *my* baby."

Breaking free, still laughing, Elijah half turned to her, that sweet baby smile carving out a dimple in his cheek. "Mom, you're so embarrassing."

"Yup," Lauren said, mussing his hair and grabbing her car keys at the same time. "That's my job."

CHAPTER THREE

GRETCHEN

Now

Lachlan Gibbs, the rising star of the Boston PD's Internal Affairs Department, answered after one ring.

"Marconi's about to be arrested," Gretchen said, not mincing words.

Thick, staticky silence greeted her; then the line went dead.

Gretchen cursed again, tossed her phone onto the passenger seat that was probably still warm from Marconi's body, and jammed her key into the ignition. The beautiful thing about not being a slave to emotions was that in times like these she could actually think straight, gather her thoughts.

But, if she were being brutally honest with herself, there wasn't much to find there.

Despite the fact that over the past year Marconi had become something close to a friend, Gretchen only really knew two hard facts about her.

The first was that her family was all dead, and she hadn't seemed too cut up about it on the few times Gretchen had brought it up.

And the second was that Marconi was dating Lachlan Gibbs.

Even when Gretchen and Marconi spent time together outside of working cases, Marconi tended toward reticence when it came to personal information. Gretchen wasn't the type to talk about someone else's life if they weren't going to offer the details up themselves. That's just not how she was wired.

She would have had to have been blind and an idiot not to notice Marconi's thick defenses, though. At times, Gretchen had been let inside them. On occasion, she'd gotten herself pushed right back out. She would have had to have been blind and an idiot not to know Marconi had shadows in her eyes.

But Gretchen had no idea whom Marconi would kill if given the chance.

That was, *if* she'd killed someone. Gretchen was far from convinced despite her initial promises to Marconi that they could get rid of the body.

Gretchen managed not to clip any cars or pedestrians on the way back to her apartment, and as she let herself in, she glanced at her phone to see if Lachlan had called back.

Nothing.

She pressed her thumbs into her eyes to get herself to focus as she swayed in her entryway. How long would it take for the cops to catch up to Marconi? Why had she used her last minutes of freedom to find Gretchen only to tell her goodbye and nothing else useful?

If either of them were the sentimental type, maybe Gretchen could have bought that excuse. But that wasn't them. They expressed their friendship through snark and pizza.

Plus, Gretchen could easily visit Marconi in jail. There was no reason to act like they'd never see each other again. That made Gretchen pause.

People said goodbye when they were planning to kill themselves.

The taste of metal bloomed on her tongue as she bit her cheek until the skin broke open.

Her phone rang.

"Are you watching?" Lachlan asked.

Gretchen didn't answer, just reached for her remote and turned on the closest news station. She swallowed the mix of saliva and blood in relief.

Marconi's face greeted her. It was gritty bystander-shot camera footage, but Gretchen would recognize Marconi anywhere.

She was on the sidewalk outside the police station, her shoulders pulled back unnaturally, hands clearly in cuffs. Uniforms were on both sides of her.

The chyron blared that a Boston Police Department detective had been arrested in connection with a murder up in Waltham.

The victim—Owen Hayes—was male, forty-nine years old, white, leaving behind a wife and child. Motive for the killing: unknown.

"God, you're useless," Gretchen spat into the phone.

"She called the head of IA and turned herself in," Lachlan said. "It was all over before I even got to the station."

Gretchen wanted to slap him, gut him with that serrated blade from the restaurant, even. What good was it that Marconi was sleeping with the rising star of Internal Affairs if he couldn't sweep a murder charge under the rug for her? "You didn't do enough. Why is it on the goddamn news ten seconds after it happened?"

Lachlan ignored the question. "She came to you. She told you something."

Which was the only reason Lachlan had bothered to call her back at all. He wanted what she knew; otherwise he would have locked her out of the investigation entirely.

Likewise, Gretchen had no loyalty to Lachlan Gibbs. In fact, he hated her, thought her the worst kind of person with nothing to offer the department except a bad reputation. The only reason she'd called him in the first place was because she'd been hoping he could help Marconi avoid this exact spectacle.

Now that it was a done deal, there was no need to keep Lachlan in the loop whatsoever.

"Nope, just a premonition," she said as cheerily as she could before she hung up and blocked his number.

———

Twenty minutes later, Gretchen found herself standing outside Marconi's apartment. She wouldn't have much time until the BPD obtained a search warrant for the place.

A month ago, Gretchen had made herself a copy of Marconi's keys—something she did with anyone she had constant and continual contact with on a semidaily basis, just in case. Some people might have deemed the practice creepy and/or invasive, but Gretchen was proud of her foresight. It meant she now had access to the condo without making it look like someone had broken in.

The living room was dark and as tidy as it always was. Marconi didn't have a lot of personal items, Gretchen realized now. She'd decorated with paintings and bright colors on the walls, knickknacks and tchotchkes to make it feel lived in. No one would come in here and think there was anything suspicious going on. But the closer Gretchen looked, the more obvious it was. There were no personal photos, no books scattered over side tables, no junk mail piled up.

This apartment could have been anyone's.

Gretchen had seen this kind of thing in homes of people in witness protection. Enough of a personality to fit in, not enough to draw attention.

How had Gretchen not noticed that before?

Right now, it worked in her favor. Anything important, anything Marconi cared about, would stand out among the bland nothingness.

Who was Owen Hayes to Marconi? Gretchen silently asked the apartment.

It gave her nothing helpful in return.

Marconi's computer sat on the desk tucked perfectly into the corner by the window. It was obviously tempting, but she knew she wouldn't get any information from it. A few months ago, they'd been working late on a case in the apartment, and when Marconi had gone to get their takeout, Gretchen had tried to log on to the laptop. Just out of curiosity.

It had been completely locked down with two-factor authentication. Maybe the police would be able to scrounge something off it. That was beyond Gretchen's skill set, though.

Instinct told her that Marconi wouldn't keep anything crucial on there anyway. Most likely, she used it for online shopping and boring social media posts.

Gretchen's eyes traced over the living room, the little galley kitchen. Marconi wouldn't hide something where anyone could stumble over it. She wasn't a believer in plain sight doing the trick to keep important things safe. She was a believer in dark spaces and hefty locks.

Marconi was also a believer in her own ability to protect what she cared about.

Which meant anything of value would be kept in the bedroom.

It took Gretchen ten minutes to find the hidden panel in the bed-side table. It took her less than a minute to extract the thumb drive that had been stashed there, return everything to how it had been, and then leave the apartment as if she'd never been there at all.

She didn't bother to wipe down what she'd touched throughout the place.

Anyone working the case knew Gretchen's fingerprints would be all over Marconi's life.

CHAPTER FOUR

MARTHA

Before

Apples with swollen bellies littered the ground beneath Martha Hayes's boots.

Fall had come and nearly gone, and Martha had arrived too late to save these souls. She kicked one just to watch it roll, but instead it broke apart, its rancid guts spilling out from broken skin.

They would have to pay to remove the carcasses.

How much did something like that cost?

Thick arms wrapped around her, pulling her back against a once-beloved barrel-shaped chest.

Owen's chin came to rest on her shoulder, his stubble brushing against her sensitive skin. She couldn't remember how many times she'd told him to keep his face clean-shaven.

He'd long ago stopped listening to her.

"I think we'll like it here," he said, breath already saturated with whiskey.

When they'd been younger, she'd found his drinking appealing. It was hard to imagine that she had, their lives so changed since then. But she'd liked the way he would bring a flask to the fancy restaurants they'd pretended they could actually afford. Liked how he'd laughed, as warm as the rum in her belly. Liked how she'd giggled along with him.

She rested her hand on top of her womb.

Owen hadn't noticed that she'd stopped drinking.

I think we'll like it here.

Martha wanted to ask if he would stop now. But did something as monstrous as what lived in Owen ever go away? Didn't creatures like that thrive in the dark, where Owen tried to keep it caged?

He tried, she knew he did.

It wasn't his fault that the monster was bigger than both of them.

"Come on, I'm freezing my balls off," he growled, and Martha nearly rolled her eyes from the vulgarity, no longer finding it so charming.

His workman boots crushed another one of the apples as he turned back to the house, but he didn't even pause.

Martha stared at the ground and thought once more that they would have to pay to remove the carcasses.

How much did something like that cost?

CHAPTER FIVE

GRETCHEN

Now

By the time Gretchen made it back to her apartment, thumb drive safely hidden in the inside pocket of her blazer, the media had leaped on Marconi's arrest with vigor, detailing the case with glee poorly hidden behind slick lips and thick fake eyelashes and serious expressions.

The details played on repeat.

Around 8:00 p.m., someone had entered the home of Owen Hayes of Waltham, setting off the alarm. By the time the security company dispatched the police ten minutes later, Hayes was on the carpet with two bullet holes in the back of his head.

No intruder had been found at the scene.

The wife and daughter had been out to dinner, and the hostess had been able to confirm both had been at the table for a half hour in either direction of that ten-minute window of time.

When the police reviewed footage from the Ring camera on the Hayeses' front door, the only person captured entering the house was Boston Police Detective Lauren Marconi.

In their feverish excitement, the reporters failed to note that the back door and windows could have also served as entry points for an intruder. That there could have been someone in the house before Marconi had gone in.

The bleached-blonde anchor with the nasally voice instead focused on the fact that the execution-style murder seemed to rule out self-defense. Marconi wouldn't be able to use that as a possible excuse if all this went to trial.

Gretchen thought about the blood crusted in Marconi's nail beds, the smear on her shirt. She had touched the body. Left her prints on it.

Sloppy, careless.

From the cases they'd worked together, Gretchen knew that was out of character. Marconi was plenty of things, but sloppy wasn't one of them.

Did that mean Marconi was more likely to be guilty or less?

She would guess the latter. If Marconi had gone into that house to kill Hayes, she would have made sure to wear gloves, to keep away from spatter, to avoid the goddamn security camera.

Gretchen dug out her computer—plus the converter she'd need to make the thumb drive work on it—and with her free hand grabbed her phone. She dialed the number she'd blocked only an hour ago.

"Who is he?" she asked when Lachlan answered. She was almost surprised that he did.

"No one," Lachlan bit out. "A fucking no one."

"Yeah," Gretchen agreed, cataloging the way he swore. In the many years that Gretchen had known Lachlan Gibbs, he'd never once dropped an obscenity harsher than *damn*. Maybe that's why he'd picked up the phone—too agitated to even be bothered to block her. "Who is he?"

"I told you—"

"You told me nothing," Gretchen cut in. Irritated now. She longed to hang up on him. But she breathed instead, thought about the endless void that was this mystery haunting both of them now. "Who is Owen Hayes?"

"No one," Lachlan repeated, the staccato cadence of his own voice revealing his impatience. Neither of them respected the other or enjoyed working together, but it was clear they'd formed a little partnership whether they liked it or not. That's what happened when you needed something from someone. "He's boring as hell, a middle-aged pencil pusher. Until about eight years ago, he owned a farm in northern Vermont. From there he moved his family to Waltham to do freelance bookkeeping for a variety of small businesses." Lachlan must have heard her next question. "Not the mob. Nothing more salacious than a mom-and-pop grocery store."

Gretchen tapped her fingers against the wood of her desk. "Do we know what brought him here?"

"Not yet."

"Was Marconi ever in Vermont?" Gretchen asked, but mostly to herself. She leaned forward to wake up her computer, to open a search page. "Where'd she transfer from?"

Marconi had joined the Boston PD only a year prior, and she'd never been forthcoming on where she'd been before. All that Gretchen had been able to tell was that she hadn't been a local.

"Amherst for eight years," Lachlan said. A beat passed, and Gretchen heard typing in the background. He hadn't known much about Marconi, either.

What did that say about their relationship?

Or, really, what did that say about Marconi?

Marconi's reluctance to talk about personal information had struck Gretchen as normal for a woman working in a chauvinist-dominated field.

Now it was obvious that Marconi had gravitated toward Gretchen for the very reason that she was someone who would pry only when she sensed a mystery that could be solved or when she could use a tidbit for future manipulation efforts. Beyond that, Gretchen had no interest in anyone's messy emotional life as long as it didn't relate to her.

Lachlan swore under his breath, and Gretchen knew what was coming. "Eight years ago she transferred to Amherst from Montpelier." He added unnecessarily, "Vermont."

"Does Hayes have a record?" Gretchen asked. "Anything?"

She could practically hear Lachlan debating whether to divulge the information. Once upon a time he would have cut out his own tongue before sharing anything with her, but the circumstances had changed. Normal people thought they were so above the cost-benefit ratio that defined her life, but when it came down to it, they were no better than her.

After a beat, he gave in, probably knowing it would come out in the tabloids at the very least. Those vultures always found the dirt. Sometimes Gretchen even fed it to them.

"A recent domestic-disturbance tip that fizzled into nothing," Lachlan said. "When the police got there, the wife was confused at what could have even prompted the call."

"Obviously she was going to say that if she got cold feet."

"Call was anonymous," Lachlan said, unruffled by Gretchen's tone. "Vague. I'm looking at the transcript now and I . . . almost believe her."

"What aren't you saying?" Gretchen asked.

"I think there's a chance Lauren called it in," he said. "As a way to get cops into the house. She was . . ." He stopped, cleared his throat. "Lauren was using BPD resources to keep tabs on Hayes. I have to believe it wasn't a new pattern."

Gretchen ran her hand over her mouth. "What kind of resources?"

"Database privileges," Lachlan rattled off. "Drive-bys."

Gretchen pulled the phone away from her ear, put it on mute, and then hurled an expensive vase at the wall. The thing shattered, the glass raining down on the floor.

If it had just been a few searches on the computer, the prosecutor couldn't have built much of a case around that. Most cops had some personal vendetta they kept track of. But drive-bys . . . those were harder to hand-wave away.

That was manpower. And the chief of police didn't take kindly to being used.

Gretchen unmuted once more.

"That's quite an easy story to tell, isn't it?" When it came to trial by jury, too often a well-told story mattered more than the truth.

"Not sure it's just a story," Lachlan said, quietly. "If she had it out for this guy, who's to say she didn't just snap?"

Gretchen would be the first person to say anyone was capable of murder, the first to say things didn't have to make sense for them to actually have happened. But there was something about it all that wasn't adding up. Every time she reached for why, though, the reason dissolved.

"What is she looking at?" Gretchen needed to know what she was working with here. "Sentencing-wise."

"No chance at a self-defense plea. It was an execution-style shooting," Lachlan said, grim and sure.

Which meant life without parole. There would be no pleading down if Marconi was found guilty. And Gretchen would put good money on Cormac Byrne snatching up the case. With an eye on the White House, the sharklike district attorney had a track record of going hard on cops who found their way into the courts. While normally Gretchen enjoyed him tearing into the department, in this case it didn't serve her purposes.

He would try to make an example out of Marconi.

"No," Gretchen said.

"Excuse me?"

"No, Marconi won't be going to jail." She said it slow and clear because she was talking to an idiot.

Silence. And then: "Gretchen, she—"

"You're a shit boyfriend, you know," Gretchen cut in.

Lachlan cleared his throat, and she wondered if he was swallowing the urge to lash out at her. Maybe he saw them like they were in a lifeboat together—more painful to keep up the vitriol than to just try to get along.

"You saw her," he said. "She didn't even clean up."

"I saw a police detective who happened upon a crime scene and whose instincts kicked in so that she checked the body for a pulse," Gretchen said, letting him hear every ounce of her contempt. Because she had no problem making this as thorny as possible. "But no, you're absolutely right, Detective Gibbs, I should write her off as dead and gone already."

"It doesn't matter what I think, Dr. White," Lachlan said, and before she could hang up on him, he added, "I'm not on the case."

The news shouldn't have shocked her, but it did. "Why the hell not?"

"You know why."

The rational side of her, the one that had kept her sociopathic impulses in check for thirty-eight years, told her to keep her mouth shut. But despite her bravado, she knew she wasn't completely in control of herself at the moment. Choosing release valves was probably beneficial for them all in the long run. "Because you're screwing her."

She thought that might be his breaking point. But he probably saw himself as too good to get ruffled by her. It was a powerful thing—what stories people told about their own personalities.

"Yes" was all he said.

"It kills me to point this out," Gretchen said, "but you're the best person to investigate the case."

"Because you're the arbiter of ethics when it comes to police cases," Lachlan drawled. So not all his edges had been sanded down.

"Please, I'd do a better job of it than you lot do," Gretchen said. "If Marconi wanted to kill someone, do you think she'd get caught?"

Marconi wasn't some bumbling amateur here. She worked as a homicide detective in Boston—a city that specialized in such things. If she'd wanted someone dead, no one would have ever found the body.

You're going to think I was framed.

But if Marconi really had killed Hayes, why would she have even bothered to talk to Gretchen? It was like telling someone not to think of a pink elephant—of course they were going to think of a pink elephant, that's how the brain worked. Marconi saying Gretchen shouldn't assume she'd been framed only introduced the idea into Gretchen's mind.

It didn't help that two of the biggest cases they'd worked together had involved suspects who looked like they were guilty as hell only to be found innocent later.

"That's the argument you're making?" Lachlan asked. "What, are they calling you as a witness for the prosecution?"

"The argument I'm making is that she's being framed, you absolute jackass." Gretchen's skin felt too tight around her bones. She'd gotten complacent in mostly working with Marconi over the past year. They'd bickered, they'd teased, but they'd always fit somehow. More than Gretchen ever had with anyone else. "Every single person in Internal Affairs is going to assume she's guilty and act accordingly. Her only chance is if you take the case."

Silence.

Gretchen scratched at her wrist too hard, enjoying the sharp little sparks of pain that raced up along her nerve endings.

She'd never given Lachlan much credit. While she could acknowledge that he had a brilliant mind, it wasn't a flexible one. He thought in black and white, of good guys and bad guys, and there was no in between. There was no place for someone like Gretchen White in his orderly little world.

No matter that she'd never hurt anyone irreparably, never willfully murdered anyone, never committed a major crime beyond self-defense. No matter that she actually tried harder than most people not to do any of those things because she didn't have the wiring that told her implicitly that it was wrong.

Normally, Gretchen didn't care. But she needed Lachlan now as a liaison to the department. No one would assign her to the case officially, but Lachlan wouldn't be able to help himself. He'd want any information she had, and she would make him trade for it.

She made her voice go butter soft. "You're her chance. Her only chance."

"And you're a manipulative shit," Lachlan shot back, and Gretchen bit her bottom lip to keep from grinning because he hadn't hung up. "I'm not going to work on the case, but I'll keep my ear to the ground."

"Do better than that."

"That's what you're getting," he said, the finality in his voice clear. She had a feeling that if she pushed him, he'd take a leave of absence or something equally melodramatic.

When she didn't argue, he quietly asked, "What if it turns out she's guilty?"

Gretchen rolled her eyes. This was going to be a long few days.

"Then we start downloading blueprints for the state prison system."

CHAPTER SIX

LAUREN

Then

When Elijah had turned six, Lauren had let him watch *Star Wars* for the first time. That's all she could think about as she drove the long dirt road to one of her last stops for the night, the snow pelting her window, the sky a dark velvet backdrop that could have been the infinite universe.

It was nearing nine at night, and she'd been on duty since eight that morning, after she'd dropped Elijah off at Sandy's. School had been canceled preemptively, and when Lauren had kissed them both goodbye, they'd already been busy plotting what movie marathon to put on for the day.

The SUV skidded and lurched as the tires hit an ice-slicked ditch, and Lauren's fingers tightened around the wheel, knuckles white.

Her headlights had been made mostly useless by the storm, but she continued on anyway. She was answering a domestic-disturbance call, a tip from a neighbor. Although she'd vaguely recognized the street name, she hadn't pictured the farmhouse being so far out of town.

With the properties the size they were, it was strange that a good Samaritan would have heard anything to warrant contacting the police. Even on a clear night, she wasn't sure she could *see* the closest neighbor.

But still, even though all she wanted to do was go home, crawl into bed, and sleep for twelve hours, she couldn't just write the call off as illegitimate.

The house loomed, stark and white and picturesque against the storm. The barn stood to its side along with a small windowless shed. Just like most working farms in the area, this one had shifted toward tourism and apple picking in the past few years, with gaudy advertising painted on the side of the barn, the word HAYES peeking out through the snow.

Lauren pulled as close to the porch as she could before jumping out.

Her boots sank into deep powder, the drift coming nearly to her knees, jeans already clinging to her legs from too many stops just like this one. She cursed herself for not bringing more than one extra pair.

The cold cut into her bones almost immediately. With most blizzards, the flakes came down deceptively gently, but not this one. The storm raged with its full force, wild and fierce and terrifying. Nature at her most daunting.

The enticing heat from the car beckoned, but she slammed the door and ran for the steps. This was her last call, and it was likely nothing. A false report, someone hearing screams where really there was only wind.

She rapped on the screen and then rang the bell for good measure, bouncing to stay warm. Living in New England had a way of toughening a person up, but tonight was cold even for the heartiest Vermonter.

Just as Lauren started contemplating knocking again—or better yet marking this down as a waste of time and climbing back into the SUV—the door swung open.

A man stood there, backlit by some distant glow from inside the house. From what she could see of him, he was medium height, medium weight. Brown hair. Average.

Lauren grappled for her badge, flashing it in a distracted gesture. "Evening, I'm Montpelier police officer Lauren Marconi. Just checking to make sure everything's okay out here."

The man didn't say anything.

She still couldn't see his face.

"We had a report that there was a disturbance on the property."

Nothing.

Lauren shifted her weight onto the balls of her feet.

"Who is it?" a woman's voice called from somewhere behind the man.

"A cop," the man answered without taking his eyes off Lauren. He didn't let her in despite the vicious wind that cruelly found every gap in her clothing. "I think there's been some mistake."

Lauren couldn't tell if he was talking to her or the woman, but it didn't matter. In the next moment, the voice had a face. The woman was nearly as petite as Lauren's own five feet one. She had a sweetheart face, and dark shoulder-length hair with severe bangs that reminded Lauren of that famous actress who was quirky and beautiful and very popular. Zooey Deschanel, some distant part of her brain supplied.

In situations like this, Lauren had learned early on how to quickly scan for signs of abuse. Bruises being the obvious thing to look for, but there were others, too. Body language, the way the couple touched or didn't touch. Too-bright voices or brittle voices or raspy ones—the kind that betrayed meaty hands around a vulnerable throat.

But this woman had the open, friendly demeanor of someone surprised with a visit from long-lost relatives.

Abuse victims could be the best actors, though. They had a lot of practice.

"Do you mind if I just take a quick look around?" Lauren asked, shifting so that she was pushing them back into the hallway simply with her presence. It was a trick she'd learned as the scrawniest kid on the playground, and it served her well as a beat cop.

"Of course not," the wife said, her hand patting at the husband's chest. His expression didn't give at all, his brows and the corners of his mouth pinched. He was not pleased with this development, but eventually he did step aside, waving Lauren in completely.

"Our daughter just went down for the night, if you don't mind being quiet," the wife said, with the wide, pleading eyes of every parent Lauren had ever met. "It took a while because of the storm."

She gestured toward the window near the door, where they could see the trees bowing beneath the weight of snow and ice, and as if on cue, the house groaned in protest of the elements.

Lauren sent her a half smile. "I understand."

And she did. Elijah hadn't made it through an entire night until he'd been three years old. Even now he was a fussy sleeper, ending up in her bed several times a week. She didn't have the will to force him back to his own room, too aware of how quickly the years would go. How he'd eventually stop seeking comfort in her.

Most of the lights in the farmhouse were off, but Lauren simply switched on her Maglite, shining it into the dark corners of the sitting room, the dining room, the playroom. She ended her little tour in the kitchen.

"I'm sorry," she said, turning to the pair, who had yet to disengage from each other. "I didn't catch your names."

The woman smiled brightly. "Owen and Martha Hayes."

"Have either of you heard anything strange this evening?" Lauren asked, as she took stock of the kitchen. Everything was clean, put away. But it didn't have the obsessive feel of an abused spouse used to violence at the mere sight of a crumb. The dish towel was crumpled around the stove handle rather than straight; a few shoes were sloppily kicked off by the back door. Lauren turned back to the pair. "Anything that would warrant a call from the neighbors?"

The two exchanged a look. It was Martha who answered. "Honestly, I don't even know how *they* could have heard anything strange. I can't hear myself think in this storm."

Lauren studied her closer, now that they were in the light. She seemed older than she'd first appeared in shadow—thin lines by her eyes and mouth that had Lauren placing her in her mid to late thirties. Still, she seemed eager to help and a little confused. Exactly what Lauren would have predicted on the drive up.

"It is strange," Lauren agreed. In other circumstances, she would have paid a call to the neighbors, as well, to verify the complaint. But she would be lucky to even make it back down the road right now. "Is there anyone else in the house? Other than your daughter, that is?"

"Yes," Martha said, quick and rushed, like this was a test. "My sister and her boy are here visiting from Burlington."

"They've already gone to bed?" Lauren asked, something not sitting right about this place.

The dark rooms.

The quiet.

The nearly silent husband.

"A long travel day," Martha offered.

"From Burlington?" Lauren asked, not meaning for it to be aggressive. But both of the Hayeses tensed.

"Traveling with a kid is always a challenge." Martha paused, cocked her head to the side. "As I'm sure you know."

A shiver slid along Lauren's spine, and she made some noncommittal sound, cursing herself for her earlier *I understand*. She'd faced down plenty of criminals who guessed at her having a child when they wanted to threaten her. It just seemed odd coming from this tiny woman. "Was there any particular reason for the visit?"

"My nephew's birthday and my daughter's are only a week apart," Martha said, any hint of tension completely gone from her voice. Lauren wondered if she'd imagined it. "We celebrate together every year."

28

Lauren nodded as she once again scanned the room, not even sure what she was looking for. Her eyes snagged on the basement door. The paint was thick and messy and covered the gap where the door would swing open. Working farmhouses, even ones that had capitalized on the apple tourism popular in the area, always made use of every bit of space they had.

She jerked her chin toward it, but turned to watch their faces as she asked, "Is that your basement?"

Martha's hand flexed against Owen's chest, in a blink-and-miss-it reaction. The man hadn't spoken since Lauren had stepped into the house, but he twitched at the question.

Lauren's fingers drifted toward her gun as she noted the back door, the darkened hallway.

Exit routes.

"We just don't want Julia wandering down there by herself," Martha was saying by the time Lauren switched her attention back to the wife. "We haven't been down there in *years*."

"Do you mind if I take a look?"

"Actually—" That was Owen. A deep rumble, a shift forward. Lauren redistributed her own weight, readying for an attack. He stopped, stilled.

The wind outside curled thick fists around the house as they all stood locked in some silent tableau.

"Officer, honestly, I'm not even sure if we could get the door open," Martha said, that happy voice dripping with sincerity as if they weren't one wrong move from having a gun drawn. Either the woman was oblivious or she had a lot of practice operating as normal in a tense situation.

Both options were less than ideal.

Lauren eyed the door again. Was it really painted shut, or did it just look like that? "And there's no outside access?"

"Gosh, no," Martha said, hand to her throat. "Can you imagine a curious seven-year-old with that kind of temptation?"

And the thing was, Lauren could. Everything they'd said so far made sense. There was nothing inherently suspicious about a basement door that didn't open. There was nothing inherently suspicious about this couple. Owen Hayes, the reticent Vermont farmer; Martha, his more socially inclined wife who didn't get much adult interaction. Offhand, Lauren could name several friends who mirrored that dynamic.

People also acted strangely in bad weather.

Maybe she should count herself among that group. Maybe she was letting the cold and the dark and the storm get to her.

"Well, I'll leave my contact information just in case something else comes up." That was the most she could do sometimes. Even when there were obvious bruises and broken bones—if a victim insisted it was a fall down the stairs that left them with a bloody lip, Lauren's hands were tied.

She might hate it, but that was life.

Still, that frisson that had tickled the nape of her neck during this interaction shouldn't completely be ignored. When she got back to the station, she'd run a check on the couple. "Y'all be safe tonight, you hear?"

Neither of them held their hand out for her business card, so she placed it on the counter, nodded once, and headed for the front door. As she went, she subtly searched once more for signs of a disturbance.

There were none. Just the normal detritus found in a home with a young girl and visiting relatives. Discarded shoes. Jackets piled on a side table, forgotten toys left tipped over in doorways.

The pair trailed in Lauren's wake, Martha going on about the candles they had at the ready just in case, their reliable generator, the beans and preserves in their pantry. Then they all stepped out into the night, and Martha gasped.

Lauren didn't audibly react, but she did curse silently.

During the short time she'd been inside, a tree had fallen across the driveway.

There was something grim in the pinch at the corners of Martha's eyes, even though her smile was warm. The disconnect was startling in the way of a missed step. "I suppose you'll be staying with us tonight."

CHAPTER SEVEN

GRETCHEN

Now

After Gretchen hung up on Lachlan, she pulled up another contact on her phone. Muscle memory, almost. It was hard breaking a habit after more than a decade of practice.

She stared at the name. Detective Patrick Shaughnessy.

Gretchen had a neat mental filing cabinet filled with folders for everyone with whom she interacted—their traits, their flaws, their strengths, their habits, both good and bad. It helped her understand the world around her, to move through it more easily.

Shaughnessy had taken up several drawers—which made sense considering she'd met him when she'd been only eight years old and he'd been the lead detective on her aunt Rowan's murder case. He'd spent the next three decades casting her as a killer who had gotten away with a terrible crime because her family was wealthy and influential. And that should have made her hate him.

Probably if she had been normal, she would have. But her brain wasn't wired that way, and so they'd moved on from their original dynamic to colleagues, and from there to something like friends.

Then she'd found out what had really happened the night of Rowan's death. All the information that she'd cataloged about him for thirty years had to be ripped out of those drawers and set ablaze, ash and fury the only things left behind.

After Shaughnessy's funeral—the one she hadn't attended— Gretchen had considered deleting the number altogether. But in the end she'd decided that would mean she cared about him too much.

So now, every once in a while, she found herself on the verge of calling a dead man, simply to chase that sense of normalcy that only his ever-present suspicion had provided.

Gretchen tossed the phone to the floor and buried her face in her hands.

Everything felt untethered in a way that she knew to be dangerous.

She associated this sensation with holding a gun to Shaughnessy's head, with confronting Viola Kent, the little psychopath who everyone had thought had brutally murdered her mother. With pressing a palm against Marconi's throat to feel the blood rush beneath her touch.

Like Gretchen had done her entire life, she'd held on to her control in each of those interactions.

While that grip had been shaky at best when she'd pushed Marconi up against her Porsche, Gretchen had managed not to seriously injure her.

She'd also managed not to kill Shaughnessy.

That was always the goal.

Marconi had forgiven her because she knew that you couldn't just play with fire on a daily basis and not expect to get a few burns. If Gretchen were neurotypical, she might have realized sooner that the thrill Marconi got from walking that fine line with Gretchen meant the detective wasn't as stable as she appeared.

In any other situation, this revelation would have made Marconi all the more interesting to Gretchen. But she'd had to go and get herself arrested—which was a nearly unforgivable mistake.

Gretchen worked so damn hard to keep herself out of jail. Sometimes it felt like every minute out of every day that she spent around other people was a struggle. Not every interaction provoked rage—in fact, most didn't. But she had to be on guard about the one that might.

And living like that was exhausting.

Then Marconi just went and called the police on herself, without even taking into consideration how it would affect Gretchen's life.

Don't investigate.

Gretchen surged to her feet, paced to ease the tingling discomfort in her legs that she absently diagnosed as some kind of psychosomatic symptom of anxiety she rarely felt.

Maybe it wasn't fair to say Marconi hadn't thought of Gretchen. After all, she'd known Gretchen wouldn't be able to *not* investigate.

It's the bed she made, some part of Gretchen whispered. *Let her lie in it.*

If Marconi wanted Gretchen to let her rot in jail so bad, maybe Gretchen should just step aside and let it play out.

The idea itched at her brain, its jaggy spikes irritating the gray matter.

The belief that sociopaths couldn't have friends was a common misconception. Gretchen could say she'd been almost popular at certain times of her life—for some reason grad school had really suited her especially. Her fellow students had always taken her blunt, awkward statements as dark humor.

More often than not, she'd inevitably sabotage those connections—through neglect or boredom or a realization that the person was more trouble than they were worth—but there had been a few that had lasted beyond that stage.

Gretchen plucked at her lower lip as she realized that two of those carefully selected few were now dead.

And one was about to go to prison for life.

People called *her* reckless, immoral, erratic. Yet here she was, the remaining soldier when the rest had been blown to bits by their own choices. That's why, objectively, she knew it was foolish tying yourself to someone in the long run in any way that mattered. Shrapnel had a way of fatally nicking bystanders.

Maybe she really should cut her losses. She had enough inherited money to buy a private island in some warm part of the world where she could forget about this mess, forget about Marconi, by the time her first margarita arrived.

But Gretchen had never been able to walk away from a mystery.

She crossed to the kitchen, desperate for something stronger than coffee to drown out the truth that she couldn't stamp out. It wasn't the mystery that she couldn't walk away from.

It was Marconi.

And the reason that Gretchen was awake in the middle of the night, desperate for clues to point her in the right direction, was because Gretchen knew firsthand what happened to cops who got put in jail.

After all, Shaughnessy had made it only two weeks into his prison sentence for the role he'd played in Rowan's death before someone had slipped a shiv in between his ribs. Shaughnessy had been at the tail end of his career, though, when he'd been arrested, with plenty of enemies to show for decades' worth of policing a city full of mob wannabes and thugs. Marconi was younger, newer to the area, as well. But in jail a cop was a cop, and there was a good chance she'd eventually pay a fatal price for having worn a badge.

Gretchen wasn't capable of true fear, but she could still worry about how her life might change if Marconi were killed.

Her younger self would be appalled.

Passing as normal had always been a point of pride, especially in those days before she'd established herself as a valued consultant. She'd spent her insomniac nights poring over body-language videos, soap operas, sitcoms, Harlequin romance novels, anything that could teach her how to not give herself away as *different* the minute she opened her mouth.

But while passing might have made her feel smug, she had never wanted *to be* as weak as everyone else around her. Normal people got attached so easily, bonding over a shared love of a coffee drink or a movie or a boy bander in one moment and calling each other for rides to the airport in the next.

As much as she'd studied cultural trends in an attempt to mimic those shorthanded pathways toward relationships, she'd still never understood why people walked around with their soft bellies exposed to the world, handing out knives to anyone they met without thought or caution.

She didn't even feel guilty when she used the ones they'd given her.

Now, though, she knew with sickening clarity that sometime in the past year she'd handed Marconi a blade.

Shaughnessy had once upon a time held one, too.

He'd done more than that, even. He'd been a guardrail. His watchful eye had always kept the most violent of her urges in check. She'd had the need to prove to him just how wrong he was about her, and that had always outweighed even her temper. While she didn't have a built-in sense of consequences, she had been absolutely determined that she could never let him see her break. That had always helped her navigate society in a way she found pleasurable and satisfying.

After his death, she'd worried she'd fly off the cliff, no longer constrained by the immovable steel of his judgment.

But then Marconi had been there.

Her judgment had been softer—expectations of greatness instead of expectations of disappointment.

Marconi had never looked at Gretchen and seen a killer.

Gretchen, at the very least, could acknowledge she owed it to Marconi to return the favor.

CHAPTER EIGHT

LAUREN

Then

Lauren's hand reached for the gun beneath her pillow while she was still halfway asleep.

Her fingers curled around the grip as her mind blared warning sirens without fully processing what had startled her.

A girl about seven years old stood directly in front of Lauren, eyes pools of shadows in the darkness.

"Hi," the girl whispered.

Christ. If she hadn't had practice with Elijah waking her up at night this same way—simply by standing and staring—Lauren wasn't positive she wouldn't have kicked out in an instinctive self-defense move, groggy and on edge at the same time.

Exhaling roughly, Lauren sat up.

"Hi." Her voice came out scratchy, and she glanced at the cheap clock radio on the side table. Four a.m. At least the power hadn't gone out yet. Small mercies. "Do you need help getting back to your room, hon?"

The girl—Julia, Lauren remembered Martha saying—pursed her lips and rolled her eyes. "I'm not a *baby*."

Lauren almost laughed at how universal that childhood disgruntlement could be, how Elijah had said something exactly like that just yesterday morning. "I know. But it's hard in the dark sometimes. To find your way."

That seemed to do the trick, because the girl tilted her head, thoughtful, one of her braids catching on her shoulder. "I guess that would be okay."

Even though Lauren had no idea where the girl's bedroom was, she stood and held out her hand.

She nearly flinched at the contact. Despite the relative warmth of the house, Julia's fingers were cold against her own.

"Are you excited school might be canceled tomorrow?" Lauren asked as they stepped into the hallway. The moon had provided some light in the bedroom, but here it was inky black. For one ridiculous heartbeat, Lauren fought off the urge to turn around for her gun.

"Mama teaches me here," Julia said, and Lauren felt more than saw her shrug, thin shoulders brushing against Lauren's hip.

"Oh yeah?"

"Yeah," Julia said, swinging their joined hands. "'Cause Papa doesn't want us to leave."

"For school?"

"Ever." Julia dragged out the word with an exasperation only children seemed to manage to deliver perfectly.

Lauren stopped. "Ever?"

"Me and Mama stay here," Julia said, tugging on Lauren's hand to get her to keep going. "Well, sometimes Mama sneaks us out. But we're not supposed to talk about that."

Lauren dropped to a crouch. Her eyes had adjusted to see the broad strokes of Julia's face, but not any reactions that might provide insight. Still, she asked, "Julia. Does your papa hurt you?"

Julia dropped Lauren's hand and put her own little one to Lauren's shoulders, pulling until Lauren leaned forward. Julia went up on tiptoes, her mouth by Lauren's ear.

"He yelled real loud at me once," Julia confessed.

Lauren pressed her lips together, tried not to react. "And did he do anything else, hon? To hurt you?"

"No, silly," Julia said, shifting back with a little giggle now that her secret had been told.

There didn't seem to be any guile in her answer, but Lauren pushed a little. "Why did he yell?"

"Mmmmm, can't tell," Julia said, a young slyness creeping into her voice. "It's a secret."

"Lots of secrets, huh?" Lauren said lightly.

Maybe Lauren could prod her into it. Children were notoriously bad at withholding information. Elijah not only couldn't keep a secret, but he would actively tell others the information even if they hadn't asked.

But she was tiptoeing toward an ethical gray area and sprinting headlong toward a legal one.

Julia was clearly an odd little bird. She'd walked into a stranger's room in the middle of the night and had taken Lauren's hand without thinking. But she didn't show any signs of abuse. Nor could Lauren exactly arrest someone for wanting to homeschool their kid.

"All right, hon, is this your bedroom?" she asked, jerking her chin toward the nearest option.

"Yup," Julia said with a little jump, before nudging the door with her bare foot.

Once inside, Lauren flipped on the light.

She was tired of shadows.

The room was perfectly normal for a girl Julia's age. There were dolls scattered about, drawings pinned to the wall, an overflowing bookcase. Absolutely nothing suspicions.

Brianna Labuskes

Lauren sighed, annoyed with herself. There was vigilance and then there was paranoia.

For a seven-year-old in rural Vermont, it probably *felt* like she never left the house. Lauren just wanted that itch she'd felt from earlier to mean something. She wanted her instincts to be proven right.

But weird did not equal criminal.

Julia let go of Lauren's hand and skipped toward the bed. Lauren followed behind, unable to resist tucking Julia in, just like she would for Elijah.

Julia blinked up at her, a sweet smile tickling out a dimple in her cheek. "Are you one of the boys' moms?"

Lauren paused. "What do you mean, hon?"

"The boys never have their moms."

A darkness twisted, writhed beneath her skin. Her voice shook when she asked, "Which boys?"

The girl smiled as she tugged a ratty teddy bear up beneath her chin, her eyelids already heavy, sinking half into sleep. When she answered, it was a whisper. "The ones in the basement."

CHAPTER NINE

GRETCHEN

Now

Although Gretchen had wanted something harder than coffee, she settled for it anyway, using a mug the size of her head. It was past midnight now, and Gretchen wasn't going to be getting any sleep tonight.

She settled back down at her desk and pulled up the folder that had been on the thumb drive hidden in Marconi's bedroom.

In it were four Word documents, all labeled with boys' first names. Gretchen hovered over the first.

JOSHUA

Her phone rang, and she ignored it.

When she opened the document, she realized it wasn't an official police report, but rather Marconi's personal notes. There was no picture included, just stream-of-consciousness words that could barely be called complete sentences.

At the top was Joshua's full name, and beneath it the scattered details of his case. Joshua Westwood had been eight years old at the time he'd gone missing a decade and a half ago.

One thing in particular caught her eye as she quickly skimmed the paragraphs: Marconi's prime suspect in the kidnapping had been Owen Hayes.

That tidbit confirmed Gretchen had been right about this thumb drive, its importance. Pleasure slipped into her veins, soothing and familiar, and she sighed over the fact that she was planning on keeping this secret for now. The chance to gloat about being right was nearly as delightful as *being* right. She knew enough about herself to admit that the many, many, many times she'd been called arrogant, cocky, and superior were well earned.

It wasn't her fault that she was so good at this, though.

She went back to the beginning of the document and read more closely this time.

Joshua Westwood had disappeared from a grocery/gas station in the middle of Vermont.

Right after that was a note from Marconi.

Gas station a half-hour drive from Owen Hayes's farmhouse.

That made Gretchen pause. It was a minor but telling detail, making it clear that Marconi already thought Hayes was guilty of the kidnapping when she'd composed this file. Right off the bat, Marconi was connecting the evidence to Hayes even when the evidence didn't actually warrant it.

Had it been the third or fourth note included, Gretchen wouldn't have thought anything of it. But it was the first thing Marconi had put down.

Gretchen blew out a breath. *Confirmation bias.* It came as both an echo and a warning siren.

She had said that so many times in the past she might as well have tattooed it on herself. She'd said it plenty to Marconi, who'd only ever nodded and stared at her with a curious expression and serious Bambi eyes.

It didn't take her level of intelligence to guess that the four other files contained information similar to Joshua's. This was Marconi building a case against the man she'd just been arrested for shooting execution-style.

Gretchen recognized the roots of an obsessive vendetta when she saw it.

For the first time since she'd seen Marconi in the passenger seat, Gretchen let herself truly consider that Marconi might be guilty.

I did it, okay?

It hadn't been long ago now that Gretchen had been forced to reckon with the fact that she might not be as good at reading people as she liked to believe. Shaughnessy had taught her that. What she'd always seen as disdain had been guilt; what she'd seen as suspicion had been his own self-loathing. She'd believed him to be the most morally righteous among them, but really, he'd just been a coward with a savior complex. A dime a dozen in her line of work.

Sometimes logically she knew all the studying in the world would never fill the gaps for her. No matter how many facial-expression videos she watched, no matter how she trained herself to recognize vocal intonation, she would always be handicapped when it came to actually understanding other people.

It was as if she could read the words while still not comprehending the sentence.

But no.

That wasn't the case with Marconi. Gretchen might not know personal facts about the woman, but she hadn't completely mistranslated her, either. Not the way she had with Shaughnessy.

Marconi was smart, she was rational, she was flexible. And she would not have killed Hayes in cold blood just because she suspected he was a serial kidnapper.

Gretchen shook her head and continued reading.

Joshua Westwood's abduction had not been caught on security footage, though the cameras had picked up Owen Hayes's truck at one of the pumps not long before the boy was snatched. No one had been in the passenger seat.

That was certainly more concrete than his farmhouse being within driving distance of the gas station. Gretchen settled in a bit, slightly reassured. The next note was under ALIBI.

Made sure to make purchase at hardware store five mins. later.

She pulled up a map of the two addresses listed. From pump to parking lot it would have been maybe three minutes without incident. Another one to two minutes to walk into the store, grab something, and make the purchase. That wasn't a lot of time, and someone sympathetic to Hayes might say it meant he couldn't have been the one to take Joshua Westwood.

Gretchen was sympathetic to no one.

It was tight, but not impossible to imagine.

According to Marconi's notes, the police had interviewed Hayes because he'd been at the store around the time of the kidnapping, but agreed that his alibi checked out and removed him from the prime-suspect list.

If Marconi's notes were up to date, no one had ever been arrested, the case now ice-cold.

The phone rang again.

She ignored it, toggling back to the main folder on the thumb drive.

The next document was simply labeled NATHAN.

His full name was typed across the top of the page with messy, off-the-cuff notes from Marconi beneath it. *Nathan* was really Nathaniel Parker, and he'd been nine years old when he disappeared.

He'd been attending a friend's birthday party in a small town just over the border to New York. Eighty miles from Montpelier.

Nathan's house had been only three blocks from the birthday boy's. The mother at the party said he'd left at three in the afternoon, and she'd watched him until he'd turned the corner onto his street. Nathan's mother had expected him home at four, so only then did she start to worry.

Marconi's note below the official details was that Hayes had been caught that morning on a red-light camera three towns over.

In the area, she'd written.

It wasn't exactly damning evidence, but it was curious. Being in the vicinity of one kidnapped child could be written off as coincidence. Twice could be a pattern.

But again, Gretchen was struck by the fact that Marconi had an agenda here.

She heard Lachlan's voice: *Lauren was using BPD resources to keep tabs on Hayes.*

Gretchen's phone rang.

The third document was labeled CALEB.

Caleb Andrews had been eight years old at the time of his disappearance, three years after Nathan's kidnapping. None of them had occurred on the same dates, which seemed to indicate that if they'd all been taken by the same person, the day itself wasn't special.

Caleb had been the child of a single mother who worked long hours. One afternoon there had been a gap in between when a babysitter could watch him and when the grandmother could come over, and the mother had made the decision to leave him alone in the house for an hour.

When the grandmother had arrived, she'd immediately phoned the police. But the kidnapping could have occurred at any time during that hour.

Hayes's alibi was Martha.

The wife? The girlfriend? Marconi hadn't included a surname, which made Gretchen think it was the former. In the history of violent killings, plenty of wives had given their husbands fake alibis. Gretchen glanced at the TV screen to see if they were still covering the case. Would they interview Martha?

It was too late, though; the station had switched to those informercials that filled the witching hours when only insomniacs and night workers were awake.

Still, it made Gretchen wonder what the wife was like. If Hayes really was guilty here, if he'd taken at least four boys, what kind of person covered for a man like that? Was she a victim? Was she a coward? An accomplice? Or maybe a little bit of all three.

Gretchen hovered over the last name as her phone rang once more.

"Christ, what do you want?" she snapped as she answered it, clicking into the last document.

"Did you know?" Lachlan's voice came through broken in a way she'd never heard before.

"Know what?" Gretchen asked, mostly distracted.

She wasn't one who could easily identify feelings. She had them; they just tended to be riotous and hard to understand. But this one she knew well.

I did it, okay?

Across the top of the otherwise blank document was one name.

ELIJAH MARCONI

"She had a kid, Gretchen," Lachlan said, one beat behind with his revelation. "And she thinks Hayes killed him."

CHAPTER TEN

LAUREN

Then

Lauren sat cross-legged on the bed in the Hayeses' guest room, phone clutched in one hand, gun in the other, as she stared at the closed door.

The ping of a text came through.

Elijah's asleep, will call when he's up.

And then Sandy proved how well she knew Lauren.

What happened?

How to put any of it into words? Lauren didn't bother trying, simply tossed the phone on the bed in front of her and glanced at the clock. She'd made it through the night.

A chain saw roared to life outside.

Adrenaline pulsed through her veins down into the soles of her feet. She scrambled to the window, pulling back the lace curtain.

In the early dawn light, Lauren could make out the silhouette of Owen Hayes. A sharp-toothed saw whirred in the air above his head as he lifted it and then brought it down on the offending tree. The one blocking her escape.

She wondered if he would have been out there all night if it wouldn't have looked suspicious.

Then she headed for the hallway.

With Owen occupied, Lauren would either have a stab at the basement door or at Martha.

Either one could be insightful.

She was still half-convinced she'd dreamed the encounter with Julia, half-convinced that, had it happened at all, the girl was a little liar, like kids could so often be.

As she walked, Lauren shoved her phone in the back pocket of her jeans and tucked her gun into the underarm holster that she covered up with her jacket. The stairs creaked beneath her weight.

When Lauren swung into the kitchen, half her attention on the basement door, Martha looked up with a smile that was warm but slightly subdued from the one she'd flashed last night. Lauren might have been imagining it, but the skin beneath Martha's eyes was smudged purple, like she hadn't slept at all.

The woman stood over the massive black stove that dominated the room, three different cast-iron pans going at once.

"Good morning," Martha greeted. Softer than how she'd talked the evening before. Everything about her muted, along with the golden light of dawn.

Me and Mama stay here, Julia had said.

"Morning," Lauren managed in return. She had a thousand questions, and none that wouldn't send Martha fleeing back behind that friendly facade from yesterday.

Martha jerked her head toward the counter. "Coffee's over there."

A mug with No. 1 Dad painted on the side sat at the ready next to the pot.

He yelled real loud at me once.

"Your daughter came into my room early this morning," Lauren said as she poured the cup.

"She has busy feet, that one," Martha said, smiling down into whatever she was cooking. "Sorry if she disturbed you." She flicked Lauren a glance. "You must know what it's like."

Lauren tried not to tense at the obvious fishing. Once might be a coincidence, but twice? Martha was trying to figure out if she had a kid.

The boys never have their moms.

Lauren wondered if she'd gotten this all wrong. She'd come in with the idea that this was a domestic-abuse situation, but that certainly wasn't the only scenario that could be playing out here.

If Julia knew about boys in the basement, there was almost no way Martha didn't know about them, too.

That was, if there *were* any boys in the basement.

Lauren wasn't convinced either way, though she couldn't help but think of the cold case currently sitting on her desk. Peter Stone, eight years old, from Burlington. Maybe that was what was making her jumpy here.

She leaned back against the sink, cradling her mug, studying the tense line of Martha's back.

When Lauren didn't latch on to the obvious conversational bait, Martha flicked a glance over her shoulder. "Julia drives my sister to distraction whenever she visits."

And with that, all of a sudden Lauren remembered the other guests. The sister, the nephew.

Maybe Julia had gotten confused? Or had told herself a little story about her cousin? If Martha could go on a fishing expedition, so could she.

Lauren set her coffee aside.

"Julia did mention something about boys . . ."

Martha stilled. Just for a second, but long enough that Lauren didn't think she'd been imagining the reaction.

"My nephew, probably," she said, pointing the spatula to the ceiling. "His father passed away when he was quite young, so he's stayed with us for some long visits before." With abruptly jerky movements, she twisted off all the burners, and turned, mirroring Lauren's position—leaning back, arms crossed over her chest. Her eyes drifted up again, like she could see through to the second level. "He's had some behavioral issues my sister couldn't handle herself."

Lauren knew her surprise must have shown. "Oh."

"Right." The corners of Martha's mouth tightened as her hand drifted down, her pinkie finger resting just below her belly button. "Boys are hard."

Had they met on a playground or in a parenting class, Lauren would have laughed and said, *Tell me about it.* Instead, she couldn't help but glance toward the basement.

The back door banged open, wood slamming against wood as the frigid air rushed in to do battle with the warmth of the kitchen.

Owen's beard was crusted with snow, and he wore the Vermont uniform of heavy-duty jacket, heavy-duty boots, heavy-duty gloves.

"Tree's cleared. I'll start the plow—you can follow down the drive."

Martha cast a look at the breakfast she'd been making and then met Lauren's eyes, offering a half smile. "A slice of bacon for the road?"

"Thank you, no." Lauren's boots had been placed by the door, and she had to step into Owen's radius to grab them. He didn't shift away like most people would, granting personal space without thought. Instead, he stood his ground. Lauren shifted her attention back to Martha as she shoved her feet in, not bothering to waste time with the laces. "I appreciate the hospitality."

"Thank you for checking up on us," Martha said, smile faded. "It's appreciated."

Lauren tried not to read into that, but a little part of her did anyway. A cry for help could be as subtle as a few well-chosen words.

"If you ever need anything, just give me a call," Lauren said, quietly, even though, of course Owen could hear her. "You have my card."

"We do," Martha said, but then she turned her back, her hands flying into motion, Lauren dismissed.

She lingered, though, just for an extra second.

Just in case.

Then Owen grunted, and Lauren realized any window of opportunity she'd had to pry had passed. She followed him out the door, into the snow. Into the still-raging storm.

The plow was already idling in front of her SUV.

With each step that sank into knee-deep powder, Lauren scrambled for something, anything to say to make sure she wasn't about to just leave a family to the whims of an abuser.

"Do you have any idea who called in the tip last night?" Lauren shouted, half her question swept away with a gust of wind. Owen had heard, though. He must have, because his stride faltered, and she caught his profile for the first time since they'd walked outside.

"No," he finally answered when they both stopped by her vehicle. He rested a hand on the top so she couldn't open the door. "But they should know that I don't take kindly to people messing around in my business."

The threat wasn't even subtle. And it wasn't directed at the tipster, clearly.

The posturing was an obvious show of aggression that had one intended audience member.

Lauren thought about Martha's gentle fishing. The two had taken different approaches, but the message still felt the same.

And it made it clear they were operating as a team to protect their privacy.

"Noted," Lauren managed through gritted teeth. Then she yanked the SUV's door open, forcing him to step back whether he liked it or not.

As he climbed into the plow, Lauren's eyes flicked to the farmhouse in the rearview mirror.

A curtain fluttered in one of the windows on the second floor.

A pale face peeked out at her from behind the frosted glass.

Julia.

Lauren couldn't suppress a shiver that had nothing to do with the cold, and wondered if it wasn't necessarily the boys in the basement she had to worry about but rather the girl in the window.

CHAPTER ELEVEN
GRETCHEN

Now

The story couldn't be easier for a jury to understand.

Detective Lauren Marconi believed that Owen Hayes had killed her son, Elijah, nine years ago and gotten away with it. Since then, she'd followed him to Boston, stalked him, pursued him relentlessly, and even abused police privilege, all in the hopes of one day enacting a revenge that had slipped through her fingers in Vermont.

I did it, okay?

It took her a moment to realize she was about one second away from throwing her phone against the wall, and the only reason it didn't follow the same fate as the vase was because she didn't want to waste time running out to buy a new one.

She exhaled and focused on loosening her grip as Lachlan rattled on, his voice tinny through the speaker, unaware that she had stopped listening. It didn't matter, anyway; he was simply mansplaining his way through the tale DA Cormac Byrne would spin in court. As if Gretchen couldn't see it as plain as day herself.

The jury would be sympathetic, of course—hell, even Cormac would be sympathetic.

But, he would remind them, we can't have vigilantes running around taking the law into their own hands. Especially when they're backed by a badge and taxpayer dollars.

Marconi would be found guilty the second this news hit the press.

"Does the media have it?" Gretchen interrupted Lachlan midsentence. He had been explaining how one of his colleagues had called the Montpelier Police Department to see if Marconi and Hayes had any previous interactions. Gretchen didn't care.

After a clearly disgruntled silence, Lachlan muttered, "Not yet."

"They will," Gretchen said, mostly to herself. "But how long do we have? Does it even matter?"

"Does what matter?"

Gretchen rolled her shoulders, irritated that she wasn't talking to Marconi. They had always been in lockstep with each other on cases in a way Gretchen hadn't appreciated until it was gone.

But she needed to find a way not to burn this tenuous bridge with Lachlan. It would serve her in the long run to keep him on her side. Also, because she had something he wanted, he seemed to be willing to at least grudgingly keep her updated. Who knew how much she could push him before he decided the information she had wasn't worth it.

Gretchen sighed to express her displeasure, but explained as patiently as she could. "Do we care if the public has found her guilty? As long as we prove her innocence before she gets in front of a jury. It will be a moot point by then."

Silent pity as loud as words answered her, and Gretchen's blood pounded against the thin membrane of her temples.

"You've given up on her already," Gretchen mused, keeping the anger out of her voice. It wouldn't serve her purpose. He'd respond better to a good shaming. "And you call me the monster."

"That's not . . ." But he trailed off again because he couldn't deny it.

She laughed, amused by all these people in her life who thought they were so righteous. Why had she ever been fooled into thinking someone who sat themselves on a high horse actually belonged there? Marconi deserved so much more than Lachlan Gibbs and his spineless doubt. "She didn't kill him, *Lachlan*."

"Just because you think she would have gotten away with it doesn't mean she didn't kill him," Lachlan said, and she pictured this conversation ad nauseam. It had her longing for Shaughnessy, even. "Things happen. That's not exactly the solid defense you think it is."

"Things happen," Gretchen repeated. "I think I want that printed out on a sign—it can go right next to my 'Live, Laugh, Love' crocheted pillow."

Lachlan made some kind of frustrated sound, and Gretchen hummed in agreement. She hated this. If she hadn't already been convinced she needed to clear Marconi's name, this conversation would have been the impetus. Without Marconi, this was her future if she wanted to continue consulting with the BPD.

"Mock all you want," Lachlan said, abruptly sounding exhausted. "That's not going to help Lauren."

Gretchen bit back a barbed retort about how little he was doing to *help* Marconi.

"Let me get this straight," she said instead. "You think Marconi—who left such a paper trail of her stalking that it was found within the hour of her arrest—walked into this man's house in full view of a security camera she must have known was there because of the aforementioned stalking. And then she shot him execution-style, completely undercutting any argument she could have made about self-defense? You think that was her play? After nine years of planning?" She shook her head despite the fact that he couldn't see her. "Because, honestly, I called you a shit boyfriend already once, but now you're just outright insulting her intelligence."

"You know better than anyone that rage doesn't always listen to reason or logic," Lachlan said, already sounding braced.

"If rage didn't listen to reason, you wouldn't be breathing right now," Gretchen said, calmly. Because she goddamn could.

"Not rage at all life's irritations," Lachlan said in such a patronizing tone Gretchen figured he was baiting her. Which, more than anything, made her not want to react at all. "Rage at someone killing your kid. If she found something definitive—off the top of my head, I'd guess the trophy he'd kept from Elijah's killing—you can't say she wouldn't have pulled a gun on him."

"And made him kneel before shooting him in the back of the head?" Gretchen asked, and she could all but see Marconi's lightning-quick smirk of approval at the point made. If she concentrated on that instead of the seething pulse in her chest, she might make it through this conversation without proving Lachlan right. "Tell me what that looks like."

"Controlled rage," Lachlan replied.

"So now it's so uncontrolled that Marconi, a woman who is coldly capable of plotting revenge for nine years, became so erratic as to be goaded into murdering her son's killer, but controlled enough that she paused during the confrontation to get him on his knees and walk behind him."

Lachlan clicked his teeth together. "What's the story you'll tell, then?"

Gretchen closed her eyes, pictured a man on the floor in front of her. A gun in her hand. She thought of the way she stored her own anger in an unlocked box so she could tap into it as needed, but not be a slave to it.

She saw Owen Hayes's face. Not scared, she didn't think. Relieved, maybe. It had been a long life. Getting away with killing little boys wasn't exactly a cakewalk.

Still, he was an animal, and animals in the face of death couldn't help themselves. They bit and howled and fought with every ounce of strength left in their bodies.

Owen would be plotting a way to get the gun from her from the moment he saw it.

She'd come in from the window or the back door because she knew about the cameras. He was in the living room, alone, watching TV.

He was bigger than her, but that didn't matter because she knew his nearest gun was in the kitchen. His fists were weapons, though, and she wouldn't get close enough for him to use them.

On the floor, she would say. *In the middle of the rug.*

Away from lamps or heavy books or anything he could throw at her to disarm her.

Hands behind your neck.

She circled behind him, peeling open the top of the box, the first tendril of rage seeping through the gap, electrifying her skin, her blood. The rush of it was intoxicating. She didn't bother with caution as she let the rest loose. It seeped into her like a drug, so heady she got dizzy with it.

This man killed her son. He hurt him, tortured him, broke him. And then hid him.

Why now, why now? That was Gretchen's voice instead of the killer's, and it came too loud. She silenced it. If she let herself get distracted, Owen would seize the opportunity.

Because he was strong, and he knew why she was here. He knew a bullet had his name on it no matter if he cooperated or not.

Just tell me where he is, she said as if that were the reason she was here. *I won't kill you if you tell me where he is.*

But that was his game: hiding them so they would be his forever. Otherwise he would have dumped the bodies in a ditch, desecrated for the world to see. These boys weren't for the world, though.

His fingers twitched against his thigh, his body tensed.

Her finger tightened on the trigger. Just as he shifted, perhaps to lunge at her, she fired.

Blood and brain spattered against the rug. A still-warm body slumped forward onto the floor, the nose cracking with the force of impact.

The beast that had been let loose from the box roared its success.

And that's when everything crystallized—why Gretchen was so sure in her conviction that Marconi was innocent. She hadn't been able to see it at first, but some part of her must have cataloged the evidence.

"You're right, it was controlled rage," Gretchen finally answered Lachlan. "It just wasn't Marconi's."

CHAPTER TWELVE

MARTHA

Before

Martha pressed her face to the cold tile of the bathroom floor as her tears collected in a small puddle beneath her cheek.

The baby had given up. It had set them both free.

She closed her eyes and thanked God again and again and again.

It was the third miscarriage, and she was starting to think some divine entity *knew* that a child shouldn't be brought into this house.

A heavy fist banged on the door, rattling the lotions and perfumes that were in the cabinet next to it.

Martha scrambled to sit up, scooting back against the far wall and swiping at her wet face as she did. She swallowed three times to make sure the wobble was gone from her voice.

"Something's not sitting right," she managed, the toilet paper wadded up between her legs saturated with blood.

"Are you . . ." He trailed off. "Do you need . . ."

What Owen thought he could offer in terms of help she would never know because this was how he got when presented with the fact that she was a human being. With things like bowels and a colon, a functioning stomach and gut bacteria.

"I'm going to take a bath," she called out, the last bit breaking as her uterus cramped and her lower back spasmed. She thought of the olden days, when women were given wood to bite down on, and wished for a spoon. Even cracking her teeth would be preferable to him walking in because she'd cried out.

"You're sure?"

"Mm-hmm," she gritted out.

Martha closed her eyes, held her breath, prayed.

The floorboard squeaked.

A child ties you to a man, her mother used to lecture her.

Never let a man do that to you, she would say.

Martha ran the water until it was hot enough to scald her skin and then crawled over the edge of the old claw-foot tub, her favorite part of the farmhouse.

She pinkened on contact, the steam curling up into the cold bathroom, the air humid now.

Pressing a hand to her belly, Martha thought about the lure of the water, the way she could simply dip beneath it, let it rush in and fill her lungs.

Three days ago, they'd driven into town for supplies. The hardware store had been across from a park, and Martha had told herself not to look.

But she couldn't help it. She'd spent so much time not looking.

Her eyes had slid to her husband's face.

His eyes had been on the swings.

When later he asked why she'd lurched out of the car, the back of her hand pressed to her mouth to keep the vomit down, she'd lied.

And he'd pretended to believe her.

CHAPTER THIRTEEN

GRETCHEN

Now

"You can't know that it wasn't Lauren," Lachlan said. Accused, really.

But underneath the words, she heard the plea. *You can't know that . . . can you?*

Gretchen finally could, though.

It was the blood.

It had been on Marconi's nails, smeared on her shirt. If she'd been the killer, there would have been no need to touch the body.

Even operating on an adrenaline high, Marconi would have known Hayes was dead had she been the one to fire the gun twice into the back of his head.

The only reason she would have thought she'd needed to check for a pulse was if she'd stumbled onto the scene a minute too late.

Telling Lachlan any of that, though, would mean revealing that Marconi had come to her before driving to the police station. For now, that was her only leverage to keep Lachlan working with her.

So instead she said, "You're right, I can't." And then she hung up the phone.

The walls of Gretchen's apartment crept closer each time she blinked, her lashes heavy. Once upon a time she could have rolled from an all-nighter into a professional workday into another all-nighter with only the aid of some good cocaine. But age was a nasty mistress that even she had to acknowledge.

She didn't have to kowtow to it, though, so she grabbed her jacket and keys and headed for the street.

Gretchen had few friends, but she did have a network of people who tended to be helpful when consulting on a case. One of those people was Fred—full name Winnifred James—and she was probably Gretchen's most valuable asset.

Although Fred could afford a much swankier place, she lived in a dank basement beneath a town house on the edge of a sketchy neighborhood because she never wanted to become one of those *richy-rich jag-offs who wipe their butts with hundred-dollar bills just because they could*. Gretchen never pointed out that there was a happy middle that Fred could surely find acceptable. It wasn't her life.

Despite the ungodly hour, Gretchen felt no remorse as she pounded on the door until it was yanked open. Fred squinted at her, a baseball bat held casually over one shoulder, her hair in a messy bun.

"I'm adding a thousand dollars to whatever you want for waking me up," Fred said, but turned, leaving the door open for Gretchen. Half of the apartment housed what Gretchen had always called command central. It was just one ten-year-old monitor with a fancy laptop docked to it, but Fred could work miracles with the setup, and so Gretchen had always shown the proper respect when she was in the inner sanctum.

If there was one thing Gretchen could appreciate in other people, it was talent.

"Don't pretend you weren't awake following every tiny development," Gretchen said, dropping into the extra chair Fred set up next to her own.

Fred's eyebrow twitched, but Gretchen knew that was the only acknowledgment she'd get.

"What do you need?" Fred asked, as if she didn't know.

"I have four names for you. Boys," Gretchen said, rattling them off without needing any notes. She'd memorized them the first time she'd read them. "They went missing between nine and fifteen years ago in Vermont."

Fred whistled low and soft after Elijah's name, but she would never leak the detail to the press. Like Gretchen, she had a strong sense of the cost-benefit ratio. Whatever she would have gotten paid by the media would pale in comparison to what Gretchen forked over year in and year out.

"Hayes was the kidnapper, I presume," Fred asked.

Gretchen pressed a thumb into her eye until she saw bright sparks. Everyone was going to draw the conclusion. It was inevitable, and Gretchen couldn't lose control of her temper each time it happened. Just because she knew how dangerous confirmation bias was didn't mean it wasn't an integral part of the human brain.

"Don't go in thinking that," Gretchen said. "For now, I just need information on them, their cases, any gossip at the station at the time, maybe. If you're as good as you think you are."

"As if you would come to me if I weren't," Fred shot back.

It was true. Gretchen worked with only the best; she accepted nothing less than impressive from the people she voluntarily surrounded herself with. "Charge what you want."

The order was foolish, sentimental. Part of their relationship depended on bargaining, even though Gretchen had so much money that none of it mattered.

Fred did some jerky thing with her shoulders. "It's on the house."

So maybe they were both a bit stupid when it came to Marconi. The woman had a way of burrowing herself under the skin of people she decided were worth it.

For some reason, Gretchen fell into that column.

"Can you get me any current addresses and employment for the victims' parents?" Gretchen asked.

Fred's hands stilled over her computer, but then she nodded. "Sure. Including on Elijah's?"

"The father," Gretchen said, rolling her eyes. "I think I know where Marconi is employed."

"But not much about her, huh?" Fred ventured with a lack of tact that matched Gretchen's.

"People put too much weight on the past," Gretchen said, more than she would give anyone else who would likely handle her too delicately right now. Fred was many things, but delicate wasn't one of them.

"I'm sorry, aren't you the woman who defined herself by a murder that happened when she was eight?" Fred countered, proving Gretchen's point beautifully.

"And look where that got me," Gretchen said. "I know Marconi just fine."

Even she could hear the defensiveness in her words, and she huffed out an annoyed breath. She *did* know Marconi. Marconi didn't have the artifice to fool someone as observant as Gretchen.

But Gretchen hadn't known about the drive-bys, the light stalking.

"Can you stand your family?" Gretchen had asked her once.

"Maybe if they were alive," Marconi had said. Gretchen remembered that it had sounded empty, not as if she were devastated but as if she'd been reciting a basic fact.

"All dead?"

"Just me left," Marconi had said.

And Gretchen had dropped it at that.

The lie had come so easy for Marconi. Or the half lie. Did it count as one if Marconi had told the truth in a misleading tone? When had Gretchen started worrying about semantics like that?

She stood, antsy once more. "Email me the results."

Fred spun to study Gretchen. "You going to be okay without your Sancho Panza?"

"Look who you're asking," Gretchen said, her car keys biting into her palm for some reason. She glanced down at her fist and realized it was clenched.

"I am," Fred said.

A hot flush crept up the back of Gretchen's neck. If she were normal, she would say it was embarrassment at being seen so clearly, but she didn't feel anything so pedestrian. "Get me that information."

She didn't wait for a response—just took the stairs back up to street level at a jog.

That untethered sensation was back, and she needed the fresh slap of night air to feel steady again. She leaned against the wall outside Fred's apartment and pictured herself only hours earlier doing the same thing outside the restaurant.

Her date. It was funny how everything could change so fast. She couldn't even remember his name now.

That space in her mind had been carved out, refilled with other ones.

Joshua, Nathaniel, Caleb.

Elijah.

There was always a chance that Hayes's death had nothing to do with the fact that he might have been a serial predator. Marconi was a good Major Crimes detective operating in Boston. She'd made plenty of enemies who could have clocked her interest in Hayes and come up with an easy way to frame her.

It was something Gretchen had considered a time or two herself with people she'd wanted to take out of some equation or other.

But the bigger possibility was that a serial killer had died because he was a serial killer.

Marconi was simply taking the fall for someone else's revenge scheme.

When people who involved themselves in violent crimes ended up murdered, the two things did tend to be linked.

Why now?

The question had been a persistent whisper against the inside of her skull all night.

Elijah Marconi had been taken nine years ago—the last of the boys in Marconi's file—and there hadn't been any more victims to add to the thumb drive, so what had instigated the killing?

Perhaps there were more victims. Boston was exponentially bigger than Montpelier. Hayes would have had a hunting ground that he could hide within, taking boys who wouldn't be missed, or ones from different neighborhoods so as not to create a pattern.

If he'd taken the wrong child, he might have earned himself those bullets in his head.

Gretchen admitted that particular narrative did not bode well for Marconi. She had the means, the experience, and the motive to get rid of Hayes. So did a lot of other people, of course, but if Gretchen had been looking at this case without personally knowing any of the players, she wouldn't have even bothered wasting her time with it.

Revenge was a drug that everyone craved. People lived for revenge, died for it, killed for it. Understood it.

If Marconi had told her about Elijah, about Hayes, Gretchen would have helped her get rid of him, and done it with pleasure. The world should not weep for monsters.

But don't you then become a monster yourself? She heard the argument in Lachlan Gibbs's voice and rolled her eyes.

That high-and-mighty stance was all well and good until someone killed your kid. Gretchen could absolutely believe that Marconi could have been planning to take Hayes out all along.

What she could not believe was that Marconi would have gotten caught doing it.

Gretchen pictured another scenario.

Marconi in her car, the night fading around her. Bored, but atten-tive, because Marconi couldn't half-ass anything.

What was she even doing there? She'd been watching Hayes for years, and he hadn't slipped up yet. What did she think she'd find? What did she think she'd see?

Had she checked her phone, read that threatening text message Gretchen had sent during her date from hell? Had she smiled? Maybe then glanced up, seen movement.

Someone entering the Hayes house through the window, or the back door, depending on where Marconi had parked.

Instinct would have kicked in.

Maybe she'd heard the shots when she'd still been on the street. That would explain why she'd been so sloppy as to go in through the front door when the Ring camera must have been so obviously there.

The big question, then, was if Marconi had seen the real killer.

There was a slim possibility that the person had gotten off the shots, escaped back through whatever entry point he used to get in, and Marconi had missed him by a few seconds.

The other option was both more interesting and more infuriating.

Marconi had seen the guy and was taking the fall for that person.

There were only so many reasons anyone would do such a drastic thing. Love, of course, even though that word was simply empath short-hand for a particular cascade of brain chemicals.

It did seem possible that Marconi was protecting Elijah's father, whoever that was. They must have been teenagers when the boy had been conceived, and there was nothing as potent as young love on a developing brain. Marconi's synapses had probably built themselves around the idea that the man was worth dying for, and so it had become a foundational part of who Marconi was.

Gretchen could almost paint that picture and be satisfied with it. But if Marconi had been carrying a torch for him—one that burned bright enough to obscure all her common sense—how had she so casually started dating Lachlan Gibbs?

Perhaps it wasn't the father. Perhaps there had been a friend, another person who was lovingly called *Aunt* or *Uncle* by the kid and was family in everything but blood. That person might have taken up the mantle of revenge without any of Marconi's restraint. And how could Marconi not protect them when they had killed on her behalf?

Neither scenario was impossible—or even implausible, for that matter—but they didn't quite sit right.

What remained? Guilt, blackmail, or a plan that Gretchen couldn't yet see.

A part of her wanted to believe Marconi had some secret scheme, and was simply waiting for the right time to unleash it. But why wouldn't she have clued Gretchen in?

Since the events with Shaughnessy, Gretchen had felt unmoored about many so-called truths in her life, but she would never doubt that Marconi, as of right now, trusted her. If there was a plan in place, Marconi would have said something other than *Goodbye* in the Porsche.

Gretchen dismissed blackmail almost immediately, as well. There were few fates that could be worse for Marconi than the one she was currently in. Even certain death might be preferable.

So that left guilt.

While Gretchen found the emotion to be utterly useless, she also could, at a distance, recognize its unmatched power. Her own life—so deeply and irrevocably shaped by Shaughnessy's guilt—was proof of that.

This picture seemed much clearer, steadier, more believable.

Foolish empath that she was, Marconi was covering for the real killer because she took responsibility for whatever had driven them to murder.

Gretchen thought about the victims' names, thought about a cornered serial killer and all that he might do if he sensed someone closing in on him, thought about the way parents' grief could hit bystanders, innocent or not, with the force of a tsunami, destroying everything in its wake.

There were still too many blanks for Gretchen to actually rule anything out. But she knew one thing to be certain.

If Marconi's investigation into Hayes had in any way led to the death of another child, Marconi would have taken that blood onto her own hands.

And that was a wrong she would have done anything to right.

CHAPTER FOURTEEN

LAUREN

Then

Connecting with Rafi, who worked shifts that could be as erratic as Lauren's, wasn't always easy. They could go two weeks without seeing each other.

It didn't help that Lauren wanted to take whatever relationship they were trying to build slow. Screwing around with Elijah's father wasn't exactly her brightest move, all things considered, but she was smart enough to keep *this* hidden from their son at least.

The stars aligned a week after the blizzard, and they spent Lauren's lunch break at the Maple Leaf Hotel on Pearl Street.

When Lauren shimmied back into her jeans, Rafi lit a cigarette, the sheet pooling at his waist.

There had always been something feral about his looks: thin lips, big eyes, a tiny underbite. But age was smoothing it all out into a face that was almost conventionally handsome. Women were always drawn in by his thick dark hair and intense focus, ignoring the imperfections that Lauren liked about him best.

"You ever going to let me see the kid?" Rafi asked as he always did, blowing smoke out of one corner of his mouth. The cigarette was why they never went to places that weren't missing at least three letters from their signs.

"Maybe when you stop calling him 'the kid,'" Lauren said, shoving her feet in her boots and shrugging on her heavy winter jacket. Vermont was its own special kind of hell when it came to the cold, and despite the fact that the storm had passed, there was still a frostbite advisory on, the kind of weather where ski resorts recommended customers not have any bare skin exposed to the cold.

Lauren could rarely manage that, but she hadn't lost a finger or chunk of her nose yet, so she figured that's what mattered. Vermonters were made of hardy stock.

"Elijah," Rafi overpronounced. He'd thought the name pretentious seven years ago, and it hadn't grown on him. Lauren hadn't given a shit then, and she certainly didn't now.

"Why rock the boat?" Lauren asked, yanking on her hat. Rafi had just gotten off his shift and didn't seem to be in any rush out the door. Meanwhile, Lauren was backlogged on her reports from the storm, had that cold case from Burlington waiting for her, and was trying to pull all the information on the Hayes family that she could find without raising too many questions from her boss.

That was all on top of her day-to-day duties, which too often involved monitoring the tricky stop sign by the high school that no one ever saw. As a midlevel uniform, Lauren didn't exactly get the glamorous assignments.

"Why rock the boat to . . . see my son?" Rafi asked, snuffing out the cigarette with an annoyed little jerk of his wrist. "You act like I'm some dangerous influence."

Lauren had already begun to sweat beneath her winter gear—a death sentence in this kind of weather—and she just didn't have the energy for this. Mostly because Rafi was right. They'd been seventeen and eighteen when she'd found out she was pregnant, and Rafi had panicked. He'd gotten himself a sixteen-year-old girlfriend and a drug habit and had rubbed both in Lauren's face until she'd kicked him out of her life.

He'd come crawling back about two years ago, after his own father had died. He'd cleaned up his life, gotten a job as an EMT, gotten a real apartment and everything.

Still, he hadn't pushed for visitation rights until recently.

Over the years, Lauren had let him see Elijah at holidays and a few other occasions that were always highly monitored, but his interest had always seemed lackluster at best. The only thing crappier than not seeing your dad was seeing your dad while he couldn't even pretend he was having fun in the process.

She wouldn't put Elijah through potential heartbreak just because Rafi all of a sudden wanted to play house.

Lauren had been perfectly happy with the arrangement, how it had been. She had enough money to buy Elijah a new pair of shoes when his own started to wear through, and Elijah had enough of her stoic personality not to sink into despair when his father would forget to send a birthday card. They'd both set their expectations a long time ago to nonexistent when it came to Rafi.

Sometimes she wondered what had changed, wondered what had Rafi champing at the bit to get custody rights now when he'd never wanted them before. If she hadn't been sleeping with him, she would have guessed a new girlfriend had been the impetus. Lauren had seen that on the job before. A deadbeat dad's new lover wanted the dude she was sleeping with to be better than he obviously was so she pushed him to spend more time with his kid.

And maybe that still was the case. Lauren couldn't swear she was the only one in Rafi's bed. Their hookups were so irregular that it wouldn't surprise her if she was in actuality the mistress in this situation. She hadn't heard any gossip around the station, but that didn't mean anything.

She tried to think back to when the subtle hints had first started. It hadn't been right away. That first night, they'd crossed paths at the

Dark Rose, each having weathered a particularly brutal shift. Lauren had kept pace with Rafi on tequila shots and then trailed him out of the pub once they'd hit the double digits.

The decision had been one of the stupidest she'd made in recent memory, but she'd repeated it only a month later. It had taken another two for Rafi to start asking about Elijah. First, it had been only vague questions about his friends and his school. Then he'd started talking about seeing Elijah more often, without Lauren around, even.

Maybe he'd created a pretty little fantasy of a nuclear family in his head. Neither of them had come from that cookie-cutter mold. Lauren had been raised in an increasingly dire series of foster homes while Rafi had grown up with an opioid-addicted mother and a grandmother who'd managed to just make it to his eighteenth birthday.

She'd thought him as cynical as she was when it came to the idea of a picture-perfect family.

He seemed to be proving her wrong, though.

"Can we do this some other time?" Lauren asked, waving a frustrated hand down her body. The corner of his mouth twitched in resigned acknowledgment. They'd both been born in Vermont; they knew the danger of standing around too long in winter clothes. Sweat killed in below-freezing temperatures.

Feeling guilty or magnanimous or something, Lauren crossed the room, rested her palms on the headboard, and kissed him with more heat than a goodbye deserved.

"Soon," she murmured against his mouth before pulling back. And then she snagged his packet of cigarettes and dropped them into the bucket of melted ice water on her way out. He yelled an ineffectual protest, and she flipped him off just as the door nearly closed on her hand.

She grinned all the way to the SUV.

Her mind was stuck back in the room, back on Rafi's push for *more*, and she blamed that distraction for why it took three blocks to realize the white pickup she'd clocked near the hotel was now following her.

CHAPTER FIFTEEN

GRETCHEN

Now

As the sky lightened into dawn, Gretchen pushed off the wall outside Fred's apartment and walked south toward the river. Her next destination was only a handful of blocks away.

She found Ryan Kelly exactly where she'd expected: sipping a—most likely whiskey-laced—coffee at the South Street Diner. His face was bathed in pink neon, and he had at least four newspapers spread out on the table in front of him.

Gretchen had met Kelly years ago, when he'd been fresh out of journalism school and thinking he was going to do big things and take down big names. Then he'd realized the *Boston Crier* was nothing but a soap opera in print, and the shine had quickly dulled. Gretchen found his complete lack of giving a shit endearing, and he found her brutal honesty hilarious. A match made in heaven, practically.

Like everything else in this town—and Gretchen's life, really—the relationship was symbiotic. Gretchen gave Kelly tips before other reporters, and Kelly gave her the gossip on the street for the low, low price of alcohol.

From the sidewalk, she scanned the other diners. Three eightysome-things sat clustered in a front booth, while a big man in flannel had taken the last stool at the counter. Besides them and the waitress, the diner was mostly empty.

The bell tinkled overhead as she stepped inside.

Kelly didn't look up until her thighs squeaked unattractively on the seat's vinyl.

He lowered his newspaper, only his eyes showing. They crinkled at the corners when he said, "What do you have for me?"

"Coffee, hon?" the waitress asked before Gretchen could respond. Gretchen flipped the cup in front of her in response and, at the woman's silent eyebrow raise, ordered scrambled eggs and pancakes.

She waited until she and Kelly were alone again. "A bottle of the most expensive liquor you can dream up."

Kelly laughed, and toyed with one of the six empty half-and-half containers in front of him. He was a fidgeter, always in motion. "I never thought I'd see the day I'd turn down that particular offer."

Gretchen took a hefty swallow of her coffee to avoid showing any reaction. She figured his price would be steeper than usual. She just hadn't wanted to play her hand too soon. "What do you want?"

"A scoop on that bestie of yours," Kelly said, now with one arm stretched along the back of the booth. The picture of nonchalance. The effect was ruined by the sheer hunger in his eyes, the kind he could never hide. He was a vulture; that was his nature.

"As if you have anything to warrant that kind of trade," Gretchen scoffed, deliberately dismissive. This dance was familiar, and usually fun. Right now she was exhausted, and her metaphorical emotional muscles that were already mostly atrophied were strained nearly to their breaking point. She stared out the window so she wouldn't give any of that away with her expression.

Everything was saturated with dawn's rose-gold tint, and she wondered idly how long this would take. Wondered what she would do next, each move a part of some high-stakes chess game where she couldn't see the board, the pieces, or her opponent.

Kelly had rolled up one of the newspapers and was drumming it against the table. They both kept silent as the waitress dropped off Gretchen's plate, refilled her mug, and then departed once more.

With careful precision, Gretchen began demolishing her stack of pancakes.

"Here's my counteroffer," Kelly finally said, and Gretchen waved magnanimously to get him to continue. "I'll keep you updated during the rest of the investigation, whatever we have even before we go to print."

It was more than Gretchen had expected. For all that Kelly had a scavenger's soul, in his chest beat the heart of a 1920s ace reporter, with starry eyes and deep-rooted ethics. On some things at least. Never before had he promised her advance warning to this extent.

Gretchen took a moment to savor the combination of butter and sugar and dough as she considered. This was a fine line to walk. It was helpful to have the inside scoop on what gossip had made it to the press, but giving away too much could burn her bridge with Lachlan.

What she needed was a juicy tidbit that wouldn't affect the case but would seem big.

One thing came immediately to mind.

She wasn't always an expert in predicting how any one person would react to something, but she *was* certain that Marconi would do physical damage if Gretchen let the tidbit slip.

On the other hand, Marconi was in jail, and if Gretchen didn't clear her name, she would remain there, would possibly die there. If, by chance, Marconi ever found out what Gretchen leaked and came at her with fists flying, at least that would mean Marconi had beaten the rap.

So the cost-benefit ratio still worked in favor of divulging the secret.

"Marconi was sleeping with Detective Lachlan Gibbs," Gretchen said, without even a single pang of guilt. "The rising star of the Internal Affairs Department."

Kelly's ragged inhale proved her assumptions correct. The detail was juicy, and it looked more important than it was. Lachlan had already recused himself from dealing with the investigation and put it on record with his supervisor. Kelly would probably have to run a follow-up tomorrow after the BPD's overworked PR team reamed the *Crier*, but for a full day he'd have the most-read article in town. A boon for both of them.

Gretchen loved logic.

"You're one ice-cold lady, you know that," Kelly said with a smile.

"I know that very well, thank you," Gretchen replied, trying to hide the laughter in her voice. She'd won this round even if he couldn't see it yet. Even if it meant Marconi would punish her later. Maybe someone else would believe the choice to be ethically ambiguous at best, but that's why Gretchen was good at this.

"I don't have anything you don't right now," Kelly admitted with a shrug as he removed the flask she'd known he had in his jacket pocket. He topped off his coffee with the liquor. "But I'll keep you updated."

Gretchen dabbed at the corners of her mouth, then stood up. "You do that."

"Hey, you owe me for breakfast," Kelly called after her. Gretchen flipped him the bird over her shoulder and sailed out the door, the bell tinkling once more.

Once she reached her car, Gretchen finally let herself stop thinking. She sank into the welcoming embrace of leather and perfume, the back of her skull cradled by the headrest. Her body ached despite the sugar rush. Her bones, her muscles, her tendons, each beating pulse reminded her that she was mortal. If she listened close, she could hear the quiet slog of tired blood thudding through her veins, her arteries.

Sleep beckoned, but so did a mystery. And thus far in her life, the latter had always won.

Today it did, as well. Tomorrow it might not.

Her phone dinged with an email, and she swiped it open.

Fred.

Just the basics, the subject line said.

In it were four separate attachments, each aligning with one of the boys' names in Marconi's file, and Gretchen went straight for Elijah's.

There had been an Amber Alert issued when he'd gone missing, which didn't surprise Gretchen. Nor was it shocking that the dad—Rafael Corado, according to the file—was listed as the possible abductor. Custody disputes were often at the heart of kidnappings. Random violence wasn't quite as common as Lifetime movies would have you think.

Corado had turned himself in nearly as soon as the alert had gone out, though. The cops had searched his car and triangulated his movements for the day using cell phone records. The only suspicious thing that had pinged was that he'd been at Marconi's apartment an hour before Elijah had been taken.

Marconi herself had vouched that she'd been there as well and that Elijah had not been.

That was . . . curious. And it made her wonder about her theory that Marconi might be protecting him by taking the fall for Hayes's death.

Had they been sleeping together the whole time they'd lived in Vermont, or had they reconnected for an afternoon tryst while their son was getting grabbed by a serial killer? Or was Gretchen making an innocent visit between coparents far more risqué than it had been?

For now, the reason Rafael had been with Marconi that afternoon was irrelevant because it still wasn't an alibi. Rafael had left the apartment before the time Elijah had been taken—between 3:05 and 3:15

p.m.—and though Rafael had said he headed straight home, there hadn't been anyone there to verify that.

The kid had been seen leaving the school building, and then he'd been lost in the shuffle of the parent pickup line. When Sandra Bowen—a family friend—had arrived to get him at 3:15 p.m., he had been nowhere to be found.

That window was incredibly tight. And it would have been even tighter had Bowen not been delayed because of a traffic accident three streets over. She'd told officers that she'd had to take a detour that added five minutes to the trip.

With kidnappings, that was plenty of time.

Still, if it had been a stranger, the man would have had to spin some kind of story to get through to a cop's kid. Gretchen would have pulled the *Your mom's been shot, she's in the hospital asking for you, get in* trick, and she had a feeling their perp had done just that.

All this spoke of practice and experience.

These were not crimes of opportunity. They were planned.

Which meant a seasoned serial killer had deliberately targeted a cop's kid.

Gretchen sucked in air and slammed the palm of her hand into her forehead.

Careless, sloppy. She'd thought that about Marconi touching the body, but she was just as guilty.

She had been assuming that Elijah's disappearance had triggered Marconi's interest in Hayes. But what if . . .

What if Marconi's interest in the missing boys had been what made Hayes go after Elijah in the first place? What if he'd wanted to either distract or punish Marconi and had come up with the perfect way to do so? Why else would he have taken a cop's son when he clearly hadn't been hurting for victims?

That was just asking for trouble.

Hadn't Gretchen just been thinking about guilt and bloody hands? Hadn't she *just* settled on the idea that Marconi wouldn't ever forgive herself if she was even indirectly responsible for getting an innocent child killed?

What if that child had been her own?

Gretchen had been basing all her scenarios on the idea that Marconi had been aware of her actions and in control of herself in Hayes's house. But what if she had learned something that had made her snap, made her disconnect from reality?

Dissociative identity disorder diagnoses had become all the rage a handful of decades back after that movie with Sally Field came out—an idiotic and irrational trend, as the disorder was extraordinarily rare. What wasn't rare was *dissociating*. Plenty of people would experience it in their lives, especially during, after, or in connection with some kind of major traumatic incident.

Had Marconi fired the gun without realizing it? Had she come back to herself only to find a body at her feet? Her guilt and grief and shame the missing piece to all this, an explanation for all the careless mistakes Gretchen couldn't ignore.

The story was intoxicatingly easy to tell.

But . . .

Her hand crept to the passenger seat, pressed against the fabric there. Marconi had been so composed, so coherent. The markers and symptoms weren't hard and fast, of course, but there had been nothing about her behavior to suggest she'd just come out of a dissociative episode.

Gretchen curled her fingers into a fist. If Marconi had kil—

She didn't let herself finish the thought.

There were other stories to tell that made just as much sense. Gretchen simply had to find them and hope that Marconi would stay alive long enough for it to matter.

CHAPTER SIXTEEN

LAUREN

Then

The driver of the white pickup that had been following Lauren since she'd left the hotel was nothing but a smudge behind a sun-glinted windshield. She could read the license plate just fine, though.

Lauren grabbed for the radio and called it in, taking a few left turns in a row to make sure she wasn't being paranoid. There were plenty of white pickups in Vermont, and this one was nothing special.

When she realized the driver wasn't even trying to blend into the rest of the traffic, she decided to stop doubting herself. This was an intimidation tactic.

The radio crackled. "Officer Marconi? That truck is registered to Garrett Adams of 42 Elmwood Avenue."

Part of her had been expecting it to be Hayes, so the name threw her.

"Anything else you need?" the dispatcher asked.

"No, thanks," Lauren said, but she didn't put the radio back yet, her eyes drifting to the rearview mirror. "Actually . . ."

"What's up?"

"I answered a domestic-violence call-in about a week ago, the first night of the storm. Around nine p.m.," Lauren said. "Is there any information to go along with it?"

"No, nothing, hon," said the dispatcher, whose voice Lauren finally recognized as an older woman named Ruth. "Area code was from California. Tip was anonymous."

"Okay, thanks," Lauren said, before reholstering the radio, her fingers drumming on the steering wheel.

Up ahead was a tight alley, and at the last second, she took a quick right to turn down it.

As expected, the truck followed her in.

Once she got about halfway, she slammed on the brakes and threw the SUV in park. In the next heartbeat, she was out of the car, advancing on the truck.

The driver hadn't been expecting a confrontation—that much was clear by the way the back end fishtailed from the abrupt stop.

In a flurry of movement, the man reached his hand over the passenger seat.

Gun? Lauren wondered, Elijah's face flashing into her mind. There was a reason she would be chewed out for not following procedure here. People got killed this way. She rolled onto the balls of her feet, readying to dive back behind the makeshift shield of the SUV, which she'd parked at a strategic angle for this very reason.

The man hadn't been going for a weapon, though. He'd been looking behind him, checking for obstructions. The tires screeched as he reversed out of the alley and back out onto the street. He disappeared from sight in the next second, leaving Lauren standing there, feeling foolish and inexperienced and stupid.

Lauren cursed but knew that unless she wanted to initiate a potentially dangerous sirens-on chase and haul him in, it was a lost cause for the moment. It was tempting to do so anyway, and she would have had she not gotten the license plate.

For now, that would suffice.

When she made it back to the station, Lauren ignored several people who tried to pull her into idle chitchat.

She threw herself into a chair in front of the desk she shared with a couple of other uniforms whenever they needed to do research.

While she was tempted to dive right into the databases, sometimes the simplest method was the best. So she pulled up a Google page, typed in **Garrett Adams** and **Montpelier**, and got her answer in the form of an article from about nine years earlier.

Local Boy, 9, Missing; Police Suspect Foul Play.

Lauren sat back, rubbing a hand over her mouth.

The boys in the basement.

The article was short on details but mentioned that Garrett Adams owned a diner in town, that his son, Damien, usually walked the three blocks from school by himself and one day didn't make it home.

When Lauren switched over to the official database, an earlier police report came up.

Two weeks before Damien had gone missing, he'd been approached by a strange man who'd talked with the boy for several minutes before getting spooked by a passerby.

The report noted that Garrett Adams had been convinced through Damien's description that the strange man had been Owen Hayes.

Detectives noted that Hayes hadn't been able to provide an alibi beyond "running errands in town," but also made sure to put down that Damien hadn't been able to identify him in a photo lineup. All they'd had to go on were Garrett's suspicions, and so they'd seemed to dismiss Hayes as a suspect pretty soon after.

Then, two weeks later, Damien had been taken.

Lauren pulled up the official missing person's report.

Garrett and Damien lived in a two-bedroom apartment above the diner, and cops had torn it up searching for evidence that Garrett might have been the one who'd killed his kid. They hadn't found anything, and Garrett had a solid—though not airtight—alibi for the window of time Damien had gone missing. There'd been a big retirement party at the diner, and multiple witnesses could attest to him being out in the main room most of the afternoon.

That also explained why it had taken him a little bit of time to notice Damien hadn't come home.

Uniforms had canvassed the area, looking for anyone who'd seen something strange. They'd talked to Owen Hayes several times. Local community leaders had organized search groups for the first few days after Damien's disappearance. No leads panned out, though.

Lauren could see the quiet resignation in the notes as days turned to weeks turned to months. No body, no clues, no suspects. How could a nine-year-old boy just disappear from the streets of Montpelier? How could no one have seen anything?

But life wasn't one of those procedural shows. Sometimes bad shit happened and the villains got away with their crimes.

At the bottom of the file was a note linking Damien's folder to another one a few counties over. She copied and pasted the info into the search bar.

Joshua Westwood. Eight years old, reported missing during a short stop at a gas-station convenience store, where his mother swore she'd looked away for only one minute.

Lauren grabbed a pen to jot the name down. The interesting thing to note was that he'd also been approached by a strange man about a week before his disappearance. Ashley Westwood, the mother, hadn't been able to identify Hayes at first but later picked him out of a photo lineup.

The detectives had reached out to Owen Hayes, noting that he'd been caught on camera at the gas station only a few minutes before

Joshua had gone missing. But he'd produced a receipt from a hardware store across town. When the cops had interviewed the cashier, the boy had said he'd remembered talking to Hayes for several minutes and nothing had seemed off about him.

Toggling back to Damien's file, Lauren saw one last note from the detectives before it had been archived as inactive.

Hayes had called the cops on Garrett Adams about three years ago when the man had parked himself outside the farmhouse for several days straight. Adams had been threatened with a restraining order but agreed to back off. There wasn't anything in the file since then, so she assumed he'd complied. Except . . .

It had never made sense that someone had called in a domestic dispute on Hayes that night of the storm. The closest neighbors to the farmhouse were a mile away. Even if the person had driven up to the place by accident, they wouldn't have been able to hear shouting over the wind.

What if the anonymous caller had been Garrett Adams on a burner phone, desperate to get someone to take his suspicions seriously?

Now he was following Lauren to see if she was going to do anything about Hayes.

Had he believed she would find something? Or had he just been banking on the fact that Hayes had a way of provoking suspicion all on his own?

A foot lightly kicked her desk.

"I called your name a couple times," Investigation Division Chief Imani Abaza said, when Lauren's eyes snapped up to hers.

"Sorry," Lauren said, shaking her head to try to clear the fog. "I'm . . . yeah, sorry. Did you need me?"

"No, but I did want to see what had you racing in here." Abaza's attention caught on Lauren's computer screen.

Lauren grimaced. Abaza was tolerant of the cold cases Lauren picked up in her spare time, but that grace only went so far when they were short-staffed and behind from the blizzard.

"Don't you have paperwork to finish?" Abaza said, and although it came out fairly neutral, Lauren still flushed.

She glanced around to make sure no one could overhear. There were two other cops at their desk, a detective from Vice and an officer who was right on the cusp of a promotion to Major Crimes. Something Stevens, she remembered now. Maybe Joe. He was trying not to be obvious about the way his gaze kept drifting to them. Months ago, Lauren had clocked him as ambitious, misogynistic, and jealous.

"Can we talk in your office?" Lauren asked, leaning back in her chair to meet the division chief's eyes.

Abaza nodded once and turned. Lauren followed a few steps behind so that Abaza had already situated herself behind her imposing desk by the time Lauren was closing the door.

"I have kind of a wild hunch," Lauren said as she sat, resting the folder on her knees. "This could be absolutely nothing. And before I even explain, I should tell you I'm basing this on a seven-year-old's nighttime babbling and a weird feeling. You might not even want to waste your time hearing it."

Abaza studied Lauren, everything about her perfectly still. Lauren had learned long ago that Abaza had absolutely no tells. She didn't fidget, didn't flinch or wince or tug at her ear or tap her fingers on the table. No matter what emotion she was feeling, she always held herself as composed as marble. Finally, she waved a hand. "Lay it on me."

Lauren slumped back in the chair, a broken spring digging into the meat of her thigh, and she explained. The anonymous tip, the Hayes farmhouse, the basement, waking to find Julia by her bed, hearing about the boys who came to the house without any mothers, Martha's subdued manner when she'd been alone with Lauren. The way Owen had booted her out at the earliest opportunity.

Finally, she got to the pickup truck, and for the first time Abaza's eyebrows pulled into a disappointed vee.

"You shouldn't have done that without backup, Marconi."

Lauren tried not to sound defensive. "I know, you're right. But when I got back, I searched the name of the owner. Garrett Adams."

"And?"

"And he thinks Owen Hayes is responsible for the disappearance of his kid," Lauren said. "He was even cited for harassing Hayes about it a few years ago."

Abaza drummed her fingers on the table. "I'll have Tobias and Smith go talk to him."

It was a dismissal. Lauren tried to hide her frustration, but Abaza knew her too well.

"This isn't your purview, Officer Marconi," Abaza said, gentle but firm. She called Lauren by her title only when she wanted to impose her will on her. "Leave it alone. And if Adams or Hayes bothers you again, I want you to call it in immediately." She paused, studied Lauren's face. "You're not on Major Crimes yet. You'll have plenty of cases like this once you get there."

No, Lauren was going to be stuck pulling over harried parents who were too busy to see a stop sign right in front of their own faces. Or taking notes for detectives like Tobias and Smith, if she was lucky.

But complaining about it would get her nowhere.

"Thank you," she murmured, standing up.

When she went back to her computer, she erased her search history and tried to put both Damien Adams and Joshua Westwood out of her mind.

She managed for most of the day; she managed when she made Elijah dinner and gave him a bath. She managed all the way up to her second glass of wine, when she pulled out the rusty hand-me-down laptop she hardly ever used and started her own file on the boys in the basement.

CHAPTER SEVENTEEN

GRETCHEN

Now

Gretchen had another stop to make following her conversation with Ryan Kelly, but first she needed the appropriate armor. And so she detoured to her town house.

She headed straight to her closet, her fingers trailing over silk and wool until they landed on the dress. The perfect dress.

The red fabric draped in a way that gave her athletic body soft curves it didn't naturally have. Maybe it should have washed out her pale coloring, but instead it made everything about her pop, made her skin look all the more creamy in contrast. She paired it with a cherry lip and a generous hand with the foundation to cover the purple smudge of exhaustion beneath her eyes. She smoothed down her white-gold bob into rigid submission, to get the perfectly polished look she knew would make her target particularly weak in the knees.

Then she stepped into stilettos with bottoms that matched the dress—and her Porsche—perfectly. After one last satisfied glance in the mirror, she grabbed her keys once more and headed back out to the street.

It took Gretchen only fifteen minutes to get to her destination, half of what it would have been had she obeyed traffic laws, and she parked next to a shiny black Jaguar that would have to be traded in for something more sensible if its owner was actually serious about his political ambitions.

Gretchen grinned as she ran the tip of her key along the back flank of the car, the perfect paint job giving way beneath her pettiness.

The amusement stuck with her all the way on the elevator and through the lobby.

The secretary tried to stop her, but Gretchen ignored the shouts, stepping into District Attorney Cormac Byrne's office without even knocking.

He glanced up, anger brewing in the space between his carefully manicured brows, but it dissipated as quickly as it gathered once he caught sight of her. He rolled his eyes, and she realized he was on the phone only when he murmured, "I have to call you back," before hanging up.

Cormac stood, and crossed the room, his long legs eating up the space quickly. He kissed each cheek and gripped her arms. "I was expecting you at least an hour ago."

"That's because you always overestimate your own importance," Gretchen said, side-stepping him and rounding the desk. She lowered herself into his expensive leather chair and crossed her legs so that the edge of her stockings and the beginning of her garters peeked out.

"Yet here you are," Cormac said, amused instead of irritated as he took the chair meant for visitors. It was far less comfortable, intentionally so. Cormac might work for the government, but he was a shark at heart. He could have made buckets of money as a defense attorney, especially in this town. But he had buckets of money already—his family, the Mayflower kind—which actually seemed to mean something here. "I can't deny it would be fun to watch you attempt to beg, but I'll save you the indignity. I'm going to push for life."

The only regret Gretchen had about keying his Jag was that she hadn't made the cut deeper.

"You know about begging, don't you?" Gretchen purred, her fingertips brushing against her collarbone before dropping to her thigh. His eyes followed the movement, as she'd intended. But he didn't blush like she'd hoped at her reference to the nights they'd spent together when they were both too lazy to find someone else.

Like plenty of powerful men Gretchen knew, Cormac liked to give up power in the bedroom. He didn't trust her enough—or at all, really, and wisely so—to provide her with anything that could actually be used to tarnish any of his future campaigns, but she knew enough to make him uncomfortable.

Except, Cormac was a politician's son, a politician's grandson. A wannabe politician himself. It would take more than innuendo to get him to react negatively when in public. And despite their trysts, he would consider her "public."

"What do you want, Gretch?" Cormac asked, and she tried not to ruffle at the casual nickname.

Gretchen dropped the seductive act, sitting forward to lean her arms on his desk. "Hayes kidnapped and killed little boys."

"No, he didn't," Cormac corrected without missing a beat. "He was an initial suspect in a string of kidnappings in another state. And he cleared his name through alibis." He paused, donning a supercilious air, and she knew she was going to hate whatever came next. She was proven right when he continued. "We have a justice system for a reason."

"Oh right, that flawless United States justice system," Gretchen said, nearly laughing. "It could never make a mistake. How foolish of me."

Cormac surprised her by not putting up a fight. "Touché. He had jury duty for at least one of the kidnappings, though."

"One of the suspected kidnappings," Gretchen shot back. "And what's more likely? That the one boy was unrelated to the other disappearances or that Hayes was innocent of all of them?"

"I've looked at one or two of the cases," Cormac said. "I'm not convinced there was even a serial killer operating in the area, let alone that it was Hayes."

Gretchen huffed out a disbelieving breath, and then realized what he'd said. "How many cases have you pulled from that time period?"

"I'll show you mine if you show me yours."

"Seven," Gretchen bluffed.

His thick brows shot up. He was irritatingly handsome in that polished, Massachusetts JFK kind of way, and he could speak volumes with just his well-defined features. "Nine. And that's all you're getting out of me."

"Nine," Gretchen said. "But you don't think there was a serial killer there?"

"Vermont has one of the highest rates of missing persons reports per capita," Cormac said, ever the smooth politician.

"Right, no need to consider they were all of similar ages and from a relatively small area." Gretchen couldn't hold back the sarcasm despite the fact that she was here for a favor. "That could complicate the story you're telling. Wouldn't want that."

Cormac lifted one shoulder, unfazed. "I still like the father for Elijah Marconi's death."

"He was cooperative," Gretchen pointed out, even though she knew what he would reply with.

"A little too cooperative," Cormac shot back. "And he was at the kid's house before he realized his son was at school instead."

"So was Marconi," Gretchen said. "And what about the other boys?"

"I think Corado probably took advantage of a pedophile operating in the area," Cormac said easily. Gretchen hated how quick he was. Conversations with most people usually made her all too aware of the constant need to hold tight to the reins of her temper. But Cormac was clever, keeping her engaged in parrying without her thinking too much about the sword in her hand.

"And killed his kid to get back at Marconi?" Gretchen asked. "How do you think he got away with that?"

"He had a girlfriend who knew Elijah. The kid would have gotten in the car with her," Cormac suggested. "It would have been easy."

"Is that a supposition or fact?"

"Supposition, Your Honor." He flashed her that charming grin that made his perfect dimple pop. "But does it really matter? Owen Hayes was investigated and found to be innocent. And Detective Marconi continued her campaign of harassment against him until it escalated to murder."

Gretchen looked away, her eyes landing on the Monet on the far side of his office. "You're going to have to tone down the excessive markers of wealth if you want to get into the White House on a progressive platform."

She didn't have to look to hear the grin in Cormac's voice. "You're here to give me political advice now? What do you charge for that?"

"On the house," Gretchen said, plucking up one of his fountain pens. She imagined sinking it into that soft spot on his neck where his pulse fluttered beneath lotioned skin. She let him see her imagining it. "Were there any missing boys near Hayes's house in Waltham?"

The amusement dropped out of his expression. "No."

"That you've found yet." Gretchen tapped out an uneven rhythm on the legal pad in front of her. Cormac liked the trappings of days gone by. Nothing was written on the paper, though, which about summed up Cormac better than she ever could.

"Was it her gun that was used to kill him?" Gretchen asked, hoping to catch him off guard.

His mouth pinched in and he sighed. "I shouldn't."

"But you will."

"One freebie, and that's it," Cormac said, pointing at her. "Bullets didn't match her registered firearm."

There was that at least. It might mean that the frame-up hadn't been intentional. Or it could just mean the real killer had been banking on the fact that it would be assumed Marconi had an unregistered weapon somewhere.

"What about the wife?" Gretchen asked.

"The wife?"

Gretchen scoured her memory. She knew she'd heard the name sometime over the past twelve hours. "Martha."

He laughed, though she wasn't sure why. "She has an alibi."

"Wives have hired hitmen for less," Gretchen pointed out.

"I'll look into it," he said, and she could tell he was humoring her.

Gretchen dropped the pen, stood, and crossed the room to stand in front of Cormac. She patted his cheek so that it brought a flush to his skin.

"Good boy," she said, and had the satisfaction of finally getting a reaction from him. Dilated pupils, a barely noticeable—but still there— hitch in his breath.

She grinned, showing too much incisor for it to read as anything but predatory, and then started for the door, letting her hips sway with each step.

"Hey," he called out. Always needing the final word. "I'm sorry about Shaughnessy."

Gretchen froze, her fingers already curled around the door's handle, everything slipping slightly out of focus. People thought sociopaths didn't have feelings, but that wasn't true. She just didn't experience them the way others did.

Right now the rage came as a tightness in her chest, but the grief came as a tremble in her hand, a new dryness in her throat.

She understood people more than anyone gave her credit for. They saw her diagnosis and forgot she had a doctorate in psychology.

This was Cormac's return thrust to her pat on his cheek, for making him feel vulnerable and small. There were few things in life Cormac Byrne hated more than that.

And so he'd reminded her that he'd been the one who had sent Shaughnessy to prison, where he'd been killed by a rusty shiv.

She didn't bother turning around. She wasn't sure she could control her face at the moment.

"I'm not."

CHAPTER EIGHTEEN

MARTHA

Before

A coffee cup slid into sight, catching on a crack in the diner's laminated table.

"I didn't order that," Martha said, staring at the cup.

"On the house."

Martha's eyes snapped up to meet cold blue ones.

Garrett was angry. She shouldn't have come here, she knew that.

When he saw the tear streaks, though, his mouth relaxed out of its pinched annoyance. His expression still wasn't exactly welcoming, but it was warm enough that her heart started beating once more. "Thanks."

It came out a whisper, but he nodded once and let her be. She'd tucked herself into a back booth, the shadows swallowing her away from any hungry eyes. Montpelier acted like a small town sometimes—she couldn't count on someone not mentioning this visit to Owen.

That's why Garrett was angry. He didn't like it when she risked her own safety. Risked her freedom, if she were being honest. How much would it take for Owen to start restricting her movements? They only had one car, and he kept a careful hold of the keys.

Still, the few times she'd been allowed to drive into town, she hadn't been able to stay away from Garrett Adams.

Martha drank the coffee Garrett had poured. Black because he was mad at her, hot because he couldn't help himself.

Then she stood, made like she was heading toward the bathroom. At the last second, she ducked into the darkened hallway that led to a small closet-size office. She didn't bother knocking, just stepped through the door.

Rough hands grabbed her, pushed her. The intensity so different than it was with Owen. Lust rather than some dark and twisted contempt.

Her back hit the wall, and then Garrett's mouth was on hers, all hot, seeking desperation.

As he pulled back, he nipped at her lip, nearly drawing blood.

Then he rested his forehead against her shoulder, panting.

She palmed the nape of his neck, closed her eyes, felt them breathing together.

Garrett finally bit out, "You can't be here, Martha."

"I know," she said, more an exhale. She thought about the bathroom a few nights back, the blood and the tub and the desire to sink beneath the water. She wondered if it had been Garrett's baby who had refused to come into her household. Wondered if, had it been born, she would have driven herself crazy with the not knowing. "I missed you."

They'd stopped all this, and she should have left it that way.

They'd started up a few weeks after Martha had moved to town. She'd had a fight with Owen and ended up in the only open bar in town. Back when she'd actually been able to drive away without needing to ask.

Garrett had ordered her a water.

She'd begged him to take her back to his place.

They'd met up only a handful of times since then. Always after Martha remembered the way Owen would look at the playgrounds for too long.

What did it say about her that she never stopped him? Never said anything? Never tried to actually run or leave an anonymous tip with the local police chief?

All she ever did was pretend she hadn't seen. Pretend she didn't know.

And then she would find someone with big, rough hands and quiet, soulful eyes who could make her brain go quiet.

A monster lived in her. A different breed than the one that lived in Owen. But it was there nonetheless, ready to feast on her cowardice, on her need to please.

Martha dug her fingers into Garrett's hair, tugged until he lifted his head, until his mouth came down on hers once more.

She needed to forget the monster, and Garrett was perfect for that.

Afterward, she straightened her dress and stepped out of the office without saying anything else.

Instead of returning to the diner, Martha made a left to head for the back exit.

Only she stopped, blocked.

A boy stood there. Floppy haired with one missing front tooth, the rest of them too big for his mouth. "Who are you?"

Martha smiled, though it probably came out shaky. "A friend."

She didn't need to ask the boy's name.

CHAPTER NINETEEN

GRETCHEN

Now

Gretchen's phone lit up on the Porsche's passenger seat as she wove through the traffic lining the streets near Cormac Byrne's office.

The screen flashed DICKWAD, and Gretchen grinned, pleased in nearly the same way as she had been while digging her keys into Cormac's Jag.

Release valve was how she'd described the impulses to Marconi. There was only so much pressure a person could keep inside them until they burst. But committing harmless, petty acts helped burn off some of that tension so that Gretchen could function on her most stressful days.

"What do you have for me?" Gretchen asked as the phone connected to her car's speakers.

"I just got a call from the prosecutor's office," Lachlan said. Of course, he was calling her to chastise her. Pointing out what other people had done wrong was the part of his job he loved the most.

"Snitches get stitches," she murmured.

"I'll be sure to remember that when Byrne's body turns up in a ditch somewhere."

"See, that's your problem," Gretchen said as her back tires skittered on a particularly vicious turn. "You think his body would be found. You lack creativity, and that blind spot is killing you on this Marconi case."

"You know what most classic literary heroes die from?" Lachlan asked.

"From being boring," Gretchen said, already done with this conversation.

"Hubris," Lachlan corrected.

"Oh, thank you, Homer." A horn honked behind her, and Gretchen flipped the driver the finger out the window. "Am I to take it you're attempting to draw some parallel to me?"

"I always knew you were clever."

"You know what else those heroes have in common?" Gretchen asked, and then continued without waiting for an answer. "They're fictional."

"As if your giant ego isn't your Achilles' heel."

"I think my Achilles' heel is my complete lack of empathy for other people," Gretchen said cheerfully. "In case you wanted to know, yours is that high horse you ride around on until your balls get swollen and sore."

"Delightful picture you paint there," Lachlan retorted dryly.

"Yet Marconi found them appealing for some reason," Gretchen mused. "Though I can't imagine she'll take you throwing her under the bus well."

"I didn't throw—" He cut himself off with an annoyed grunt, and she grinned. This was already going better than her exchange with Cormac, which had left her feeling twitchy and raw. She didn't enjoy not knowing whether she'd won a conversation. Some people might argue that you couldn't win a conversation, but those people weren't her.

She decided not to think about the fact that she could draw a straight line from Cormac's mention of Shaughnessy to her extra-salty attitude toward Lachlan.

"Why did you call?" Gretchen demanded.

"You leaked our relationship to the press."

"Oops?"

There was a beat of silence. Then: "I assume you got something from it."

"Whatever the tabloids scrounge up on the case," Gretchen offered easily.

"A fair trade," Lachlan said.

Gretchen was almost disappointed at the lack of a fight. "I thought you'd give me more shit than that."

"Sorry, you acting like the trash-fire human you are is low on my list right now," Lachlan retorted. "But I can try to work up some surprise if it would make you feel better."

"You better be careful. I might start thinking you're flirting with me," Gretchen said, amused at his attempts at cruelty. People with a conscience were rarely any good at it. She'd grown up with two narcissists and a serial killer in her household. Taunts like Lachlan's stung as much as a mosquito bite. Even less so, if she were being honest.

"Not even if you were the last person on earth," Lachlan said, though there was humor in his voice now.

"Right back at you, darling," Gretchen cooed. "Still, you're the one calling me."

"To make sure you're not doing anything to get Marconi into even deeper water," he countered. He was probably telling the truth on that front. She'd been half-curious about what other reason he must have for working with Gretchen beyond finding out what Marconi had said. Keeping her on a leash was certainly more effective when the line of communication was kept open.

Not that she cared what he was attempting to do. Let him think he held the leash. He'd find out at some point that it was just his imagination. "So is this you just slapping me on the wrists? Or did you have something actually useful to impart?"

"Mostly the wrist thing." But Lachlan took a breath as if preparing to give bad news. "The judge didn't grant bail."

"No surprise there."

"No," Lachlan said. "But it does mean no one will be able to see her until she's processed. Being that it's Friday, that means, at best, Monday."

So there was no hope in grilling Marconi this weekend, then. "Even with your badge?"

"Even with my badge," he agreed. He seemed to sense something in her tone. In a hushed voice, he asked, "What are you planning?"

"Oh, now he wants in on the prison break," Gretchen said, banging an illegal U-ie with one hand on the wheel. "Where are you?"

"The station."

"Do you have a go bag?" Gretchen asked, half wanting him to say no, half wanting him to make some remark that would have her turning back to her previous destination. But she knew his badge would get her in places that merely flashing a consultant business card wouldn't. Especially since they would have no jurisdictional rights whatsoever.

"Of course," he said, though it came out hesitant.

"Well done, you," Gretchen murmured. "Meet me outside in"— she glanced at the clock, glanced at the gridlock in front of her—"ten minutes."

"Uh, no," Lachlan said. "I'm not leaving the city, and I'm certainly not going anywhere with you."

"You've recused yourself. They're keeping you informed as a courtesy, but you're not going to be able to actually do anything with the investigation." She paused. "You just want to sit around with your thumb up your ass?"

"Always lovely," he murmured. "Still not getting in a car with you."

The only reason she hadn't hung up yet was because Lachlan's authority and badge would be useful enough that the energy she was expending to convince him was worth it. "Do you know my solve rate?"

"Let me guess, it's impressive," Lachlan said, and she all but heard him rolling his own eyes. "I don't care."

If he didn't view her as the asset she was, then she'd make use of his contempt. "Fine, I'll go without you."

He cursed, like she'd known he would. He'd already revealed that he didn't want her running wild all over this case, which is why people should keep their thoughts to themselves. Otherwise they could be used as leverage.

There was nothing he could do to stop her from taking a road trip. If he wanted to keep an eye on her, he'd have to come along.

Without even acknowledging the truth they both knew, he said instead, "Dare I ask where we're going?"

There were times in investigations that Gretchen could see too many paths forward. Each would tug at her belly, pull her along so that she ended up split in too many directions. That was already happening with this case.

And in those instances, the best place to go was back to the beginning.

Where it had all started.

Gretchen smiled as she answered. "Montpelier, Vermont."

———

Lachlan was as obnoxious a passenger as he was a colleague. He did that thing with his foot where he stomped an invisible brake, and Gretchen couldn't help but compare him unfavorably to Marconi. The woman had yet to flinch even once from Gretchen's driving.

"What did Lauren say to you?" Lachlan asked as she merged onto the highway toward Vermont.

She glanced at him. He didn't quite fit into the Porsche, too tall and lanky for the bucket seat, his knees pressed comically against the dash, his shaved head nearly brushing the top. Still, he somehow pulled off *disgruntled dignity*, just as he always did, his white button-down starkly pristine against his dark skin, his dove-gray trousers tailored to perfection, everything about him pressed and polished.

"Do you think if you just spring that question at random enough times you'll surprise an answer out of me?" Gretchen asked, her speedometer creeping toward one hundred.

Lachlan gripped the passenger side door. "What I think is that it might distract me from my impending death."

Gretchen rolled her eyes. "Such a drama queen."

But the question reminded her of what had been lurking at the back of her mind since Cormac had given her the real number of victims the authorities knew about.

There had been only four names on that thumb drive.

Joshua Westwood.

Nathaniel Parker.

Caleb Andrews.

Elijah Marconi.

If there were at least nine boys, why had Marconi included only those other three in the file she was keeping on her son's killer?

Whom had she left out, and, more significantly, which were more important: the excluded boys or the ones who had made the cut?

Of course, Gretchen couldn't rule out the possibility that Marconi had simply missed some of the victims. But if Cormac Byrne's team could identify nine boys over the course of only a few hours, Gretchen guessed Marconi had found more than three in her time investigating Hayes.

When Gretchen reached behind the seat to get her phone from her bag, Lachlan made an absolutely undignified sound and grabbed for the wheel.

She grinned at him and hit call on Fred's contact. Before Fred could say anything, Gretchen warned, "You're on speakerphone, and Gibbs is in the car with me."

"Are you driving out of the city to more easily hide his body?"

Gretchen sent Lachlan an assessing look. "Jury's still out."

"I'd like to remind you that threatening a police officer's life is punishable with up to a year in jail," Lachlan said dryly.

"Mmm, worth it," Gretchen said, then turned her attention back to Fred. "Anything on Hayes?"

"His childhood is pretty much the cliché of what you see in all the serial-killer origin stories," Fred said, almost on a sigh. At best, she tended toward misandry; at worst, she bent fairly close to Gretchen's own diagnosis. But she had too much of a soft spot for child-abuse victims to ever get herself on the sociopathy spectrum. "Dad was a Vietnam vet with PTSD demons. He beat the crap out of Hayes and the mother so that they both landed in the hospital several times a year."

"Was he ever charged?"

"Nope," Fred said, letting the *p* pop with disgust. "Lots of clumsy falls down the stairs, according to Mom, who decided to exit stage left via two bottles of temazepam when Hayes was nine."

"Nine," Gretchen murmured.

"Yup," Fred agreed. Right around the age the boys were being taken. "That left Hayes alone with dear old Daddy for nine more years before he got the hell out of Dodge. He went to a small college in Vermont on a full-ride scholarship. Met Martha Turnbull there, married her once they both graduated."

"Anything that looks suspicious after that?"

"Not even a speeding ticket," Fred said with an edge to her voice, and Gretchen hummed knowingly.

Lachlan cleared his throat. "I'd like to be the voice of reason here and point out that not having a record does not make someone suspicious."

Gretchen rolled her eyes and took the phone off speaker. "Yeah, ignore him. He thinks like a cop."

"You're not far from thinking like a cop these days," Fred poked.

"Slander," Gretchen said on a fake gasp, enjoying talking to Fred after a morning full of Kelly and Cormac and Lachlan. "Anything on the missing boys?"

"His victims," Fred said as she seemed to be pulling something up. "All right, here we go. You said there were four Marconi mentioned?"

"Joshua Westwood, et cetera," Gretchen agreed, just to get her to move along. Lachlan made some annoyed sound beside her—probably because she'd referred to three of the victims as "et cetera." She rolled her eyes. He was so sensitive. "Byrne said it might be more like nine boys."

"Yeah, that seems much closer to what I'm finding," Fred confirmed. "It all started about a year after Hayes and Martha moved to Montpelier, and then it's about one boy a year for the ten years he was in the area."

"Active but not escalating," Gretchen mused.

"Yeah," Fred said. "And he was really careful."

"What do you mean?"

"Only two of the boys were from Montpelier, and those were eight years apart," Fred said. "The others were from different jurisdictions, and he made sure not to take two in a row from any one county or city. I even found a likely case just over the border in New Hampshire."

"Which is how he operated as an active serial killer in a small state for ten years," Gretchen said, following Fred's logic.

"With a very specific victimology—boys between the ages of seven and nine, most with single mothers. Well, in one case, a single father, but all in one-parent households. Similar in appearance," Fred said. "I'm not sure I can draw any conclusions here but . . ."

"You know I love it when people trail off midsentence," Gretchen said.

"Elijah fits the victimology, but he doesn't fit the timeline," Fred said, unruffled. "His kidnapping was about three months after the boy before him."

It wasn't hard to guess that Fred had come to the same conclusion Gretchen had earlier. "Elijah was punishment for Marconi digging into Hayes's business."

"I mean, it's just a theory, but yeah," Fred said.

Part of Gretchen longed for a whiteboard or even just a wall to draw on so she could identify patterns in the cases. She wanted to see the boys' names, the locations from where they'd been taken, the months that Hayes had spent in his cooling-off periods—as if she were working any other serial-killer case.

Except they weren't trying to catch a serial killer. They were trying to figure out who had murdered *him*. Lachlan would call her callous for it, and as much as it pained her to prove him right, she couldn't help but think that she didn't even need to know these extra boys' names. There was a chance that the boys Marconi had created files for were important in some way, but at the end of the day, when it came to understanding serial killers, there was only one victim who mattered.

"Who was the first boy who disappeared?" she asked.

"His name was Damien," Fred said, without missing a beat. "Damien Adams."

CHAPTER TWENTY

LAUREN

Then

Garrett Adams owned the diner on Elmwood Avenue, the one that still served outrageously cheap coffee in the era of Starbucks. He catered to the locals instead of the tourists, and that much was obvious given that there was only one car parked in the lot despite it being a Friday at noon.

The battered sedan belonged to old Sam Jones, who was known for his perfect attendance record at the minor league baseball team's home games.

Lauren tried not to stop as she drove by the place, but her SUV ended up next to the sedan. Abaza couldn't fault her for getting her caffeine fix.

Sam didn't even look up when Lauren walked into the diner, but Garrett Adams did.

She compared his current self to the pictures that had run in that nearly decade-old article. The time between the kidnapping and now hadn't been kind to the man. He wasn't old—early forties, at most—but he had deep lines in his weathered face. There were wide swaths of silver in his overgrown beard that matched the salt at his temples. His cheeks were hollowed, his face gaunt.

His flannel shirt was clean, as were his big, calloused hands. Lauren would never think to call him unkempt, but she had the impression that if he didn't have a business to run, he would have drifted closer toward that description.

Beyond his looks, there was just something *hard* about him, as if he'd seen too much of life. And she supposed he had.

He'd frozen when she walked in, his fist tight against the rag he'd been using to clean the counter, but after a long, tense moment, he sighed and jerked his chin toward one of the swiveling stools.

As she crossed the room, she unwound her scarf, shoving it in her bag. Garrett's back was to her—he'd reached for a plain white coffee mug and grabbed the caffeinated pot without even asking.

She welcomed the cup with a small smile, inhaling the warmth and the rich scent while she waved away the creamer.

They hadn't said anything to each other yet. Lauren knew it should be strange, but somehow it wasn't.

While she drank her coffee, Garrett drifted to the far end of the counter. He carried on a hushed conversation with Sam, which seemed to result in Garrett comping Sam's lunch in order to hustle him out of the diner.

Lauren nodded once at Sam's jaunty salute, and then shifted her attention back to Garrett until she heard the tinkle of the bell.

"You can't be following me," Lauren said, without preamble once they were alone.

Garrett looked away, and she could swear there was a tint of pink in his cheeks. "I wasn't."

"Sure," Lauren said, resting her forearms on the counter. "It must have been someone else that took that truck of yours—the one that's right now parked around back—and trailed me through the city. Then they must have returned it. Mighty nice of them, wouldn't you say?"

His lips disappeared into a thin, white line as he met her eyes. His were a faded, white-washed-denim-type blue, she noted absently.

Ropy tendons flexed in the arms he'd crossed over his chest, and she wondered how much willpower he was exerting in not losing it on her completely.

"I wouldn't have to follow you if you people did your goddamn jobs," he said, voice raspy as if he didn't use it much.

"You can't be following me," Lauren said again, calmly. The weight of her gun against her hip reassuring, though she realized she wasn't frightened. Despite his bulk, Garrett clearly had impeccable control.

It was almost like watching a stallion, one that had been broken but had also just been insulted. Raw power, rage, and grief for a lost wildness. And yet a fierce grip on all of it.

Garrett tugged at his beard, his knuckles thick and cracked from the cold. "All right."

Lauren raised her brows. "That's it?"

He cut his eyes back to meet hers. "You going to do something about Hayes?"

"Why do you think there's something that needs to be done?" Lauren asked instead of answering.

"You seem too smart to think there isn't."

"I want to hear it from you," Lauren said.

"I've told that story a hundred times and look where it's gotten me." Garrett tossed the rag he'd still been clutching, nervous, agitated energy rippling beneath his skin.

"You've never told it to me," Lauren countered.

That got those faded blue eyes back on her. Somewhere beneath the mountain-man beard he might have been handsome; somewhere beneath the years of anger and mourning, he most certainly had been.

He seemed to make some decision, and in a few long strides he came out from behind the counter and flipped the lock on the door, muttering something that sounded like *Screw it* under his breath.

When he returned, it was to sit on a stool a few down from hers, his long legs spread around the side, leaning his palms on the vinyl seat as he stared at her. "I was having an affair with Martha Hayes not long before Damien's disappearance."

If Garrett had straight up punched Lauren in the face, she would have been less shocked. "Huh."

His mouth twitched at that. "Yeah."

Her mind had gone completely blank at the admission, so she didn't even have a follow-up question to ask. He didn't wait for her to come up with any.

"There's more as to why I think it was Hayes," Garrett said. "But I'd never mentioned that part. And I should have."

"Why didn't you?" Lauren managed to get out.

Garrett grimaced. "Even if I was wrong about Hayes being guilty, he would have killed Martha if he'd found out she was sleeping with me. And at the time, I cared about that."

"You don't anymore?"

He looked away, didn't answer. After a beat he said, "You know Hayes tried to take Damien and failed before he succeeded, right?"

"I know a strange man approached him, yes," Lauren said as carefully as possible.

"Look, I know what Hayes looks like," he said, and then deliberately met her eyes. "Believe me. I had to."

Because of the affair, he was implying.

"But Damien didn't say it was him, correct?" Lauren pressed. "Just described him."

"Down to a shirt I was familiar with." The leash keeping his frustration at bay was clearly fraying.

"Mr. Adams . . . ," she said as kindly as possible.

"No, don't do that," Garrett said, voice tight. With anyone else, she would have expected a finger pointed in her face, but he remained still. "Don't use that tone."

They sat in tense silence.

"There was another parent," Garrett continued before Lauren could ask anything else. "Ashley Westwood. Her son was named Joshua."

"I read about her," Lauren said.

Hope and something else she couldn't quite read flickered into his expression, but then was extinguished as quick as it had come. "You've been looking into the cases."

She sighed, not wanting to make promises she couldn't keep. "Just tell me about Ashley."

He looked like he wanted to argue, but then he nodded.

"I showed her several pictures, she picked out Hayes," Garrett said, a stubborn tilt to his jaw. "He'd talked to her son at a McDonald's one time, started walking away with him. Acted confused when she asked him what he was doing."

In some distant part of her brain, Lauren cataloged how strange it was that Hayes had talked to both boys in daylight, out where anyone could have seen him. Was he careless? Or was he counting on people being less suspicious in the middle of the afternoon?

"She didn't recognize him at first, though," Lauren pointed out. "Only later. After you told her it was him, right?"

Again, he nodded. "And by that point Ashley was . . . what they probably called an unreliable witness."

"What do you mean?"

"You have to understand what it's like at first," Garrett said, his eyes pleading now. "Nothing makes sense. You can't think right, time jumps around." He paused, took a deep breath. "She'd accused a lot of people by then. The mayor, I think. That had been after seventy-two hours without sleep. She was institutionalized for her own safety."

Lauren sighed, understood why the cops had done their due diligence with Hayes and nothing more.

"You're thinking what they all think. That we're grasping at straws," Garrett said, and she nearly buckled at the sheer resignation in his voice.

"I just . . . want my boy found. I need to bury his body right. Not let it rot up in that farmhouse of theirs."

Of theirs.

"You think Martha is involved?" she asked.

His throat worked as if he were swallowing answers he didn't want to put his name on. "Does looking away make her guilty?"

Lauren felt too young to answer that question. If Hayes had really taken those boys, what would it be like living with him? Martha might be just trying to survive and keep her daughter alive. There could be a fine line between labeling someone a victim and labeling them an accomplice, and Lauren didn't know precisely where she would draw it. "What changed your mind about her?"

"When I realized Hayes probably used her to get Damien," he said without a single tremor of doubt.

She could feel the tug of certainty, of wanting to believe him. But she could also see that he'd told himself a story a long time ago, and facts didn't really play a part in it. He thought Hayes was guilty, and there would be no dissuading him.

Instead of arguing, she asked, "What did you think I would find in that house?"

He shrugged. "Nothing."

"So why did you send me in there?"

"Not you," Garrett clarified. "Just . . . someone, anyone."

"Okay," Lauren agreed easily. "But why?"

"Honestly?" He met her eyes. "Because now you're hooked."

Lauren hated that he was right.

CHAPTER TWENTY-ONE

GRETCHEN

Now

There was always something about the first victim. That was Serial Killer 101.

And Gretchen knew that course well.

Oftentimes the first victim was actually connected to the killer in some way. A girlfriend or love interest that had delivered a rejection, a family member, even someone who had crossed into the killer's life just long enough to trigger the psychopathic rage that had been brewing for years.

The first victim was usually the killer's sloppiest work, as well. They didn't have the practice that would come with each subsequent kill. They would be working on a high—of adrenaline and fear and euphoria all mixed up into some heady sludge that blurred the senses.

The killer would try the hardest to hide that victim, but they hadn't had the experience that would later inform them that the ground was too hard in February, or burning a body down to ash was a lot harder than building a campfire.

Even serial killers heading toward certain death protected that first victim in a way they didn't the others.

So who was Damien Adams?

And was he really the first boy?

"We're going straight to the Montpelier Police Department," Lachlan said from the passenger seat as they crossed into the city limits. Gretchen wondered how long he'd been holding that in.

He probably expected a fight, but Gretchen wanted him occupied anyway. She wouldn't bother wasting her time making nice with the locals—she doubted the MPD could give her anything she couldn't get from Fred. Lachlan would handle the diplomatic bullshit, which was why she'd brought him in the first place, and she would do what she wanted.

"Yes, we'll report to the principal like the good little children we are."

"Just like that?" Lachlan asked, raising his brows.

Gretchen punched the destination into her GPS and reconsidered. "Yes."

"You're lying," Lachlan observed.

"Well noted," Gretchen murmured.

"You're going to drop me at the station and disappear, aren't you?"

That was, in fact, exactly what she'd been planning. "No, I would never."

Lachlan's knee bounced up and down as if he was readying himself for something. "Can I ask you a question and get an honest answer?"

"Why would you think I could promise you that?" Gretchen asked, genuinely surprised.

"How did you and Lauren work together?"

Gretchen's fingers tightened on the wheel, and she jerked around a corner a little too close to the curb. "Screw you."

"No, I'm not being . . ." Lachlan made a frustrated sound. "I'm actually not being an asshole here."

"That's a first," Gretchen said, because it was a softball. Then she looked over at him. His expression seemed . . . thoughtful, if she had to put a descriptor on it. "Marconi likes me. You don't."

"That's it?" Lachlan asked.

"Uh, yes," Gretchen said, lifting one shoulder. "Have we met? I have narcissistic tendencies." She paused. "I mean, it doesn't help that you're a humorless, sanctimonious prick."

"You care about her," Lachlan observed as if Gretchen hadn't said anything. "This whole time you were working together, I thought you were screwing with her because she's an easy touch. But you care what happens to her. How does that work?"

Gretchen slammed on the brakes a little too hard outside the Montpelier Police Station. "Here's your stop."

In one quick move, she leaned over him and opened the door, pushing it so it swung out.

"It's your stop, as well," Lachlan pointed out, his arms crossed over his chest.

"Give them my love," Gretchen said as she revved the engine and unsnapped Lachlan's seat belt.

Lachlan scowled in a way Gretchen was sure he'd practiced in the mirror, before finally shrugging. "Answer your phone when I call you."

Channeling one of Marconi's signature moves, Gretchen gave him a thumbs-up that she flipped into a single finger as soon as he turned to climb out of his bucket seat.

Before he shut the door, though, she said, "Hey, Gibbs."

He bent down, met her eyes. "Yeah?"

"The fact that you think Marconi is an easy touch is why you and I will never work well together," Gretchen said. And with that, she peeled off into traffic, assuming he'd get the door shut.

At some point during the drive out to Vermont, Fred had texted Gretchen the address to the old Hayes farmhouse. It was about twenty minutes away, and Gretchen spent the time deliberately not thinking.

There was already too much information, and she felt what should be wisps of theories firming up into something solid beneath a lack of sleep and a narrow band of details.

That wasn't a good thing.

Gretchen knew how dangerous it could be to become enamored with a certain idea.

When the GPS announced her turn, Gretchen decided to risk taking the driveway. There was some merit to the idea of finding a side road and creeping onto the property from the back, undetected. But it had been too many hours since she'd slept, and since then she'd had to put up with too many hours of Lachlan Gibbs.

She was going to cut herself a damn break.

The gamble paid off.

There weren't any other cars parked in front of the farmhouse. That didn't mean it was empty—it was clearly occupied by new owners if the flower boxes in the windows were anything to go by—but it was a good start.

Gretchen climbed out of her Porsche and checked the tiny trunk. Not only was there a pair of sturdy boots waiting for her but also the go bag she liked to keep tucked into one of the corners.

"Thank you," she whispered to her past self as she contorted her body to reach the zipper on her dress. She'd worn it to knock Cormac off his game, not to go stomping around some apple farm in Nowhere, Vermont. Without any sense of shame, she was left standing in her bra, panties, and stockings, which she quickly unhooked from her garters. It took a few minutes to step into the designer jeans, white button-down top, and blazer she'd brought along, but the delay was worth it.

A recent rain had turned the ground soggy, and Gretchen sank into the muck as she headed toward the porch. Before she got to the steps, she stopped, hands on hips, and let her eyes track over the property.

If Martha was involved, the burial site could be located in the house itself. A cellar or basement, perhaps.

If she wasn't, Hayes might have used an outhouse—a barn or shed—to hide the remains.

But in the distance, a line of overgrown orchard trees drew her attention.

Bodies had a way of becoming nutrients to root systems like that.

She would start there.

CHAPTER TWENTY-TWO

LAUREN

Then

Chlorine saturated the air at the community rec center's indoor pool, the mugginess inside the room nearly unbearable after the crispness of the cool night air.

Lauren unwound her scarf as she found a spot on the bleachers, her eyes locked on the doors to the changing rooms.

Now that she'd gotten—unofficially—involved in the Hayes case, she hadn't liked to let Elijah out of her sight more than necessary.

But when he'd turned seven, he'd started insisting he could use the men's changing rooms by himself, the five minutes it took for him to lock up his swim bag some kind of important marker of maturity in his own head.

While she knew some parents would balk at the little freedom, Lauren had found it endearing. Her baby was establishing boundaries and exploring the world. Plus, there were always at least five or six other boys in there getting ready for practice. Usually he'd spot one of his friends before he even stepped through the door.

It had never worried her overmuch before.

Tonight, she'd seriously considered dragging him back into the ladies' locker room with her even though the inevitable tantrum would have been nasty.

These were the times she hated being a single mom. They were rare, few, and far between. But they came in moments she hadn't expected. She'd braced for changing every diaper, for the physical toll of being the only caretaker of an infant, for the loneliness that came with celebrating the milestones by herself. She hadn't prepared herself for things like driving to CVS with a toddler who was projectile vomiting because she needed to get meds and had no one to leave him with.

And she certainly hadn't prepared herself for times when she'd be pulled into an investigation of a serial killer who targeted boys only a little older than Elijah.

Lauren fished out her phone, checked the most recent text from Rafi for perhaps the hundredth time.

I don't want to take you to court, Laur, but I will.

Beneath the knee-jerk anger she felt over the threat lay fear, deep and dark and bottomless. She didn't actually think any sane judge would take Elijah away from her and give him to Rafi. At most, it would be a partial custody sort of thing, and she guessed the judge would be sympathetic to her concerns that the visits should be supervised.

It still felt out of her control in a way she hated when it came to her son. When Rafi had started floating the possibility of seeing Elijah more, Lauren should have made it happen on her terms. Rafi was Elijah's father, after all, and from what Lauren could tell, he'd actually cleaned up his act. She should have given him a chance.

His text made her want to dig her heels in further, but she knew that wasn't the right move.

A flash of movement caught the corner of her eye, and she stowed her phone back in her pocket. Putting it all off again.

In the next second, Elijah stood in front of her in his Spider-Man trunks and goggles already pressed into his eyeballs so that he looked like a little alien. Her little alien.

"Hey, goofball," Lauren said, ruffling his already-ruffled hair. "Ready for practice?"

"Yup," Elijah said, his smile showing off the missing tooth he'd lost two days ago. "I have to tell you something first."

"'Kay," Lauren said, leaning forward so that he could whisper in her ear. He cupped his hands around his mouth so that none of the words would escape, his breath hot against her skin.

"There was a man in there."

Every part of Lauren went taut, her thigh muscles bunching, the fine hair on the nape of her neck lifting at the hint of a predator. She kept perfectly still.

"Yeah, did he talk to you?" she asked, her voice trembling.

"No, he talked to Jason," Elijah said, his hands still cupped against her ear. "The man said Jason's mom was looking for him out front. But he doesn't have a mom. Just two dads."

At that, Lauren almost did stand. "Did Jason go with him?"

"No," Elijah said, and she heard the pride in his voice. "I yelled, 'Stranger danger,' like you taught me."

Lauren pressed her lips together to hold in something that would have landed somewhere between a laugh and a sob. "Did he go away?"

"Yup," Elijah said, straightening, his little shoulders pulling back. "Mr. Jonas came over to see what was wrong and then went after him."

"Oh, baby," Lauren murmured, and wrapped her arms around him, pulling him so tight he stumbled into her lap. She buried her face in his sweet-strawberry hair and felt the rabbit-quick flutter of his heart. Her heart. "You did good. You did so good."

Elijah pulled back, a sly twist to his mouth. "Can we stop at Dairy Queen on the way home?"

At that, Lauren did laugh, though it was watery. "Of course, baby."

Lauren turned to the woman a few feet away who was busy pretending not to watch the exchange. "Hey, Della? Would you mind keeping your eye on Elijah for me?"

When Della nodded, eyes wide, Lauren pressed one more kiss to Elijah's temple, told him to go find his coach, and then took off, heavy winter boots clattering against the metal bleachers.

Fluorescent lights buzzed overhead as she ran out into the hallway that took her to the lobby.

"Did you see a man?" Lauren asked the ancient woman who sat guard behind the front desk. "He might have been moving fast, heading for the exit. Jonas Wilson would have been following not far behind him."

The woman's mouth pursed, but before she could answer, Jonas reentered the building from outside.

"Oh good," he said, spotting her. The swim-parent community was small enough that most of them knew what she did for a living. "Did Elijah tell you?"

"Yeah, did you see the man?" Lauren asked, already moving past him through the little wooden stall that acted as some sort of ineffective security gate.

"No, no one was out there," Jonas called after her, but she wasn't about to take his word for it.

She scanned the small parking lot. There weren't more than a handful of cars, and only one of the trucks had its lights on. Toward the far corner.

Lauren unholstered the personal gun she'd started to wear ever since the farmhouse, and took off at a careful run, keeping the cars between her body and the idling truck. It was so cold out that her fingers ached from it, but the pain was distant, easy to dismiss.

She rounded an SUV and then a sedan, her body crouched low, her boots doing their job on the ice-slicked pavement.

Staying out of the golden glow spilling from the lampposts above, Lauren was nothing but a shadow, creeping up on the truck from behind.

The plate was from Vermont, most of the numbers obscured by mud. She noted the ones she could see, along with the make and model of the vehicle. Then she used the muzzle of the gun to rap on the door.

"Police, open up," she called.

Nothing.

"Sir, step out of the vehicle."

Nothing.

She eyed the surroundings.

Concrete curbs blocked the truck's exit to the front and the side. She blocked him from backing up, as long as he didn't want to run over her in the process.

"Sir." She rapped on the side of the truck again.

The squeak of a window. Not automatic, she realized, but the hand-cranked kind.

And then a terrified face peered out at her. "Ma'am?"

In a rush, the adrenaline left her body. She exhaled roughly and dropped her weapon so that it pointed at the ground.

"Shit," she muttered. It was a teenager, pockmarked and floppy haired, stinking so strongly of weed she could probably get a second-hand high. That was why he'd hesitated when she'd banged on his door.

Bloodshot eyes blinked at her slowly. "I wasn't . . ."

Waving away the lie, Lauren reholstered her gun. She scanned the parking lot, but nothing had changed in the handful of minutes it had taken her to get to this truck. The rec center stood alone on a country highway, a line of trees in the distance offering the obvious escape route.

Hayes had probably parked on some maintenance road back there. Or maybe he'd had a head start and hightailed it out of the parking lot before she'd even made it outside.

Just to be thorough, she glanced into the truck and then back into the cab. It was empty.

Coughing from the smoke, she glanced at the kid. "What are you doing here?"

"My little sister has gymnastics practice," he said carefully, like he wasn't sure he was forming the right vowels. "I was dropping her off."

"Did you see anyone run out of the building?" Lauren asked, and his eyes darted to the space over each of her shoulders as he shifted uncomfortably.

"No."

Lauren went back on high alert. "What did you see?"

"No, no, no," the kid rushed to correct her. "I really meant no. Because um. I couldn't see, um, with . . ."

He waved at the weed smoke lingering in the cab, and she swallowed an annoyed curse. It wasn't that he was hiding something; he just still hadn't caught on that she didn't care about the pot.

"Are you driving your sister home?" she asked, trying to decide if it would be worth it to bust him. If he was going to have a child in there, she'd have to.

He shook his head, that mop of almost curls falling into his eyes. "No, ma'am. My mom's coming to get her later."

She studied him for a moment, but she'd been out here now for nearly ten minutes, her eyes off Elijah. It wouldn't be easy to lure him from a swim practice where at least a third of the parents were watching from the bleachers, but wouldn't that be a perfect way to distract her? Create a false alarm and then swing back to snatch your actual target?

"Don't drive for a while," Lauren said, doing her best to be a responsible member of the MPD. And then she took off at a light jog toward the building once more. She'd run the kid's plates when she got into work tomorrow to make sure he didn't have any priors. But there were bigger fish to fry.

Jonas was still waiting for her inside, and grimaced when she shook her head. "Who would have thought it could happen here?"

She knew he didn't mean the rec center itself. He meant Montpelier, Vermont, where they all knew each other well enough that it almost felt like a small town.

But that meant they'd become complacent. Damien Adams and Joshua Westwood and how many others proved otherwise.

Lauren turned to the old woman—AGNES, her name tag read—to find her already watching them closely. "Ma'am, can I get a list of the members who came in tonight?"

Agnes hunched up her shoulders. "You're going to need a warrant."

From the depth of her soul, Lauren cursed the recent spate of crime shows that made women like Agnes spout off things like that. "One of those members approached a young boy in the locker room and tried to entice him out of the building. Are you sure you can't let me see the list?"

The rec center was lackadaisical with their entrance policies, especially for people who came often. Someone could just say he forgot his ID and they'd wave him through. At most he would have had to sign his name—but that wasn't always checked against a photo, depending on who was watching the desk.

Agnes went a little shifty-eyed behind her thick lenses. "I'm going to get a cup of water."

Lauren didn't blink at the non sequitur, just nodded slowly.

"And leave this clipboard with the sign-ins right here," Agnes continued, nudging the sheet forward.

On that cryptic note, Agnes shuffled off toward the water cooler in the far corner of the lobby. Lauren glanced at Jonas, who shrugged, and then she took out her phone to take a picture of the list.

It was short: only three names from today.

That same sensation from when Elijah whispered, *There was a man*, sank into the hollow spaces of her body as her finger paused on one of the entries.

Garrett Adams.

CHAPTER TWENTY-THREE

GRETCHEN

Now

Swollen apples hung heavy on the branches in the orchard behind the farmhouse, the rotting ones having already succumbed to gravity.

Fermentation and death saturated the air, leaves crunching beneath Gretchen's boots.

How would the deadweight of a body feel against her shoulder? Would she stumble beneath the burden?

Her blood would be hot from the recent kill, from the way a knife slid into flesh like butter, from the fear in his eyes, the tears on his cheeks.

Where would she dig?

The far corner. It would be the most obvious, but it was the most obvious for a reason. Workers would be less likely to stumble upon it, as would visitors if Hayes had ever opened his orchard to the public.

It seemed implausible that Owen Hayes would let strangers tramp around his burial ground if it was out here, but serial killers could be arrogant to an extreme. Hayes had been caught on videotape at the abduction site of one of the victims, and he still hadn't cooled off at all.

When Gretchen made it to the end of the row, she stopped and turned back to the house once more, glanced at the barn, the shed. It would be a long way to haul a body, but Owen Hayes had been a farmer at the time, used to manual labor. He'd have been able to carry the boys easily.

Gretchen searched the ground at her feet as if it would offer up clues. Some part of her had hoped the rain would have pushed the bones to the surface, even if that hope was foolish.

She thought about the little baggie in the glove compartment of the Porsche.

Two years ago, she'd been invited to a body farm near Quantico, Virginia. She'd invited Dr. Leo Chen, the coroner for the Boston Police Department, to go with her, and the managers of the establishment had been naive and had allowed them to wander around alone.

Dr. Chen hadn't exactly kept an eye on her—and vice versa, to be honest—and in a moment of brilliance, Gretchen had snagged a phalanx from one of the corpses.

Who knew when a stray human bone would come in handy?

She could hide it in the ground here, call in Lachlan, say she found evidence of a burial site. By the time the dust cleared, she'd either be able to confiscate the phalanx or write it off as having fulfilled its purpose. No one would be able to trace the thing back to her.

But she was only about 40 percent confident that this was the location Hayes had chosen. And if she burned this opportunity, she would be screwing herself over for the rest of the investigation.

So, instead, Gretchen headed back to the house, slow-walking the row between the trees, eyes darting to every shadowed grove.

The porch's wooden steps groaned beneath her weight as she made her way toward the window. She detoured to the door and found it locked, as predicted. A large window was right next to it, though, and the glass looked modern enough—not like some farmhouses where it was thick and warped and more likely to break bone than break itself.

Gretchen shrugged out of her blazer and wrapped it around her fist, her arm.

The window shattered, not on the first punch or the second or third. She was just considering using her foot instead when it finally gave way.

Her fingers ached, the bruises inevitable, but she didn't think anything was fractured.

She shook out her hand as she reached through with her other and unlatched the window. After that it was just a matter of pushing it up and avoiding the shards as she stepped through the empty pane.

The silence inside the house pressed against Gretchen's eardrums in that way you could always tell when no one was home.

Someone lived here, though. There were shoes in the wicker basket by the door, a used pan on the back burner of the stove. Photos hanging on the wall.

Gretchen swiveled, taking in the rest of the kitchen, her eyes lingering on the basement door that sat slightly ajar, the paint-coated lock dangling from it like a loose tooth.

She crossed the room, nudging the door farther open with her boot. Idly, Gretchen wondered if a normal person would feel fear. She had never understood the emotion—for good reason, considering all the research done on sociopaths showed they weren't able to produce the same hormonal cocktail that inspired the sensation.

All Gretchen could feel was curiosity.

Darkness greeted her at the top of the stairs. They were deep and narrow, and she had to hold on to the railing lest she trip and break her neck. That kind of calculation she'd learned to factor into her behavior, not because she could internalize the consequences of being careless but because she knew that if she was, it could incapacitate her for days or even months. It was like when she'd been a teenager and had to leave out sticky notes to remind herself to use pot holders so she would be able to function after cooking herself dinner.

When she got to the bottom, a metal string brushed against her forehead. She groped for it and tugged.

"Let there be light," she murmured as the bare bulb flickered into existence.

The basement was exactly as she'd been expecting.

Cinder block walls, a dirt floor. A crawl space that seemed to promise untold horrors.

Her breath puffed out, and she took a moment to watch it dissolve into the next. No one had bothered to install heaters down here.

The shadows beckoned her, and she crossed the room, flipping on her phone's flashlight to try to cut through the darkness.

The crawl space on the far side of the room was elevated, waist level, so that she had to bend to duck her head inside.

If there were ever a perfect spot to bury bodies, this would rise to the top of the list.

Gretchen brushed her hand against the loose dirt, wondering how deep she'd have to go to find bones.

She thought of the baggie in her car.

Then she pulled up a contact on her phone.

"Hypothetically speaking," Gretchen said as soon as Cormac Byrne answered, "if someone broke into a house and then dug around in the basement to find murder victims, would that be admissible in court?"

"Gretchen . . ."

"That's not a no," she said.

A beat. "You know it doesn't matter if he was a serial killer, right? Murder charges aren't dependent on the victim's character."

She could make the argument that it *did* matter. The jury would automatically be more sympathetic to Marconi if her lawyers could show Hayes had killed five, ten, fifteen boys. Marconi wouldn't get off completely—Byrne was right about that—but anything would help.

Cormac knew that as well as she did, so she didn't bother wasting her breath.

When she didn't say anything, Cormac heaved an unattractive, put-upon sigh. "Maybe, but it would be messy and undercut the evidence you found. If you really think there's something there, go about it a better way."

Gretchen flicked the end-call button almost before his last words were out, and looked around.

This was it.

His burial ground.

One of the traits that had secured her spot on the sociopathy spectrum had been a grandiose sense of self. What she called a healthy respect for her own brilliance, doctors labeled abnormal. When she'd become a BPD consultant, she'd known that could be a weakness, one that would, ironically, mean she would end up solving fewer cases.

So she'd trained herself, carefully, assiduously. Always, always, always checking and rechecking her self-esteem against logic.

But . . .

This was it.

It was exactly where she would have put the bodies.

Gretchen took the stairs faster than was safe.

She didn't bother with the shard-covered window, instead twisting the dead bolt and flying out to the back porch. To the shed.

The doors opened with an annoyed groan.

A well-used shovel had fallen to the floor, half-hidden behind a discarded bucket and the built-in tool bench.

Gretchen stared at the thing, and spent a long minute wondering how much she really cared that Marconi was rotting away in jail. Then she let herself think about the mystery, Cormac's derision, Lachlan's pitiful frown.

The need to be right.

And she grabbed the handle that was stained with something she fervently hoped wasn't pig shit.

Back in the crawl space, she had to maneuver herself to get any leverage on the shovel. It wouldn't be easy for someone even a handful of inches taller than her to bury victims back here.

She pictured the wife. Then the daughter. It would be tight for either of them but not impossible.

Had serial killing really become a family business, then?

The blade of the shovel struck cold ground that didn't give at all, but Gretchen was nothing if not stubborn.

It took an hour to hit the first bone.

Something bright, sharp, and fierce dumped into her bloodstream. Maybe a normal person would think about the boy those bones had belonged to.

But Gretchen wasn't normal people. The only thing she cared about was making sure it wasn't some beloved pet. That would certainly ruin her plan.

After she confirmed the skull she'd hit was human size, she joyfully abandoned her digging, the calluses on her palms already pulsing in the places she gripped the shovel, her hand already achy from the window.

In the kitchen once more, she stopped scanning until she found the perfect tool—the toaster, just beneath the pretty frilly curtains that looked extremely flammable.

Gretchen grabbed a handful of paper towels, shoved them into both of the slots, and set the toaster to high.

Then she headed back to the shed to set everything to rights, stashing the shovel exactly where she'd found it, wiping down the door handles.

By the time she made it back to the kitchen, thin, black smoke crawled up from the toaster, but there were no flames.

She darted glances between the clock and the appliance for five minutes, hoping for something dramatic.

Google wasn't helpful beyond confirming her belief that the toaster was, in fact, a fire hazard. It did not give any tips, though, on how to actually create a fire using one. She made a mental note to write a post about how to do it when all this settled down. She'd get Fred to work on the SEO so that it ended up on the first page of results. No one should be stuck in this position when the information had to be out there somewhere.

After more smoke that she worried might prematurely set off the alarm, Gretchen used a pair of tongs to rescue the scorched paper towels. She dropped them in the sink, dousing them before yanking open one of the kitchen drawers. It took three tries to find the lighter.

She held the thing to each of the curtains and sighed, happy and satisfied, when the fabric caught and held the flame.

The sight of it soothed the irritation within her that was burbling way too close to rage. She'd never been attracted to arson in particular, but the inherent destructive nature of fire always seemed to resonate somewhere deep in her gray matter, some primitive holdover satiated.

Gretchen wasted a couple of seconds making sure it wouldn't just burn out before grabbing the singed paper towels from the sink and crossing to the door. She relocked the dead bolt and then carefully maneuvered herself out the broken window.

Once outside, she dug out her phone and dialed 9-1-1.

"Hi, yes," Gretchen said, before rattling off the farmhouse's address. "I smelled smoke and broke in through a window to try to put out the fire. I was too late, though. Please send help."

She hung up before shifting to get a better view of her work.

It was less than impressive, if she was being honest. But the first responders would have no choice other than to turn up, and then break down the door and check the place out.

They would forget about how weak the flames had been when they saw what was waiting for them downstairs.

Fifteen minutes later she heard the sirens.

Ten minutes after that, she stood in the now-open doorway as too many firemen loitered in the kitchen, all giving each other knowing looks.

Look at this hysterical broad. Calling in a fire that could have been put out with a home extinguisher.

"The basement," Gretchen murmured, pinching the skin of her inner thigh hard through her jeans pocket to get tears to spring to her eyes. "I smelled smoke there, too."

The biggest guy, the one with the buzz cut and tree-trunk thick biceps, did a terrible job at hiding his disdain. But he shrugged when she didn't trip over herself with apologies for being a pain in his ass.

It took three minutes for the shout to come.

"You guys better get down here."

CHAPTER TWENTY-FOUR

LAUREN

Then

Elijah was so tall now that he no longer needed a little booster step to brush his teeth.

Lauren sat on the closed toilet lid, watching him spit foam into the sink, unable to take her eyes off him. He needed new pajamas soon, but he'd become obsessed with *PAW Patrol* and the firefighter Dalmatian on the show. No matter how many times she'd explained to him that she could buy the exact same pair, only bigger, he'd gotten that stubborn set to his jaw she recognized all too well from a mirror.

He grinned at her now, showing off his newly clean teeth, and then took off for his bedroom.

She followed at a slower pace, picking up a towel to toss in the laundry bin as she went. Stopping in the hallway, Lauren took out her phone, texting Sandy.

Hey can you come stay with Elijah for an hour? Emergency . . .

Sandy texted back almost immediately. **On my way.**

Lauren pressed the phone to her chest, not sure how she would function without her friend, and then followed Elijah into his bedroom.

He was already shoving his legs beneath his *PAW Patrol* com-forter—which had the whole cast of pups on it—having grabbed his book from the floor, where they must have dropped it last night. It was a chapter book about a young boy sleuth and his faithful dog, and Lauren was dreading the day Elijah would move from subtle hints about getting a pet into full-on begging.

When she'd asked him earlier to describe the man who'd approached Jason in the locker room, he'd simply shrugged and said he'd had brown hair. Lauren had tried for more details, but kids tended to see adults in broad strokes.

So instead of pressing him further, Lauren read him three chapters of the book as she waited for Sandy to arrive.

The woman let herself in, calling Lauren's name softly from the doorway. Lauren disentangled herself from Elijah's sleeping form and crossed the room.

"I owe you," Lauren said, but Sandy waved her off. "Like, so much."

"You know I don't mind."

Lauren squeezed her arm in silent thanks and took one last look back at Elijah. Then she headed downstairs, shrugged into her coat, and snagged her keys. By the time she was halfway to Garrett Adams's diner, she realized she'd been going through the motions in a blind haze of rage.

She didn't bother parking between the lines, too angry to worry about anything but getting to Garrett.

The CLOSED sign rattled against the glass as she pounded on the door. If she needed to, she'd start honking her horn to get him out here. She had lost any desire for diplomacy the second she'd seen his name on the intake sheet.

But extreme measures weren't necessary. A figure took shape in the darkened diner, and in the next moment, the door was yanked open.

Garrett all but snarled at her, clearly having been on the verge of sleep himself. Although it wasn't late, Lauren distantly realized that diner life meant he probably got up well before the rest of the world.

"What?" he bit out.

Lauren didn't bother answering, just used all her fury to bodily push him up against the closest wall. She didn't have the best angle, but she'd long ago learned how to use what she had to overpower men who would otherwise loom over her.

"Jesus," he said, his hands going to where her fingers curled around his throat. "What the f—"

"You've crossed a line, Adams," Lauren said in a whisper.

He brought his arm up, twisted it over hers, and brought his elbow down, breaking her hold. Lauren winced and stepped back. Considered drawing her gun. But he didn't go for her, just stood there leaning against the wall, panting. Not from her hand on his windpipe, she gathered, but from surprise, confusion.

"What the actual fuck?" He got it all out this time, though his voice was raspy.

"You follow me around, fine," Lauren said. "You come after my kid, we have problems."

"Come after your . . . What?" Garrett shook his head. "No, I didn't . . ."

The denial made white dots pop in the corner of Lauren's vision. "Don't. Lie."

"Honestly." Garrett held his hands up, placating. And then something slipped into his expression. Hunger? No, that wasn't quite right. Hope, maybe, was closer. "Hayes came after your son, didn't he?"

And there it was. Exactly the fear that had lingered in the back of her mind even after seeing Garrett's name on the sign-up sheet. Hayes knew that Garrett suspected him, might have even seen Lauren's visit to the diner the other day. Using Garrett's name had been a pointed threat.

I don't take kindly to people messing around in my business.

Lauren stumbled back, reached out for a chair, and dropped into it, letting her head fall below her heart. Fainting wouldn't be advisable in a situation where Garrett could still just be lying.

If he wasn't, though . . . that meant she'd put Elijah on the map for a serial killer. This was her fault.

"Not my son," she said, staring at the pristine linoleum instead of him. "A boy he was with."

Garrett laughed. "If you believe that, I've got a bridge in Brooklyn to sell you."

Lauren knew he was right. Just because Hayes had talked to the other kid didn't mean this wasn't a message directed at Lauren.

Garrett continued, pity clear in his voice. "You really think it was a coincidence that Elijah just happened to be standing there when Hayes talked to the other boy?"

Everything sharpened as her sluggish thoughts snagged on something. She looked up slowly. "I never told you my son's name."

He stilled.

In the next heartbeat, she was on him again, hand back at his throat.

"I never told you my son's name."

He blinked at her, not even trying to break free this time.

Lauren's mind raced through the events of the past two weeks, combing over each moment, until the realization came, slicing through her flesh.

"You knew I was in the area the night of the blizzard," Lauren said, her fingers spasming against his neck. "You waited until I was the closest cop around and then called in the tip." His expression was calm, patient. "You knew he would go after Elijah."

"Insurance," Garrett managed to get out. "I needed you to care."

"How did you . . . ?" she breathed out, not even sure what she was asking.

"Tell me you wouldn't do the same," Garrett said, that broken-stallion energy quivering, barely constrained. He could break her hold if he wanted—he'd already proved that. But he let her keep him pinned against the wall. "If Elijah was murdered—"

"Get his name out of your goddamn mouth."

And he . . . laughed. "Tell me you wouldn't do anything to avenge him."

Neither of them breathed, blinked.

"It's Hayes's pattern, Lauren," he whispered, almost gleeful. "He contacts his victims first."

"He didn't contact Elijah," Lauren said, but she heard the desperation in her own voice. "He didn't."

"Tell yourself that all you want." He was talking easier, and Lauren realized her hand had dropped from around his throat. "It doesn't make a difference."

Her knuckles met the nearly unmovable force of a jaw; his head snapped back.

In the silence that followed, he rubbed the pad of his thumb against the trickle of blood where bone had broken open skin. The smear of red had her swallowing bile.

His eyes were hooded, his mouth twisted into some terrible smirk. "He contacts them first."

CHAPTER TWENTY-FIVE

GRETCHEN

Now

"Byrne's such a narc," Gretchen said as Lachlan stormed toward where she stood in the front yard of the farmhouse, the righteous indignation all but coming out of his pores.

"He didn't need to call me." Lachlan rounded on her, his back to the emergency vehicles and the sobbing woman who currently lived in the serial killer's old den.

Her husband was patting her arm in an ineffectual manner, gaping idiotically at the people streaming in and out of his farmhouse.

They had arrived back about an hour after the firefighters had found the first body.

"You think I wouldn't have heard about this while at the station?" Lachlan asked, with a jerky wave of his arm.

She glanced at him, ran her eyes over his long frame, as if assessing. "You can be pretty oblivious."

He shook his head. "You just happened to spot a fire while driving by."

"Of course not," Gretchen said easily. "I started the fire."

Lachlan groaned, took two angry steps away, and then spun back, jabbing a finger toward her face.

She pictured biting it off, could almost taste the bloom of copper on her tongue.

"I will gladly help the Montpelier Police Department arrest you," Lachlan said, in a weird, angry whisper. "Don't test me."

"So scary and intimidating," Gretchen offered in a deadpan tone. "I think they're a little busy."

"They won't always be busy."

Gretchen rolled her eyes. "What were you going to do? Try to lecture a police chief into giving a damn? When he ignored this case for years and let Hayes kill who knows how many kids even after Marconi pointed them in his direction?"

Lachlan's jaw swiveled, like he had been going to attempt to do just that but didn't want to admit it. "People listen to reason. And the chief retired. The woman in charge now had been Lauren's direct supervisor, and she had her suspicions about Hayes. You would know all of this if you had followed procedure."

"I'll follow procedure when you pay me to consult on this case," Gretchen said. "Until then, I'm doing you a favor by letting you tag along to any of this. You're welcome, by the way."

"Right, thanks ever so much," Lachlan said, but some of the outrage had bled out of his voice. He turned to stare at the house.

"Hey, I saved you the effort of getting a warrant." Gretchen nudged him with an elbow. She was bored of the sniping, and at the same time could see it escalating. One thing she knew how to do when entering any conversation was find off-ramps. "You really should thank me for this one. And," she added smugly, "I didn't even have to plant anything."

He grimaced. "Did you know the bones were there?"

"What are you talking about? I just smelled some smoke," Gretchen said, lips twitching.

"And the firefighters just happened to find a skull sticking out of the ground, right there waiting for them."

"Lucky that." Gretchen shrugged. "Funny how he got away with it for so long when he was so sloppy about hiding his victims."

"Apparently the retired chief was a good ole boy," Lachlan said, with a fake little twang. "And he went fishing with Hayes. Detectives always did the bare minimum anytime a finger got pointed, but it might explain some of what looks like incompetence in this case."

"Did the new chief . . ." She lifted her brows in a request for the name.

"Imani Abaza," he supplied dutifully.

"Did Abaza say anything about the wife? Or daughter?" she asked.

"Martha and Julia," Lachlan said. "No one thinks they were involved."

"But the bones were in the house."

"John Wayne Gacy had thirty-three bodies in his crawl space," Lachlan countered.

"And Gacy's wife knew about them," Gretchen said. "Or at least knew he was bringing teenagers to the garage to have sex with them. She let him explain away a smell in the attic as a leaky sewer pipe. And she wasn't an idiot."

"Yeah, okay, I get your point," Lachlan said after a beat. "Not involved doesn't mean they don't know it was happening."

"Does Abaza have a file on all this?" Gretchen asked. The crime scene techs would be a while here, and there wasn't much left for her to do until the scene was completely processed.

Just as Lachlan started to answer, a tall woman with a long dark braid strode toward them, blazer flapping open.

She had a no-bullshit air about her. Women like that could always see through Gretchen's smoke and mirrors where men in similar positions of power couldn't.

"Speak of the devil," Lachlan murmured.

"Gibbs," Abaza greeted Lachlan, completely ignoring Gretchen. As expected.

"You found something," Lachlan said. Not a question.

Abaza crossed her arms over her chest, surveyed him. "This is just a professional courtesy. I'm not inviting you onto this case."

Lachlan gave a curt nod, and Abaza continued.

"We've found four separate sets of remains," she said. "The dogs also targeted the back corner of the orchard as a possible secondary burial site."

Gretchen smirked at that. She liked being proven right more than most things in life.

Abaza's eyes flicked to Gretchen for the first time. "Don't think your little stunt fooled anyone."

"It didn't need to fool you," Gretchen said, eyes narrowing. "It was what was needed to get you legal access to the house. You're welcome." She was annoyed no one had praised her ingenuity yet, to be quite honest. And because Abaza had no ground to stand on, she added, "The house of the serial killer you let operate under your nose for ten years. The same serial killer who murdered one of your own officers' kids."

There was the tiniest twitch of a muscle in Abaza's jaw, but she didn't acknowledge the jab. She simply turned her attention to Lachlan. "You'll need to find a ride back to town."

Without waiting for a reply, Abaza turned and strode back across the lawn, barking orders at some low-level uniforms as she went.

"Should Marconi be worried?" Gretchen fake-whispered, just to annoy him. She jerked her chin toward Abaza. "About a potential rival for your affections?"

"You're exhausting," Lachlan muttered as he headed toward the Porsche, which had by some miracle not been blocked in.

"It's part of my charm, darling. And you better be nice to me. I could leave you here." Gretchen slid into the front seat. He'd only just closed the door when she revved the engine and swung wildly close to the unnecessary ambulance. It's not like there was anyone to save. "What else did you learn during your time following procedure?"

Whatever it was wouldn't be on par with unearthing a serial killer's burial ground, but she didn't think she needed to point that out with all the evidence of the find still there in the rearview mirror.

"There were complaints against Hayes, some stalking and harassment accusations that never really made it to an official file," Lachlan said without even hesitating to run his calculations first. He was probably too used to answering questions posed by his partners to even remember why he wouldn't want to share everything with her. Or maybe she was just wearing him down inch by inch. "Starting about two years after he moved here, and obviously, ending when he left."

"And he moved right after Elijah Marconi was killed?"

Lachlan nodded. "About six months later."

"Can we put a rush on the ID for Elijah?"

"Depends on how clean the finds are," Lachlan pointed out. "They could be a jumble. Especially if there's more than one burial site."

Gretchen sighed in acknowledgment. "It's going to take a while to sort that mess out."

They both knew they would be lucky if there was a total victim count within the week, let alone identification or cause of death for each boy.

They needed answers sooner than the forensics would give them up.

When Gretchen took a left into town instead of a right toward the police station, Lachlan sat up straighter. "Wrong way."

"Is it?" Gretchen asked casually.

He didn't say anything until she swung into a parking spot. "What are we doing here?"

"Everyone thinks one of the victims' parents is the killer, right?"

"And by that you mean Lauren. Yes, everyone thinks Lauren is guilty," Lachlan said slowly, following her out of the car.

She pretended that he hadn't said anything and gestured to the diner in front of them. "Now we just have to figure out which one it is."

CHAPTER
TWENTY-SIX

MARTHA

Before

When people who had drowned were resuscitated, they said there was a moment, one moment, where they saw God.

Or peace, if they were agnostic.

Or the universe, if they were scientists.

It didn't matter. The biological cascade was the same: the body flushed the system with serotonin and endorphins to try to blunt any pain before death. As a result, the victim often experienced a euphoric sensation akin to a religious experience in the seconds before their soul departed the earth.

Martha couldn't remember if she'd ever believed in heaven. She didn't anymore, of course. She believed in the void, in the hopefully gentle extinguishing of life.

More than anything, though, she longed for that euphoria, dreamed of the heartbeats before death slunk in.

She rolled over at the sound of Owen stirring in the bed beside her, propped her head on the pillow, traced his features with her eyes, and wondered if this was that pocket of space. Wondered if she'd given in to the tug of the water and she was just here, floating, waiting for the final rush of it into her lungs.

Owen blinked up at her, groggy still, the golden predawn light making him softer than he'd been in years.

Martha pressed her palm flat against his heart, listened to the steady pump of it beneath sinewy muscle, his body so steady and sure. If she could crawl into the cavern of his chest, if she could hide there, she would, she realized. Everything out here was too much, too scary and loud and complicated.

There was Garrett's face when he'd stepped out of his office and seen her with the boy.

There were the fingerprint bruises on her hips, her punishment for staying in town too long. A reclamation of ownership in the only way men knew how.

There was yesterday morning, when she'd found Owen standing downstairs in their basement, staring at the crawl space that she'd begged him for the past two years to fill in.

There was the scarf that hung beside her mirror, the one she draped over the glass whenever she could so she wouldn't have to look at her own face.

Martha had only so much she could hold inside her as her organs rotted and her blood curdled.

She just wanted to rest now.

She let her hand tap out the gentle thump of his pulse.

A corner of his mouth ticked up, and she could read the confusion there just as easy as she could read the pleasure.

"Morning," he rasped out, lifting his palm to cup the back of her head.

Martha didn't wait for him to tug her down for the kiss. She dived in herself.

When her lips met his, euphoria sparked in her nerve endings, and she had one last coherent thought before succumbing completely.

Why had she been fighting this for so long?

CHAPTER TWENTY-SEVEN

GRETCHEN

Now

Garrett Adams could have been on a magazine cover as the poster boy for a Vermont diner owner. He had a thick salt-and-pepper beard and wore flannel and a wool beanie pulled low over his forehead.

As Gretchen and Lachlan walked in, he waved to all the empty tables and booths. "If you can find a seat."

The delivery was so dry Gretchen almost missed the humor in it.

She beelined for the counter, hitching herself up onto one of the stools. Garrett eyed her grumpily and sighed, as if having a customer were the deepest grievance he could encounter in his life. Then he poured her a cup of coffee.

Gretchen rarely liked people on sight, but she could make an exception.

Wouldn't that be interesting if he'd killed Hayes and then let Marconi take the fall for it? What did that say about her own judgment?

Though to be fair, she'd long ago accepted that she was terrible at telling if someone was what society deemed *good* or *bad*. It mattered far more how they interacted with her.

Garrett didn't look especially tired or twitchy, though. And Gretchen was pretty sure that he could clock them as law enforcement. Especially Lachlan.

While someone like her might be able to murder a person and then drive home and operate as if nothing had happened, it would be difficult for normal people to do so.

That didn't mean Garrett Adams was innocent of killing Hayes, but it was something to note at least.

Gretchen took a deep swallow of her coffee despite the fact that she was so strung out that it would do little other than make her more jittery. Then she set her mug down hard, drawing Garrett's eyes back to her. "Do you know who killed your son?"

Garrett stilled, and Lachlan made some kind of groan-like sound behind her, but to his credit, he managed to cover it well. She could rarely call him unprofessional.

She tried to study Garrett's reaction beyond surprise, but that beard of his did a lot of heavy lifting in terms of shielding his emotions.

The silence hung between the three of them, but neither she nor Lachlan rushed to fill it. They both knew that this was when suspects made mistakes, the social tension digging too deep into their skin.

Finally, Garrett nodded once. "Yup."

"Who was it?"

He put down the plate, then leaned his hands on the counter. Not close to her, not even looking at her. "That's a complicated answer, ma'am."

"I've got time," Gretchen said.

"Yeah, well, I don't." Garrett jerked his chin toward the coffee. "That'll be two bucks."

"Pricey," Gretchen murmured, but slapped a five down on the counter and waved away his offer of change. "Did anyone else in town suspect Hayes killed those missing boys?"

"Did I say I suspected Owen Hayes?"

"You didn't have to," Gretchen said with a confidence that felt shakier than it had a minute ago.

Garrett laughed, though it was humorless. "Sure."

Gretchen wasn't about to let that reaction go. They had a crawl space full of bones on their side. "If it wasn't him, who was it?"

He squinted at her, and she tried to imagine how he'd reacted to Marconi interviewing him. That would have been nine years ago. Had he always been this hard?

"Come back with a subpoena and I'll tell you what you want to hear," Garrett muttered, and Gretchen filed that phrasing away. *I'll tell you what you want to hear.* That had been deliberate. "Until then, get the hell off my property."

"Just one more second of your time." Lachlan swooped in. "May I ask where you were last night at approximately eight p.m.?"

"You can," Garrett said easily. "Doesn't mean you'll get an answer."

"My name is Detective Lachlan Gibbs, with the Boston Police Department," Lachlan said, voice tight as he reached for his badge.

"You're a long way from home, Detective." Garrett didn't bother even looking at the gold flashed in his direction. "And a long way from your jurisdiction."

Gretchen flipped through her mental catalog, the one she kept about social norms. New Englanders were tight-knit with their communities but reticent with outsiders. In theory, Marconi had been a part of this community, which might mean Gretchen could use her as an in.

"I'm not a cop," Gretchen said, drawing Garrett's attention back to her. "I'm friends with Detective Lauren Marconi."

Again, that humorless laugh as he shook his head. "Lady, if you think that's going to help your case, you know even less than I thought."

Delicious curiosity, sweet and tantalizing, crawled into her veins. "Tell me what I don't know."

"You don't know that sometimes things work out just as they should."

"Hayes is dead and Detective Marconi is in jail," Gretchen said slowly, trying to follow.

"Exactly," Garrett said, and held her gaze for a second too long. Then he blinked and looked away. "Now get the hell off my property. I won't ask again."

———

"Well, if we're looking for someone who might have framed Marconi, I think we have a top suspect," Lachlan said as they stood on the sidewalk outside the diner.

Gretchen didn't bother to take her eyes off the big windows. Garrett had gone back to wiping down the counters, his movements easy and unbothered. Was he a phenomenal actor? Or was he a man at peace with how justice had been delivered?

She thought about the potential reasons she'd come up with for why Marconi, if she'd seen who had shot Hayes, might take the fall for that person.

She thought about what she'd landed on.

Guilt.

But Garrett's son had died years before Elijah had been taken, probably years before Marconi had ever heard the name Owen Hayes. Why would Garrett hold Marconi responsible for the child's death?

It didn't make sense.

Gretchen glanced at the truck parked in what looked to be the owner's spot. It had a thin layer of pollen on the windshield, probably hadn't been driven for at least a day. That wasn't exactly definitive proof that Garrett hadn't left Montpelier last night, but again, it was something.

That, added to the way he had answered her questions, had Gretchen shrugging. "I don't think he killed Hayes."

When Lachlan turned on her with barefaced incredulity, she cursed herself for forgetting whom she was talking to.

Marconi would have rocked back on her heels, hands shoved in her pockets. *"That was weird, though, right?"* she would have said.

She wouldn't have tried to intimidate Garrett with the implicit threat of her badge like Lachlan had, either, right when Garrett had clearly been shutting them down. She would have pulled some random fact about him from thin air, asked coolly if he knew what it meant, watched dispassionately as he fumbled for an answer, thrown off balance. They would have gotten something more. Because while Gretchen's brain was unmatched in the logical game of hunting a killer, Marconi was unmatched at interviewing them.

Gretchen slid Lachlan a glance, and tried, for research's sake, "That was weird, though, right?"

He stared at her like she'd spoken Greek, and she sighed, not bothering to wait for an answer. "He seemed quietly happy at the circumstances. If he'd done it, he'd have worked harder to pretend otherwise."

"You know that how?" Lachlan pressed. "He could just be an arrogant son of a bitch who doesn't think he'll get caught."

The problem with Lachlan was that sometimes he made fair points.

Gretchen decided to take a page out of Garrett's book. "Sure."

"You don't think that," Lachlan said, falling into step behind her as she started toward the car.

"I told you why I don't think he did it, and you gave your own theory," Gretchen explained like he was a five-year-old, because she knew the tone would needle him. "That's how conversations work."

He rubbed a hand over his face, in what was becoming a familiar gesture of exasperation. "Where do you want to stay for the night?"

It was only then she realized how late it was.

He was right, they needed to get a hotel. But everything in her rebelled at the idea of stopping now. "Your budget and my budget are not in the same league."

"It's funny you think you're not paying for my room," Lachlan shot back.

Gretchen couldn't help the amused twitch of her lips at that. "Sure."

"You like that response too much," he noted.

"I have to admit it is more effective than I would have previously realized," Gretchen mused. "Find a hotel. You're right, it's on me."

"And the drinks."

Lachlan dutifully pulled out his phone and found what was likely one of the best Montpelier had to offer—the higher end of one of those national chain hotels.

Gretchen honestly didn't care. When they checked in, she scoped out the fact that it had a bar, and, really, that was all that mattered.

As they turned away from the counter, key cards in hand, Gretchen pushed Lachlan's shoulder and jerked her head toward the little room off to the side. "Come on."

"One whiskey and I'll be unconscious," he said, but he was surprisingly docile as he followed her to a circular leather booth near the entrance. A waiter wearing a suit far too fancy for the place didn't blink when Gretchen ordered the most expensive bottle on the menu and directed him to just bring them two glasses along with it.

"Is this what you and Lauren do after a long day?" Lachlan asked, an odd blankness to his voice. She eyed him and wondered if he was covering up jealousy.

She thought about the pizza place she and Marconi went to after solving a case, the sweaty beers clinking together.

"Not quite," she murmured, letting him draw his own more salacious conclusions because that information wasn't his to own.

He tensed beside her, but then laughed quietly to himself. "I walked right into that one."

"It was practically a written invitation," Gretchen agreed, sloshing too much liquid into his tumbler and then just as much into her own. The burn was smooth and hot and settled in her belly. She couldn't remember if she'd eaten anything that day—she did vaguely remember those pancakes with Ryan Kelly, but that was over twelve hours and several bodies ago. She waved the waiter back over to put in orders for two burgers.

"Why are you being thoughtful?" Lachlan asked, tongue a little looser than it had been. She side-eyed his drink and noticed it was almost empty. She topped him off again.

"You have a troubling tendency to think in binaries, Detective Gibbs," Gretchen said, her own tongue probably looser than she'd like, as well. Still, what did it matter? It was all true. "You've slotted me into the one marked 'terrible.' Which hurts my feelings, of course." She held up a hand, cutting him off. "You're going to say, 'What feelings?' You're tediously predictable."

He rolled his eyes. "Is there a point to this lecture?"

"You know why Marconi is such a better detective than you are?" Gretchen asked, and though she knew objectively the words were too harsh, she wasn't actually aiming to maim. "She would never be surprised that I ordered her a meal."

"Nothing surprises Lauren."

For the first time in a long time, Gretchen wondered if that's because the woman was numb. Looking back through the lens of new information, Gretchen could see that Marconi was rarely just plainly happy. She laughed, smiled, joked, did all the appropriate things for normal conversation, but there was always a heaviness about her. Gretchen had called that darkness *shadows*, but maybe that was an inaccurate term.

To have shadows, you also needed light.

"I could say that ordering you food ultimately benefits me in the long run," Gretchen said, sitting back and swirling her drink. "It keeps you focused and your sugar levels more balanced, which means you'll be both in a better mood and better at your job."

Lachlan zeroed in on the important part. "You could say?"

"If I'd thought through why I was doing it," Gretchen said, shrugging. "Sure. Mostly I was ordering a burger, and you're here, too. It's actually not as complicated as you make it seem."

"Aren't you supposed to be wholly selfish, though?" The alcohol was doing its work, clearly. He was rarely this blunt. "Isn't that at the heart of the sociopath thing?"

"You know, Ted Bundy used to talk people out of committing suicide," Gretchen said. She squinted into the distance. "And he's, like, way higher on the spectrum than me."

The "way" stretched far longer than it should have, and she glared briefly at the bottle of whiskey. Neither of them was a lightweight, but neither of them had slept, either. That, plus the stress and the empty stomach, and this could end with both of them bleeding out on the floor, emotionally speaking.

Which, right now, sounded like a fun distraction. She reached out and tapped a finger against the delicate skin of Lachlan's temple. "You're too rigid."

He didn't move away, just studied her as he plucked at his lower lip. He was trying to decide if he should engage or not. She let him have space for his deliberations.

"It's why I'm in Internal Affairs," he finally said after another hefty swig. "Gray areas are dangerous when it comes to ferreting out bad cops. It fits me better than . . ."

Lachlan waved the glass around, and she thought back on the day. The way he'd followed procedure at every step to the point of getting nothing accomplished; the way he refused to try to get added to Marconi's case; the frustration that had thrummed beneath his skin both at the Hayes farmhouse and out on the sidewalk outside the diner.

She knew she had an inclination to make everything about her. It had gotten Gretchen in trouble plenty of times. But for the first time all day, she realized that Lachlan's stressed-out behavior might not just be a reaction to her presence.

Her world shifted slightly, not shaking but rearranging just so, like she'd slipped on ice but caught herself before falling.

Lachlan wasn't a great cop; he didn't even want to be.

"Before you get too smug, you would be terrible at my job," he pointed out, and then smiled gratefully at the waiter and the burgers he was carrying. "So what's next?"

For the first time, Gretchen heard the question as neutral instead of loaded. Strange, that. How such a small piece of information could change so much.

She popped a fry in her mouth and chewed thoughtfully.

Guilt, the voice whispered.

"Maybe we should figure out why Garrett Adams blames Marconi for his son's death."

Lachlan's knife clattered to the table. "He doesn't."

But it came out as surprise rather than disbelief.

"Of course he does." She lifted her eyebrows. "Why else would he be so happy she's in jail?"

CHAPTER TWENTY-EIGHT

LAUREN

Then

Following the confrontation with Garrett Adams, Lauren swung by the station to run a more thorough search on missing boys from the state.

She knew the detectives Abaza had assigned to the case were competent, but she wasn't about to trust Elijah's safety to them, not when they didn't really care about the investigation beyond being ordered to look into it.

After she'd identified a handful of potential victims within a hundred-mile radius, she returned home and relieved Sandy, who waved off the invitation to just sleep in the guest bedroom.

Lauren put on a pot of coffee and sat down at the rickety kitchen table that eight years ago she'd been so proud about being able to buy. It had seen so much since then. Smeared applesauce and spilled glasses of wine, high chairs that morphed into booster seats, homework and glitter art projects. It all went so slow in the moments, in filling up days with activities to keep the kid entertained. But she also felt like she'd blinked and Elijah was no longer a baby.

She booted up her old laptop once more and opened her Word document on the boys in the basement.

Before she added any, though, she reached for the stack of papers she'd printed out at the station.

DELANEY, MICHAEL was first.

In terms of a victim profile, he was perfect. He fit the age, had a single mother, had been taken in broad daylight. No body found. He even looked like the other boys, with light-brown hair and the rounded cheeks of youth.

Only, there was no mention of an incident before his kidnapping of him being approached by a strange man. That didn't mean it didn't happen—clearly there was some incompetence bordering on neglect at play in these cases. Why were so many of them cold? Why were so many incomplete?

But it was interesting.

She made it through three more before she found a boy who'd been approached by a man a few days before he'd been taken.

Lauren stared at his file for a long time. Then she shifted so she could reach for her laptop once more. She wasn't sure what she was thinking, but she wasn't about to ignore her instincts. Not right now. Not when Elijah was in danger.

She decided each boy would get his own document, so she opened a new one, which she labeled simply as CALEB.

It took another four files before she found another boy who'd been contacted first. Nathaniel Parker. In the interviews, his mother referred to him as Nathan, and that's what she labeled that file.

By the time she'd waded through the fifteen files she'd identified as possibly being connected, she had a gnarly headache brewing behind her left eye, the sun was starting to creep in the window, and she had three boys in addition to Damien Adams who had been contacted by Hayes.

That didn't mean the others hadn't been Hayes's victims, but these were ones she could be sure about.

Slowly, she added one more Word document to the folder.

She titled it ELIJAH.

It wasn't a shock when Abaza called Lauren into her office the morning after the confrontation with Garrett.

He hadn't seemed the type to report her, but as she stared at a stone-faced Abaza across the desk, Lauren had to admit that she didn't know Garrett Adams well. She shouldn't have assumed that.

"Lauren," Abaza started, a brutal kindness in her tone. Lauren had been expecting a slap, but somehow this was worse. "What were you thinking?"

"I was thinking that Garrett Adams needed to be hauled in for stalking charges," Lauren said as calmly as possible. "This wasn't his first incident. He followed me after the blizzard. He harassed Hayes."

"That doesn't give you the right to attack him," Abaza said.

Lauren disagreed, but kept that to herself. "It won't happen again."

"Look, you're shaken up over what happened with Elijah yesterday," Abaza said slowly. "Understandably so, of course, but—"

"You think I've lost my objectivity."

"Honestly?" Abaza stared her down. "I don't know if you ever had it to begin with. You come back after one spooky night with a seven-year-old girl in a farmhouse, and all of a sudden you think there's a serial killer loose in our town?"

When Lauren tried to defend herself, Abaza held up a hand. "*And* I explicitly told you to stay away from this case. I knew this was going to happen."

Lauren couldn't argue with that. She'd known she was playing with fire. But the unfairness of it burned. "I thought Garrett Adams had come after my son. You expected me not to confront him?"

"I expected you to do what I'd asked and call Tobias and Smith," Abaza said, her tone unyielding. "Or for god's sake, Lauren, me. When did I become your enemy?"

Somewhere around the time Lauren had identified fifteen missing boys within a hundred-mile radius and a credible local suspect who had never been taken seriously. Lauren didn't say that, though; she wasn't even sure it's what she felt. But she was angry and defensive, and her worst thoughts were going to come to the surface.

"What was the thought process last night, Lauren?" Abaza asked, when Lauren didn't say anything. "That's right, there wasn't one. What if Garrett Adams *had* meant to harm you? What if he wanted to provoke you and then get you alone?"

"It was Hayes—"

"Stop it," Abaza cut in. The emotion in her voice alarmed Lauren more than the words themselves. "Stop it. You've gotten tunnel vision when it comes to Hayes. I didn't want you on this case before, and now . . ."

Something dark and heavy coiled at the base of Lauren's spine. "Now *what*?"

"I think you should take a few days off," Abaza said.

It wasn't a suspension, and it wasn't the firing Lauren had half braced for. But it stung.

"There's a pattern here," she said as unemotionally as possible. "If you would just look at the files."

"I will," Abaza assured her. "*If* there's a serial killer operating out of Montpelier, that's absolutely my top priority." She paused, leaned forward. "But you're my priority, too. I'm not doing this to punish you."

Lauren laughed in disbelief. "Fooled me."

"This isn't going into any kind of personnel file," Abaza reassured her. "It's staying between us. I just think you could use some of those built-up vacation days. You have plenty." Something like disbelief or annoyance must have been plain to read on Lauren's face, because Abaza continued in a harder voice. "Just take a beat, Lauren."

"Take a beat," Lauren repeated, the words feeling foreign in her mouth. "Wonder how many kids can die in the span of a beat."

"Not as many as you think," Abaza said, the coldness back. "That's the point."

"Right." Lauren exhaled her irritation, then stood. There was no use fighting this. "Right."

"I'll see you in a week, Detective Marconi," Abaza called out.

If Lauren stopped, she would have done something unprofessional. So she just nodded, swung by her desk to grab her bag, and then headed out the door. She felt the hungry eyes of her colleagues on her back, but she ignored them all, even the sympathetic ones.

It was only when she was in the safety of her SUV that she let out the frustrated scream that had been building in her chest. She gripped the wheel so her hands didn't shake as she tried to think beyond *hurt* and *desperation*.

Her eyes slid to the files she'd printed last night. They were still sitting there on her passenger seat.

"There was another parent . . . ," Garrett Adams had said. One who had seen Owen Hayes talking to her son only weeks before he'd gone missing.

Take a beat.

Lauren chewed on her lip, thought of the consequences should she be found out, thought of Elijah tucked into his *PAW Patrol* comforter, and then with a trembling hand, she punched into the GPS the address she'd found for Ashley Westwood.

CHAPTER
TWENTY-NINE

GRETCHEN

Now

Gretchen made sure to set her alarm to an ungodly hour so she could sneak out of the hotel without Lachlan knowing.

They might have had what he probably deemed a soulful bonding moment the night before, but Gretchen had no warmer feelings for him this morning than she did yesterday.

And anyway, overnight Fred had sent Gretchen the address for Sandra Bowen—the "family friend" who had been picking Elijah up from school the day he disappeared. Gretchen wasn't sure there was anything the woman could add to the investigation, but it was a box that needed to be checked.

Gretchen's drive across town was easy, and the traffic was light.

The squat, all-brick apartment building wasn't anything to write home about, but it seemed well maintained.

Once inside, Gretchen took the creaky elevator to the third floor and, after two wrong turns, found the right door.

There was a scuffling sound that followed her knock, and then the tiniest sliver of space.

"Yes?"

"Sandra?" Gretchen asked, trying to peer into the nothingness.

Silence, and then the squeak of hinges. "Who's asking?"

"I'm a friend of Lauren Marconi's," Gretchen said, taking the risk that Marconi hadn't burned all her bridges here.

The door opened to reveal a woman in her mid to upper thirties. About Marconi's age.

She had teased honey-colored hair with turquoise streaks through it, a full face of makeup despite the early hour, and shadows beneath her eyes that even her generously applied foundation couldn't cover. She wore velour sweatpants that Gretchen would bet had something cheeky printed across the butt, and a plain white crop top that showed off her aesthetically pleasing body.

Going by visuals alone, she couldn't be more opposite from Marconi, yet something about her made Gretchen want to smile in an extraordinarily rare bout of camaraderie. Marconi didn't like the boring ones—clearly never had.

"You're not one of those tabloid reporters?" the woman Gretchen presumed to be Sandra asked.

"If I were, I would tell you I wasn't," Gretchen said. "But no, I'm not."

"I guess you probably wouldn't have told me you'd lie," Sandra mused. She threw in an extra syllable to most of the words in a way that would normally irritate Gretchen but this time didn't. "But if you're that good at messing with my head, you probably deserve to get whatever information you want."

Gretchen laughed. "I do appreciate that logic."

Sandra's bubble-gum-pink-slicked mouth slanted up at one corner, and she held up two fingers, intertwined. "Me and logic. Famously best friends."

A yap came from somewhere behind her, and she rolled her eyes. "Shut it, Tequila. I swear to God."

The dog did not in fact "shut it," and Sandra turned away from Gretchen, heading back into the apartment. Gretchen followed.

The place was neat and tidy if a little run-down at the edges, the TV at least a decade old, the couch sagging from stuffing lost long ago. Bright paintings—landscapes and photographs and mixed-media art—hung on the walls, giving the place a pop similar to that of its owner.

Like she had when she'd first gone to Marconi's apartment, Gretchen had the urge to touch, rearrange. Maybe she already viewed Sandra as an extension of Marconi, a place to leave fingerprints, as well.

"Mimosa?" Sandra called from the kitchen, and Gretchen smirked, pleased with this visit already.

"Sure."

Lachlan had been right about Gretchen's new affinity for that word.

Sandra pressed a plastic champagne glass into Gretchen's hand and then disappeared once more. She reemerged with a mean-looking Chihuahua tucked under one arm and her drink in the other hand.

"If we're drinking together, I suppose you should call me Sandy," she said. Then with dancer-like grace, she arranged herself into a tufted blue monstrosity of an armchair, pulling her legs up as well so she could dump the dog in her lap.

Through missing teeth, he hissed at Gretchen, a sound she hadn't realized dogs could make.

"Don't mind Tequila—he's all bark," Sandy said, bopping him lightly on the nose. "Fifteen next week, if you can believe it."

"Hmm," Gretchen murmured, deciding the safest place to perch was the coffee table. "You knew Marconi."

"Poor Lauren," Sandy said with a little pout before downing half the mimosa. She stared at the glass sadly. "Should have made a pitcher."

"What happened with Elijah?" Gretchen asked.

Sandy's eyes filled but didn't spill. Gretchen had always found the skill mesmerizing, and had never been able to quite manage it. Crying itself was ugly enough that many people didn't like doing it in public, but it was a useful tool when it came to manipulating others.

"I know Lauren thinks it was that man," Sandy said, her fingers absently stroking Tequila, who was still glaring at Gretchen with little beady eyes. Dogs had never liked her. They sensed the void. "But I'm not so sure."

"Who do you think it was?" Gretchen asked for curiosity's sake. If Marconi thought it was Hayes, so did Gretchen, but it was interesting to get other perspectives.

Sandy leaned forward, and when she spoke it was in a conspiratorial whisper. "Rafi."

"The husband?"

"Elijah's father," Sandy corrected, sitting back again. "They never married."

"Why not?" Gretchen asked.

"You said you're friends with her." Sandy's eyes narrowed, another flash of that intelligence Gretchen suspected was closer to the surface than the woman wanted people to think.

"She's tight-lipped these days," Gretchen said, trying to sound reassuring. "But this could help her."

The debate played out clearly in the dip of Sandy's brows, but then her face smoothed over. "Rafi was no good up until maybe a year before Elijah was taken."

"Drugs?" Gretchen guessed.

"Yeah, just a dick all around, you know?" Sandy was warming to the topic. "He rubbed the girls in Lauren's face, got all caught up in the wrong crowd." Her mouth twisted, the memory clearly sitting sour. "Lauren was so convinced it was that serial killer who was after Elijah she didn't even notice what was happening."

Confirmation bias. "What was happening?"

"He got a girlfriend," Sandy said. "While he was messing around with Lauren. The girlfriend was pushing for him to get at least part-time custody of Elijah."

"But then why would he kill the kid?" Gretchen asked.

Sandy shook her head, big eyes framed by her sooty lashes. "Straight-up kidnapping gone wrong?"

Maybe. "Where's he now?"

"Still in town," Sandy said. "The nerve of him. I spit on the sidewalk when I pass him, though, don't you worry."

And that reminded Gretchen of another question. She dropped friends easily, but people like Marconi were stupidly loyal. Gretchen had seen that in action herself.

"Why aren't you still friends with Marconi?"

"Who says I'm not?" Sandy asked, an affronted hand pressed to her collarbone. Then she slumped a little in her chair. "She doesn't like thinking about this place. About Elijah. And I'm a big ole walking neon sign of memory."

"Is her family really dead?" Gretchen asked.

Sandy winced a little at the lack of tact, presumably, but didn't quibble. "Yeah, she was a single kid of single kids, and her parents died when she was still a kiddo. She had to make it on her own. Stubborn little bird."

Bambi, Gretchen mentally corrected, pleased that her nickname lined up so perfectly to circumstances.

"How'd she meet you?" Gretchen asked, even though it probably didn't have anything to do with the case.

"Treated herself to a manicure." Sandy flashed her own dagger nails that had elaborate scenes painted on them. "Sensed a kindred spirit in that one immediately."

Gretchen was annoyed at the hot flash of emotion she objectively identified as jealousy. "That day that you didn't get to Elijah in time, was there anything you can remember that was out of the ordinary?"

The shame and pain Sandy couldn't hide came like a menthol balm against a burn Gretchen didn't want to admit had stung.

She wanted to leave fingerprints on Marconi's things. Even if those fingerprints came in the form of bruises.

Did that make you feel better? she heard Marconi's dry voice ask. *Throwing your tantrum.*

"Just that detour." Everything about Sandy had dimmed, and she matched the dilapidated couch now more than the color on the walls. "Otherwise, no. I didn't see Rafi or anything like that."

"Have you ever heard of Garrett Adams?" Gretchen asked. She hadn't forgotten what she'd said last night—they needed to figure out why he blamed Marconi for his son's death.

Sandy's open expression shuttered, her eyes going shifty. "His boy was taken, too."

There were only a handful of times Gretchen had ever been envious of other people. Now, she wished for Marconi's interviewing skills. Gretchen ran through her catalog, searching for a way to pry whatever secret Sandy clearly held close to her chest.

"You don't like him, either?" Gretchen tried.

Sandy took a deep, shaky breath. "I don't know him."

"You know *of* him, though," Gretchen pressed.

"Lauren blamed him partially," Sandy said in a rush, like she knew she shouldn't be giving out this information but couldn't help herself. "I used to wonder if she was projecting onto him what she felt toward me."

The psychologist in her was instantly fascinated by the idea, the sociopath even more so. What must that be like to emotionally blame a close friend for the death of a child but at the same time know that you couldn't actually do that and survive?

She thought back to the quiet pleasure in Garrett Adams's eyes when he'd learned Marconi was in jail. How had Marconi shifted that anger, the rage, that she couldn't express to Sandy onto a target that could take the heat?

"Why did she blame him?"

"He sent her into that man's house," Sandy said, and this didn't sound like a secret. This sounded like Sandy was confused as to why Gretchen didn't already know the information. "That first night that got Lauren hooked on the case. Garrett Adams was the one who'd called in the anonymous tip."

"Garrett sent Marconi in particular?"

"That's what she seemed to think," Sandy said, lifting one shoulder. "They had a big blowup—actually a couple of them—after Elijah was, well. After."

"Do you know anything about Garrett's son, Damien? His disappearance?"

"No," Sandy said. "No one knows much about Garrett Adams. He moved to town a few years before his son went missing and owns the diner. People don't ask a lot of questions 'round here."

"What about Damien's mother? Was she ever in the picture?"

"If she was, she was long gone before the two got here," Sandy said, lifting one shoulder in a shrug. Uninterested. "Garrett was a hot commodity when he came to town. No wedding ring, a single father? And with that body?" She fanned herself. "I'm not gonna lie, I hit on him myself."

Gretchen raised her brows. "Successfully?"

"No, he only had eyes for Martha."

The words didn't make sense at first, and then they did. "Martha Hayes?"

"Mm-hmm." Sandy leaned forward with the eagerness of anyone who had good gossip to share. "They were having an affair."

"Did Owen Hayes know about it?"

"Can't imagine he didn't," Sandy said. "Not to . . . Well, I'd hate to say it. But I think some part of Garrett got off on, you know . . ."

"Screwing the wife of the man he thought killed his son?"

Sandy grimaced. "Yeah. Sounds terrible when you say it out loud, doesn't it?"

It sounded interesting more than anything. "Did it start before or after Damien's disappearance?"

"Before, I think," Sandy said. "Who knows with those types of affairs. But there was gossip going around when they all moved here."

That made Gretchen pause. "They came here around the same time?"

Sandy tipped her head to the side. "Yeah. Guess that's kind of weird."

Montpelier wasn't a small town, but it wasn't exactly a hub of activity, either. Maybe it was just another coincidence, but it seemed worth noting, considering how their lives had become so entangled. "Do you think Garrett is the kind of man to have killed Hayes?"

"Who can say what type of person anyone is?" Sandy asked. "He's quiet, keeps to himself. But don't all the neighbors say that once they realize the guy next door is a serial killer?" She paused. "I mean, he doesn't have a temper, if that's what you're asking. Even when Lauren would go in on him, she said he'd always stay real calm."

Gretchen didn't know what to do with any of that. Sandy was right: you couldn't guess what a person could do in any situation until you put them into it.

"What do you mean 'go in on him'?" Gretchen asked.

"Misdirected anger," Sandy said with the particular overenunciation of someone who'd heard the phrase from a therapist. She tapped one dagger nail against her chin. "Lauren ran into Garrett not long after Elijah was taken, and there were some fireworks. If I'm remembering correctly, it happened at one of those vigils Ashley held every year."

The name had Gretchen straightening. "Ashley Westwood? Isn't she one of the missing boys' mothers?"

"Yeah," Sandy said, rolling her eyes. "And now she's Rafael's wife."

That surprised a "What?" out of Gretchen.

"I guess they bonded over their missing kids or whatever," Sandy drawled, sounding contemptuous but not suspicious. "Anyway, Ashley is one of those, like, PTA"—Sandy elongated each letter—"moms. She always held memorials and search parties for all the missing boys."

"Did Marconi know her?"

"Oh yeah," Sandy answered without pause. "Lauren actually liked her. Ashley was one of the few people who bought into Marconi's theory about Hayes."

"Why don't you think it was Hayes?" Gretchen asked.

"I guess it's hard to imagine that *we* had a serial killer in our midst. It sounds more like a movie," Sandy said. "Losing a kid messes with your head. I think it would be easy to create a monster to hunt rather than admit that sometimes bad shit just happens."

"That would be true," Gretchen murmured—because Marconi wasn't here to stop her—"if we didn't just find a graveyard in that particular monster's home."

CHAPTER THIRTY

LAUREN

Then

Ashley Westwood's house looked like it had been lifted out of a Nancy Meyers movie.

And Ashley herself could easily star as one of the tastefully rich and immaculately put-together women who seemed to populate all those films.

Her spotless white button-down was tucked into artfully faded designer jeans, her glossy red hair just touched her shoulders, her makeup was subtle but carefully enhanced her gold-flecked green eyes, and her body had been clearly molded by six-days-a-week Pilates workouts.

Thick, but manicured, eyebrows rose as her gaze swept over Lauren's beat-up jeans, her boots, her heavy workman's jacket. "I'm not expecting a delivery."

Lauren almost laughed, would have had she not just been ordered to *take a beat* by her boss. "I'm Lauren Marconi with the Montpelier Police Department. I'd like to ask you a few questions if you have a minute."

Shock and grief chased each other across Ashley's expression before she nudged the front door all the way open. She led Lauren into a spotless, white marble–heavy kitchen that had copper-bottom pans hanging like artwork over a massive island in the center.

"Water?" Ashley asked, dipping into a fridge stocked with Evian bottles.

"No, thanks."

Ashley still took one for herself and then gestured for Lauren to sit on one of the farmhouse-chic stools across from her. "You've talked with Garrett Adams, I suppose."

Lauren schooled her own features to cover her surprise. "Why do you ask that?"

"He and I are the only ones left banging the drums," Ashley said, with a small, sad smile. "And even my arms are getting tired these days."

"Banging the drum about what?"

Sighing, Ashley leaned her forearms on the table, the unopened water clutched in both hands.

"Do we have to play this game?" When Lauren didn't say anything, Ashley continued. "I guess we do. We're the only ones who still think Owen Hayes is responsible for our sons' deaths."

"Out of who?" Lauren couldn't help but ask.

"I don't know what you mean."

"You said you're the only ones left," Lauren said, the phrasing interesting. "There were others before?"

"Oh." Ashley tucked a strand of hair behind her ear. "The other parents. For a while there, we managed to convince them, too."

"The parents of Hayes's victims?"

"Yes," Ashley said. "Not all the boys who disappear are because of Hayes. Or likely not, from what I can tell." She shot Lauren a wry look. "I'm not a cop. But I think I've got a pretty good list going."

"Why did they stop banging the drums?" Lauren asked.

"Hayes has a way of producing alibis." Ashley shrugged. "And I had a way of making myself look crazy. So . . . when it comes to believing people . . ."

"Garrett Adams is pretty believable," Lauren offered.

Ashley laughed, harder than Lauren would have expected. "That's a kind take on the situation. Most people see him as a stubborn ass. Think he's hard up about Martha and getting his revenge by pointing fingers at Hayes."

"They were together?" Lauren posed it like a question even though she knew the answer.

"If that's what you want to call it," Ashley said, and Lauren heard the bitterness there. Jealousy? Though Lauren couldn't imagine the picture-perfect woman with the mountain man from the diner. "Martha used him whenever she wanted to forget the fact that her husband kidnapped and killed little boys and she could do nothing about it."

"How do you know that?"

"It doesn't take much to add two and two and get four," Ashley said, lifting a careless shoulder, any emotion muted. Lauren wondered if it was an act. Wondered if maybe it was prescription pills dulling the reactions. "It wasn't any secret back then that Hayes hit her. Controlled her." She paused, stared at the marble countertop, shook her head. "I almost don't even blame her."

"For not doing anything?"

"Yeah," Ashley said, meeting Lauren's eyes. "What would you do if you'd married a serial killer?"

Anything other than nothing, Lauren wanted to answer. But what did she know? She was still sleeping with the person who wanted to take her to family court. Men made you do stupid things. She yanked hold of the conversation once more. "Why are you still convinced it's Hayes, then? Why are you left?"

"I saw him," Ashley said with quiet certainty. "He tried to take Joshua once and failed. Then no one did a goddamn thing about it, and he succeeded on his next attempt."

Lauren thought about the alibi Hayes had for Joshua's kidnapping. The hardware-store receipt. It would have been messy trying to make that all work, but not impossible. "You had trouble identifying him at first?"

Ashley swallowed, her fingers fidgeting at the water bottle's label. "I'm sure it was him. He has a small scar bisecting his eyebrow." She touched her own.

Lauren pictured Hayes. Ashley was right.

"And you noticed it?"

"I was trying to memorize any details I could before the man got away from Joshua," Ashley said, chewing on her lip. "But that didn't help the cops much—it's not like Hayes lives near here—until Garrett showed me a picture of Hayes."

"But at first—"

"Look, I know," Ashley cut in. "I'm the definition of an unreliable witness. But . . . I just needed a second, you know? I was too emotional to really process anything at the time. Then, when I did notice the scar, it was already too late. No one was going to believe me."

There were so many ways Garrett could have nudged Ashley into remembering "a scar" that hadn't actually been there on the man from McDonald's. Lauren was starting to get a clearer picture of why the rest of the parents had edged away from the theory.

She started to pick at her own reason for suspecting the man.

Julia was at the root, of course. But what had she said?

He yelled real loud at me once.

Are you one of the boys' moms?

The ones in the basement.

Lauren thought about the No. 1 DAD mug on the counter and the way Elijah had thought werewolves were real for a solid six months after she'd accidentally let him watch a movie too scary for his maturity level.

If Garrett and Ashley were the only two who identified Hayes as the culprit and Ashley admitted that Garrett had been the one to point her in that direction, couldn't it be that Garrett was acting out a vendetta? Or at least trying to build credibility for a pet theory that he couldn't prove with actual evidence?

Had Lauren been led on a wild-goose chase?

You think I've lost my objectivity.

I don't know if you ever had it to begin with.

"You're doing it," Ashley said quietly.

Lauren cleared her throat, embarrassed and off-balance, having forgotten exactly where she was. "Doing what?"

"Thinking we're crazy," Ashley said, resignation laced heavily into her tone.

"I don't think you're crazy," Lauren said as gently as possible. "But eyewitness accounts should be taken with a grain of salt for a reason."

"Why are you here?" Ashley asked, abrupt and annoyed.

Why *was* she here? "I'm worried my son's next."

Ashley's eyes narrowed. "Hayes talked to him?"

"Someone did," Lauren said, newly careful now. *Confirmation bias.* She'd seen it written in enough detective study books to know it was a dangerous thing. When you started shaping the evidence to fit your suspect rather than approaching it with a blank slate, innocent people ended up in jail. "Did the police have any leads on Joshua at the time of his disappearance?"

"They spun their wheels for a few weeks," Ashley said, a bitter twist to her mouth. "And then wrote it off as a vagabond passing through."

"But his body was never found," Lauren said, and internally winced at her own bluntness.

But Ashley's expression didn't falter. "Exactly."

It bothered Lauren. That none of these disappearances had sent red flags up higher, that the FBI hadn't been at least consulted. That there hadn't been a task force.

Still, she knew that less than 50 percent of violent crimes were ever solved, and that was of the 40 percent that were actually reported to the police. Homicide had the highest rate of clearance, but that was only impressive considering less than 20 percent of lesser crimes were solved.

Hayes—if it was Hayes—seemed to have a long cooling-off phase, and while they all fell within a somewhat contained radius, the victims had been taken from different neighborhoods, different suburbs. Their parents weren't all of the same socioeconomic demographic.

She thought about that missing boy, the cold case that she'd just started working before the blizzard. How many times had she put off looking at his file now? Sure, she'd had a wild couple of weeks, but even in the days following the storm, she hadn't managed to get to it.

It was drilled into detectives' heads that after seventy-two hours a missing-child case often became impossible to solve. No one wanted to admit that, though. And then when the parents—rightfully—couldn't accept that, they were given no support. Ashley had been institutionalized; Garrett had been threatened with a restraining order.

Lauren studied Ashley's face, the strain there, the lines, the years of grief and struggle and perseverance. Ashley had let Lauren into her home even though she'd known, or at least suspected, that Lauren would doubt her.

She thought about Garrett's resigned sigh.

I've told that story a hundred times and look where it's gotten me.

You've never told it to me.

And Lauren stopped. She took a beat.

"Tell me about Joshua," she said, instead of picking apart Ashley's theories further, as if doing so would make Elijah any safer. "What was he like?"

For the first time, Ashley smiled.

CHAPTER THIRTY-ONE

GRETCHEN

Now

Gretchen stripped everything Sandy had told her down to one key takeaway.

Rafael Corado had been emotionally involved with his son and/or Marconi at the time of Elijah's kidnapping. If she was working off the premise that the most likely suspect in Hayes's death was a parent, Rafael was just as likely to have done it as Marconi.

More so, even, considering he wasn't bound by a sworn oath to uphold the law.

She checked her phone. Four missed calls from Lachlan—she wondered if he felt betrayed at being left behind—and two texts from Fred.

Figured you'd want this, the first read.

The second contained a current Montpelier address for Rafael Corado.

How much do you charge for mind reading? Gretchen texted back. Maybe she would have been ruffled by Fred being a step ahead of her if it wasn't so obviously the next one to take.

Don't tempt me, Fred replied a second later.

Gretchen laughed and tossed the phone onto the Porsche's passenger seat. Fred enjoyed the negotiation game almost more than the money. Gretchen wouldn't be surprised if TELEPATHY showed up as a line item on her next invoice just because Fred thought she was clever.

The house at the address Fred had sent was modest, but in a seemingly good neighborhood. There were three newspapers piled up on the sidewalk, and the driveway was empty.

Had Rafael left in such a rush he'd forgotten to stop his newspaper delivery?

She parked at the curb and climbed out of the Porsche. While she figured it was pointless, she knocked on the door, rang the bell, and then knocked on the door some more. If someone was home, they would have heard her.

She looked back over her shoulder, scanning each of the nearby houses. The neighborhood was quiet.

Except . . .

Movement.

Across the street, one porch down. An older woman was watching Gretchen, peering out from behind a column like it would actually do anything to hide her.

Considering the woman didn't dash inside when she realized she'd been spotted, Gretchen guessed she hadn't really been trying to go unnoticed in the first place.

"You're looking for Rafi?" the woman asked once Gretchen crossed the street. She was even older than Gretchen had figured from a distance. Eighties at least, heading into her nineties.

Perfect. Women like her loved their entertainment, and Gretchen could promise that at least.

"Do you know where he is?"

"Gone," the woman said, shaking her head. "Coffee?"

"Sure," Gretchen said with a private smile, thinking of the offer of mimosas from Sandy.

The woman—Dorcas "call me Dori" Palsgrave, a strong New England name, if Gretchen had ever heard one—settled them onto a plastic-covered couch with an eye-wateringly bold floral pattern and patted Gretchen on the knee. Gretchen exaggerated her position with the investigation, but Dori was clearly eager to talk and needed little reassurance on that front anyway.

"Do you know where Rafael went?" Gretchen asked again.

"He hightailed it out of here a few days ago," Dori said, eyes wide behind the rim of her cup. They weren't cloudy or dulled with age, but sharp and assessing. She knew this was interesting information to dole out.

"He didn't tell anyone where he was going?"

"No, he did not," Dori said, as if it were a personal affront. "He dropped the cat with Mrs. Turner down the way. Said it was an emergency. Didn't say how long he'd be gone."

An emergency. Right before Marconi had been arrested for Hayes's murder.

They had found something.

The thought came fully formed as if someone had whispered it in her ear. *They* had found something.

Marconi and Rafael had been working together to take Hayes down.

Don't investigate.

It would explain the mistakes that were the reason Gretchen had so steadfastly believed in Marconi's innocence. Marconi would never be that sloppy in killing someone, but a random civilian?

I did it, okay?

Gretchen's pulse fluttered against her wrist, too fast.

Marconi might actually be guilty.

She swallowed hard, bit the inside of her cheek. Maybe it had all been Rafael. Maybe Marconi had seen him going into Hayes's house and had rushed in to try to stop him.

Gretchen blinked and found Dori watching her with a speculative twist to her mouth.

"Can I show you a picture?" Gretchen asked.

Dori made a production of putting her reading glasses on—they'd been hanging from a lanyard around her neck.

With just a few swipes, Gretchen found a picture of Marconi saved on her phone. They'd been at the pizza place where they went to celebrate solved cases, and Marconi had made some sort of snarky remark that she'd been too pleased with herself about. She was wearing her classic amused smirk, eyes laughing at Gretchen. Though she was classically beautiful, she tried to hide it under her bangs and her thick brows and a bare face.

It was there, though, in the cut of her jaw, in the slope of her nose, in the freckle at the corner of her mouth.

Gretchen stared at the picture for a beat longer, then held out the screen to Dori. "Do you recognize her?"

"Oh yes," Dori said after a theatrical moment of studying the picture. She plucked the reading glasses off her nose and let them drop down. "She came by the day before he left town."

Everything around Gretchen—the radiator's hissing, the footsteps of curious cats above them, the low hum of passing cars—went perfectly silent.

They had found something, she thought again. And then corrected herself.

Marconi had found something.

Why now? Gretchen had been wondering from the start. Here was an answer. What if Marconi had found something that proved beyond any doubt that Hayes had killed Elijah? And then she'd told Rafael, unwittingly stoking some murderous rage that had been simmering for nearly a decade.

Or . . . not unwittingly. Maybe Marconi had known exactly what she was doing. Maybe Rafael had a temper, maybe he had a hair trigger when it came to his son's death. Maybe Marconi had tossed a grenade and then, when it blew apart her world, regretted it so deeply she took responsibility for the fallout.

Or maybe Marconi might have been sloppy with the kill because she had been desperate to make sure she got to Hayes before Rafael did.

Gretchen was so fucking tired of *maybes*.

Without quite realizing how she did it, Gretchen extricated herself from Dori's house. When she was back on the street, she pulled up a recent contact on her phone and hit call.

Cormac answered after one ring.

"It was the father," Gretchen said. "Rafael Corado."

Silence and then a sigh. "Gretch."

"Don't call me that," she snapped. Shaughnessy was the one who used to call her that, and she wasn't in the mood. "If you're selling the story that Marconi wanted revenge, it's just as believable that the father wanted that as well."

"Right," he said, drawing out the word. "Except he wasn't caught on camera entering the house."

"There were other points of entry," Gretchen said, annoyed that everyone seemed so hung up on the footage.

"You just don't want it to be Lauren."

"Don't call her that," Gretchen snapped again, not even sure why she was angry, only recognizing the warning signs well.

Apparently, so did Cormac. "Call me back when you're feeling civil."

And then he hung up.

Gretchen screamed, startling a flock of birds into taking flight from the power lines above her head.

It was only then she noticed Lachlan, leaning against a dark SUV he must have rented once he'd realized he'd been left behind at the hotel. He'd parked in front of the Porsche, as if that guaranteed she wouldn't drive off without acknowledging him.

"Should I be worried about my personal safety?" Lachlan asked, eyeing her, clearly sensing the rage that was popping as bright-red splotches across her brain. "What happened?"

"Why are you *here*?" she asked instead of answering, pacing so that she didn't claw at his face just to feel the blood beneath her fingernails.

"Logical next step," Lachlan said, with a wave toward Rafael's house. "Can I take it from your murderous expression that you discovered something?"

Her eyes darted between Dori's porch, Rafi's newspapers, Lachlan's raised brows. Before finally admitting what had her so close to the edge she could feel the rush of air beneath her toes. "She might have killed him."

Lachlan's eyes dropped closed as he exhaled and rocked back, absorbing the statement like a punch. "Shit."

"You thought she was guilty anyway," Gretchen said, aware her words were coming out too fast. As was her breath. "This doesn't change anything. It doesn't change anything."

"Jesus, Gretchen." And Lachlan made a fatal mistake then, reaching for her.

The minute his fingers touched her arm, Gretchen reacted on pure, blind instinct.

In the next heartbeat, Lachlan's back was pressed up against the Porsche, his gun in her hand, her forearm pressed up against his jaw, exerting what she knew would be uncomfortable pressure.

"Don't. Touch me," Gretchen gritted out. Then she reached deep, so deep, to get herself to step away from this precipice that only had craggy rocks waiting for her at the bottom of it.

She needed help, though. She'd always needed help. That was her problem.

First it had been Shaughnessy, then Marconi. But neither of them were *here*. They weren't . . .

"You're panicking," Lachlan said, and she searched his tone for an emotion she could identify from her catalog. Surprise. No, not quite that. Disbelief. "You're actually panicking."

Gretchen pressed up against his throat, thought of how she'd had Marconi in a similar position recently, and nearly laughed.

Marconi hadn't even blinked those Bambi eyes, hadn't flinched. She'd let Gretchen into her apartment with bruises still on her throat.

The hot wave of uncontrollable anger receded, crashed down and receded, crashed down and receded. Gretchen felt it go, slowly, so slowly, and dropped her arm as soon as she could.

She stepped away from Lachlan, out of reach. That was the thing about sociopathic urges: they burned out as quick as they'd come. Something she would always be grateful about.

"Shit," she breathed out, feeling the sticky residue of adrenaline clinging to her insides. But she was back in control, mostly. She forced out, "Sorry."

Wow, an actual apology. Did that hurt? She heard Marconi say.

You don't get to speak, she snarled back at her imaginary Marconi.

Lachlan just nodded, his eyes wary and his expression curious as he watched her start pacing again on a tight path in front of him. "You really didn't think she killed him. I thought you were, you know, being stubbornly obtuse."

Gretchen whirled on him, but didn't attack. "She wouldn't have gotten caught."

On one of her passes, she held the gun out, butt first, to Lachlan. He took it, reholstered it.

"Even the best killers make mistakes," Lachlan said.

"Not these kinds of mistakes," Gretchen said, and she could hear that she was reassuring herself rather than him. Why had Marconi had blood on her, though, if she'd been the one to shoot the man?

It had been Rafael with the gun, was why.

"What changed your mind on whether she did it?" he asked, and she spared the briefest moment to acknowledge that he could have been more of an asshole about all this.

Still, that didn't mean she had to tell him what she'd learned from Dori. She took a second to actually think instead of reacting like a cornered animal. In the end, what did it matter? He already thought Marconi was guilty.

"She visited Rafael the day before Hayes was killed," Gretchen finally said, rolling the dice. Lachlan drew in a breath. "And Dori didn't make it seem like she was a frequent visitor otherwise."

"They were in on it together." It was the obvious conclusion; she wasn't surprised he'd gotten there.

She studied him, realizing only then what all this meant for him personally. Marconi being in touch with the father of her child.

Was she so hung up on Rafael that she'd take the fall for him? Gretchen watched as the thought came and went, a shiver of pain behind Lachlan's otherwise stoic expression.

"You think so, too," he pushed when she remained silent. "That they were in on it together."

"Maybe," Gretchen said, then corrected herself. "No. Maybe. No."

Again with the *maybes*.

"Well, as long as we're clear about that," Lachlan said, and she could all but hear the effort he put into making the joke. There was a wound there beneath that tough shell, and Gretchen, being who she was, wanted to pluck at its torn edges, pour salt into the gape of it, and watch the ways he flinched.

She fought the instinct with every part of herself. "Marconi might not have known what he would do."

"Maybe." Though he sounded doubtful. Before Gretchen could say anything else, Lachlan pushed off the SUV, stepped closer, his eyes locked on her face. "But why were you panicking?"

"Why does that matter?" she shot back, scratching at her skin.

"You could spin this easily," Lachlan said slowly instead of answering. "Conspiracy to commit murder rather than murder. Byrne just has to chase down Corado. Maybe neither of them will be charged to the full extent if the defense can introduce sufficient doubt over which of them did it."

He was right—of course he was right. This was probably good news.

"But you're still panicking," Lachlan observed, though he said it more to himself than to her.

She bared her teeth but kept her distance. He was closing in, getting too near to the right answer.

"Marconi said one time that you kept yourself under control because you didn't want to prove Shaughnessy right," he said. "You didn't want to become the monster he thought you were."

Gretchen's nails dug into her palms at the idea of Marconi telling Lachlan anything about her.

"And then Marconi stepped into that role." Lachlan was picking up speed, though she noticed he kept his hand hovering near his weapon. "You keep yourself under control because you don't want her to stop working with you."

The disappointment, Gretchen thought but didn't say. She didn't want the disappointment.

Her eyes were too dry now, and she wanted to rip them out.

Ever so carefully, Lachlan continued. "But if she can cross a line you thought she would never cross, what's to stop you from acting on your very worst impulses?"

Gretchen stopped, met his gaze, saw the grim realization there. "Absolutely nothing."

CHAPTER THIRTY-TWO

MARTHA

Before

The pregnancy stuck this time. Martha hadn't even bothered praying.

Julia Christine Hayes was born at 3:14 in the morning in the nursery, the second bedroom to the right on the top floor of the farmhouse. Martha's sister, Hannah, helped deliver the baby, her own petulant son sulking in the corner, impressed only by the sight of the bloodstained sheets.

When Hannah announced that it was a girl, Martha had to swipe at her wet cheeks and pretend it was the hormones.

Martha pressed tear-soaked lips to Julia's forehead, whispering over and over again, "Thank God."

Owen showed a passing interest in the baby, enough to soothe the wrinkle line in Hannah's brow. But he handed her off quickly and disappeared downstairs. He didn't find the sight of Martha breastfeeding intriguing, but rather something to look away from. Something almost embarrassing despite the fact that it was his wife, his daughter.

"You'll be okay?" Hannah asked the night before she left, her son on the cot, sleeping already, Julia in her arms.

"We'll be okay," Martha said, the lie tasting rotten on her tongue. But she must have delivered it convincingly because Hannah smiled, rubbed a thumb along Julia's cheek, and then handed her back over.

When Julia was six weeks old, Owen let them come into town with him. He dropped her at a park, told her to stay there, and then drove off.

Martha waited until his truck rounded the next corner before placing a hand on the back of Julia's head so she wouldn't jostle the baby while she walked.

Her feet knew the way too well.

Martha didn't go into the diner, didn't dare.

But she stood on the corner and watched as others did.

She saw him moving inside, a shape more than anything, and thought of the headlines from two years back.

Local Boy, 9, Missing; Police Suspect Foul Play.

Julia's heart beat against Martha's own.

It was only when Garrett glanced up sharply as if sensing he was being watched that Martha moved.

Back into the shadows that had become so familiar and dear.

CHAPTER
THIRTY-THREE

GRETCHEN

Now

Gretchen had thought Ryan Kelly would conveniently forget their arrangement—he was a tabloid reporter, after all. They weren't known for their integrity. But it was his name that lit up her phone as she drove back into town, away from Rafael Corado's house, Lachlan following in his car behind her.

"What do you have?" she asked, too raw for an attempt at pleasantries.

"Well, hello to you, too," Kelly said, too bright, too cheery. "Was that an apology I heard?"

"Please." Gretchen rolled her eyes despite the fact that he couldn't see her. She liked this, though. Felt back on solid ground where there had been only quicksand before. "You got a promotion, I'm sure."

"And then the threat of a demotion the next day," Kelly shot back, though she could tell he was playing it up. "When we had to run a clarification to the story that Gibbs had already recused himself from the case."

"Right, because that paper of yours is concerned with high-minded journalism."

Kelly laughed. "Touché. All right, I actually have something for you."

Gretchen gripped the wheel. "It better be good."

"As if I would call you for anything less," Kelly said. "There's some whispers. About the wife."

"Martha."

"Bingo," Kelly said. "Nothing is really bubbling to the surface—most eyes are on Marconi."

"But?" Gretchen pressed.

"There's a scoop, it's not mine, but it's coming out any minute now," Kelly said. "The wife bought an unregistered gun from a local dealer. About six months ago. It's a 'he said, she said' thing, I think. But . . ."

Gretchen whistled low. "That's damning."

"If it's true."

She didn't bother to say she didn't care either way. What she was doing was collecting stories. If she couldn't definitively prove Marconi hadn't been involved, what she needed was reasonable doubt to do the work for her.

"Did you hear about the bodies?" Gretchen asked, because that was part of Martha's story. A woman who had snapped after finding out her husband was a serial killer was juicier than anything they could squeeze out of the Marconi narrative.

"Oh, do tell," Kelly murmured, and she gave him what she could about the burial ground.

By the end, Kelly laughed. "I feel like we've really taken our relationship to the next level on this one."

"You couldn't handle next level with me, darling," Gretchen said. They'd slept together a time or two when they'd both been bored, and it had been fine, though nothing earth-shattering, neither of them putting much effort into it.

But the harmless flirtations were as much a part of their symbiotic relationship as the exchange of information was.

Gretchen hung up and then mindlessly wove her way through the streets back to the hotel.

The rage and what she distantly realized was fear were both gone, burned out completely, nothing but the hint of ash in their wake. If Marconi was guilty, it was because she was covering for Rafael, which fit with Gretchen's worldview even if she couldn't understand it.

Right now, she needed other viable suspects, though.

And here was Martha Hayes handing herself to them on a platter.

Had she actually done it? Had she killed her husband?

She'd been having an affair with one of the victims' fathers. What did that mean? Would Garrett have killed his lover's husband, eight years after the two had moved out of town?

That didn't seem as likely as Martha finally breaking after nearly two decades of watching her husband kidnap and kill young boys. Or . . .

Or maybe it wasn't Rafael and Marconi who had been working together.

Maybe Martha had hired, begged, or blackmailed Garrett into killing Hayes for her while she established an alibi for herself.

If that were the case, why would Marconi tell Gretchen not to investigate? Wouldn't she have wanted Gretchen to solve it instead? There was no way Marconi wouldn't have known Martha could plead down her sentence. The idea of battered wife syndrome still carried weight with juries. Her lawyer could even argue that it *had* been self-defense: she'd simply been able to gain hold of the weapon and shoot Hayes before he turned on her once more.

There was still that slim possibility that Marconi hadn't seen the killer. What if it had been Martha, but Marconi had thought it was Rafael instead? Marconi had known Gretchen's path would lead straight to Elijah's father, and for some ridiculous reason, Marconi wanted to protect him.

Gretchen pulled out her phone, redialed Cormac. "Has Rafael Corado been found yet?"

Silence and then a sigh. "I can't give you details, Gretchen."

She tried to decide if that was a yes or no, and couldn't. "Are you at least looking for him?"

When he didn't say anything, she slapped her hand against the dash. "Give me *something*."

"There's a cabin in his name. Up past Stowe, near Canada," Cormac finally said, and she could tell he thought he was throwing her scraps. She didn't care. "We're going to check to see if he's there."

It was all she would get. She hung up and pulled into the hotel's parking lot.

When she turned off the ignition, her hand crept into her pocket, her fingers fondling the black thumb drive she'd kept on her person since she'd found it.

Why were there only four names?

Gretchen got out of the car, waved Lachlan down. For all that he winced at her driving, he'd been only a few minutes behind her.

"I need your badge," she said when he rolled down his window.

"You know, the similarities *are* uncanny, but I don't think anyone's going to buy that you're a six-foot-three Black man named Lachlan Gibbs," he said dryly.

"You are the necessary evil that comes along with the gold," Gretchen said. "Stop being amused by your own wit and get in the car."

"You're lecturing me on wasting time being amused by my own wit," Lachlan said, brows raised.

"Yes, yes, pot, kettle, let's go," Gretchen said, and he smirked but dutifully climbed out of his SUV and into her Porsche.

"You've calmed down."

Gretchen snapped her teeth at him, but didn't disagree. She had decided that Marconi was either innocent or being stupid about a former lover. Both made her feel like her world order had been reestablished—which was the thing that mattered to Gretchen.

When she didn't say anything, Lachlan looked her way. "Should I even ask why you need a badge for whatever you're doing?"

"Don't worry, it's nothing too scary, I promise," Gretchen said, patting his thigh with as much condescension as she could put in a single gesture.

"Oh, screw you," he muttered, but it came out laced with humor, the same way Marconi would flip her off.

Gretchen didn't have room in her head to think about that, though. "We're going to the police station."

"Why?"

"I thought you loved it there."

"Why are we going to the station, Gretchen?" he asked again.

She chewed on her lip. Answering that question meant laying out one of the cards she'd been keeping tight to her chest. Gretchen wanted to pull the official files for the boys Marconi had singled out, but then she'd have to tell Lachlan that she'd broken into Marconi's apartment and hidden something from his Internal Affairs buddies. She doubted he would take kindly to the information.

Lachlan seemed to sense the reason she was stalling. "I'm not on the case, if you remember."

"Yes, but you have that pesky tendency to still care when I break the rules."

He didn't argue, and she made a face because they both knew she was right. It was quite literally his defining characteristic. He couldn't bend, he couldn't see gray, because then he wouldn't be who he was. And she didn't have to like it to admit that he had a point—when you started making exceptions in the type of job he had, there was only one way for it to turn out.

"What if we were talking about a hypothetical case instead?" he suggested slowly.

"Well then, that's a horse of a different color, isn't it?" Gretchen said, pleased. "Let's say hypothetically someone broke into a murder suspect's apartment before the police could seal it off."

Lachlan groaned and slumped against the door, but didn't interrupt.

"And then hypothetically that person found something that related to said murder," Gretchen said, wiggling her eyebrows obnoxiously.

"I'd say that person should have turned over the evidence to the investigators," he said, because he was one of those people who couldn't help themselves.

"This brilliant hypothetical police consultant knew that it would be far more useful to hold on to it herself," Gretchen said. "Because the aforementioned hypothetical murder suspect had already been found guilty in the minds of even her closest allies."

"But—" Lachlan started to argue further, but they'd just pulled up in front of the station. In the second it took him to realize that, Gretchen was already out the door and on the sidewalk. He had to scramble to keep up with her as she jogged up the steps and into the lobby.

His long legs didn't make it easy to stay ahead of him, but she was particularly determined, as she didn't want to hear whatever he'd been about to say. She did, however, let him catch up just in time to flash his badge at the bulldog woman at the front desk.

While the woman eventually let them through, she must have called Abaza right after, because the chief was waiting for them just outside the swinging doors of the bullpen, arms crossed, looking like she'd been awake the entire night.

Considering a serial killer's burial ground had just been found within her jurisdiction, Gretchen figured it was a fair assumption that Abaza hadn't gotten any sleep.

"Why are you here?" Abaza asked Lachlan, once again ignoring Gretchen. As if Gretchen cared. It let her scan the room, which had clearly seen an influx of federal agents since yesterday. The FBI didn't need those windbreakers they loved so much to stand out. You could spot one by how they walked around as if they owned the place.

Any cordiality and goodwill Abaza had been able to offer before their descent had clearly been used up.

"We need a conference room," Gretchen said, making sure not to frame it like a request.

"That's it?" Abaza asked, gaze flicking between them. "We're a little tight for space, but there's an empty one down the hall, to the right." She studied them for one more long minute. "Don't make a mess."

"We could have set something up in one of our hotel rooms," Lachlan pointed out as they both turned back to the hallway.

"Yes, but our hotel doesn't have an archives room with all that beautiful, beautiful information stored in it," Gretchen said easily. She stopped outside the room she figured Abaza had meant.

The space wasn't much—a single metal table, two plastic chairs, a whiteboard, and some markers. She could probably touch each wall with only two steps in either direction. But it would do.

She uncapped one of the markers and wrote four names on the board.

Joshua Westwood

Caleb Andrews

Nathaniel Parker

Elijah Marconi

As she stared at the victims' names, she thought about all the *maybes* she'd collected over the past two days. Maybe it had been Rafael who had killed Hayes because of something Marconi had told him. Maybe it had been Garrett Adams or another parent, one they didn't even know about. Maybe it had been Sandy, eaten away with regret about the detour; or Martha, tired of watching her husband kill children; or even the daughter. It couldn't be a treat living with a serial killer as a father.

Or maybe it had been Marconi, and Gretchen was just *stubbornly obtuse*, as Lachlan had put it.

Gretchen blew out a frustrated breath.

They needed to strip away the maybes.

She hadn't wanted to take this approach, hadn't wanted to even learn any of the boys' names. But Marconi had kept this thumb drive hidden beside her bed. She'd moved to that apartment only a year ago, which meant as recently as that she still thought this thing was important enough to protect.

So what were they missing?

"All right," Lachlan said from behind her, "I'm going to go ahead and take a wild guess that this is the information our brilliant but hypothetical consultant found."

Gretchen threw a look over her shoulder. "You're not just a pretty face, are you?"

"All I hear is you acknowledging I have a pretty face," Lachlan said, dry as dust.

"If only the personality didn't ruin it," Gretchen said, scrunching her nose. "Maybe I'd actually see what Marconi was thinking."

He smirked as she turned back to the list.

"If there were nine total—which is what the DA's office has—why did Marconi care about these particular four boys?" The question was more rhetorical than anything.

She thought back to the thumb drive.

The first three boys all had notes and details included in their Word document, but Elijah's had been empty.

Gretchen grabbed the eraser, hesitated, then took Elijah Marconi off the bottom of the list.

She circled the remaining boys and tapped the re-capped marker against the board, turning back to Lachlan, who was watching her with a surprising amount of patience.

"Whatever's going on here," she said, pointing over her shoulder, "those names hold the answer."

CHAPTER THIRTY-FOUR

LAUREN

Then

What Lauren needed was actual evidence against Owen Hayes.

Elijah hadn't been able to describe the man in the locker room the night before. Before he'd gone to school, Lauren had actually shown him a picture of Hayes. He'd stared at it for a long time and then offered her a shrug and a blank expression.

Beyond the fact that Elijah had been targeted after Hayes had warned her to stay out of his business, all she had was a handful of missing-boys cases that may or may not be related.

Lauren needed to actually start working the case. It seemed like Hayes had some alibis for Damien's and Joshua's kidnappings, but that just meant he could have an accomplice. Had anyone bothered to talk to him about the other victims? Had he been asked where he'd been when they went missing?

But Lauren couldn't start digging until she made sure Elijah was safe. So when she got back into her car after her talk with Ashley Westwood, she headed to the fire station, mostly on autopilot. Not quite believing this was the step she was going to take, but not seeing another alternative.

When she arrived, she found the shadows and waited, watched Rafi pull in with his ambulance, opened her own door when he stepped out of the station in a civilian top and jacket.

He was staring at his phone, tossing his keys in the air, when she called out to him.

It caused him to stumble. "Lauren. Is Elijah okay?"

The concern warmed the ice chip she carried around in her with Rafi's name on it. "He's fine." She paused. "Right now."

Rafi squared up as if he needed to brawl with some unknown force to protect their son, and Lauren almost wept with it. "What's wrong?"

She licked her lips, glanced back at her SUV. "Can you follow me home?"

The delicate muscles near his mouth twitched in his attempt not to have a reaction. "You've never invited me over before."

"I know," she said.

He nodded once and gestured toward their cars, not far from each other.

The drive back to Lauren's didn't take long, and Rafi stayed close on her tail.

He shook off her offer for water, but trailed her into the kitchen. She grabbed a bottle, leaned back against the stove, and studied him.

Nerves. That's what she saw, in his hands, in the careful stillness of his body. He was waiting for her to yell at him.

"I think Elijah's been targeted by a possible serial killer," Lauren said without preamble, the words so far-fetched they landed like lead weights between them. It took another fifteen minutes to fill Rafi in on what was happening, about the incident at the rec center the night before, and he only half believed her when she was done.

"I don't know, Laur." He ran his hands through his hair. "That sounds crazy."

She could blink at him for only a second, wondering if the rest of the world had lost all sense. "A grown man approached our son in the locker rooms. Apart from anything else, that should have you on edge."

"It does, I am," Rafi said, his shoulders pulling back. "I want to kill someone. But . . ." He glanced at her through his lashes. "You said he didn't talk to Elijah."

"It doesn't matter," Lauren said, frustrated, actually feeling the bricks being built one by one in the wall she used to keep him out. This had been stupid, to go to him. "It was a warning to me."

"But you said he contacts his victims sometimes," Rafi said, like he was talking to a wild animal. "Don't you think it's more likely that was what was happening? And that we should have someone check on Elijah's friend?"

Lauren waved that away. "We obviously assigned a patrol to him last night. He'll have protection for the next month at least. I don't care about him—I care about Elijah."

Rafi exhaled and leaned back against the counter, the galley kitchen so narrow his feet bumped against hers. "Okay, I'm sorry, tell me what we should be doing."

Her eyes traced each of his so-familiar features, the ones she could see echoed in Elijah's face. "Can you answer me something first?"

He pressed his lips together and then sighed, guessing what it would be without her needing to say it out loud. "It's my new girlfriend. Well, not new anymore. But she thinks I should have more visitation rights than I do."

"What's her name?" Lauren asked carefully so she didn't reveal any emotion.

Lauren and Rafi had been in a hotel room a week ago, their sheets sweaty, their hands busy. But hadn't she had that very thought as she'd been getting dressed that day? That a new girlfriend was pushing him to get custody? Lauren had dismissed it, because she'd been foolish enough to assume Rafi really had changed his ways.

"Does it matter?" he asked.

She could tell he thought it was a jealousy thing. "Yes."

"Look, I don't need you to go running a background check—"

"I need to know if she's involved in the goddamn case, Rafi," Lauren said through gritted teeth. She wouldn't put it above Hayes to use Martha to do his dirty work. Garrett had been having an affair with her before his son was taken. Martha could have easily been reporting back to Hayes, could have helped him take the kid. Was it so hard to believe that history would repeat itself here?

"Oh Jesus, what?" He seemed so baffled, and she wondered what it was like to live in that world. Where no one lied to you to do you harm. "We met a year ago."

"What. Is. Her. Name?"

"Jennifer Cochran. Jesus," he said again.

Lauren exhaled and shoved her trembling hands into the pockets of her jeans, feeling both ridiculously and justifiably paranoid.

You think I've lost my objectivity.

I don't know if you ever had it to begin with.

"I might need you to take Elijah on a trip somewhere," she said, ignoring the echo of Abaza's warning. "Maybe for a week, two. If you can get the days off."

The request had a metallic tinge to it so that it tasted wrong. But she couldn't protect Elijah herself and catch his potential killer at the same time. Rafi wasn't exactly a cop, but he had medical training, and he was big enough to stand a chance against potential threats. That was better than sending Elijah away with someone like Sandy.

He cocked his head. "You trust me to take him away from you?"

No, she thought. "No," she said.

"I'm the better of two evils, huh?" His mouth twisted wryly.

"Can you get the time off or not?"

"Yeah, yeah, of course." He glanced at his watch. "I have to cover a morning shift tomorrow, but after that? Can you have a bag ready to go for him after school?"

"Where are you going to take him?" she couldn't help but ask.

"Uh, the hunting cabin?" Rafi said. "Up near the border."

She closed her eyes. He'd shown her photos of the place. There were guns on the walls, trees spreading out for miles around it. "Perfect."

"I take it I shouldn't let anyone know."

"Please," Lauren said. "Not even Jennifer."

He reached out for her quick as anything, snagged her wrist, reeled her in so that her body bumped up against his. He wrapped an arm around her, pressing a kiss into her hair. "I'm sorry."

"It's not me you owe the apology to," she murmured into the collar of his shirt.

She could feel the deep breath he took, and she braced herself.

"Can we talk custody when this is all over?"

Lauren pictured him in the parking lot, pictured him a few minutes ago.

Tell me what we should be doing.

"Would you kill for him?" she asked without really meaning to.

He didn't hesitate. "Yes."

She took her own deep breath. "Then yes. We can talk about it."

Rafi kissed her temple hard. "Hey," he said, tilting her away from him, "where's he now?"

"At school." Lauren glanced at the wall clock. "But Sandy's picking him up any minute now."

CHAPTER
THIRTY-FIVE
Gretchen

Now

Lachlan proved to be proficient at the thing Gretchen had brought him along for—using his badge to get them access to things.

In this case, it was the files of the three boys, besides Elijah, Marconi had noted on her thumb drive. It helped, Gretchen was sure, that there was so much confusion with the FBI flooding into the office that the man in charge of the archives hadn't even bothered to try calling Abaza to authorize Lachlan making copies of the files.

"You know, I feel like even *I* could have just waltzed in there and gotten these," Gretchen said as she grabbed for Joshua Westwood's folder. His name was the first listed on the thumb drive, and so he was a place to start.

There wasn't much in there that hadn't been included in Marconi's notes. Certainly nothing that stood out as remarkable.

She held the folder up and waved it in Lachlan's face. "Trade?"

From the vaguely frustrated expression he wore when he glanced up, she figured he hadn't found anything notable, either.

Two pairs of eyes were always better than one, though. And so they swapped.

After they'd gone through all three, they sat back.

There was a tiny wisp of *something* nudging at Gretchen's intuition, but every time she reached out to grasp it, it dissolved into nothingness.

She stared at the spot where she'd erased Elijah's name, could see the bit of fuzz of leftover marker still clinging to the board.

"How persuasive do you think you can be?" she asked, toying with her phone but not calling the person she wanted to yet.

"Fairly," Lachlan said. "The key is to know you're doing the right thing."

Gretchen made a face at that, but said, "We need Elijah's folder."

"I thought—"

"Yeah," Gretchen said. "But we need Elijah's folder."

He sighed, pushed away from the table. "I'll try."

"You're a hero," she said, making sure he heard the sarcasm layered into it, and he huffed, part humor, part exasperation.

The second the door closed behind him, she had her phone at her ear.

"I don't think I have anything new for you," Fred answered.

"You've pulled up information on Owen Hayes, I presume," Gretchen said.

"Yeah, a nice dossier, though it's not that interesting, if I'm being honest."

"He was in Vermont before he moved to Montpelier, right?" Gretchen asked. "Ever since college."

"Brief stint in Connecticut, it looks like," Fred said.

"Small town?"

"Uh, some place called Waterbury," Fred said. "Population a little over one hundred thousand."

"What was the time period?" Gretchen asked, circling closer to the wisp, coming behind it.

"Lived there for two years before they moved to Montpelier," Fred dutifully reported.

"I don't think his record is as clean as it looks," Gretchen said, knowing this was going to be a big ask. "Is there any way you could run a search on those two years in that city and see if you find . . ."

"A predator?" Fred guessed when Gretchen trailed off. "Reports of a strange man approaching young boys?"

"Exactly," Gretchen breathed out.

"I can try." Fred didn't sound hopeful or pessimistic. When she said she would try, she meant just that. "Give me an hour, maybe longer."

"Thanks," Gretchen forced out, because she was grateful. That word just sat rusty in her toolbox.

"Yeah, don't mention it," Fred said, popping what sounded like a gum bubble at the end of that and then hanging up.

Twenty minutes later, Lachlan was back with two folders.

"I like this, directing people to do my will," Gretchen mused, as she took Elijah's file. "Whose is the other?"

"Damien Adams." He held up a hand. "For contrast."

She stared at him, and he lifted his brows.

"What?" he asked.

"Just surprised you came up with a good idea."

"What I heard is that you think it's a good idea," Lachlan quipped again, and Gretchen laughed, pleased that he didn't get ruffled by the jab, as he would have only yesterday.

"We'll make an adequate substitute for Marconi out of you yet," Gretchen said, and he squinted at her.

"I actually think I followed that."

"Terrifying," Gretchen said. "That you're spending enough time with me to understand."

"Who would have thought?"

Gretchen hummed, and then proceeded to ignore him.

Elijah's file was more detailed than the other boys', mostly because Marconi's statement read like that of a cop on the case.

Marking her spot, Gretchen glanced up. "Have you heard of the 'rec center incident'?"

Lachlan shook his head.

When she just went back to reading, he knocked on the table, and requested, "Details."

Gretchen thought about brushing him off, but then shrugged. "A man approached Elijah's friend in the locker room the day before Elijah was kidnapped. But the guy fled after Elijah called out to an adult. When Marconi chased him into the parking lot, there was no one there except a teenager smoking pot in his truck."

"Jesus." Lachlan sat back in his chair.

"I think . . ."

She broke off and reached for the three other files.

Flipping through the pages, she stopped at the right place for each of them and then pushed them all across to Lachlan.

"They were all approached by a strange man in the days and weeks before their kidnapping," she said. "Including Elijah." She glanced at the folder in front of him. "What about Damien?"

"Yeah, same. Notes that the father ID'd Hayes as the perp based on the kid's description, but Damien couldn't pick Hayes out of a photo lineup."

Gretchen drummed her fingers on the table, and then arranged her features into something that could pass for pleasantly beseeching.

He grimaced at her. "You want the rest of the files for Hayes's potential kills."

She smiled brightly, and he shook his head.

"They haven't even identified the victims in the farmhouse yet," he pointed out.

Gretchen pulled up the list of the nine cases that Fred had sent her the day before. "I bet this is a pretty good start."

Lachlan stared down at her phone and then looked back at her. "I don't want to know where you got this."

"See, again with the closed-mindedness." Gretchen tsk-tsked. "A detective worth their salt would be dying to know where I got that information."

"I'm not that kind of detective," Lachlan murmured. Then he emailed the list to himself. "I'll be back."

It took him a half hour this time.

"Did you get the files?" she asked when he stepped back into the room.

Lachlan nodded. "Five of them."

Gretchen held her hand out for one, and they both settled in. It took them an hour and a half to get through all the folders.

When they finished, Gretchen sat back. "No strange men mentioned."

She drummed on the table, trying to force this tidbit into what they knew about the rest of the case, then called Fred without bothering to get Lachlan out of the room again.

"Hey, I was in a rabbit hole," Fred said as a greeting.

"A productive one?" Gretchen asked.

"I think so." There was clacking on the other end, Fred pulling something up on her screen. "So you are a genius."

"I know."

Fred laughed. "There was a string of incidents reported six months after Owen Hayes arrived in Waterbury. They were scattered over a twenty-mile radius, and no one seemed to ever put them together, according to the newspaper articles around that time."

"They were all treated as one-offs?" Gretchen clarified, surprised.

"No, a few were linked," Fred said. "But, you know, I'd find a mention of two, and then a month later find another incident, but the reporter didn't call back to the first two—things like that."

"Any police reports?"

"Yeah, I ran a search on the crime blotters in all the local papers," Fred said. "I'd say there were about fifteen mentions of potential predators. At least thirteen of those could have matched Owen Hayes's description."

Gretchen whistled low. "But he's a pretty average-looking white dude."

"Exactly," Fred said. "So maybe a handful were him. Maybe none. But I searched the year after he left, and the incidents dropped by half."

"Circumstantial but damning."

"Here's the thing," Fred barreled on. "There were no unsolved missing-boys cases from the time he lived in Waterbury."

"So he didn't escalate to kidnapping and murder until he got to Montpelier."

"From what I can tell, yeah," Fred hedged. "There might be something I missed."

"But probably not," Gretchen said, because Fred didn't tend to make mistakes. "Did you run the same search on Montpelier papers once he got here?"

"You know I did," Fred said, a hint of smugness in her voice. "And you don't really see an uptick there until 2008, when Damien Adams went missing."

"I hear a 'but.'"

"But they ticked up in Burlington, Vermont, right after Hayes moved to Montpelier," Fred said, and Gretchen could hear the smirk. "Which is thirty minutes away, in case you aren't looking at a map. Which means Hayes might have—"

"Been using Burlington as his hunting grounds instead of Montpelier," Gretchen finished for her.

"Right."

"So what made him switch to Montpelier?" Gretchen wondered out loud. "Why take the risk?"

Lachlan, who had been listening in, grimaced and held up Damien Adams's file.

There was always something special about the first victim.

CHAPTER THIRTY-SIX

LAUREN

Then

Sandy crouched down in front of Lauren, a mug of soup cradled between her hands, her long nails clicking against ceramic.

Lauren stared through her.

Her knees were drawn up to her chest, her arms wrapped tightly around her shins, the metal of the cabinet door pressing into her spine.

"It's been four days, hon—you have to eat," Sandy said, just above a whisper. There were plenty of people moving in and out of Lauren's shitty little apartment that she'd once upon a time been proud she could afford. Now she saw every stain, every sag, every reminder that she was a shitty parent who couldn't even protect her own kid.

"You can't find him if you starve yourself to death."

Lauren's hand lashed out without her even thinking about it, the cup shattering against the tiled floor, noodles and broth pooling in the grout. The three uniforms who'd been drinking coffee in the corner dropped silent and then shuffled out of the kitchen.

Embarrassed, Lauren thought distantly, by the erratic display.

She chewed on the inside of her cheek until she tasted blood.

The fresh bloom of pain came as a relief, almost. She deserved it, but everything about her ached so much that she'd gone numb, her body refusing to recognize the gnawing in her stomach, the dried-up eyes, the burn in muscles held at the ready for four days straight. All that had become background noise.

Sandy dropped to her butt in front of Lauren, not seeming to care about the soup soaking into her jeans. "You've gotta sleep, hon."

Shameful, hateful words sat at the ready to be unleashed, and Lauren only *just* held them back. They hurt to swallow, the jagged edges of them slicing up her throat even more than it had from the yelling that had occurred on the first day and the second day.

They would lodge themselves so deeply in Sandy's skin, though, that they might kill her. And even here, in hell, some distant part of Lauren knew she didn't want to fatally wound.

In her most rational, lucid moments she knew the truth, anyway. Sandy wasn't to blame for this.

Lauren was.

———

Lauren had found the old maintenance road that ran behind the Hayeses' orchard on the fifth day after Elijah had gone missing.

She waited two more days before she used it.

The moon was so full that she didn't need her lights, the iced-over ruts jostling her but not throwing her off the path.

The bare limbs of the apple trees came into view, standing out in contrast to the denser evergreen woods that surrounded the orchard, and Lauren carefully maneuvered the SUV so that it was facing back the way she'd come, in case she needed a quick exit.

When she hopped out of the car, her boots sank into the snowbank on the side of the road.

Déjà vu crept over her, sliding into the gaps of her coat, slinking in against her skin. It had been less than a month since that night she'd been called out to the Hayes farm.

Since she'd been *sent there*, a voice corrected. By Garrett Adams.

This time, she had her gun already unholstered, pressed against the outside of her thigh.

Her progress through the trees was slow, but she moved like a shadow, not disturbing even the creatures of the night who were keen observers of any intruders upon their domain.

The farmhouse acted as a beacon in the darkness, golden light spilling from the windows in contrast to the silver caressing the snow from above.

A picture-perfect postcard of a Vermont winter—the death, the rot, the evil of this place all hidden by the soft glow.

If she listened close, she thought she could even hear the wind-chime laugh of a little girl.

How long did Hayes keep the boys alive? None had ever been found. Maybe he killed them right away, which would almost be a blessing. If she found Elijah in that basement, he would have been held by a monster for seven days.

Lauren realized her breathing had gone erratic only when stars popped at the edge of her vision.

This wasn't the time to think about that.

Abaza had refused to get a warrant for Hayes's place. There wasn't any evidence tying him to Elijah's disappearance. He'd even volunteered his alibi—security footage again. He'd been at a car dealership across town, and he hadn't once left the place during the ten minutes it had taken to kidnap Elijah.

"He has an accomplice," Lauren had argued, because it was so obvious now. She hadn't said she suspected Martha.

"You've had a target on that man's back for weeks and have not found a scrap of evidence," Abaza had said with a calmness that had made Lauren

want to throw her own badge on the table. *"We can't just go after him because of a gut feeling."*

Lauren knew the whispers that had followed her out of Abaza's office. That she was hysterical, that she'd latched on to some poor man because she couldn't handle the fact that her kid was probably dead.

She shrugged them off.

There was a stretch of open land between the orchard and the back porch. If she was unlucky, Owen or Martha might glance out at just the wrong time.

But there was no other option.

Taking a breath, she started to run, keeping her body angled low.

The snowdrifts caught at her ankles, her knees even, and each inhale came as a dragging wheeze, the frigid air crystallizing the water in her lungs.

The backyard stretched, expanded, and then all at once snapped back to a mere few feet.

In the next heartbeat, she found shadows to hide in once more.

Lauren crouched by the steps, catching her breath, slowing her pulse so that she could hear something beyond her racing heart.

When her thighs were no longer trembling, she stood, took the stairs, trying to dodge the kitchen lights.

She pressed her back flat up against the space next to the back door, and closed her eyes, listening.

Muffled shouts, explosions, and then wild laughter.

A television, she told the raw nerves that screamed at her to either curl up in a ball or kick in the door.

She reached out, tested the knob. It gave, but the door didn't.

Dead bolt.

Lauren reached up with her free hand to yank the bobby pins out of her pocket.

The actual picking of the lock would require two hands, so she weighed her options, found no good one, and reholstered her gun.

Immediately, she missed its weight in her palm.

Taking one more breath, she pushed away from the wall and stepped in front of the door.

The world stilled and went blurry at the edges as she met the cool, assessing gaze of Martha Hayes through the single pane.

Run.

Fight.

Run. Fight. Run. Fi—

Lauren did neither, just stood there, paralyzed, caught in that stare.

All she could do was watch as Martha slowly, ever so slowly, lifted her hand and unlocked the door.

CHAPTER
THIRTY-SEVEN

GRETCHEN

Now

The obvious answer to the first-victim question was that Owen Hayes had found out his wife was cheating on him. That had been the psychological trigger that had made him escalate from his disturbing but misdemeanor-level predatory behavior to kidnapping and murder.

It would have been so easy for Hayes to give in to the more violent urges once he'd found out that the man who was sleeping with his wife had a child the same age as the boys he preferred.

Everything coming together like that would have created a perfect storm for someone with that kind of darkness brewing inside him.

There were several curious things that stood out to Gretchen, though. First and foremost, why Damien hadn't been included on the thumb drive. While Gretchen knew she shouldn't be taking the thing as gospel, it still struck her as strange that she'd found a pattern connecting the five boys, yet Damien had been left off it.

Her eyes drifted back to the names written on the whiteboard in their little conference room. "What if those boys were his failed attempts?"

Lachlan had been quiet as she'd been thinking, his chair rocking back on two legs. He let it slam to the floor. "He got caught in each one."

"A passerby, another boy in the locker room, Ashley Westwood in that McDonald's," Gretchen listed off on her fingers. "That's why there aren't mentions for a strange man contacting the other victims. It wasn't his MO. It was him making a mistake."

"And after each of the failed attempts, he set up a decently solid alibi for every kidnapping the police asked him about," Lachlan said.

"Except Damien's. That's just the wife's word," Gretchen said, grabbing for the folder although she'd memorized most of the facts for all the cases that had been on Marconi's thumb drive. "The first, the sloppiest."

Lachlan plucked at his lower lip. "That means he has an accomplice, right? Someone to do the dirty work while he sets up an alibi."

"A pinch hitter."

"Nice," Lachlan said with an approving nod. Then with grim certainty offered, "The wife."

Gretchen thought about the gun, then about the rumor that Martha was having an affair with Garrett. But she shook her head. "I don't know."

Lachlan huffed a disbelieving laugh. "You said back at the farmhouse—you said Martha probably knew."

"I mean, you don't have a dozen kids buried in your basement without knowing," Gretchen said. "But she was his alibi. It seems weird to use the accomplice who steps in when you fail as your alibi."

"What? It makes perfect sense."

"No, because then she's on the detective's radar," Gretchen said. "And a wife isn't a good alibi in the first place. If she were the accomplice, he would have found someone to vouch for his whereabouts who wasn't her."

"You said the first victim is the sloppiest."

Gretchen tipped her head. "True."

"And what if Hayes coerced her," Lachlan said, gaining speed with his theory. "Or what if it was something akin to Stockholm syndrome."

"First of all, Stockholm syndrome isn't a real thing," Gretchen said. "It was a diagnosis created by a misogynist and police sympathizer to explain why a female hostage wasn't in awe of the detectives who screwed up her rescue."

That seemed to catch him off guard. "Really?"

"Yes, and it's been used to strip autonomy from women ever since," Gretchen said. "Sometimes women are villains, sometimes they're complicated accomplices. But they aren't suffering from some syndrome that doesn't actually exist."

"Okay, but what if Hayes used their kid to get Martha to cooperate?"

"Damien was taken before Julia was born," Gretchen pointed out.

Lachlan stood, started pacing. "Try this: She covered for him on Damien's kidnapping because he somehow made her believe she could be implicated. The moment she did that, he had actual leverage over her and got her to participate in the ones where he'd been identified. Fast-forward to now, and for whatever reason she senses Lauren closing in on them."

"Martha buys a gun," Gretchen said, because why not see where this will lead? "She claims Hayes had been abusing her for years and that she finally snapped. He goes to the grave with the secret that she'd helped kidnap and kill the boys all along."

"Martha Hayes gets maybe a year in prison," Lachlan continued. "Maybe five. But either way, a pretty light sentence in comparison to what she'd be facing had Lauren actually discovered something damning."

That's where things fell apart, though. "But why would Marconi take the fall for her?"

"I've stopped thinking I know what Lauren would and wouldn't do," Lachlan said, and for the first time she heard the pain in the words. She had been reading it slightly wrong—as jealousy or disbelief or something not quite identifiable. Again, she was forcibly reminded that no matter how much she trained herself to understand normal people's emotions, she wasn't a natural at it.

"You like her." Gretchen had the realization out loud.

"I'm sorry—were you under the impression I didn't?" he asked. "We were in a relationship."

"Are," Gretchen corrected. "Except you aren't 'in a relationship'— you were screwing each other."

"Even if that were true, I tend to like the people I sleep with." He paused. "I'm guessing you don't."

"It's not a prerequisite, no," Gretchen said idly. "Actually, it probably would complicate things."

"Unbelievable," he muttered. "But yes, I thought . . . well it doesn't matter."

He made a face like he couldn't believe he was telling her all this. She couldn't quite believe it, either. This was edging close to emotional ammunition should she ever need it.

"On that note, why *didn't* she tell you anything helpful?" Lachlan asked. "I assume she didn't."

"Not so much," Gretchen said. "She told me that she did it, that she wasn't framed, and that I shouldn't investigate."

He stared at her. "All of which you ignored spectacularly."

Gretchen grinned. "If she thought I'd just let her go to jail, she doesn't know me as well as she thinks she does."

"Hmmm."

Gretchen's amusement dissipated. "That sound meant what, exactly?"

"Just, most people would expect you to cut your losses," Lachlan said, shrugging. "I did. She's one of the few people in the world who knew you wouldn't. And tried anyway."

When Gretchen didn't say anything to that, Lachlan continued pacing. "Maybe she was just tired of waiting for the world to know Hayes was a killer."

"She could have just said something," Gretchen offered, a little dryly.

Lachlan ignored her. "She knew you didn't care about jurisdiction. You were her best shot at finding the bodies." He stopped, swiveled toward her. "She wanted Elijah's body found."

"But she said—"

"She said, 'Don't investigate.'" Lachlan stopped, swiveled toward her. "Right? Those were her exact words?"

Gretchen considered lying but couldn't find a reason to. "'Promise me. Don't investigate.'"

"Because she killed Hayes," Lachlan said, serious and grim. "Lauren has spent nine years trying to prove Hayes killed her son, and yet no one would believe her. But she was tired, she was done waiting. The only way anyone would listen to her is if she killed Hayes herself."

"I take back that 'you like her,'" Gretchen said. "You clearly don't even know her."

"Look, I know she's a little more . . . flexible . . . than I'd like when it comes to some of the decisions she makes while on cases." Lachlan held up a hand before she could say anything. "I just wouldn't put this past her. And, to be honest, it seems like she did a favor to the world, getting rid of Hayes."

Gretchen thought about the resolution of Viola Kent's case, of the resolution of her own. Sometimes Marconi could bend the rules, but the reason Gretchen had panicked when she'd doubted Marconi's innocence was because the woman didn't ever break them entirely. Not when the stakes were this high. She wouldn't just kill someone because she'd grown tired of waiting for the justice system to work.

Whether or not Gretchen agreed, that was a system Marconi ultimately believed in.

Gretchen knew better than anyone that even people on the highest of moral grounds could be brought low, knew that everyone was capable of murder in the right circumstances. But she just couldn't get behind Lachlan's reasoning here. Marconi lived in gray areas, but she wasn't irrational.

They found something.

"Will Byrne tell you if they found any local victims in Waltham?" Gretchen asked, her brain plucking at the tangled threads. If Martha had been in on the kidnapping, then it was unlikely the two had gone silent just because they'd moved to Massachusetts.

As an answer, Lachlan pulled out his phone and typed something out. It took only about thirty seconds for the thing to vibrate with a return text.

"No local victims yet," Lachlan said. "And apparently they found three more sets of remains at the Hayes farmhouse in addition to the one you, uh, stumbled upon."

"Why did he stop?" Gretchen asked, and then waved away her own question, answering it out loud in case Lachlan wasn't as quick as she was. "BPD and Byrne not finding local victims doesn't mean there aren't any."

"But it's interesting, isn't it?" Lachlan said, sitting forward. "You would think they'd have a spate of missing boys from somewhere within driving distance of Waltham. But nothing."

"Boston's big," she said, though it sounded inane. "Lots of missing boys."

"But he has a type, clearly," Lachlan said, gesturing toward the files. "Someone would have noticed a pattern."

"It took someone eight years to notice one here, and Montpelier is smaller than Boston."

The energy seemed to go out of him as the truth of that sank in. There were always more missing kids than there were resources to find them. "We're spinning in circles."

He wasn't wrong. Gretchen couldn't even figure out which case she wanted to pay attention to. Hayes's murder. The missing boys.

The accomplice.

Something niggled at her. Everything was foggy, running together, even. She'd read so many files that she was struggling to keep the details straight now. But there had been something in one of them.

She stood so she could reach all the folders and started flipping through the pages.

Searching.

When she found it, she closed her eyes, exhaled.

"What if the accomplice isn't Martha?"

She shifted the pages for Lachlan to read.

"The rec-center incident?" he asked after a few seconds of skimming.

"The kid smoking pot," Gretchen said, with an absolute sense of certainty. "What if he's the accomplice?"

CHAPTER
THIRTY-EIGHT
LAUREN

Then

Martha didn't linger by the door, simply unlocked the dead bolt and then turned and walked out of the kitchen.

Lauren couldn't breathe, couldn't move, could barely feel her fingers. But the jolt of adrenaline that came with the shock of what had just happened pulsed through her, waking up her sluggish limbs.

In the next moment, she was through the door, in the kitchen, her gun redrawn.

The TV still blared, covering the squeak of linoleum as Lauren crossed the room to the basement door that was no longer painted shut. In fact, it was almost ajar, like it had been prepared just for Lauren.

It was the first thing that made her hesitate.

Because maybe Martha wanted her husband to be caught. That would explain her unlocking the back door. But this? This smelled like a trap.

Hayes would have noticed if his lair had been breached.

Lauren kept her eye on the darkened hallway as she ran the probabilities in her head. What if Hayes had kidnapped Elijah to lure Lauren here in the first place? What if she'd just walked directly into a serial killer's den without having told anyone else where she was going? What if she would die next to her son, be buried next to him?

That part didn't sound so bad. It would be better than the interminable hell she'd been living for the past week.

And that pushed her to lightly nudge the door open the rest of the way.

Because she didn't care if she did die tonight, didn't care if she'd been played. If there was even the tiniest chance that Elijah was still alive, she had to try.

There was not even a hint of light coming from below. Lauren risked taking one hand off the gun to grope for a railing, her fingers finding unfinished wood.

The stairs were steep and narrow, and Lauren took her time even though everything in her strained to get down there, move faster, move faster. Find Elijah.

A string bumped against her forehead, and she grabbed for it, throwing light into the bare basement with one desperate flick of her wrist.

A part of Lauren truly believed Elijah would be there, tied to a chair, curled up in a ball, even, hands bound, but *there*. Breathing. Alive.

There was nothing but dirt.

It wasn't even a big room, no dark corners that had to be searched. Except . . .

Except a crawl space in the back.

Her fingers trembled on the gun, her mouth flooding with saliva as a precursor to the bile that would be the only thing in her stomach to throw up.

If Elijah wasn't bound on the ground, he would be there, beneath the dirt.

Lauren crossed to the elevated space without conscious thought, no longer trying to be quiet, no longer being careful.

Elijah was dead. He had to be.

It was only when she peered into the space, desperate eyes searching for fresh tracks, did she remember the Maglite she had strapped to her thigh.

The bulk of it was heavy in her hand as she toggled it on, the beam cutting into the darkness, hitting up against a back wall.

"You won't find anything."

Lauren spun on her heel, flashlight in one hand, gun in the other.

Even once Lauren realized it was Martha and not Owen, she didn't lower the weapon, nor did she take her finger off the trigger.

"You're lying," Lauren said.

Martha smiled softly, her face thrown into some strange relief beneath the force of both the bare bulb above her and the Maglite that Lauren held. "You needed to see for yourself." She paused, met Lauren's eyes like she had through that pane of glass earlier. "I know what you think."

"That your husband has been kidnapping and killing young boys," Lauren said, not bothering to soften that blow. If Martha was going to try to pretend her family was innocent, Lauren wasn't going to use kid gloves on her. With this little display, Martha was moving herself from victim to accessory.

"Where are they, then?" Martha asked, with a gesture toward the crawl space. "Do you want me to get you a shovel?"

Lauren called her bluff. "Yes."

"You won't find anything," Martha repeated, and it came so close to pity that Lauren shook with it. "If Elijah was there, there would be fresh dirt. You know that."

"Why would I trust anything you say?"

Martha tilted her head. "Julia said something, didn't she? That made you think this."

The boys in the basement.

Lauren didn't answer.

"A seven-year-old's imagination. What other evidence do you have against my husband?" Martha asked, sounding reasonable, calm. Like she didn't have a gun pointed at her chest. "A few coincidental interactions?"

Lauren blinked, so tired, so hungry, so worn that her thoughts weren't easily accessible. What did they have pointing to Owen Hayes as the perpetrator?

She shook her head. She'd been building a case, and Hayes had retaliated by taking Elijah.

Although had there really been any evidence?

Martha was watching Lauren, closer to her than she had been a minute ago.

Had Lauren closed her eyes that long? So that Martha had been able to get within arm's reach?

Sloppy. This whole thing had been so sloppy.

She had a gun. Martha didn't.

She had training. Martha didn't.

But all of a sudden Lauren felt trapped. She shifted, felt the wall against her spine.

"Where are they?" Lauren whispered.

"They're not here," Martha said just as quietly.

Then Lauren heard the sirens, and Martha smiled.

CHAPTER
THIRTY-NINE
GRETCHEN

Now

Lachlan clearly didn't share Gretchen's sense of certainty about the kid in the rec-center parking lot.

"That's quite the leap," he said, his eyes flicking between the file and Gretchen's face, sounding like he wanted to believe her but couldn't quite make himself actually do it.

"To the only person in the parking lot after a predator contacted Elijah?" Gretchen asked, lifting one brow in a maneuver she'd practiced in the mirror. She whipped it out only for special occasions where she really wanted to transmit her disbelief, making it all the more effective. "If you want to talk about sloppy mistakes, there you go. Marconi should have followed up on that."

"Her kid was taken the next day."

"Look at that timing," Gretchen said with a little wave.

"I know you didn't have a normal childhood," Lachlan said, getting agitated now. "But pot smoking in parking lots is a pretty well-documented favorite pastime of youths."

"Like you were really out there toking," Gretchen said, amused at the image. "What better way to hide, though? Light up, pretend that's why your hands are shaking, and not because you were caught trying to snatch a kid."

"But there had to be other cars in the parking lot," Lachlan pointed out. "Imagine this—Hayes runs out, hides in the back of his own truck, waits until Lauren goes back inside, and drives off. Why would the teenager have even turned his lights on?"

"To distract Marconi," Gretchen realized. "Maybe he wasn't the person who actually went into the rec center. Maybe he was the diversion. Look this way at a kid breaking the law, not at the other trucks in the parking lot."

Lachlan cursed softly, which she took as him admitting she was right.

"See."

"I'm not sold, but, yeah, you're right—that is plausible," he admitted. His eyes dropped to the files on the table. "Who is the kid, then?"

Gretchen squinted, trying to call up the timeline. The rec-center incident would have happened nine years after Damien Adams had gone missing. That would put him at the right age if Hayes had kept him alive instead of killing him.

She pictured Garrett Adams in his diner, pictured that quiet satisfaction that Marconi had been arrested.

Standing on the sidewalk, watching him, she'd wondered how he could have blamed Marconi if the kid had died before Elijah had even been born.

What had Sandy said? That Marconi and Garrett had gotten in blowups after Elijah's kidnapping. Sandy had made it seem like Marconi had been the instigator, but what if it had been Garrett?

What if the reason Garrett Adams blamed Marconi for his son's death was because Damien had still been alive when Elijah had been taken? What if Marconi *had* been responsible for Damien's death because she'd seen him in the parking lot of the rec center?

Martha could have easily let that particular secret slip just before leaving town.

Gretchen laughed, a small huff of disbelief, and when Lachlan raised his brows in question, she shook her head. "It was Damien. The first victim."

Lachlan's curious expression settled quickly back into skepticism. It seemed to be his default around her. "Now you're off the rails."

She flicked away the knee-jerk irritation of essentially being called crazy. Genius was often labeled as such, after all.

And for once, she didn't feel like arguing. She wasn't even that confident about her own theory, and had no interest in convincing Lachlan before she felt more on solid ground with the idea.

To make sure she wasn't getting blinded by her own preconceptions, she grabbed her phone once more.

Fred had run her search on the crime blotters for incidents where Hayes—or some perpetrator, at least—had talked to boys in Burlington. But if they were looking for an accomplice who would have been around sixteen to seventeen years old at the time Elijah was taken, they needed a list of boys who'd actually been kidnapped.

Gretchen fired off a quick text. **Any kids missing from Burlington in those first years?**

Fred texted back a thumbs-up emoji, which Gretchen took as assurance that she would look into it.

Meanwhile, Gretchen dug out her wallet from her bag, shifting through the business cards she kept in one of the pockets, her fingers stilling over the one she'd been looking for.

It had sat behind the rest of them since she'd gotten it months ago, during Shaughnessy's trial.

Lachlan's eyes were heavy on her as she finally plucked it out, but he didn't ask whom she was calling.

Gretchen put it on speakerphone because she didn't want to bother with Lachlan's questions when she was done.

"Daniels," a husky voice answered after one ring.

If Lachlan was surprised, he hid it well. But she knew he knew that Zachary Daniels was the man on the other side of the phone. *Former FBI guy turned sellout* was how Lachlan had explained Daniels to Gretchen once. He hadn't been wrong. Daniels had left the FBI to write a series of bestselling books on serial killers, tapping into the general public's insatiable cravings for information about the monsters. Now he lived off his speaking tours and consulting gigs with all the big cable serial-killer shows.

But Gretchen wasn't the type to care about that kind of thing, not like Lachlan, whose principles would have been offended by Daniels's decision to chase after money instead of chasing after bad guys for a government salary.

What she'd hesitated over was the fact that once upon a time he'd been something close to friends with Shaughnessy.

He'd never fully turned on him, either, not even on the witness stand.

"Hello?" he asked after she'd been quiet longer than was socially acceptable.

"This is Dr. White," Gretchen said, erecting the barriers she relied on in situations where she couldn't get away with being caustic and quick. "I have a few questions for you if you have the time."

Although she would have done it anyway, it wasn't presumptuous asking for the favor. When he'd handed over his card, he'd told her not to hesitate to use it. She wondered if he felt any guilt for missing the signs that Shaughnessy was a piece of work, or if he actually cared enough about Shaughnessy that the loyalty extended to her.

"Of course," the reply came after only a few seconds of hesitation. Then Daniels cleared his throat. "Does this have anything to do with Owen Hayes and Detective Marconi?"

Gretchen ignored the question. "What can you tell me about serial-killer protégés?"

Without missing a beat, Daniels launched into lecture mode. "Well, probably the most well known were the 'Beltway Snipers.' John Allen Muhammad and Lee Boyd Malvo. Although, to be clear, some people argue that they were spree killers instead of serial killers."

The Beltway sniper attacks in the DC area had occurred when Gretchen was in college, but she still remembered them well. Probably because, once caught, the men had been the main subject for several weeks of her abnormal psychology classes. Gretchen had been fascinated by the fear they'd inspired far more than the killers themselves. The way they'd cradled an entire metropolitan city in the palms of their hands had been captivating in a specific way that Gretchen found too tempting.

"But honestly," Daniels continued, "it doesn't matter much here. The urge to take on a protégé doesn't necessarily intersect with the urges that make someone a serial killer. The latter simply twists the former into something ugly."

"They see a boy or teenager in need of a father figure and step into the role," Gretchen guessed.

"Exactly," Daniels said. "The desire for a son, or son-like character, is certainly prevalent outside of predatory men, but those predatory men make it so that they're teaching that son to kill or kidnap or rape, et cetera. Have you heard of the 'Candy Man' killer?"

Gretchen would bite off her tongue before admitting she didn't know every detail of a notable case. "I have, but my friend Lachlan here hasn't, so why don't you explain?"

She winked at Lachlan when he rolled his eyes.

"Sir, I'm Detective Lachlan Gibbs of the Boston Police Department," Lachlan cut in. "I took a class from you a few years back. We're much obliged for your help."

Gretchen considered calling him out on his ass-kissing tone, but decided the interruption wouldn't be worth it.

"Ah, well," Daniels said, and Gretchen laughed because if that wasn't a polite way of saying *I don't remember you at all*, she didn't know what was. "Anyway, Dean Corll—a.k.a. the Candy Man—was one of those early-1970s serial killers. Murdered twenty-eight boys in a three-year period."

"Let me guess, he was known for giving the local kids candy."

Daniels made a sound of agreement. "He was one of the worst serial murderers of the time. But why I'm mentioning him is that he recruited one of his would-be victims to become his protégé."

Again, that wisp tried to become something tangible, but Daniels continued before she could fully hold on to it.

"Corll paid Elmer Wayne Henley—the protégé—two hundred dollars for any boy he could bring back to Corll, and more for 'good-looking' boys."

"What a gem," Gretchen murmured.

"Right," Daniels said, with that dark amusement that everyone who worked around serial killers seemed to have in order to stay sane. She wondered if he'd adopted any of the techniques she had to fit in. "Anyway, Corll even ended up killing one of Henley's good friends, and Henley just brought him another friend to rape and kill, so I'm thinking the money was just icing on the cake for him."

"Did Henley do any of the killings himself?"

"At least six," Daniels said. "And, you know, tortured at least a dozen others."

Lachlan whistled low.

"You want to hear something wild?" Daniels asked. It was obviously rhetorical, so Gretchen just waited. "Henley was the one who killed Corll in the end. And after shooting him, he said his only regret was that Corll wasn't alive to appreciate how well Henley had done. The protégé killing the mentor."

Gretchen's eyes found Lachlan's. His face reflected her own gut punch.

Through the loaded silence that dropped between them came Daniels's voice, laced with surprise as if he'd just realized exactly what he'd said. "Oh shit."

CHAPTER FORTY

MARTHA

Before

A poster advertising dog-walking services had ripped in half, revealing the boy's photo underneath.

Martha stood paralyzed at the end of the cashier lane, the ice cream she'd just bought melting, the condensation soaking into the paper bag she held.

When she started to feel her legs once more, Martha took the four unsteady steps to get to the bulletin board hanging on the grocery store's wall. Along the way, she bumped into a young mother's shopping cart and earned a muttered curse. But she didn't pay it any mind.

Slowly, Martha hooked a finger into the space created by the dog-walking poster and tugged.

The paper gave way easily.

And there was Peter.

His big green eyes, that freckle on his right nostril.

The baby fat had melted away a while ago. Now his face was leaner, older, his hair close-cropped. She wondered if his mother would recognize him if she walked by him right now. If Martha had brought him into the store, would he even draw one suspicious look?

MISSING, the poster blared above his picture, before giving a run-down of his statistics. His height, his weight, the clothes he had been wearing when last seen back in Burlington.

It didn't mention that he'd snort chocolate milk out of his nose if the knock-knock joke was good. Or that he was most ticklish on the left side of his rib cage, or that he liked dinosaur facts the best but would settle for stories about cowboys and the Wild, Wild West.

She exhaled when the first tear dripped off her chin, down to her collar. Her shaking hand swiped at her cheeks.

Could you really cry when you were drowning? Could you feel the tears as something separate than the water, waiting to rush in?

"Ma'am?"

Martha turned to find a uniformed cop standing at her side, expression sympathetic. But he kept a hand on his belt as if he couldn't rule out that she was about to violently lose it in public.

"Sorry," she said, swallowing the shame that lived too close to the surface always these days. "I, uh . . ."

She jerked her chin toward Peter's picture, letting the cop fill in the gaps.

He did, his hand dropping from his hip, his eyes going shifty. Still worried about an outburst, but not of the violent variety. Men never did know what to do with a grieving woman.

"Can I call someone for you?"

"No." Martha mustered up a deliberately wavering smile. "I'm . . . not far from home."

"You let me know if you change your mind, you hear?" the cop said, offering his own bland smile. His gaze flicked to Peter, lingered, and her pulse raced against the thin skin of her wrists. But then he gave Martha one last shrug and sauntered away, plastic bag in hand. He hadn't even been on duty, she realized.

The nerves that had come alive at his presence, at the sight of Peter, overwhelmed her.

She made it to the trash can outside just in time.

CHAPTER
FORTY-ONE
GRETCHEN

Now

Gretchen's phone beeped with an incoming call, and she used it as an excuse to hang up on Daniels without answering any of his questions.

"I have a case I'm going to send you," Fred said, as soon as Gretchen answered. "His name is Peter Stone, and he's from Burlington. Might not be connected at all, but he went missing the same year Hayes moved to Montpelier."

There was some static in the silence. "What aren't you saying?"

"I set a program to trawl through cases and flag any that had Marconi's archival access code attached to them," Fred said. "For anything she worked on in the year before she got transferred to Amherst."

"Smart," Gretchen said. "What made you think of that?"

"Just something I can have running in the background." There was a pause. "Also, I may have called the MPD yesterday pretending to be working on Hayes's case."

Gretchen laughed, loud and long. "Fantastic."

"Yeah." The amusement on Fred's side clear as well. "Anyway, the person I got was chatty. He told me that when Marconi was a uniform, she had this habit of picking up cold cases in her spare time. Most people thought she was a suck-up because of it."

"She was studying to become a detective," Gretchen said, absently defending Marconi.

"Right, well, we know that, but it probably didn't go over well with her fellow—male—uniforms who weren't as gung ho. Doesn't matter," Fred said, shaking it off. "It got me thinking that it was kind of strange for Marconi to just . . . stumble, if you will, over a serial killer."

"Very strange."

"Unless—"

"Hayes got nervous about one of those cold cases," Gretchen said.

"Right, so this Peter Stone popped up from my search, *and* it matches Hayes's victimology," Fred said, with a shrug in her voice. "And Marconi pulled the file only days before the blizzard that seems to be at the start of her trouble with Hayes."

Something was *off* about that, but Gretchen couldn't quite pinpoint it yet. "Send the file to me?"

"Done," Fred said, and then hung up.

It took a few seconds for the email to load, and then the picture took another few. When it did, she touched the screen gently. He looked so much like Damien Adams they could have been brothers. Hayes had a type.

She held out her phone to Lachlan. "Peter Stone. Lauren was looking into his case before all this started."

"Damien might not have been Hayes's first victim."

Gretchen didn't acknowledge the obvious statement, annoyed. Not necessarily with Lachlan but with herself. Why was she taking everything at face value in the case? Was this how others fell so easily into confirmation bias? Because they actually cared about the outcome?

But that couldn't be right. She hadn't felt this way when she and Marconi had been working Gretchen's own case.

This was because Marconi was sitting in jail right now, and every minute that passed meant that she could end up like Shaughnessy, his death too fresh to do anything but imagine a similar situation for Marconi.

Gretchen hadn't cried when she'd heard that Shaughnessy had been killed. Of course she hadn't. Instead, she'd poured herself a glass of his favorite Scotch and sat by her window and watched the evening turn to night, turn to dawn. She'd thought she'd let him go; she'd thought she'd been free of the man, finally, when he'd confessed to all the ways he'd meddled with her life. Quietly, from the shadows.

When he'd confessed to all the ways that she'd been wrong about him.

Sometimes, she wondered if that was what hurt the most—being wrong.

Sometimes, she wondered if she just hadn't ever listened closely when she lectured others on the fact that sociopaths had feelings, too.

Gretchen breathed deep now, and pictured Marconi's blood snaking its way through the tiles on the shower floor, running down the drain. Imagined the crack her head would make when hitting the floor while limp and gutted. Imagined sightless Bambi eyes.

It made Gretchen long for the weight of a knife in her own hands to defend, to avenge. But visualizing Marconi's death also let her finally put the prediction aside. If that was going to happen, it was going to happen.

What Gretchen could do was actually get her head in the game and stop letting everything else cloud her vision.

"Maybe the teenager in the parking lot wasn't Damien," Gretchen said to the room more than Lachlan. "Maybe it was this kid."

"Maybe it was no one," Lachlan pointed out, ever the voice of reason. "You're relying too heavily on gut instinct and storytelling."

She lifted her brows. "Storytelling?"

"It's a problem we have in IA," Lachlan said, sounding tired. "People like a good story, and if one doesn't exist, they fit the facts into a narrative that they're used to. I can't tell you how many times I've heard something to the extent of 'It just makes sense.'" He ran a hand over his shaved head. "But *stories* make sense. Life doesn't. You're telling yourself a story right now, but you're not basing it on anything."

The concept intrigued her. As ever, if Gretchen's brain was engaged with something, it was easier to ignore her more irrational impulses.

"We have to do that, though," Gretchen countered. "If I couldn't tell myself a good story, then I would never be able to solve any homicides other than the most blatantly obvious."

"Evidence," Lachlan argued. "That should tell its own story."

"You're still interpreting it, though. There's no way to separate our instinct for storytelling from crime solving," Gretchen said.

"There *should* be, though."

"You're too used to Monday-morning quarterbacking and hindsight," Gretchen said. "You don't get that benefit when you're actively working a case."

"I'm used to it, but it allows me to see how often good detectives get it wrong because they jump to biased conclusions," Lachlan said, unruffled.

"I take it you think I'm making assumptions," Gretchen said.

"Absolutely." Lachlan tipped back onto two of the chair's legs. "You hear of a boy that could be one of Hayes's victims, assume that Hayes kept him alive as a protégé, and that he became the teenager in the parking lot smoking pot. The assumptions in each step of that logic are hard to even comprehend."

Gretchen held up a hand and counted off her fingers. "Hayes had an accomplice, you agree?"

"Yes, he has too many alibis to be the only one taking the boys," Lachlan said, but continued before she could keep going. "But it could have been Martha. It could have been a fishing buddy. It's not necessarily a protégé."

"Fact two." Gretchen folded down a finger. "The only other person ever stopped during one of these incidents connected to Hayes was a teenage boy between the ages of fifteen and eighteen."

"How do you figure his age?"

"He had to be old enough to have a license," Gretchen said. "Since he was alone in that truck. And, making a tiny leap here, if he looked younger than driving age, I'm guessing Marconi would have done something about the pot."

"Marconi wasn't thinking clearly at the time, though," Lachlan argued. "And it's rural Vermont. Kids learn to drive a lot younger out here."

"No, Hayes wouldn't have risked him getting stopped for something as dumb as driving underage," Gretchen countered. There *was* a tendency to credit serial killers with more intelligence than they had, but Hayes had evaded capture for a decade and a half now, even with police attention on him. Stupid mistakes weren't part of his DNA.

Lachlan's doubt was still obvious, but he just nodded. "Okay, fair."

"That means if this kid was Hayes's protégé-slash-accomplice, then he would have been one of Hayes's earliest victims," Gretchen said. "Maybe Peter Stone, maybe Damien Adams. But after that, they'd be too young to match up with the teenager in the parking lot."

"Isn't that the sticking point, though?" Lachlan asked, a little roughly. "Why are we even connecting the teenager to the incident in the locker room?"

Gretchen fought the urge to snap at him. If she were being brutally honest with herself—which she sometimes tried to be—it was moments like these that she needed a Lachlan Gibbs type. It forced her to comb through the background noise in her mind to find the seed, the thing that made her so certain she was right. Something beyond her own delusions of grandeur that by now she was fairly good at acknowledging.

"The license plate," she finally said with a smug smile.

"What about it?"

"Do you know how hard it is to obscure a license plate to the point where it's useless?" Gretchen asked.

"Sure," Lachlan said. "It's something we teach rookies to be on the lookout for during highway patrol."

Gretchen grabbed for Elijah's file, where the report was written out in the excruciating detail of a thorough cop, which Marconi was, even when she was distracted. Gretchen flipped the papers around so Lachlan could see. "Marconi noted that there was mud covering most of the numbers and letters. That when she ran the make and model when she got in the next morning, it came up with too many results."

Lachlan plucked at his lower lip. "But it's rural Vermont."

"In January, though. Which makes it frozen rural Vermont," Gretchen corrected. "Where's the mud coming from? Maybe if it had been road salt or something like that, it'd be more believable." She paused, let him see her frustration. "You *just* said you teach rookies to look for that as suspicious behavior."

"That reasoning would never hold up under legal scrutiny," Lachlan said.

Gretchen bit the inside of her cheek until she tasted copper. "It doesn't *need* to. Take off that IA hat of yours."

"But it fits so well," Lachlan said, with a tiny grin that broke some of the tension Gretchen hadn't even noticed was building.

She rolled her head side to side to crack her spine, the pop of air and bone easing some of that frustration that had coiled beneath her skin. If she actually wanted to make progress here, what she had to do was look at Lachlan's behavior analytically.

He was a pain in the ass, sure. But why?

Because he found the problems.

There were people in the world who went house hunting and saw the beautiful wallpaper and fully redone kitchen, and there were those who saw the slight sag of the wooden floors, saw the splotches of old leaks on the ceiling. Lachlan was the latter, and he was meticulous and stubborn about it. Which meant he dug in when pushed.

She needed a different strategy.

"What happens if I'm wrong about this?" Gretchen asked.

Lachlan blinked at her. "I don't . . ."

He trailed off, and she refused to help him. His eyes darted down to the folder, and then up to her face, and then back down. She simply raised her brows when he glanced at her again.

"We might go down the wrong path," Lachlan said slowly, like he was feeling it out.

"What happens if we do that?"

"We lose time that Lauren doesn't have," Lachlan said, with a little more confidence.

"So what should we do instead?" Gretchen asked with faked patience. She could appreciate Lachlan's need to find the flaws in every-thing; what she couldn't stand was that he never seemed to be able to offer any suggestions. A critic without any creativity himself.

"Is this what you and Lauren do?" he asked, proving her right. He didn't have any idea what to do next, other than poke holes in all her scenarios. "Game out wild theories?"

Gretchen rolled her eyes. "Yes."

"Okay," Lachlan said slowly, and Gretchen tasted victory. Sometimes she impressed even herself. "Fine. Let's say it was Hayes's protégé in the parking lot. Does that mean it was Peter or Damien?"

That, Gretchen didn't have a feel for. She still thought Garrett's behavior might be explained by the protégé being Damien. But that was only if she wasn't misreading the situation.

The chair screeched its protest as Gretchen pushed back from the table. She didn't bother to wait to see if Lachlan would follow, simply headed out of their little conference room, down the hallway, toward the bullpen.

Abaza glanced up when Gretchen stepped inside her office. The room was full of people: a few in those FBI windbreakers, a few in street clothes, and a couple of MPD uniforms. The FBI agent with a shockingly thick head of pure white hair had clearly been midsentence.

"We need to put a rush on two of the victims' IDs," Gretchen said.

"Dr. White, now is not—"

"Sorry, Chief," Lachlan said in that diplomatic tone that she didn't think she'd ever master with all the practice in the world. "I know you're busy. But this could be important."

Abaza's eyes narrowed on Gretchen's face, and Gretchen remembered that this woman had once upon a time been Marconi's supervisor. Gretchen wondered how she felt about the arrest. If she took responsibility for it, for never solving Elijah Marconi's case.

"We're already prioritizing Elijah Marconi, considering his death might be connected to an active homicide investigation," Abaza said, very formally and clearly for the benefit of the G-men in the office.

"Not Elijah," Gretchen corrected. "A boy named Peter Stone. He was from Burlington."

Abaza glanced at her computer screen. "He's not one of the suspected victims."

"Right," Gretchen said slowly, and Abaza's mouth tightened at the tone. "That's why we need to figure out if his remains are at the farmhouse."

"No," the man with the white hair interjected. "We're doing this by the book, not catering to the whims of—" He broke off and glanced between them. "Are you even on this investigation?"

Abaza cleared her throat. "Why Peter Stone?"

"And Damien Adams," Lachlan added.

Her eyes flicked to him before returning to Gretchen. "And Damien Adams."

"One of them might have been kept alive as Hayes's protégé," Gretchen said.

"I'm sorry, 'protégé'?" the white-haired man cut in, his tone annoyed. He didn't like being ignored and dismissed, that was clear.

"Well, aren't you a waste of space. Would you like me to google the definition for you?" Gretchen murmured before turning back to Abaza, who looked like she was trying to contain a smirk.

"There's a chance Hayes kept one of the earlier victims alive to help him lure the boys to him," Lachlan offered.

The collective attention of the room shifted to the pictures of the bones from beneath the Hayeses' farmhouse.

Abaza turned toward one of the younger men lurking in the corner. "Let's do it. Contact Matthew Chapman over in Burlington for Stone's records. I have Damien Adams's."

The uniform straightened his shoulders and dashed from the room.

They all watched him before Abaza asked, "Is that all, Dr. White?"

The urge to wipe that infuriating composure from the woman's face rose in her. Gretchen acknowledged it, let herself have three seconds of imagining the ways she'd slice into Abaza's skin to cause the most amount of bloodshed, then exhaled and left the room without saying another word.

"You *know* she actually listened to you," Lachlan muttered, trailing behind her. Gretchen guessed she wasn't surprised that he'd follow her instead of lingering in the room. They'd become some weird little team over the course of the past day. "You're acting like she ignored you. But she listened to you."

"There's listening and then there's humoring," Gretchen gritted out. She didn't like explaining herself. It was one of Marconi's best qualities that she rarely needed Gretchen to do so. "She was humoring us because you were there."

"Isn't that why you brought me in the first place?"

Amusement, a quick lick of water against the flames, came and went. "Fair."

She pursed her lips in thought. "You really think this accomplice thing is a wild-goose chase?"

Lachlan stared at her for a long time before sighing. "You know what? If I've learned anything in the past few years, it's that I should never bet against you."

Gretchen grinned, pleased. "Damn straight."

CHAPTER
FORTY-TWO

LAUREN

Then

One of Lauren's favorite parts of her apartment was that her bedroom window overlooked the porch's roof. Many a night, she'd crawled out here, bundled in blankets, to study the stars, holding Elijah safely cradled against her body.

Where she could feel his heart beat against her palm.

She'd never feel that again.

Now all she had to cradle was an empty bottle of vodka.

Sandy climbed out onto the roof next to Lauren and passed her a fresh bottle of liquor. At this point, Lauren didn't even bother checking what kind it was. She took a swig and savored the burn.

It wasn't like she had work in the morning to worry about. Her little stunt at the farmhouse had gotten her a month's suspension without pay.

"You're going to fall off from here," Sandy said, clinging to the windowsill.

"As if I care," Lauren murmured.

"What would Elijah say to that?"

"Doesn't matter, he's dead." Lauren hoped that if she said it frequently, it might start feeling like something other than a hot poker directly to the chest.

Sandy inhaled roughly. "You stop that."

Tears leaked out of the corners of Lauren's eyes. "Can't."

"You're just giving up, then?" Sandy asked, and it felt like a slap. Lauren wanted to slap back at her, ask her about that detour, about those ten minutes that had allowed Elijah to be snatched up.

It seemed she had some sense left, though. "No one believes Hayes did it."

Sandy was quiet, and Lauren knew that was because she thought Rafi was the guilty one. Lauren didn't know why everyone believed that, but they probably thought her just as foolish as she did them.

"I think there's a reason loved ones aren't allowed to work cases of their relatives," Sandy said in a way that sounded like she'd practiced it. So as to not set Lauren off. "And you know Abaza is going to solve this one."

Lauren laughed, and it hurt. "Because she's done such a stellar job figuring out who took Damien Adams?"

"You said Hayes had alibis for all the kidnappings," Sandy said in that same careful tone.

"Not all of them," Lauren corrected, feeling human for the first time in days. That's how it was, she realized. When she started focusing on the case, the numbness receded. "He was only asked about his whereabouts when the parents pushed him as the suspect."

It made her remember Martha and the way she'd unlocked the door, then called the police. What had Martha been thinking?

Martha had been right about the fact that Lauren would never have believed Elijah wasn't down in that basement if she hadn't seen it herself. But they could have smoothed over the dirt. Seeing the undisturbed earth did nothing to clear Lauren's suspicions of the family. In fact, it just made her more convinced that Martha was a part of the scheme.

Of course she had to be. Julia knew about the boys in the basement. How would the little girl know and Martha not?

That left the likely possibility that Martha had done it not to persuade Lauren of anything but to discredit her in the eyes of the MPD. Just like Ashley Westwood had been discredited.

She heard Sandy's small, resigned sigh as if she sensed where Lauren's thought had gone.

"You can leave," Lauren said.

Sandy made a small, protesting sound. "Never, hon."

Please leave is what Lauren wanted to say.

Instead, she took another swig of the alcohol so she didn't throw herself from the roof just to feel a different kind of pain.

———

Abaza met with Lauren in a park on Wednesday mornings during her suspension.

It was a courtesy Lauren didn't deserve yet resented anyway.

"We've questioned all the parents from the cases you identified," Abaza said, as she handed over a to-go cup of coffee to Lauren. The weather hadn't crested freezing that morning, so they walked the paths instead of sitting. "None of them recognized Hayes."

"What about Martha?"

"They didn't recognize her, either," Abaza said, gently, like she always talked to Lauren these days. Like Lauren was made of the thinnest glass that would shatter with a single wrong word.

Lauren couldn't deny that's how she felt. "Can you talk to Julia Hayes?"

Damning silence greeted the question. Then Abaza coughed. "Lauren, I was already worried about your objectivity before . . . Well. Before."

"She knows something," Lauren cut in, before Abaza could stumble further onto all the broken parts of her. "She said the 'boys in the basement.' Why won't you—"

"Lauren," Abaza cut her off. "She's a child. She doesn't know anything."

That wasn't true. Elijah had known plenty when he'd been that age. But Lauren gritted her teeth against the argument. If she made a big deal of it, Abaza might put a patrol on Julia. Then Lauren would never have access to the only source of information she had in the Hayes household.

"I wanted to let you know we're . . . we're looking at Rafael," Abaza said, like she expected a fight.

"If you want to waste your time," Lauren muttered without much heat. "I had asked him that day to take Elijah out of town. If he'd wanted to kidnap him, he only had to wait twenty-four hours to do it with my permission."

They went quiet as a young woman with three kids beneath the age of ten passed them. She was pushing a double stroller and looking for all the world like she wanted to strangle at least one of the children.

Lauren's palms, lungs, womb, ached at the sight. How many times had she worn that exact expression around Elijah?

Abaza's hand pressed into the space between Lauren's shoulder blades, and it was only then that Lauren realized she'd stopped walking completely. Softly, Abaza nudged, "Come on."

They made another loop in silence. Abaza was the one to break it.

"I know you want it to be Hayes," she said. "Because then you have an answer."

Lauren huffed out an unamused laugh. "Yes, I want the man I suspect to be a serial killer to have taken my son."

"You know that's not what I meant," Abaza said.

Drawing in a shaky breath, Lauren nodded. "I know."

"There's only so much I can help you if you get yourself into more trouble." Abaza paused, and Lauren realized her question about Julia hadn't been as subtle as she'd intended. "Or if you contact the Hayes family in any way."

"I hear you," Lauren said, and Abaza tensed because she wasn't stupid. Lauren hadn't agreed to anything. But it was what Lauren could offer. She had nothing else to give. If there was even a slight chance of finding Elijah, Lauren would do what she had to do. Even if it meant losing her badge.

"You know Martha unlocked the door," she said even though they'd had this conversation several times before.

"And she says she didn't," Abaza countered as Lauren knew she would. "Considering we found your bobby pins on the porch, and I know that you can pick a dead bolt, you don't have much ground to stand on." She paused again. "Even if I personally believe you."

"Why would she do that, do you think?"

"Because she didn't want you stalking her for years to come," Abaza said, like the answer was obvious. Maybe it was.

"Or because she knew she could show me just enough," Lauren countered. "So that you all would be more hesitant to search the farmhouse. She did it so she had leverage over the investigation."

"Now you think she's the mastermind here?" Abaza asked after a minute.

Lauren swallowed, not sure. There had been something hollow in Martha's eyes that morning at the farmhouse. During the blizzard. And then again in the basement. "An equal partnership, maybe. He grabs the kids, she keeps them."

Abaza didn't say anything, so Lauren kept going.

"No, it makes sense with the length of time between the kidnappings," Lauren said, that same spark returning from the night on top of the porch with the fifth of alcohol and Sandy's doubt. "They keep them alive. In the basement. For a certain length of time."

"Lauren." Abaza stopped her this time, with a hand on her forearm. "You need to stop. I've seen this happen before. There's only one way this ends."

"With Hayes in jail."

Abaza shook her head, a deep sadness in the downward slant of her mouth. "No, honey, with you there."

CHAPTER FORTY-THREE

GRETCHEN

Now

"Now what?" Lachlan asked. They'd left the station, but not before collecting the files Lachlan had managed to procure for them. Those were in the back of the Porsche to make room for the fast-food bags spread out between them.

Gretchen popped a fry in her mouth, savored the salt, the fat, licked the remnants of both from her fingers.

"Would you have killed Hayes?" she asked instead of answering. "If you were in Marconi's shoes."

Lachlan laughed and then sobered. "Oh, I assumed you were messing with me. You know I wouldn't have."

"So is there anyone you'd bend the rules for?" Gretchen pressed. "Marconi?"

He swiped at a ketchup stain on his trousers, his face tucked down, mostly hidden from her.

"No," he said, softly. "Ethics don't work like that."

"What if it was the only way to stop him from killing more kids?" Gretchen asked. "What if you knew you'd never have enough evidence to catch him? What if you'd spent ten years letting the system do its work and had to watch him kill a boy a year in the process?"

Gretchen didn't believe that was what had happened with Marconi, but it was close enough that she was curious at Lachlan's answer. Men like him revered moral purity above all else, but the world wasn't pure. There were monsters out there who enjoyed hurting people, ones who would never be caught through legal means.

Lachlan shook his head softly. "I honestly don't know what you want me to say."

Gretchen laughed, amused at herself, at him. He was right—this was pointless navel-gazing. "That would be a bit like you trying to get me to admit there are moral absolutes in the world, huh?"

His mouth slanted up in a reluctant grin. "Yeah, I'm not sure we're going to solve ancient philosophical debates mid–homicide investigation over fast food."

In moments like these, Gretchen had to grudgingly admit—to herself only—that Lachlan wasn't actually as irritating as she'd once thought. She did not enjoy being wrong. "Don't knock it. Some of my best thinking comes mid–homicide investigation over fast food."

Lachlan snorted. "Fair."

Gretchen stared down sadly at her empty container. "So let me get this straight. You don't think everyone is capable of murder?" She glanced over at him. "Including yourself."

"Anyone can pull a trigger," Lachlan said, sidestepping.

"True, I suppose." She paused, turned toward him more fully. "If Marconi killed Hayes, do you think that makes her a bad person?"

Lachlan was an expert at dodging. "Why does it matter if I think she's a bad person?"

"Because I'm a psychologist and a criminologist and a sociopath, and I find it all very fascinating what lines people draw not only for themselves but for others," Gretchen said, easily. "And how they think they would act differently than the very people they judge when really they've just never been put in the same situation."

To his credit, he seemed to consider it, balling up the crinkly hamburger wrapper as he did. "I want to be able to answer with nuance, but at the end of the day, that's not who I am. Yes, I think that if Lauren killed Hayes, then she isn't the person I thought she was."

"She's bad," Gretchen pressed.

"If we're using labels," Lachlan said, a soft agreement. "This isn't relevant, though."

"Actually, there's where you're wrong. It lets me think about the case in a different way," Gretchen said. It was the truth. As much as she might be set on her own version of what had happened, considering other aspects of the investigation let everything percolate in the back of her mind. Who knew what could be unlocked that way? "I still find the nine-year gap from Elijah's death to Hayes's strange."

"Lauren was biding her time."

"And then executed—no pun intended—her carefully thought-out plan in such a sloppy way she was caught immediately?" Gretchen shook her head. "No."

"That 'just doesn't make sense,' right?" Lachlan said with emphasis to remind her of the conversation from earlier. Sometimes things just didn't make sense, Gretchen understood that. But people were also predictable in their own ways, and she had sufficient data on Marconi not to doubt her own judgment—for longer than a few minutes.

Gretchen was saved from having to answer that little slap on the wrist by Lachlan's phone ringing this time.

Abaza, he mouthed, as he answered on speakerphone.

"We've identified Damien Adams's body in the remains we found," Abaza said in that no-nonsense, clipped way of hers. "We got lucky. We ran the three dentals against the only body that was buried in the far corner of the orchard. The secondary site."

"And it was Damien's?"

"Yes," Abaza said. "The others are going to take more time, and our team is still excavating."

"Was he killed around the time he was taken?" Lachlan asked. "Do they know that yet?"

"We haven't gotten that far yet, but off the record?" Abaza said, lowering her voice. "The remains were that of a child. So not your protégé."

Gretchen sighed. That seemed to close the door on Garrett Adams blaming Marconi for Damien's death.

"Thanks. Keep us updated?" Lachlan asked.

"Hmm." That was all they got before Abaza hung up on them.

"That wasn't agreement," Gretchen pointed out.

Lachlan lifted one shoulder. "She's sharing more than I thought she would."

"She's feeling guilty," Gretchen said. "Considering she botched the investigation."

"You believe she did?" Lachlan asked, tone carefully neutral.

"Do you not?"

"I think she did all she could to protect Lauren from a reputation that would have damaged her career," Lachlan said, ever the perpetual sidestepper. "And most people would have dead-ended on Elijah's case. They interviewed all the school aides, the parents there that day. No one could remember him getting in a strange car. Hayes had security footage for his alibi." He paused, looked at her from the corner of his eye. "You know what to look for because you already know the answer. It's a lot harder when you're staring at a blank slate."

It was paraphrasing what she'd said about his Monday-morning quarterbacking. Gretchen pursed her lips, not wanting to admit he had a point.

"Damien Adams died right around when he was taken," Gretchen said, forcefully redirecting the conversation. "So, timeline-wise, that leaves Peter Stone as the potential protégé-slash-accomplice."

"Or it leaves him as a victim of some other killer," Lachlan said. The downer of their little duo. *Voice of reason,* she imagined him correcting her. "And it was really Martha who was his accomplice all along."

Gretchen couldn't deny that the Martha theory made solid sense—and would answer the nagging mystery of what the catalyst had been for the shooting. Perhaps whatever Marconi had discovered that had her running off to tell Rafael had caught Martha's attention. Shooting Hayes when she had and somehow managing to implicate Marconi meant that he took both of their secrets to the grave.

Lachlan nudged her shoulder with his. "Why do you think Damien was buried by himself?"

She didn't have an answer to that other than the fact that she'd been thinking of Damien as the first victim. The one connected to the killer more so than any other. The first victim was often personal, which meant a more sacred burial ground than dumping bones in the basement in a mass grave.

"Martha was having an affair with Damien's father." Gretchen was still feeling out the answer even as she said it. "That would have made him special in her mind. She might have taken more care with him."

"So you're buying into the Martha-as-the-accomplice theory?" Lachlan said, and she could hear the smugness in his voice.

"Not necessarily," Gretchen shot back. "There're plenty of stories about older victims—such as Martha—trying to protect or care for younger captives in scenarios like this."

"Martha wasn't a captive."

"Who's to say that?" Gretchen asked. "Just because her captivity looked different on the surface doesn't mean the situation wasn't, at its core, the same."

Lachlan didn't say anything, and so she poked him. "What's with the face?"

He looked like he was at war with himself. "That's an empathetic observation to make."

"I'm an onion," Gretchen said, baring her teeth. "I have layers."

"It's just . . . I guess I should have tried to have understood your—" He waved at her person, and she swatted his hand away.

"My diagnosis."

"Your diagnosis," he said, rolling the word around in his mouth. "Better. It seems like I've made a lot of assumptions."

"Oh, don't hurt your brain too much," Gretchen said, amused at this turnabout. "I'm unique."

"You are that," he said on a laugh. "Anyway, I guess I'm back to 'What's next?'"

Gretchen drummed her fingers on the steering wheel and then did what she always did when she was stuck. She called Fred.

"Girl, you've got to stop interrupting me," Fred said as a greeting. "I think I'm onto something important."

"Important how?"

"Not yet," Fred said, her voice clipped. "But I've got an address for Peter's mother. Go talk to her—I'll get back to you on what I'm looking into within the next few hours." She paused. "If it pans out into anything."

Then Fred hung up on her. Gretchen glared at the phone, not pleased at being on the receiving end of that particular action.

She looked up to find Lachlan watching her. "Ready for another road trip?"

CHAPTER
FORTY-FOUR

LAUREN

Then

Ashley Westwood held a memorial for all the lost boys three months after Elijah had been taken.

She held it at dusk in a vacant lot not far from the Hayeses' property. After she pressed a candle into Lauren's hand, she threw her arms around Lauren's shoulders, holding her tightly, like she would her own missing son.

Even though Lauren had met the woman only once, she let herself be hugged, burying her face in Ashley's scarf. It smelled of some expensive yet understated perfume that Lauren would never be able to afford.

"We'll get the bastard," Ashley whispered for only Lauren to hear.

Lauren stiffened on instinct—as she would have if Elijah hadn't been taken and a parent of a victim said this to her. And then she relaxed with the knowledge that, yes, they would get the bastard.

Eventually, even if it took the rest of Lauren's life.

She tried to imagine how Ashley felt now. Joshua had been gone for years. People barely remembered that it had happened at all.

Still, Ashley's voice was raw with pain.

Would Lauren always feel like that? How did anyone live holding that much hurt within themselves?

Revenge, a tiny voice whispered as she let Ashley go. That's why they woke up each morning, why they ate and worked and carried on.

Ashley's eyes slipped to a spot over Lauren's shoulder.

Rafi was there, and he was earning some sour looks from participants who didn't realize that Lauren already knew who her son's killer was. And it wasn't the man behind her.

Ashley knew, though. So she gathered Rafi up in that same embrace.

She didn't look like she could offer such solace. Everything about her was immaculate, her red hair smoothed into a chignon, her nails manicured, her coat and boots designer. She was thin, wispy almost. But her presence seemed so sturdy that Lauren couldn't help but be warmed by that promise that Ashley couldn't actually make.

We'll get the bastard.

———

The memorial evening ended with wine at Ashley's house for the parents of the victims.

Lauren was too nervous about leaving smudges on Ashley's white marble counters to actually relax, but she ended up cradling a glass that could reasonably serve as a fishbowl and leaning back against the sink. Ashley stood next to her, six bottles of Merlot waiting to be doled out.

The gentle, dimmed light was kind to all their red-rimmed eyes.

"Do they all think it was Hayes who killed their boys?" Lauren asked under her breath, her eyes scanning the room. She recognized some of the parents from the files she'd pulled, but there were at least a handful who were strangers.

Ashley was quiet for a minute, pouring another glass. She sighed and turned to meet Lauren's gaze head-on. "I think they want to believe it's him. Some of them, at least."

It came too close to Abaza's consistent refrain for Lauren not to ruffle at that. "Just because it's easy doesn't mean it's not the truth."

"I've looked at everything each of them has on their kids' disappearances," Ashley said, without any bite despite the sharpness in Lauren's own tone. "I'd say five or six probably can be attributed to Hayes."

"What makes you decide that?"

"He was seen in the area or approached the kids before their disappearances," Ashley said. "Just like with Joshua."

Lauren rolled the stem of her glass between her fingers. "Why do you let the others come to this, then?"

Ashley pursed red-slicked lips. "They lost their sons, too."

She said it as if it were simple, and Lauren couldn't speak, emotion suddenly thick in her throat.

Resentment that maybe the other parents still had a bit of hope left. If their kids hadn't been taken by a serial killer, that meant there was a chance they could still be alive.

Gratitude that at least she knew what had happened to her child and didn't have to live her life wondering, going to memorials for other boys in a desperate hope that someone would remember her own.

When Lauren didn't say anything, Ashley leaned against her shoulder in a show of solidarity. "It doesn't get easier, I won't promise that. But it won't always be this bad."

"It feels like it will."

"I know," Ashley said on a sigh. Then she gave Lauren one last sad smile before crossing the room to hand deliver Rafi's glass to him. Lauren watched the way Rafi's eyes lingered on Ashley long after she walked away, and tried to feel anything.

She was empty, though. There was nothing left to tap.

"Welcome to the club," Garrett said, sidling up beside her.

Lauren eyed the set of fancy knives that were temptingly in reach. "Walk away."

"Why?" Garrett sounded genuinely surprised.

"You did this as much as Hayes did." Her voice came out an angry hiss.

He didn't even have the grace to slink off in shame. "I didn't know this was going to happen."

"Yeah, well, when you play with fire and the world burns, it doesn't really matter what you intended," Lauren said, impressed with herself that she hadn't drawn her gun on him yet. "Walk away, Adams."

"I—"

No, everything in Lauren shouted. "One more word and I'm cutting off your balls to feed them to you."

Rather than retreating at the threat, Garrett just stood there. As if he wanted forgiveness.

"Are you a fucking sociopath?" Some part of her realized her voice was rising. Most of her didn't give a shit. "What do you want from me? You've taken everything."

Ashley was beside her in the next heartbeat, an arm winding around Lauren's waist, pulling her away. She shot Garrett a reproving look as they went.

"Why did you let him come?" Lauren asked, her throat scratchy. She must have been louder than she realized.

"I know it's hard to hear, but he's grieving, too," Ashley said quietly before dropping Lauren off with Rafi. "I'm sorry."

Rafi didn't hesitate, just pulled her tight against him, his mouth pressed against her temple. She realized how familiar, how comforting, the gesture was. She thought of that afternoon back in her kitchen. When she'd been a day too late with her request.

"I wish I'd gone right then," Rafi whispered as if reading her mind. "I wish I'd driven to the school, picked him up. Isn't it funny how one decision can completely wreck your life?"

"Funny," Lauren repeated.

He made a sound. "You know what I mean."

"A lot of people saying that to me recently," Lauren commented idly, but she wasn't actually mad.

"Do you want me to kill that guy?" Rafi asked, and she could tell he was talking about Garrett, not Hayes.

"It feels like I would cross any line to get the man who murdered Elijah," Lauren said instead of answering.

"Yet when someone did just that for their kid, you want to bury them so deep they'll never be found." Rafi followed her train of thought like he always did. No matter how many years he'd been terrible to her, some part of her knew he, at the very least, *understood* her.

"It's hypocritical of me, I guess," Lauren said into his shirtfront. She hadn't been able to pull away from the warmth he offered. "I think I've earned it, though."

Rafi sighed. "I guess we all have."

CHAPTER
FORTY-FIVE
Gretchen

Now

It took thirty minutes to get to Peter Stone's house on the outskirts of Burlington.

The woman who opened the door to them was tiny and put-together. Gretchen would guess she was in her midforties, tasteful silver streaks at her temples, a few wrinkles from lived years on her face.

"You're here about Peter," she said. It wasn't a question. "I'm Penny. Come in, come in."

Gretchen exchanged a glance with Lachlan, but they followed Penny in.

She led them to a cozy kitchen with sunny yellow walls and rooster figurines on most available surfaces. She cradled her own mug of something without offering them anything to drink.

"How do you know we're here about Peter?" Gretchen asked.

The corner of her mouth lifted. "Every time something like this happens, at least a few people come knocking."

"A serial killer being killed?" Gretchen clarified.

Penny actually laughed at that, a deep, husky sound that didn't seem like it could come out of such a bird-boned lady. "Yup. A serial killer in the news. Also, if there are ever any missing boys."

"You must have quite a few visitors, then."

"Too many," Penny agreed. "I wouldn't mind if they were social calls, but they never are."

Gretchen took a guess that wasn't much of a guess. "They all want to link Peter's case to their own."

"Something like that," Penny murmured. "Now. You think Owen Hayes took my son."

"We think it's a possibility that he not only took him but—"

"Yes, ma'am, we are considering that." Lachlan spoke over her, and Gretchen could tell by the pinch of his mouth that she'd been about to say something insensitive. Or wrong in some way.

In these situations, she usually let herself be directed away from stepping on toes. But when she looked back at Penny, the woman was watching her with a new intensity.

"Finish your thought," Penny told her.

"Ma'am—" Lachlan tried.

"No." Penny held a hand up toward Lachlan but didn't take her eyes off Gretchen. "I've heard it all by now. You're not going to have a crying woman on your hands. Finish your thought."

"We think he might have kept Peter alive and used him to help kidnap other boys," Gretchen said, eyes darting between them. Of course, she vaguely saw what had prompted Lachlan to step in; it probably wasn't pleasant to hear your son might have been turned into a mini serial killer. But she found it fascinating that this had been the moment he'd intervened—especially since he hadn't when they'd talked to Garrett Adams—and equally as interesting that Penny hadn't let him protect her.

"You think he's still alive?" Penny said.

"Maybe," Gretchen said. "There's a possibility that he's the one who killed Hayes."

Penny took a deep swallow of her coffee. "Well, that's one of the more fantastical theories I've heard."

Gretchen didn't bristle. "Did you have any suspects at the time of the kidnapping?"

"No, but—" She stopped, eyed them. "If I tell you this, I don't want you going crazy about it."

"Scout's honor," Gretchen said, and Penny rolled her eyes.

"Don't be cute," she said, but she sighed. "We went to the Hayeses' apple orchard a few weeks before Peter was taken."

Beside Gretchen, Lachlan sucked in air.

"You never told anyone this?" he asked.

"I didn't put it together until that woman killed him dead," Penny said, lifting one shoulder. "Who knows if it actually means anything."

She was so blasé about it all. Gretchen had seen plenty of houses where a child had disappeared. There were usually shrines devoted to them, their rooms left untouched for years if not decades. Gretchen doubted she would find that here.

It didn't make her think that Penny had been involved in Peter's possible death. But it painted a study of grief that was far more complex than what Gretchen usually saw.

Marconi had plastered herself in behind multiple layers of defenses, as well. Gretchen had always likened the distance she put between herself and anyone else to the moat, the drawbridge, the outer walls protecting a castle. Other people went on the offense instead.

Penny had seemed to just hunker down and admit that this was reality. No matter how much it might hurt.

"You don't seem too interested," Gretchen observed out loud. "In any of this."

"If you had the number of false promises I've had in my life, you'd be less than thrilled with every new one as well," Penny said.

"Can you tell us about the visit to the farm?" Lachlan asked. "Did you have any interactions with Hayes?"

"Not that I can recall," Penny said. There was a *but* on her tongue, though.

"Then what can you recall?" Gretchen pressed.

"The wife," Penny said slowly.

Gretchen didn't breathe, didn't interrupt even though she wanted to shake the words out of the woman's mouth.

"She talked to Peter for a long time," Penny said. "About nothing in particular. She gave him a free doughnut, and when I tried to pay, she wouldn't let me."

"That's it?" Gretchen asked, and Lachlan nudged her. She shot him a look, and he just did the equivalent of a shrug with his eyebrows. She took it to mean she'd been lacking on the tact front. The problem with Lachlan, though, was that damn rigidity in his thinking. Even Gretchen could see that Penny didn't care about tact.

"That's it," Penny said with a grand gesture. "I told you, I had never really thought it was odd until he made the news. Then I remembered."

Gretchen glanced around, looking for inspiration. The first victim was always important. She just had to dig deeper. "Do you have any photos from that day?"

"Sure do," Penny said, and then disappeared from the kitchen without another word.

Lachlan rounded on Gretchen, his eyes wide. "She was at the Hayes farm a few weeks before the kidnapping?"

"There's no chance that's coincidence," Gretchen agreed. "What was it about Peter that triggered Hayes?"

"Or Martha," Lachlan said, a grim set to his mouth, and Gretchen realized that Lachlan really had zeroed in on the wife. Gretchen wasn't as convinced.

"Here we go." Penny came back with some eight-and-a-half-by-eleven papers in her hands. "I printed off all the photos I had on my phone back then. Just in case they'd be useful. Not that they ever were before."

Without any ceremony, she pushed them into Gretchen's hand. There were dozens. "These are all from that day?"

"I used to be trigger-happy on the camera," Penny said, with a rueful glance at the stack. "Not anymore. Nothing worth taking pictures of."

They all sat with that for a beat before Lachlan cleared his throat.

"Ma'am, did the police have any idea who took Peter?"

Penny resettled herself with her mug. "His father's out of the picture. They always go for the other parent in kidnapping cases like these."

"It doesn't sound like you agreed with that premise," Lachlan noted.

"Nah, he'd moved out of town before Peter was even born," Penny said. "He hadn't even known I was pregnant, to be honest." As if she thought they were going to judge her, she added in a rush, "That was back before everyone had cell phones. It wasn't as easy to get in touch with people."

"You really didn't have any suspects?" Gretchen asked.

"Too many," Penny admitted. "I thought it was the priest and then one of his teachers and then his swim coach. None of them panned out, obviously."

Gretchen glanced down at the papers in her hand. The one at the top was blurry, just the erratic motion of a young boy on a fall day. The red and yellow of the leaves matching the swatches on his jacket. "We can take these?"

"Yup, all yours," Penny said. "Not that you'll find anything, but I can always make more for myself. They're just printed off my computer."

Penny glanced out the window, but Gretchen got the impression she wasn't looking at anything in particular.

"It'd be a shame if Owen Hayes really was his killer," she said, but almost like she was thinking out loud.

Curious beyond belief, Gretchen asked, "Why's that?"

"Two shots to the head?" Penny asked, meeting Gretchen's eyes. "What kind of death is that for someone who killed my son?"

Of course, something inside her whispered and then clicked into place. Gretchen nearly stumbled back with the enormity of that simple realization.

"How would you kill him?" she breathed out, and Lachlan made some sort of hum of distress in his throat.

"Castration," Penny said without hesitation. This was a woman who had planned this out. "Then slicing open his gut, pulling out his intestines, cutting him shallowly all over with a paper cutter, removing fingers, toes, going to work on his extremities until he realized he was bleeding to death in the worst, slowest manner possible." She paused and then her face lit up. "Oh, and first things first, I would cut out his tongue."

Some people might have thought Penny was exaggerating for effect. But Gretchen believed she would do it given the opportunity. Believed she wouldn't blink.

And it crystallized everything that Gretchen now knew she'd gotten wrong.

"Controlled rage," she'd said to Lachlan after she'd imagined how the killer must have felt confronting Hayes, how they must have tapped into the anger to shoot an unarmed man on his knees. But she was a sociopath; he shouldn't have just trusted her on that.

This wasn't the controlled rage of someone seeking vengeance. That would look like torture—it would be slow and painful and exactly like Penny had just described.

Execution-style killings weren't about emotions; they were about tying up loose ends, getting rid of problems.

There was a reason they were favored by the mob.

It was business, nothing personal.

"Gretchen," Lachlan murmured, like he would to a wild animal.

She looked up and laughed. "Mark the calendar, Gibbs."

"Why's that?" he asked, clearly nervous.

"I was wrong," Gretchen admitted, whirling and heading toward the front of the house without even bothering to say goodbye to Penny. "I have never been more wrong."

CHAPTER FORTY-SIX

LAUREN

Then

Lauren would have fought the transfer if she hadn't known she was an endlessly patient person.

Abaza stared her down now, arms folded on her desk, eyes steady, like she expected a verbal brawl. But Lauren just lifted one shoulder. "I've heard Amherst is nice."

"It will be a good reset for you."

Lauren wanted to bristle at that. Six months ago she would have. She would have argued, would have appealed to Abaza's fondness for her, even. But a lot had changed in six months.

So she didn't say anything.

To Abaza's credit, the woman had done all she could to sweep Lauren's odd behavior—since Elijah had been kidnapped—under the rug. She'd even taken Lauren back after the suspension as if nothing had happened. Then Lauren, desperate and halfway to drunk, had tried to talk to Julia Hayes when she and Martha had been in town one day.

After that, it had all been over.

Still, because Abaza liked her, Lauren's transfer would move through the system as if Lauren herself had requested it.

Everything would look very aboveboard. Especially if she wanted to actually put in for a move later on.

This was the best-case scenario, everyone kept telling her.

This was the best-case scenario, she kept telling herself.

But every hollowed-out part of her ached as she drove out of town, her roots digging into the soil where Elijah was likely buried, where he'd been raised and he'd been born and he'd been conceived.

Two weeks after she'd moved her few boxes to the stark little apartment on the edge of Amherst, the Hayeses' farmhouse went up for sale.

She would have done anything to buy it had she known about it in time, but it sold the next day, at record speed.

Amherst was blue skies and cold, but beautiful weather and friendly people, so different from her Vermont her skin itched with it.

It wasn't a place she wanted to settle, though. What she needed to do was put distance and time between herself and Owen Hayes. It would take a while. Her erratic behavior might not be on any official report, but it had made the rounds. In Amherst, she had three potential partners bail on her before a rookie apparently drew the short straw.

Reputations, once tarnished, were nearly impossible to polish up again. One way she knew to do it was to keep her head down, work hard, and brace for the long haul.

The years in Amherst passed easily. She rented an apartment, decorated it with the bare minimum not to look like a psychopath if someone were to come over unexpectedly.

Lauren established a routine. She found a coffee place, said hello to the regulars when they called out to her. She did her job well, racking up three promotions over the eight years she was there.

That part had been as deliberate as everything else. If she was going to get into the Boston Police Department as a homicide detective, she had to have an impressive résumé.

She didn't make any friends; she didn't try.

Sandy stopped texting her after the first year.

Rafi stopped after two.

He'd gotten married, she'd heard. To Ashley Westwood, and Lauren wasn't even surprised. She'd sent them a slow cooker after she'd heard the news because that's how she'd been raised. The thank-you note from Ashley ended with that same promise she liked to make years ago.

We're going to get the bastard, it said across the bottom.

Lauren didn't think Ashley even meant it anymore. It was just something to say. Like holding that memorial every year was just something to do.

Neither Rafi nor Ashley was devoting their lives to catching their sons' killer. Not like Lauren was.

They had moved on, and Lauren wasn't even sure she could blame them.

Some part of her thought she might actually be moving on, too. Some nights she'd look at the "evidence" she'd collected in those weeks before Elijah went missing and wonder if she really had anything at all. Maybe Abaza had been right and she'd fixated on Hayes simply because it had been the easy thing to do.

The first time she'd genuinely laughed at some stupid joke one of the detectives said, she went home and cried. But after that, some dam broke. Sometimes she would buy herself chocolate cupcakes because she could, or drink a single glass of wine, watching the sunset from her roof.

It wasn't forgetting Elijah, she promised herself. She'd always had a long-term plan when it came to Hayes.

And Lauren had also continued to keep her eye out for cases on missing boys. She wasn't just a mother who'd lost a son; she was a cop, and a large part of her rebelled at the idea of just letting a suspected serial killer roam free.

If Hayes had continued his killing streak in Waltham, though, he'd been far more careful about it than in Montpelier.

Sometimes a child would be reported missing, but it never seemed to fit with Hayes's MO.

They were too old or too young, obviously taken by a parent in the middle of a custodial dispute, or killed by a parent too young and too vicious to see any other way out of *being* a parent.

Abaza called her only once, about three years in, and Lauren let it go to voice mail.

"Glad to hear you're doing well, Lauren," Abaza had said. "Come visit sometime. We're only two and a half hours from Amherst, you know."

Lauren had almost laughed. As if she didn't know just how far Montpelier was from every bit of earth. That was where her heart lived.

She hadn't returned the call—she'd thought she might say something unforgivable about Elijah's cold case. But for the first time she hadn't any urge to gut Abaza from pelvis to collarbone, and she thought that might be growth.

Her transfer request to Boston was denied twice before it was approved. Finally, though, after eight years in limbo, she was granted a ticket out.

Boston was cold and gray, but she preferred that to the sunny skies in Amherst. Even if there hadn't been that many sunny skies in Amherst, it had still felt like too many.

She was partnered up with a veteran cop who didn't talk about himself much. She appreciated that, as well.

Detective Patrick Shaughnessy liked to drive, and she was fine with that. He liked when she brought him black coffee in the morning, and she was fine with that. He preferred when she did the interviewing and he observed, and she was fine with that.

Lauren was fine with it all, as long as he didn't look too deeply into the ways she was using the database she now had access to. She'd been able to tap into it somewhat from Amherst, but cops were so concerned about jurisdiction and turf that if she'd gone too deep, she would have raised red flags.

In Boston, she could pretty much do as she pleased—say Shaughnessy was signing off on it—and get as much information on Hayes as was available.

She hadn't found anything, but that didn't make her think there wasn't anything to be found.

Then she and Shaughnessy got called out to a drug overdose. The death was somehow related to a murder case Shaughnessy had closed before Lauren had even moved to Boston.

When they'd walked into the apartment, a woman was standing over the body, eyes hungry on the rigid muscles, the blue-tinted lips.

She was beautiful in a cold way, with icy platinum hair, frigid eyes, the kind of pale skin that you could see veins beneath. Even in Lauren's limited experience with wealth, she could tell each piece of the woman's clothing was more expensive than Lauren's car payment.

"Why am I not surprised to see you standing over a dead body?" Shaughnessy asked in that Boston-drenched rumble.

The woman turned to them fully, those hungry eyes landing on Lauren's face, her hair, her body. Lauren was being cataloged and judged, and the woman wasn't even subtle about it.

There was a hardness to her that Lauren found immediately interesting. In Lauren's experience, that meant there were places inside a person that were so vulnerable that finding them, hitting them, would send cracks through the entire foundation.

"Because you think I'm a killer whom you just can't seem to catch," the woman answered. Lauren searched for the humor in her voice but found none.

"A killer I can't catch," Shaughnessy repeated. "Isn't that the truth?"

Lauren didn't know if interrupting their clearly familiar banter was the right call. In Amherst, she would have faded into the background. In

Montpelier, she might have just watched, amused or irritated depending on how much she actually wanted to get to the case.

But Lauren couldn't help admit that for the first time in years she was intrigued by someone.

It was like the first sprig of green to push through burned and salted soil. A tiny flower that could be crushed out in an instant but was there, existing nonetheless.

Something other than destruction.

"You know each other?"

The woman's mouth pursed as if she were swallowing back some nasty insult, her eyes roving over Lauren. Lauren had a feeling that her fascination was not mutual. "You've got yourself a true detective there, Shaughnessy."

Maybe in another life, Lauren would have flinched away from the jab. But in this one, where she was no longer feeling numb and broken after years of just that, she wanted to laugh. There was a sense of humor there beneath the ice and disdain the woman clearly wore as a cloak.

Shaughnessy snorted his own amusement. "Detective Lauren Marconi. Gretchen White."

Gretchen flicked him a look. "Doctor."

"Dr. Gretchen White," Shaughnessy corrected, clearly a routine of theirs. "Our resident sociopath."

CHAPTER
FORTY-SEVEN

GRETCHEN

Now

Gretchen didn't even wait for Lachlan to close the door to the Porsche before pulling out onto the street, jabbing ineffectively at her GPS.

"Get us back to Montpelier," Gretchen said.

"Are you going to explain what happened back there?" Lachlan asked, but he took over the jabbing.

"This wasn't revenge." There was a shame- and embarrassment-based fury sliding into her bloodstream. "Hayes's death. That's not what revenge looks like. Revenge would have been slower and more painful."

Lachlan was silent, before he cursed softly. "Jesus, why didn't I think about that?"

"Like we've already agreed, you're not a very good detective." It helped, a little, to let some of the venom out.

"There's an easy retort to that, but I'll be the adult here and restrain myself," Lachlan said. "Considering you're well past ninety miles per hour, and I'd like to not die in a fiery crash, at least before we solve this case."

"But after is fine."

"Exactly," Lachlan said, with a little smile. "So, if Hayes's death wasn't revenge, doesn't that rule out Rafael Corado?"

"And Marconi," Gretchen pointed out.

"We're still guessing here."

"Right, well, be useful and guess yourself into an actual motive," Gretchen said, glancing at the ETA. "You have twenty minutes. Go."

"All right, execution-style, with a gun," Lachlan said, taking direction like a champ. "Means maybe a woman. Or someone who didn't think they could physically control Hayes."

"Stereotyping, but I'll allow it."

"Two bullets to the head," Lachlan continued. "You're right. That's not personal. It's getting rid of someone for the purpose of getting rid of someone."

"Without leaving a lot of evidence on themselves," Gretchen added, thinking of the blood in Marconi's fingernail beds. She had come into the room after Hayes was already on the floor and had been checking for a pulse—Gretchen had never been more sure. After two shots to the head at close range, it would have been obvious Hayes was dead. Marconi could have just walked away after the shots.

"Who would want to get rid of Hayes, but in the least painful way possible?" Lachlan asked.

And even though she'd technically tasked him with the assignment, she couldn't help but offer. "The wife. Or the daughter."

"Julia Hayes?" The surprise in his voice was clear and tinged with disapproval. "She's only . . . what?"

"Sixteen or so," Gretchen said. "Age isn't a factor when it comes to violence." He was well aware of the details of her own case. He knew about Viola Kent, too. "Plus, it would explain the gun, explain getting Hayes on his knees so she would have more control."

"What's the motive, though?" Lachlan asked.

"I'm going to go ahead and guess that having a serial killer father isn't all puppies and rainbows."

"No, I know, but . . ." Lachlan shook his head. "I guess the mother bringing a gun into the house could have been the trigger."

"Which brings us back to Martha."

"And she has an alibi," Lachlan said. "Dinner with her daughter, which doubles as an alibi for Julia."

Gretchen plucked at her lower lip, her mind combing through the possibilities. An alibi didn't necessarily mean either was innocent.

"Call Cormac."

"You'll sweet-talk him better than I can," Lachlan countered, but had his phone out. When Cormac answered, Lachlan informed him he was on speakerphone. Gretchen made a face. Contrary to what Lachlan had said, they would have gotten more information had Cormac thought he was just talking to Lachlan. But Lachlan didn't like putting a toe over the line.

"It's been two days, folks," Cormac said in that politician's tone. "And it's Sunday. I don't know what you think our office would find in that amount of time."

"Meanwhile, we've unearthed a serial killer's burial ground," Gretchen said, not wanting to reveal any more than that. "Tell me about Martha."

Silence dropped, but when Lachlan went to open his mouth, Gretchen held her hand up to cut him off. Miraculously, he listened.

After a minute, Cormac filled the space between them, like she'd known he would.

"She's clean, Gretch," Cormac said. "No weird money transfers, no secret under-the-table job to build up a stash of cash. Hiring a professional costs money, and Martha didn't have any."

That was a fair point. The last time Gretchen checked, the going rate for a hit had been about $50,000. With inflation as it was, that could have climbed even higher. "It could have been a friend."

"Right." Cormac snorted. "Martha Hayes definitely seems the type to just have assassin buddies hanging around waiting to do her favors."

Gretchen thought about Rafael. "It could have been a mutually beneficial relationship."

Cormac seemed to read between the lines. "Like she seduced one of the parents of the victims into killing the husband? How do you know you didn't just describe what happened with Marconi?"

Lachlan coughed. "Can we rein in this wild speculation by any chance?"

"Please," Cormac cut in quickly before Gretchen could get anything out. Probably for the best. "And, Gretch, you gotta realize. You getting involved in this is only hurting Marconi in the long run."

"How so?" Gretchen asked, because everyone seemed to be insinuating that without actually giving her any reason it was true.

"Because you know what you're going to find."

I did it.

"Did you look into Rafael Corado?" Gretchen asked instead of acknowledging Cormac's implicit warning.

He sighed, loud and obnoxious. "We're on it now. We had uniforms check that cabin he owns up near the border."

Gretchen perked up. "Anything?"

"Looks like he'd been there recently, but he was gone by the time the cops swung by."

"Gone?" Gretchen asked, dubious. "Or hiding in the woods until they left?"

He heard the criticism. "He's not worth the resources."

Though Gretchen had just rescinded her own theory that Rafael had been the real killer, with Marconi taking the fall for him, she was still annoyed that Cormac wasn't taking the lead seriously.

People assumed that when you were personally involved in a case, you couldn't have any good ideas about it. Gretchen could just picture Marconi screaming at the top of her lungs that Hayes had killed Elijah and with every breath damning herself to irrelevancy—a vicious cycle that would have been impossible to escape.

Except with a reset.

Marconi had been exiled to Amherst for eight years. She'd stopped screaming.

And then there had been a graveyard found beneath the house of the very man she'd been yelling about.

Not so irrelevant any longer.

It was a lesson, though. The more Gretchen screamed about Rafael, about this case, the less anyone would pay attention to what she was saying. If she'd been a man, maybe it would be different. But everyone in this conversation knew she wasn't a slave to her emotions, knew she didn't get *hysterical*, yet they were still writing her off as too emotionally involved.

Had this been any other case, and a suspect like Rafael had left town in the days before his ex-lover killed the man they both thought had murdered their child, he would have gone to the top of everyone's list.

"Send the uniforms again," she snapped back before plucking the phone from Lachlan's loose grasp and ending the call. When Cormac immediately tried again, she sent him to voice mail, then tossed the phone back into Lachlan's lap.

"Gretchen," Lachlan started.

The placating tone was steel wool over skin already rubbed raw. "You think this means it was Martha."

"She was cleaning up the mess," Lachlan said. "You said it yourself. Executions aren't personal. She needed her secrets to die with Hayes, and she took care of it quickly and effectively."

It made sense, it did. Gretchen couldn't even find a hole to poke in it beyond an alibi that could have been manufactured. Martha had obtained a gun; she'd been married to a serial killer. Marconi must have discovered something about how Martha had been involved the whole time. What better way to eliminate both threats?

The answer was like a coat that fit *just* wrong, too small in the shoulders, too wide at the waist. Almost right, but not quite.

And Gretchen, for all her love of logic, couldn't explain why.

She glanced at the pictures in Lachlan's lap, the ones Penny had given them.

The first victim. She couldn't get that out of her head. "Look through those."

"You think there's something in here?" he asked.

"No, I'm just telling you to do it for shits and giggles," she said, missing Marconi in perhaps a million different ways. She'd known they'd worked well together. It was why Gretchen was going to such lengths to clear her name. But Lachlan kept proving it right. Even if they'd had something close to a breakthrough, their jagged edges were always going to be slightly off.

"Not every answer has to be sarcastic, you know," Lachlan muttered. "In case that's something no one had told you before."

Every part of Gretchen wanted to swipe out at him, to never say an earnest thing again in any of their interactions. But she actually did take pride in being able to keep useful people in her life, and right now Lachlan Gibbs fell into that category.

What Lachlan appreciated, she'd noticed over the past few days, was having the investigative thought process explained to him. And it cost Gretchen nothing to do that.

Growth, she heard dryly in Marconi's voice.

"Martha had a long-enough talk with Peter that fifteen years later Penny remembered that it had been odd," Gretchen said. "Even if Penny couldn't pinpoint why, the visit struck her as strange. I've come to realize that parents are particularly attuned to predators who approach their children. Something happened on that day that led to Peter's disappearance a few weeks later. Maybe something was caught in those photos."

"Now was that so hard?"

"Don't push it," she gritted out, and he laughed, a warm baritone.

Gretchen let him sort through the pictures in silence as she maneuvered her way through the streets of Montpelier, heading toward the police station.

Just as she pulled up to the curb, Lachlan uttered a soft "Holy shit."

Gretchen stopped herself from reaching out and yanking the pictures from his hands. Instead, she settled for one of her least favorite words. "What?"

Wordlessly, he held the paper up. Gretchen swallowed hard as everything slotted into place.

It wasn't some*thing* that had been caught on camera.

It was *someone*.

CHAPTER
FORTY-EIGHT
LAUREN

Then

A beautiful thing about Dr. Gretchen White was that she never paid too close attention to anything that didn't directly involve herself.

It was one of the many characteristics that Lauren actually liked about the woman. She was funny and sharp and clever and had one of the best investigative minds Lauren had ever seen in action. She had a strange but compelling way of viewing the world, heavily influenced by social training via sitcoms and soap operas and Shakespeare and YouTube videos. Lauren maybe should have found her off-putting— Gretchen didn't ever bite her tongue, or if she did, Lauren didn't want to know the things that she refrained from saying.

She was never boring, though.

And the more Lauren found out about Gretchen, the more she admired the way the woman lived, teetering at the edge of her diagnosis, never willing to bend to it, but willing to force it to suit her life. She studied brutalized bodies so she didn't brutalize them herself. She said those caustic asides because she knew there was only so much poison that she could hold inside her veins. She drew lines in the sand she would never cross—not because it was morally right but because once she put her mind to something, she refused to fail.

One time, after everything had unraveled with the murder case that had hung over Gretchen's life for decades, Gretchen had told Lauren about an epiphany she'd had.

If a life is made up of actions instead of thoughts, don't I come out ahead?

Lauren couldn't argue with that. She'd done plenty of things that had fallen into the shaky middle ground when it came to ethics—including stalking Hayes and his family to Massachusetts.

Long ago, she'd realized people only knew the extent they were able to break their own moral code when they were put in untenable situations. Most people never experienced enough pressure to think themselves anything other than *good*. But how many really had the courage they thought they did? How many really had principles that would remain intact even in the face of death and destruction?

People broke. It was what they did.

So Lauren had never judged Gretchen for who she was. At least the woman had an awareness of her own limitations. Most blithely went about their days pretending they would, on a hero's journey, slay the dragon and save the princess and do it all with a heart full of pure thoughts and devotion.

Meanwhile, Gretchen would never assume it wasn't the princess who needed to be slain.

She would never win an award, though, for her observational skills outside of cases. She was self-centered in a way that Lauren found delightful.

Especially since it let Lauren finally—after nine long years of waiting—make contact with Julia Hayes.

As an added precaution, Lauren had set Gretchen up on a blind date for the next week. That would be enough to occupy her mind so she wouldn't get too curious about where Lauren was going on her weekends.

Julia Hayes was homeschooled in Waltham just like she had been in Vermont, and from what Lauren could tell, rarely left the house. She must be about sixteen now, though, so every once in a while she *was* left alone.

Lauren had followed Martha and Owen Hayes on those days that they drove away together, wondering if they were perhaps scouting for their next victim. But they'd simply been going to the big discount store down the road to stock up on toilet paper and condiments and the like.

Weeks ago, Lauren had clocked the Ring camera on the front door. But there were other ways to approach the house.

She parked a few streets over and cut through the neighborhood behind the Hayeses' place, approaching it through the backyard.

The sliding glass door let Lauren scope out the dining room and the kitchen, both of which appeared empty.

Lauren chewed on her lip. This was so goddamn stupid. She knew that objectively. What would Gretchen say to this mess?

Probably she'd have figured out how to maneuver a semilegal break-in and then get a warrant for a full-house search based on fake evidence she'd planted.

While Lauren didn't have the benefit of straddling the law so carelessly, she wasn't entirely sure this method was any better.

And wasn't that what Gretchen always argued? That being born with a conscience, with the right wiring, didn't exactly make someone perfect. They were all down in the muck; some of them were just able to admit it.

Lauren was certainly able to.

She took a breath and then gently rapped two knuckles against the glass.

Nothing.

She waited a beat. Tried again.

If no one answered, would she go in? Would she find Julia, make the girl answer questions? No matter how traumatic it would be for her.

No.

Lauren didn't seem to have many lines left when it came to solving Elijah's case, but that was one of them.

Thirty seconds passed, then a minute. The Hayeses were never gone for long. An hour, usually. Two at most.

Chewing on her lip, she glanced around the backyard. It was so different from the apple farm in Vermont. There were no wide-open spaces to hide bodies, no trees to offer their shadows as protection. But there were neighbors who were probably nosy.

There had been plenty of serial killers in history who operated out of suburban homes. The changes Hayes would have had to make to his cleanup style, though, were unfathomable.

The click of a lock.

Lauren shifted her attention back to the door, cursing herself for letting her eyes wander.

There stood Julia, peeking out at Lauren with those big blue eyes Lauren had seen only once. They lived seared in her memory.

The girl was tall and slim as a willow reed, the previous roundness of her face lost to a sharp bone structure and the hollow cheeks of a depressed teenager.

Julia stared at her with curiosity instead of fear, the same way she'd walked into a stranger's bedroom in the middle of the night. Lauren had been counting on that to have remained a core part of her personality.

"Who are you?" she asked, her voice raspy, like she didn't talk much. Lauren supposed she didn't. Stuck in this house for her entire life, as she was.

"I'm one of the mothers," Lauren said, without realizing that was going to be her answer.

Julia's breath caught, and any doubt Lauren had faded. The girl knew what she meant.

"You're not allowed to be here." Julia's voice had dropped to a whisper, and she darted a quick glance behind her. She still wore her hair in twin braids, and one of the tails flipped over her shoulder with her agitated movement.

"Julia, you have to help me," Lauren said, her voice coming out raw, pleading. "Are the boys . . . are there boys in your basement now?"

"Boys in our basement?" The girl repeated slowly before her eyes widened. "Oh."

Lauren wanted to grip Julia's arms, dig fingers into her flesh, dig the secrets out of her eyes. She curled her hands into fists instead. "Julia . . ."

"No," Julia said, shaking her head. For the first time since she'd peered through the crack in the door, she looked scared. "You don't understand."

"What don't I understand?"

Julia tugged at the end of one of her braids, chewing on her bottom lip. Clearly deciding something.

It gave Lauren insight into Hayes's decision to keep her in the house like a prisoner. Just from their two interactions, years apart, Lauren could tell the girl had no ability to hide her thoughts, no self-preservation. She was the type who liked knowing things and letting people know she knew things.

It was a dangerous combination in someone so young, and one that Lauren wished she could have exploited a lot earlier.

Softer this time, Lauren asked, "Julia, what don't I understand?"

Julia leaned forward. "The boys? It was never *our* basement they were in."

CHAPTER
FORTY-NINE
MARTHA

Before

It took Martha years to save up the money to buy the car.

She'd never given up, though, even when she'd been tempted to use the squirreled-away cash for something else, something flashier, like a gun.

There were the dollars crumpled up in jeans, the coins that she could pocket after making a purchase, the times she could forgo getting Julia a new coat to stash the money instead. Owen never paid close attention to Julia; he saw the girl only in broad strokes. If Martha said it was a new coat, he believed her.

The car wasn't anything fancy. She'd bought it, cash, at one of those sleazy dealerships on the outskirts of town. She'd waited until Owen had to go to Burlington for a day trip before locking Julia in her room with enough snacks to feed an army of toddlers. Martha had walked the three miles to the closest busy road and hitchhiked into town.

The car dealer had taken everything she had saved, except for fifteen dollars, and then given her the little sedan with a mostly empty tank.

Martha hadn't cared; she'd been busy trying to hide the fact that she was shaking.

A car.

Her own car.

The freedom it offered was nearly overwhelming. Her body ached with the idea of it; her muscles burned from nearly a decade of being ready to run.

She'd had to pull over to the side of the road to breathe. Shockingly, there were no tears on her cheeks, and when she pressed a finger to her face, she felt the dimple that she'd long forgotten about.

A smile.

She was smiling. For the first time in what felt like years.

Martha bought herself an extralarge slushy and a bag of salt-and-vin-egar potato chips at the gas station and used the remaining ten dollars to get almost half a tank. Her belly hurt from the rush of sugar and processed carbohydrates, and she didn't even care.

Months ago, she'd found a good parking spot for the car, out in the woods. It was in an old dried-up creek bed just off the maintenance road in the back. Probably it would be covered with snow in the winter, but given the state of the sedan, it wasn't like Martha could drive it in anything other than pristine conditions.

That was fine, too.

Martha knew where Owen kept his cash. Thousands of dollars' worth. Owen controlled her through fear and thus had never thought to change the safe's combination from what he'd set it as years ago.

What she'd always needed was a head start.

When Martha was ready to leave, she'd be able to trade in the sedan as soon as she crossed the next state's border.

During Owen's next trip into Burlington that neither of them addressed, Martha couldn't resist the temptation of freedom. She wasn't able to run yet, but they could do something other than stare at these goddamn walls that seemed to be closing in on her by the day.

She dragged Julia on the long walk back behind the orchard, the little girl too curious to complain. That was her baby—she watched the world like it was putting on a play for her, the only person in the audience. Martha knew Julia was an odd child, but considering she'd only ever interacted with her cousin, a boy older than her, Martha couldn't blame it on anyone but herself.

Some nights the guilt ate at her. She'd made the decision to marry Owen, and Julia was paying the price for it.

Other nights she was just grateful that Owen acted like Julia was a particularly lively piece of furniture.

In town, Martha bought Julia ice cream topped with whipped cream that went higher than the little girl's head. Martha hadn't been able to get herself anything—the five dollars for the sundae more than she was willing to spend now that she was saving for gas—but the pleasure she got from watching her little girl eat had been worth the splurge.

After ice cream, they walked through the streets hand in hand, birds out of a cage stretching their wings just because they could.

Julia said hello to strangers, who smiled back with varying degrees of judgment, surprise, and happiness at the guileless child.

"We have one more special stop," Martha said, swinging Julia's hand.

Those little owl eyes blinked up at her. "Where?"

"That would ruin the surprise," Martha chided, compulsively checking the street to make sure there was no one who would recognize her.

Coming into town was *always* a risk; being in this part of the city, even more so.

The back door was locked, of course, but the key was there, behind a loose rock in the wall. Martha let Julia retrieve it because Julia liked collecting secrets, and this was one of the biggest ones.

It was lucky for Martha that Julia never talked to Owen, seeming to sense that was one stranger who was off-limits to her.

The hallway was in shadows, but Martha knew her way. The door to the basement turned soundlessly, well oiled as it was. The sound of chatter from the front of the building soothed Martha in a strange way.

No one knew.

They couldn't see, like she'd always been able to.

Julia let go of her hand and skipped down into the darkness.

There was another heavy door here with lots of locks. Julia bounced impatiently as Martha took her time with them.

Once it was opened, Julia darted inside what Martha had always guessed was an old, reinforced bank safe.

"Hi, I'm Julia."

Martha pressed a hand over her smile at that easy greeting. No hesitation, her daughter.

"What's your name?" Julia asked.

A soft voice snaked along Martha's skin like a shiver.

"Elijah," the boy said, as brave as his mother.

CHAPTER FIFTY

GRETCHEN

Now

Gretchen's phone rang as both she and Lachlan stared down at the photos Penny Stone had given them. At the person caught staring at the serial killer's first victim.

She nearly ignored the call, but then saw Fred's name. "What did you find?" she asked.

"I was crossing my t's," Fred said. "I know how you like things to be precise."

"As if you're any different."

"Exactly," Fred said. "So, I thought, who buys a serial killer's house anyway?"

"Only creeps, if people know its history." Gretchen played along. "But anyone if they don't."

"Right, but there were accusations against Hayes floating around town. Even if just the pedophile stuff was true, people are going to be wary," Fred continued. "It got me curious. So I looked into the person who owned the Hayes property after the family left town."

Gretchen banged the back of her skull against the headrest.

This whole investigation, she'd had blind spots a mile wide.

"It was actually a company," Fred said. "Not all that weird considering that in the fall Hayes pimped out his farm to tourists. Still, it was strange enough to warrant more digging."

"Smart," Gretchen praised, because at least one of them had been thinking straight.

"The company's ownership is protected by a lot of layers," Fred said. "The simplified version is that there are things called anonymous land trusts that rich people create to protect themselves from ever being sued for their real estate investments. They hide the trusts in their LLCs, which effectively camouflages them from the public. It's not a well-known practice, and I'm pretty sure Montpelier, Vermont, hasn't been recently overrun by real estate moguls, so it was another red flag."

Lachlan cleared his throat, and Gretchen's eyes snapped to him. She'd all but forgotten his presence.

"Did you find who owned it?" Lachlan asked.

"I'm not admitting nothing, copper," Fred replied in a 1920s gangster accent before continuing as if she hadn't been interrupted. "I started pulling at the threads, and worked my way back to the LLC. Now here's where the mistake was made. The owner of the land trust has another business that's under the LLC."

"Let me guess." Gretchen glanced at the picture still in Lachlan's lap, at the man in it, staring from a distance at Peter Stone. "A diner."

"Got it in one."

CHAPTER
FIFTY-ONE
LAUREN

Then

The boys hadn't been in the Hayes farmhouse.

They had been in the basement of Garrett's diner.

"Mama would take me there sometimes to play with them," Julia said, watching Lauren with those intense blue eyes. "But then they would leave, and it made me sad. Mama sad, too. She always cried then."

Surely when the boys "left," they had been killed. Lauren searched for shame, fear, remorse—*anything*.

Julia might as well have been talking about puppies who had to go live on a farm upstate.

A distant part of Lauren realized Julia reminded her of Gretchen. She didn't think the girl was a little sociopath, but she had the same flatly curious affect that Gretchen wore when she didn't realize she was supposed to be feeling some kind of emotion.

Mostly, though, all Lauren heard was white noise inside her skull. A static disconnect, a distant blaring. Nine years. It had been nine years, and she had been so wrong that entire time.

"Why?" she managed, knowing that she couldn't linger, but unable to drag herself away.

"Mama felt bad for them," Julia said, still only curiosity in her voice. "Mr. Garrett always kept them locked down there. Just like Papa keeps us at home. She wanted us to be friends."

Something clicked for Lauren then. Julia didn't find any of this shocking because it was how she'd been raised her whole life. Kids didn't leave. That's how it worked.

"Did Mr. Garrett . . ." Lauren trailed off, trying to remind herself that she was talking to a child. She swallowed. "Were the boys ever hurt?"

"No," Julia said. "We were keeping them safe. Mama didn't want Papa getting them."

Lauren tried to follow the logic, but she felt like she was swimming through fog. "What?"

Julia's head cocked then, her eyes going impossibly wider. "They're home."

The whisper sliced across Lauren's skin, sent her stumbling back.

In the next blink, she was in her car.

In the next, she was in her apartment.

In the next, in her kitchen, cradling a bottle of whiskey between her knees.

She couldn't remember the individual steps she'd taken to get there. Had she been seen? She wasn't sure. Did it even matter anymore if she had been?

Mama didn't want Papa getting them.

Lauren's mind skittered away from the thought, her fingers clenching around the bottle.

The seal hadn't been broken—she knew that at least.

286

She didn't think it would be, either.

It had been years since she'd solved her problems with alcohol, her transfer a scar that had never quite faded.

But, God, it would be nice, she thought. To just forget for one night. To just not think about whatever the hell had just happened.

To pretend her entire world hadn't just been overturned.

That was the problem, wasn't it? Lauren had gotten so good at compartmentalizing her life, her emotions, that now when everything lay scattered on the floor, she couldn't do anything but stare at the mess and wish it weren't there.

As a detective working the Major Crimes beat, Lauren would have been destroyed had she not been able to section off those parts of her. She'd had to interview plenty of parents of missing or dead children, and the only way she'd been able to do it was to see them as creatures apart from herself. Their lank hair, their glassy eyes, the loose skin that came from sudden weight loss. None of that could be familiar, because she wasn't one of them.

She was Detective Lauren Marconi, and she could handle any investigation thrown at her.

She excelled at flying just under the radar. Good but not a superstar, quiet but resourceful. No one had ever effusively sung her praises, but no one had cursed her name at happy hours, either.

That had been as intentional as the outfits she'd worn, the way she'd cut her hair to help mask the bone structure that drew too many eyes to her face.

Gretchen had commented on it more than once. Her unplucked eyebrows, her makeup-free face, her clothes that walked the perfect line between baggy and fitted. Gretchen had thought it had to do with Lauren trying to get ahead in a man's world, and Lauren had let her think that.

The thing about Gretchen was that she usually found her own ideas so flawlessly brilliant that she could be blind to the layers that ran beneath the thing she'd—rightfully—identified as important.

There had been only a handful of times when Lauren had nearly melted down, but they had been few and far between. Instead of ducking out of missing children's cases, which could have raised red flags for anyone paying close attention, she'd leaned in. They needed volunteers for a task force? She was the first to raise her hand. They needed fresh eyes on a cold case? Lauren would be the one to stare at the gruesome pictures. Exposure helped her fortify her defenses.

She'd always taken pride in the fact that she hadn't broken.

Now she just realized that she'd put too much faith in her walls, as if nothing could raze them to the ground.

It wasn't the fact that the boys had been in Garrett Adams's basement that nearly did her in, nearly had her breaking the whiskey's seal and drowning out her thoughts until there was nothing left but silence.

It was that she no longer knew in her heart where Elijah was.

Despite the fact that she'd seen the unturned earth beneath the farmhouse a mere week after she'd assumed Elijah had been buried there, she'd always thought that was where he was resting.

White dots popped in her vision as she squeezed her eyes tight, dreading the idea of replaying that conversation. But she had to. Right now, nothing made sense.

Even though the girl was a teenager, she obviously viewed the situation through a child's lens. But she'd still given Lauren plenty of information.

We were keeping them safe.

That wasn't true, of course, if the boys had never been found again. But there must be a grain of *something* there, reality bent and twisted by a monster's mind. Martha—and maybe Garrett—had told themselves they were protecting these boys.

How on earth had they gotten to that belief?

Lauren rewound, pressed play on her own memory, rewound, pressed play, scouring each second, each sentence, each pause for what she was missing.

And every time, she stuttered over the same moment.

Mama didn't want Papa getting them.

Lauren shifted to her hands and knees, crawled to her bedside table, where there was a hidden space carved out. The thumb drive.

She hooked it up to her computer and stared at the four names she'd written all those years ago.

Her instinct had known what her mind hadn't been able to grasp.

He contacts them first.

What if . . .

What if Hayes hadn't been the particular monster Lauren had thought she was hunting but was evil in his own special form? The two men kindred spirits in devious tastes.

Hayes had a weakness for boys, couldn't help but approach them, talk to them, maybe even think about doing more. But what if he had never escalated beyond that?

Garrett Adams had known his secret because men like that could always recognize others like them. Or maybe Garrett just watched the crime blotter, or had a buddy on the force with loose lips. Cops did frequent his diner on a daily basis.

She thought about those files, the missing boys who hadn't been contacted by Hayes, the four who had, in addition to his own son.

Joshua, Caleb, Nathaniel.

Elijah, though maybe he didn't quite fit in with the other three.

Garrett had turned them into a smoke screen. A narrative, really. One that said: *If Hayes was guilty of approaching these boys, surely he could have found a way to take them, too.* No matter how many alibis he produced, Hayes had already damned himself with his earlier actions.

What if she'd gotten this all wrong, and Hayes had never killed a single child?

How easy it had been for Garrett to shift the lines, just slightly, and make Hayes a psychopath in everyone's eyes.

She thought back to that first meeting with Gretchen.

Because you think I'm a killer whom you just can't seem to catch.

That's how Lauren had viewed Hayes for nearly ten years. She would never have believed herself susceptible to such manipulation, but whoever did? Grifters got away with their cons so easily because no one wanted to think themselves a fool.

And Garrett had played these games with Lauren, as well.

When Lauren had looked at him, she had seen her worst nightmare as a parent. He'd looked at her and seen every way he could exploit that.

And it had all started that night with that anonymous call. Why had he sent her into the farmhouse?

He wouldn't have done that just to screw with her—it was too big of a risk.

She chewed on her nail as she let her eyes unfocus, the white light of the screen blurring, becoming the snow from that night.

Lauren had been tired after working all day, but nothing unusual had happened.

She thought back further, to that morning, leaning her forehead against the frosted glass, coffee cup cradled in her hands.

Movement behind her, Elijah. Her mind rebelled, pulled her away from that tender moment where she'd rocked him and called him her baby. That was hers and should be protected.

She went back further. Talking to Rafi. She'd been hopeful, she realized now. When she'd called him, though she'd pretended not to be. Even though she hadn't trusted his pushes for custody, some part of her had wanted them to mean something.

Her mind pushed that away as well. No use dwelling on that. Rafi wasn't involved in this.

Back to the window, her forehead against the frosted glass. She'd been thinking of all the ways the blizzard was going to disrupt her day, and she'd been upset.

Because of that case.

The cold case and the missing boy.

She couldn't remember his name, which was its own small tragedy. Was there anyone out there who still did? Who still banged the drum—as Ashley said—to get someone, anyone, to take his case seriously?

There hadn't been time back then to follow up on it, though. She'd been too distracted by what had come next.

Had she told someone about the boy? She must have. Everyone had been nosy back then, jockeying for Abaza's attention.

Lauren's eyes tracked back to the names on her computer. What if she'd stumbled over one of Garrett's victims? What if something about that boy had put Garrett on the offense to cover his tracks?

Her pulse slammed against her throat, her wrists, and the world started to slip sideways.

She had worked so hard in telling herself this wasn't because of her. The killer was to blame; she hadn't actually caused Elijah's death just because she was a police officer.

But maybe that had just been a pretty lie that she had desperately wanted to believe.

Lauren swiped at her cheeks, mad that they were damp. She'd heard somewhere that the structure of each tear looked different depending on what produced it.

What must hers look like? They were born of rage, embarrassment, frustration, grief—a spectrum containing too many emotions to even name.

Lauren focused on the rage. It was time to nail the bastard.

CHAPTER FIFTY-TWO

GRETCHEN

Now

Lachlan didn't get it. Despite the picture and the new information that Hayes hadn't been the only one to own the house where the serial killer's victims had been found.

Lachlan didn't get it.

"But his son went missing, too," he muttered. Then with more volume, to Fred: "What if he just bought the house because he knew his son's remains were there?"

Into the silence that followed that idea, Fred said, "Well, there's more."

Gretchen met Lachlan's eyes. "Go ahead."

"Garrett Adams is not his full legal name," Fred said. "It's Robert Garrett Adams. And on all the paperwork he goes by R. G. Adams."

"Adams being a common name," Lachlan commented, almost help-lessly. And maybe a week ago or even an hour ago, Gretchen would have murmured, *A brilliant contribution,* dripping in sarcasm. But she didn't have the energy left for it now.

"Anyway," Fred said, her tone pretty much doing the job for Gretchen, "I did a broader search on Robert Adams and R. G. Adams and came up with something."

Gretchen braced herself. "Another house?"

"Good guess, but no," Fred said. "A birth certificate."

The answer was so far from what Gretchen had been expecting that her brain tripped, tried to right itself, but still felt shaky.

The first victim is always important.

Her eyes flicked to the photo, to Garrett Adams watching Peter Stone, his beard hiding most of his expression, the poor quality of the print doing the rest of the work. Anyone glancing at the picture would likely miss him entirely.

But all of a sudden, Gretchen knew what it meant. "For Peter Stone."

"You're a smart cookie, Dr. White."

Not smart enough. Gretchen didn't say it out loud, wouldn't drop her guard like that. But it would be a bur in her skin for a long time, no matter how this case turned out.

Fred cleared her throat as if she'd heard the thought. "Anyway, Robert Adams is listed as Peter Stone's biological father. It looks like the police tried to track him down when Peter went missing, but no one knew where to start."

Hindsight. The word came back to Gretchen. It was so easy to see something as a mistake when you had more information. But the Burlington detectives would have been chasing a Robert Adams in a country full of them back before there were digital bread crumbs to follow.

Gretchen pictured Garrett. The beard, the Vermont camouflage of flannel and beat-up jeans. If he'd been clean-shaven before, he probably looked like a different person now. And Vermonters prided themselves on not asking too many questions of their neighbors.

Robert Adams had disappeared well and truly into Garrett Adams, to the extent that Penny Stone hadn't even noticed him that day at the orchard.

Why now? Gretchen had wondered after realizing Owen Hayes had been killed.

Maybe that was the answer.

Someone had been figuring it all out.

If that someone had been Marconi, why not frame her and kill Hayes at the same time. Two problems, one bullet.

Executions weren't personal.

Lachlan was talking. "So Garrett happens to be at the Hayes farm the day Penny visited with Peter. He did the math when he saw the kid."

"He realized Penny had never told him she was pregnant," Gretchen added. "Kept his kid from him all that time. That could have easily been his trigger."

"That's not an excuse," Fred cut in, a rare fire in her voice. "Just because Penny never told him doesn't mean he has a right—"

"No one said he did." It was Lachlan who stopped the tirade that Gretchen had honestly been finding interesting.

She wanted to probe at that sore spot like a tongue worrying a loose tooth. Fred had always been particularly touchy about the child-abuse cases, more so than she was about anything else, more so than anyone would guess listening to the way she unemotionally talked about death and pain and violence. There were shadows there, just like with Marconi. Gretchen wondered if she was just attracted to people who had them, or if she simply liked people who had lived through trauma and come out the other side whole.

There wasn't time for that, though. For every minute they wasted—and they had wasted plenty—a shiv could be finding its way into Marconi's rib cage.

"Right." Gretchen snapped her fingers in irritation. "Focus."

Lachlan looked like he wanted to say more—God forbid someone think he was siding on the wrong side of a moral line—but he nodded. "So Garrett kidnapped his son because he didn't think he'd win any kind of custody battle with a woman who didn't let him know he had a child."

This time, Gretchen stopped him. "If he's responsible for that grave-yard up at the Hayes Farm, then he's a psychopath. He doesn't need a reason to kidnap his son—he just needed a trigger. Which he got."

"But we're still leaping to conclusions that he was responsible," Lachlan said.

Gretchen reached over and tapped Garrett's face in the photo. "He's the father of two of the victims. At one point, he owned the house where the bodies were found. I'm not seeing a big leap here."

"Damien was buried by himself," Lachlan murmured. "He was special."

"And so was Peter," Gretchen realized, thinking about the case Daniels had mentioned on the phone. The Candy Man. He'd made the protégé bring friends over to kill. Sure, it meant easy victims, but it also could have served another purpose. "I wonder if killing Damien was a test of Peter's loyalty."

Lachlan sucked in air. "He would have been a child."

She nearly rolled her eyes at that. Considering that kids' brains—and understanding of social taboos—were underdeveloped until well into adolescence, it actually made more sense that they could be coerced into violent acts than adults. "Hey, Fred, I need to make another call."

"Aye, aye, Captain, I'll keep nosing around," Fred said before hang-ing up.

Before Lachlan could ask any more idiotic questions, Gretchen pulled up the number she'd dialed yesterday. Daniels answered quickly.

"How can I help?"

It caught Gretchen off guard in a way she couldn't name. Shaughnessy had often asked that. She had long told herself that

Shaughnessy thought the worst of her, but he'd never once hesitated to help her when she needed it. Except when it had come to her own case, of course.

Gretchen didn't do well with unexpected emotions, and so her voice came out snappier than she would have made it had she been in control of her senses. "How often do serial killers murder their own kids?"

"Incredibly rare, believe it or not," Daniels said without hesitation. "There are actually far more examples of the killers going out of their way to protect their own children. To this day, BTK's daughter says there must be something decent in her father because he treated her so well."

"Jesus," Lachlan breathed, running a hand over his head. Gretchen realized it was the same kind of reaction as Marconi rocking back on her heels. Surprise, astonishment, and disbelief wrapped up into one movement.

"There are some instances, of course," Daniels continued. "Mostly serial killers who are women. There was a black widow who once tried to fake her daughter's suicide and leave a forged note that took credit for all of the husbands' deaths."

"Smart," Gretchen observed. "She didn't get away with it?"

"The daughter survived the 'suicide attempt,'" Daniels said, with some of that dark humor. "Game over for the widow."

"And men looking for protégés," Lachlan said. "Do they ever just use their own sons?"

"Yeah, there are a few examples of that. Most famously a guy nick-named 'Crazy Joe.' He took his thirteen-year-old son on a killing spree. But you know what? He was later convicted of killing one of his kids. So there aren't any hard-and-fast rules here. Just . . . it's not as clear-cut as 'serial killer will kill his own kids.'"

He paused, and she heard a thousand questions in the silence. What he asked, though, was, "What else can I tell you?"

"Is there a reason a serial killer would move out of a house even if he used it as his burial ground?" Gretchen asked. "Supposing there was no financial pressure, of course."

"Actually . . ." Daniels sounded thoughtful. "Do you know any details about the killings themselves? Was there . . . any sexual assault?"

Lachlan met her eyes over the held-out phone. "We don't know."

"You sound like you're thinking about something," Gretchen prodded.

"There are four types of serial killers," Daniels said in that same cautious cadence. "Hedonistic and power control are the ones that get the most attention."

"That would be your typical rape-and-torture serial killers," Gretchen said as an aside for Lachlan, who mouthed a dry *Thanks* in response.

"Right. But there's also two others," Daniels continued. "Visionaries—who have God in the ears telling them to kill. And mission oriented."

"You think our guy might be one of the latter?" Gretchen asked. "Why?"

"The protégés, for one," Daniels said. "Mission-oriented killers often want to teach their protégés the right way to live and pass judgment on . . . sinners, for lack of a better word. Though, of course, their missions aren't always religious based." He paused. "And it might explain why he abandoned the burial site. The act of killing was more important than being close to the bodies. He wouldn't have gotten that stereotypical rush that hedonists and power-control killers get from desecrating their victims' bodies. Killing them would have been more of a—"

"Relief," Gretchen realized quietly.

"Relief," Daniels repeated. "The mission-oriented ones just want to . . . This is going to sound—"

"Just spit it out," Gretchen ordered, and he huffed out a breath.

"I'm used to tiptoeing around feelings on my book tours," he admitted. "The mission-oriented ones are checking off a list of people who need to die. So that feeling when you cross off an errand or something. It's more important that they've accomplished the killing than feeling a closeness to the victims."

Lachlan's hands trembled against his thighs.

"These were kids," he said, his voice breaking on the word. "How could it be his mission to kill kids?"

"You're not going to like my answer."

The corner of Gretchen's mouth twitched up. "Again, don't let that stop you."

Daniels took a deep breath. "He thought he was protecting them." When neither Gretchen nor Lachlan responded, he exhaled heavily. "That would be my guess, at least. It's actually an incredibly common urge—relatively speaking, of course—in mothers who think they're protecting their children from an abuser. There are probably a handful of cases a year."

"Christ," Lachlan breathed out.

"How does that translate to a serial killer?" Gretchen asked. Even *she* could admit when she was out of her league when it came to what they were dealing with here.

"You asked about serial killers murdering their own children?" Daniels asked. "That likely was his trigger, then. His kid experienced some kind of abuse similar to something he'd experienced."

The names on the thumb drive.

They'd been Owen Hayes's victims. And then they'd become Garrett Adams's.

What if Garrett had clocked Owen Hayes's interest in Peter that day on the farm? The same day he realized he had a child he didn't know about? What if something similar had happened to Garrett growing up?

"Again, obviously, this person's mind twisted circumstances to fit his own urges," Daniels said. "I'm not saying he was actually protecting these kids. Just, that's what he probably told himself."

Her mind was doing that tripping thing where she couldn't quite find the right question or the right answer. Couldn't even find solid ground to stand on. She knew one thing, though. "That was helpful, thank you."

"Hey, Gretchen?"

Normally Gretchen would have hung up by now. "Yes?"

"Keep my card handy."

She swallowed hard. Didn't answer and hung up. But she thought he was exactly the type of person who understood that as *I will*.

CHAPTER FIFTY-THREE

LAUREN

Then

Lauren couldn't be reckless this time. She needed to actually build a case instead of running off instinct and then taking each misdirection as a revelation.

Julia Hayes was only fifteen, and she'd been a child when she'd met the boys in the basement. No matter how sure she'd seemed when talking to Lauren, even a mediocre defense attorney could get a jury to question her credibility.

For a moment, Lauren thought about taking all this to Gretchen. Together, they'd successfully worked a number of investigations, including solving the mystery of the Kent case and closing the book on Gretchen's own past.

But Lauren hesitated. Gretchen had a way of bulldozing her way through life, and this was too raw, too tender. Too personal. Maybe later she would bring Gretchen in, but for now, Lauren wanted to protect this little piece of herself.

What she really needed was evidence and bodies. That's what would get people to finally listen, to finally believe. Lauren had burned too many bridges in the days after Elijah's death to think she could just go in and expect anyone to take her seriously now.

A conversation came back to her, one held over pristine marble counters.

"You're doing it," Ashley had said quietly. *"Thinking we're crazy."*

Lauren had never seen herself reflected so clearly in someone in that moment.

Grief had made her unreliable, just like it had Ashley. It didn't matter that the pain had faded and changed into something that could be tucked away, hidden. If you're a hysterical woman one time in your life, you're forever painted with that brush.

Ashley.

She'd been woven into Lauren's story in such strange ways. But Lauren had felt a kinship with her from the start.

She also might be the perfect person to ask about Garrett. Ashley had her own special connection to Garrett, a relationship that went beyond simply seeing an echo of yourself in another person. One that Lauren hadn't ever understood.

Why did you let him come?

He's grieving, too.

Lauren hadn't known much about Garrett back then—she remembered having that thought when he'd reported her to Abaza, something that made much more sense in hindsight. But if anyone would, it might be Ashley.

———

Ashley Westwood had always intimidated Lauren, even if Lauren had never wanted to admit it.

While standing in the modest kitchen Ashley now shared with Rafi, Lauren let herself wonder about their relationship. Had Rafi insisted on paying for half the mortgage? Was that why they'd downgraded from Ashley's mansion? It must not have been that she'd lost her money. She still wore tasteful and subtle designer clothes that reminded Lauren of Gretchen's wardrobe. People who had been born rich didn't need to be flashy about it.

"I'm sorry, what?" Ashley asked, her coffee long forgotten on the kitchen table in front of her. "You think Garrett Adams actually took our boys?"

"That's what Julia Hayes says," Lauren repeated. They'd gone through this twice now, but Lauren didn't even blame Ashley. It was nearly impossible to shift a worldview you'd cultivated for nearly a decade. A worldview that had helped you move on—not because it was pretty or nice, but because at least you understood what had happened.

"No," Ashley said, dragging it out, ending it in almost a question. "No."

The second denial was firmer. Lauren pressed her lips together. "Why would she lie?"

"She was just a girl," Ashley said. "She was confused about what was happening. It was Hayes."

"I thought so, too," Lauren said. "But Garrett made us think that."

"No." Ashley shook her head, her hair, still that same lovely shade of red, swinging against her chin. "It's always made sense that it was Hayes."

Cognitive dissonance. It was one of those fancy terms Lauren had learned from Gretchen.

People didn't like having deeply held beliefs challenged, no matter how much proof they were shown. And so they would create scenarios where the evidence was wrong.

A core belief being challenged is the psychological equivalent of being attacked by a bear, Gretchen had told her.

Looking at Ashley now, Lauren could see that. Her face had paled; her fingers had curled into fists. She didn't want to believe this because it would mean that she had been fooled all these years, that she'd been friends with her son's killer. A man who had manipulated all of them with devastating success.

Ashley would rather live in the world where that simply wasn't true.

"Why are you so sure it was Hayes?" Lauren asked, trying to find a way in.

"Because he talked to Joshua."

"How did you know it was Hayes?" Lauren pressed, already anticipating the answer.

Ashley breathed in sharply through her nose. "Garrett showed me a picture of him."

"You reported the incident," Lauren said, as gently as possible. "It was in the crime blotter that week it happened. Garrett must have been paying attention to any mentions of someone who matched Hayes's description."

"Why would he—?" Ashley pressed a hand to her lips, cutting off her own question.

Lauren wondered what Gretchen's answer would be. The woman loved motive, based her investigation technique around discovering the *why* of any murder. But she was also extremely pragmatic about people's wiring, as she called it. Some men were born to be monsters because of how their gray matter formed back in the womb. Gretchen never said that like it was a bad thing, but rather a fact of life. It was how she treated her own diagnosis as well.

"I don't think it matters," Lauren said, again as carefully as she could. "But why I'm here is because I wanted to ask if you remembered anything about Garrett in those days. Had he been in town long? Did Damien have a mother who disappeared from the picture?"

Ashley's fingers traced patterns on her coffee cup, her eyes on whatever she was drawing instead of Lauren. "I don't think it could have been Garrett. It was Hayes. We all know it was Hayes."

"He fooled me, too," Lauren said, reaching over to take Ashley's hand. The psychological equivalent of a bear attack. That probably meant Lauren wasn't going to get through to Ashley this afternoon. Not when Lauren still didn't have any solid proof that her theory was any more accurate than Ashley's. "Maybe you're right, maybe it was Hayes. I'm just . . . asking questions right now. Nothing else."

"Okay." Ashley visibly swallowed. "Um . . . I didn't know much about him back then. We didn't move in similar circles, you know? Um, I think he moved to Montpelier a couple years before Damien was taken? The mother died around that same time. Cancer, I think."

Lauren's pulse jumped and then settled. A dead wife didn't mean anything. "How do you know all this?"

Ashley cleared her throat, shifted. And something about the uncomfortable movement triggered an understanding in Lauren.

"You slept with him."

"That sounds so sordid," Ashley murmured, swiping at her cheeks even though her eyes were dry. "We . . . comforted . . . each other after Joshua's case went cold."

Bile rose in Lauren's throat, disgust making her hands shaky. Not disgust toward Ashley. Lauren could never judge a grieving parent for seeking relief, no matter what form it came in.

No, toward Garrett Adams.

This was part of his game. It wasn't just about taking the boys. He hung around, relishing the effect it had on the mothers.

The single mothers, she realized. Something had happened in his childhood, but she didn't give two shits about it. People had bad childhoods all the time and they didn't grow up to kill boys and emotionally torture their mothers.

She pictured Garrett at the memorial, sidling up to her, with hungry eyes that had devoured her every reaction. There had been no shame there, and Lauren had thought it was because he had justified his actions as righteous. Now, she realized he just wasn't capable of the emotion.

Gretchen would label him a true psychopath.

"Okay," Lauren said as neutrally as possible. She'd thought the rage had faded long ago, but now she realized it had just been locked away so neatly, so completely, that she'd protected herself from having to control the full brunt of it every waking second of her day. "Did he ever tell you where he moved here from?"

Ashley shook her head.

"Okay," Lauren said again, swiping her thumb over Ashley's knuckles. "Okay."

When she didn't ask anything else, Ashley met her eyes once more. Ashley's were big and wet, but no tears had spilled over yet. "I don't think I could live with it, if it was Garrett."

Lauren was struck by a thought. "Does he still come to the memorials?"

Ashley nodded once, twice, and a terrible, grim silence settled in the space between them.

Of course he did.

"Does he still live in town?" Lauren asked, wondering if she would go confront him if he did. That wasn't the right plan; she knew it wasn't.

"You're going to take this the wrong way," Ashley said, pulling her hand back into her own lap. Before Lauren could ask, she continued. "But he bought the Hayes farmhouse after the family left town."

Lauren exhaled, not able to form any coherent thoughts beyond the sirens ringing in her ears. "Okay."

"He sold it, though," Ashley said, as if that meant anything. "I think he just wanted to see if there was any evidence." She nudged Lauren's shin with the tip of her pump. "Don't say you wouldn't have done the same."

"So where is he now?" Lauren asked, carefully.

Ashley must have heard something in her tone. "I don't think I should tell you. For your sake."

"Okay." Lauren could find it out herself anyway. Or ask Fred to do it on the down low. "Okay."

She stood up, because she knew she wasn't going to get any more out of Ashley.

Before she could leave, though, Ashley's hand darted out and gripped her wrist, her fingerprints sure to leave a bracelet of bruises. Lauren didn't flinch, just looked down at that too-pretty face and lifted her brows in question.

"Are you going to go after him?" Ashley finally asked.

"No," Lauren lied.

Ashley knew her too well, even though they barely knew each other. It was more like Ashley knew herself, knew what it was like to be one of the mothers of the boys in the basement.

She let Lauren's wrist drop, and murmured, more to herself than to Lauren, "Yes. Yes, you are."

CHAPTER
FIFTY-FOUR
GRETCHEN

Now

Gretchen stared up at the brick facade of the Montpelier Police Station.

"If Garrett Adams was the one who killed Hayes, why would Marconi tell me not to investigate?" The question was rhetorical, but Gretchen was frustrated enough to use Lachlan as a sounding board.

"Actually," he said, and then grimaced as if he hadn't really meant to share whatever his thought was.

"Actually?" she prompted, because no way would she let him get away with pretending he hadn't said anything.

"It might still have been Marconi."

"Explain."

"Your person"—he nodded to the phone, and she assumed he meant Fred—"only figured all the stuff out about Adams now. And we only got these photos today." He shook the papers. "Marconi thought it was Hayes then—she thought it was Hayes for the past nine years. Why should we assume she realized it was Adams?"

I did it, okay?

He had to be wrong, but Gretchen was stuck. She couldn't force any of her theories to make more sense than Lachlan's, which, honestly, infuriated her. Although he was not as terrible as she'd thought going into this, she would never believe he was a better detective than her.

If there were two things she would bet on being true, they were *one*, Marconi wouldn't have had blood smeared on her if she had been the killer; *and two*, no way in hell would she take the fall for Garrett Adams, or any unknown assailant for that matter.

She was facing a brick wall. Her experience, her knowledge, and her own biases just simply couldn't create an explanation for what had happened the night of Marconi's arrest.

What she needed to do was go to the source.

"We have to talk to Abaza," she said, trying not to sound too enthusiastic about the suggestion. If she did, Lachlan would know something was up. He seemed to have a better radar for her bullshit than most.

"Yeah." Lachlan had to be caught up in the adrenaline of it all if he didn't even blink at her suggestion that they follow procedure. He was already unbuckling.

"At the very least, she can start the process of figuring out if Adams had an alibi for the night of Hayes's death," he said.

Gretchen nodded. "He won't give it over easily, but we need to get him on record."

She saw his hand linger on the car handle. Not long, just a beat. Something must have pinged in his subconscious but not made its way to the surface, because a heartbeat later he was out on the sidewalk.

"Actually, you go ahead. I have something to do," she called out when he'd cleared the car completely. He shut the door as he turned, but then he seemed to realize she wasn't coming with him. He leaned down, his face drawn tight in confusion and then irritation.

Gretchen took off, out of the parking lot, into the street.

With only one hand on the wheel, she managed to dial Fred. "Do you have a current address for Garrett Adams?"

"Oh shit, you sound—"

"I sound like I need the current address for Garrett Adams," Gretchen gritted out. "Now."

"You sound like you've ditched the cop." Fred finished her thought, not cowed. She was too used to working with Gretchen for that. Anyway, in the next second she rattled off a street that Gretchen knew was out toward the Hayes farmhouse. Garrett hadn't gone far from his burial ground, after all. Before Gretchen hung up, Fred managed to get in, "You won't do her any good beside her in jail."

Both of them knew that warning wouldn't deter Gretchen.

It didn't take long to make it out of town and then down the two-lane country highway toward Garrett's place. Gretchen wondered what Lachlan's play would be.

Because he hadn't wanted to know, he would have no way of getting in contact with Fred. That meant he would have to bring in Abaza, place a call back into IA in Boston to have them run their own search—or, if his SUV had been close, he could have tried following her.

She glanced in the rearview and saw nothing but blacktop.

That would give her some time. Maybe as much as twenty minutes before he got there.

What she would do with it, she wasn't yet sure.

Gretchen wanted to kill the man. It wouldn't be a great loss to the world, clearly. And with all this land up here, she was confident she could get away with it.

It was so tempting.

Yet that wouldn't get Marconi out of jail.

She needed his confession first.

———

Gretchen didn't have a death wish, no matter what some people thought.

Just because she wasn't able to experience fear didn't mean she had any interest in dying. It just became more of a calculation than instinct based.

And Gretchen liked her odds facing down an unprepared serial killer even though she had no backup. The solid weight of her gun holstered against her rib cage tipped the scales, of course.

She was a predator herself now, within jaw-snapping distance of her prey.

These men all thought themselves apex killers, yet they were all the same—broken boys who took their abuse out on others. While sympathy didn't come naturally to her, she could muster something close to it for people who were like herself. Wired wrong. But this went beyond that. This was a glitch that had manifested as evil incarnate, and it needed to be snuffed out.

Lucky for everyone, Gretchen didn't mind taking care of this particular problem. At the very worst, she was confident she could provoke him into attacking her. That meant her perfect streak of not killing anyone in cold blood would remain unbroken.

Technically.

And wasn't that all that mattered?

Right before she knocked on the door, she made sure her phone's voice recorder was on.

Then she rapped on the wood.

CHAPTER FIFTY-FIVE

MARTHA

Then

There was something inside Martha that attracted darkness.

At first, she had been too young to realize it. Her brother had told her she was golden, and she'd believed him. Her teacher had told her she was sweet, and she'd believed him. Her driving instructor had told her she was beautiful, and she'd believed him.

By the time Owen had come around, she'd thought she'd understood that she had something rotting at her core that drew these types of men to her.

He'd said the same things they had, and for some reason, she'd believed him.

She'd thought Owen had been the exception. Instead, he'd been the rule.

She had never thought Garrett the exception.

No, by then she'd known better.

Martha didn't consider herself an evil person. But life didn't work like the old Westerns her brother loved, the ones he'd watch with her on his lap, his hand creeping below the waistband of her pj's while their dad drank himself sick in the lounge chair beside them.

There weren't only white hats and black hats, angels and demons. There were just people, trying to live when every breath felt like more trouble than it was worth.

Martha was in the middle of drowning, though. Breathing didn't hurt anymore, or at least not how it used to.

She hadn't meant to get involved in any of this. Then Martha had walked out of Garrett's office in his diner and seen Peter Stone in the hallway.

Who are you?

Peter hadn't remembered her from the orchard, but she'd remembered him.

Garrett had followed her out, seen Peter, frozen. *What are you doing up here?*

He'd been sloppier back in those days, she realized now.

Martha had still been trying to figure out what the boy from the orchard was doing in front of her. Except it came in a flash, in a memory of a MISSING poster at the grocery store. The same one she'd seen years later, covered up by advertisements for dog-walking services.

"He's my son," Garrett had said, fingers digging into the soft flesh of her upper arms. *"Why did you have to come back here—you weren't supposed to come back here."*

There had been a second or two there when Martha had thought Garrett was going to kill her in front of the boy.

Martha pretended she hadn't seen anything, like she always pretended she hadn't seen anything.

She was an expert at it.

At the end of the day it was what kept her alive, time and again.

Then Damien had been "kidnapped," and the police had come calling. Owen had been so confused. And panicked. She was certain he had a laptop full of videos that would get him sent to prison. People like Owen didn't last long in prison.

So he'd acted guilty because he had a guilty conscience, and Martha had watched from the sidelines, curious. When the cops asked for an alibi, Martha confirmed Owen had been home. Had she been thinking clearly, she would have let him take the fall for it. What did she care if he was charged with the wrong crime? He deserved to be put away.

Martha had been flustered, though. So she'd told the truth, and when asked if she would take a polygraph, of course she'd agreed. They never had brought her in for that.

Still, Garrett had carried on with his theatrics, all while Damien had probably been locked in his own basement. It was an effective tactic, Martha couldn't argue with that. Point loudly at the known pedophile, ask why no one was doing their jobs to catch him.

He was counting on her not saying anything, and one time she wondered why he thought he could. Except he seemed to know her too well. That first night she'd told him about Owen, and if she wouldn't report that to the authorities, why wouldn't she keep silent on her theories about Garrett?

That's when she'd realized she might be able to make this shit show work for her. She would just have to give up any semblance of morality in the process.

So she'd stayed quiet as her soul had rotted in her chest—and the tactic seemed to work. In the weeks after the police came to talk to her about Damien, she realized Owen was keeping himself in check. He wasn't taking day trips to Burlington anymore, wasn't spending his evenings locked in his office downloading God knew what.

Garrett Adams and the cops had scared him. Six months crawled into seven crawled into eight. She thought maybe she'd imagined everything. Then his shoulders started to relax; he spent longer days behind locked doors.

Then Joshua Westwood went missing. The cops came around again, suggested the mother thought maybe Owen had been seen talking to her son two weeks before he'd been taken. He'd been at the gas station where Joshua had disappeared only minutes after Owen drove away.

Martha hadn't been asked for an alibi that time.

That night she'd dosed Owen's drink with three crushed painkillers and then had driven to Garrett's diner, found the key where he hid it behind the loose brick. Found the basement next. That's where Peter had come from that one time, the door open and damning.

There was an old safe room down there, the walls so thick no one could hear anyone scream.

Garrett found her standing in front of it. He wrapped his arms around her waist and kissed her jaw. No longer enraged, his violence satiated by whatever the hell this was. *I don't hurt them,* he'd promised.

He didn't hurt them when he killed them was what he meant.

I'm protecting them from him.

Martha was no mastermind, no big thinker. But even she knew that was crap. This was just the same brand of monster that Martha always seemed to be able to find in human form. What was wrong with her? Why had she been born to this life? Being able to identify them but never having the strength to slay them.

She'd nodded once, twice.

Don't kill me is what she'd thought. *"I won't tell"* is what she'd said.

This was it—this was what she could do. Garrett taking the one child meant others would be safe from Owen.

What was one sacrifice a year if it kept two monsters well fed?

How would it be any better if Martha got torn to scraps trying to stop either of them?

They would keep each other in check. It was almost funny, if your sense of humor was dark.

The days Owen had lived in fear of this nameless opponent who kept pressure on him from the shadows were some of the best in her life. His gaze rarely strayed anymore. His anger was kept in check by fear of a surprise visit from the MPD. His brain started to rewire itself to enjoy normal pleasures again.

She still plotted to leave. Because she wasn't fooled, whatever was happening between the two men could only end in flames, and she had no interest in being caught in the wildfire.

Then Officer Lauren Marconi had turned up on her porch, knocking on her door. Martha had known in an instant who had pointed her in their direction. She hadn't known why until two weeks later when she realized Peter wasn't locked in his bedroom—the one he'd been given after proving he was loyal to Garrett.

Peter had become a liability. Marconi had started looking into his case, and then later she'd seen him in the rec center's parking lot. Garrett loved control and he hated liabilities.

Martha hadn't even gotten to say goodbye.

"We need to leave," she'd whispered to Owen the night after Marconi had tried to break in looking for her son. If Garrett could take a cop's kid, he would turn on Martha next. She was a liability that wouldn't be left alive for very long.

Owen was just as spooked for his own reasons. He got their finances in order and put their house up for sale as soon as he could. He was a guilty man, after all, and that tended to make him act guilty.

They'd moved to Waltham, and Martha had to start the slow process of saving up money once more. Only, living in the outskirts of Boston made that much more difficult.

The part of her that once thought of herself as a good person made sure to keep her eye out for any missing boys from back home. For whatever reason, Garrett had gone—at least mostly—dormant in the years since they had left.

Maybe he had enough control of himself to know that without Owen there he didn't have a scapegoat. Maybe he really bought into whatever bullshit his deranged brain told him about killing those kids.

Maybe he'd really thought he was protecting them, and with Owen no longer there, he couldn't justify the murders.

Maybe she was just bad at actually finding the boys who were taken.

Owen had been so scared that he'd mostly kept his eyes to himself in the years after they'd moved. Martha was sure that laptop still had some password-protected folders on it that FBI agents would love to get their hands on, but the crime blotters weren't full of predatory men talking to boys anymore.

Just like back in Montpelier, though, the fear had ever so slowly faded.

The day after she'd seen him chatting with a child in the grocery store, she'd bought a gun.

Maybe she wasn't a brilliant mastermind, but she knew a bullet to the brain would end it once and for all. There was Julia to consider, of course, but Martha didn't intend to get caught standing over the body.

Years ago, she'd thought she'd been drowning. She'd decided she couldn't control the beasts around her, and that surely it would all end in her death if she'd tried to slay them.

Here was her moment of clarity, though. That pocket of space where the serotonin and endorphins were released, and all she could see was God or bliss or the entirety of the universe.

If she was going to die from drowning, she was going to make sure she took the monsters with her.

Martha might have something rotting at her core, but she had come to realize that—sometimes—that was a good thing.

CHAPTER FIFTY-SIX

GRETCHEN

Now

Garrett didn't answer Gretchen's knock.

He was likely at the diner. Maybe she should have gone there instead, but she hadn't wanted an audience.

She glanced at the time on her phone. It was early enough that she probably wouldn't be caught if she had a look around.

Gretchen checked one last time to see if there was anyone else lurking outside and then tested the doorknob. It turned beneath her palm, surprising her. She'd assumed she would have to pick the lock.

Her fingers lingered on the metal, a shiver rippling beneath her skin, some primal warning system for danger that never quite translated to *fear* in Gretchen's brain. She could still hear it, though.

Something was wrong.

She palmed her weapon, and then nudged the door fully open.

Death.

The stench of it slammed into her, pressing into her nostrils, onto her tongue, coating her throat. She knew what was going to be there before she even caught sight of the lifeless hand, the sprawl of limbs, the blood spatter on white walls, the bits of skull fragment on the carpet.

The kill was fresh, the body possibly still warm. Rigor mortis hadn't set in, but other side effects of death had, muscles no longer tight enough to keep the fluids and excrement locked up inside.

Gretchen hummed quietly to calm her vagus nerve, the instinct to heave in the face of blood and brains and exposed skull fragments unaffected by her diagnosis. All she needed was to add her own vomit to the mix.

Was the killer still here?

She gripped her weapon tighter as she stepped inside, swatting at a fly that had been drawn to the carbon monoxide she exhaled. It returned to the body in the next instant, greedily feasting on whatever was coming off it.

Garrett Adams's execution was no prettier than Owen Hayes's must have been.

She was no forensic expert, but, if pressed, she would say there were two bullets to the back of the head that had taken the man down.

Only, Marconi was sitting in maximum-security prison. There was no blaming her this time.

Gretchen, however, was *not* sitting in maximum-security prison and had just slipped the person who ostensibly could vouch for her innocence in whatever this was.

After pulling out her phone, she hesitated. The smart choice would be to contact Lachlan, to tell him what had happened, to make sure he knew she didn't have time to do this.

The even smarter choice was to make sure the house was clear and that she wasn't about to end up next to Garrett on the carpet.

She repocketed her phone, then swiveled, checking her surroundings.

The house had that empty feeling to it, the one where you could tell no one else was there.

Garrett's body was sprawled out, half in the entryway, half in the little front salon, his blood soaking into the plush carpet. She assessed him for one second longer and then took off, up the stairs to where she guessed the bedrooms were.

The first one she found was clearly Garrett's. It was neat, though not obsessively so. There were about a dozen flannel shirts hanging in the doorless closet, along with a couple of extra pairs of Timberland boots that she'd noticed him wearing. A picture of Garrett and Damien was the only personal item in the room beyond the ChapStick and hand lotion she'd found in the drawer beneath it.

The bedroom beside his was empty.

The one next to that was too neat.

Someone lived in it, but they'd left no mark. There was one pair of androgynous pajama bottoms in the drawers and a copy of *The Catcher in the Rye* tucked under the pillow.

But there was a smell to the room. It wasn't completely unpleasant, something separate from the stench that she could already tell was creeping in from downstairs.

It just smelled like someone had lived in this room. It smelled like a human, with their sweat and their tears and their breath.

She tried the windows, but they wouldn't budge. Painted shut. Not nearly as foolproof as security bars, but certainly less noticeable, especially since the drop from the second floor would likely result in a broken bone, at least.

Gretchen backtracked to the door, her fingers finding the indentation easily.

A dead bolt used to be there. But on the outside.

She lingered over the different-colored section.

Curious.

Her phone rang.

It surprised her enough that she laughed, an involuntary reaction to nerves she was unfamiliar with.

Cormac Byrne.

Lachlan must have called him. She imagined the conversation if she answered. There would be threats of arrest involved, she was sure.

Gretchen silenced her phone as she went down the stairs.

She stopped in the entryway, her eyes on Garrett's exposed skull once more.

Then she heard it. The slight scuff of shoe against wood.

Gretchen brought her gun up as she nudged the front door open the whole way with her foot.

She met equally startled eyes on the other side of it.

"I did that," Martha Hayes said with a jerk of her chin toward the body. "But I didn't kill Owen."

Don't investigate.

Gretchen nodded. "I believe you."

CHAPTER FIFTY-SEVEN

LAUREN

Then

Lauren watched Garrett Adams through the big windows of his diner. He delivered plates with practiced moves, laughing with his customers, pouring coffee, and replenishing napkins.

He looked so ordinary.

Half of her was fascinated by him. Horribly so, like the way everyone got into those grisly true-crime podcasts and shows. She found herself creating a backstory for him, a tragic one, of course. But every time she did that, she yelled silently at herself.

A serial killer was a serial killer was a serial killer. Lauren had no desire to give him any more justification than he deserved—which was none.

She shoved her keys back in the ignition and drove out of Montpelier, back to Boston.

The road blurred in her periphery as she, in a quasi-fugue state, desperately tried to figure out what to do next. She'd been hopeful that

Ashley would be able to tell her something useful, but it seemed now like it had been a wasted trip at best.

From her days in Montpelier, she knew how difficult it was to solve cold cases. Timelines blurred; evidence got misplaced or just dusty; detectives retired, taking with them all the information they'd never written down. The reason those podcasts had such a broad swath of material to work with was because it was nearly impossible to solve any case older than a year.

What she needed was a fresh victim. For one ridiculous moment, she thought about the "sociopath test," which wasn't really a sociopath test. The one where someone was asked, *If you met a potential lover at your mother's funeral, but didn't get their number, how would you find them again?*

By killing the father.

A nervous bubble of laughter escaped into the quiet confines of her car. She wasn't about to go murder a kid and frame Garrett Adams just to finally get him locked up. But the idea had a logic to it that appealed to the side of her that related to Gretchen too much.

Lauren dug her thumb into her eye socket and muttered a quick "Get a grip" to herself. She needed sleep. Desperately. In the morning everything might look clearer.

There was no urgency here. Garrett didn't know what she'd found out. She could take her time, actually figure out a way to put him behind bars not only for Elijah but for all the kids he'd taken.

She just needed to . . . take a beat.

Another laugh escaped, and once she started, she couldn't stop. Soon it morphed into wet, gasping sobs, and she had to pull over to the side of the road for a minute, rest her forehead on the steering wheel, and count each inhale and exhale to get control of herself.

By the time Lauren made it back to Boston, she was feeling something maybe close to hopeful—or at least in the neighborhood of it, despite the fact that she had nothing substantial to go on.

There was some beauty or irony in the fact that she'd now trusted Julia Hayes's words enough that twice it had been enough for her to launch an investigation into a serial killer.

It made her hesitate, but only for a second. Julia hadn't lied before; she simply hadn't given Lauren the entire truth.

There was a difference between the two.

Lauren's phone dinged with a message just as she pulled into her apartment building's parking lot. She climbed out of the SUV, opening the text thread as she did.

She had one new message, and it was from Ashley Westwood.

I'm sorry, I told Garrett.

"No, no, no, no," Lauren whispered to her phone, rereading Ashley's text as if it would change.

She bit off a curse, her eyes already scanning her surroundings.

Back in the city, there were only pockets of darkness holding ground against headlights and streetlamps and the ambient glow of too many apartment buildings.

But there could easily be someone lurking there.

Lauren's training kicked in. She unholstered her gun, locked her SUV, and crossed the parking lot at a jog, keys already in hand. The building's security was lackluster at best, but there was a fob system that offered some hint of protection.

Still, it took only one bored or overly people-pleasing type of inhabitant for anyone to piggyback into the lobby.

So she didn't drop her guard until she was safely behind the locked and dead-bolted door of her apartment.

Rafi was in her ear before she even fully realized she'd called him.

"Lauren? Laur? Lauren, what is it—are you there?"

"You guys have to get out of the city," she managed. "You have to leave."

"What?" Shuffling sounds came from his end, and then the ambient noise dropped away. Had he been in the fire station? Was he at work? Was he even still an EMT? She was shocked that she didn't know the answer to that. Once upon a time, for good or bad, Rafi had been in her thoughts every other minute or so. "Lauren, you're scaring me—are you okay?"

She laughed at that, couldn't help but laugh at that. "No."

"Laur—"

"Just . . ." She cut in, but then trailed off. She licked her lips, tipped her head back so that it banged against the door. "Can you trust me? This once?"

"Just this once, huh?" He sounded amused, though, not annoyed. She nearly smiled.

"Ashley might not want to go," she decided to warn him. "She won't think it's necessary."

"You've been talking to Ashley?"

The amusement had dropped out of his voice.

"Today," she admitted. "Only today."

She wondered if he was thinking about the way she'd stalked Hayes. Rafi was maybe the only person who had realized what she had been doing when she put in her time at Amherst. He was maybe the only person who had known exactly what she'd been up to by transferring to Boston eight years later.

"Lauren, is this about Hayes?"

Screaming into the void wouldn't help right now, she told herself. Otherwise she would have yelled, she would have howled. Of course it was about Hayes. *Everything* that mattered was about Hayes.

Except . . .

"No," she said, and for once it wasn't a lie. She realized Hayes had ceased to matter the second she'd found out the basement had belonged to Garrett Adams instead. "Rafi . . . do you remember where you were going to take Elijah?"

Without hesitating, Rafi answered, "Of course."

Lauren nodded, though he couldn't see her. "Do you understand?"

"Yes," he whispered.

"Don't . . . don't tell Ashley where you're going until you guys get there, okay?" Lauren said, though she wasn't sure she could trust his promise. Who was Lauren to ask anything of him? "Rafi?"

A ragged inhale, an exhale. Silence.

Finally: "Okay, I won't."

She pressed her lips together to hold back a small sound of relief. She didn't know why she cared, except that she still remembered the way Ashley had hugged her. That expensive perfume curling around Lauren along with Ashley's arms. The warmth of her, the comfort. The promise. *We'll get the bastard.*

Lauren remembered Rafi kissing her temple.

Do you want me to kill that guy? He hadn't been serious, but it mattered that he'd offered.

They were flawed, all three of them. Her, Rafi, and Ashley. Lauren couldn't say she liked that the two of them had fallen into each other and somehow had seemed to make it work when Lauren and Rafi had never managed it. Lauren couldn't even say she *liked* either of them now, Ashley sitting at that table, stubborn to the point of dangerous. Rafi fading off into the distance years ago when he should have instead become a constant.

But Lauren felt responsible for them. They were hers even when she'd had nobody.

"All my family is dead," she remembered telling Gretchen once without batting an eye over the stark truth.

Maybe that actually had been a lie, and she just hadn't known it at the time.

You didn't have to *like* your family, after all. You just had to want them to survive.

And right now, Garrett Adams knew two people in the world suspected him.

"Rafi?"

"Yeah?"

She smiled. He was expecting more instructions. Or something heartfelt. "You kind of suck."

He laughed, one sharp, staccato bark. And then, because he somehow still knew her better than anyone alive, he said, "Love you, too."

CHAPTER FIFTY-EIGHT

GRETCHEN

Now

Martha Hayes was shorter than Gretchen would have guessed from the pictures she'd seen of the woman. She had dark hair and the big eyes of a Disney character, everything coming together to make her look like naivete personified.

The gun she held, probably still hot from killing her ex-lover, said otherwise.

Never underestimate what women are capable of when given the chance.

"Why now?" Gretchen asked. Part of her brain was busy, thinking through the pieces that seemed to have clicked into place upstairs, but she couldn't help but be curious about violence, any kind of violence. This kind especially. When it was personal.

Martha took a deep, shuddering breath, her eyes flicking to the body and then away and then back again. "I was too late for Owen. I didn't want to miss my chance with Garrett."

"Too late," Gretchen murmured, not buying into this avenging-angel persona Martha seemed to have painted herself into. "Except you'd been married to Owen for how many years?"

The downside to pale skin was that it revealed so much. Marconi had the same issue.

Only, Martha didn't blush like a Disney character. Her skin went blotchy starting at the hollow of her neck. Like hives.

"You're not a cop," Martha said, instead of answering the obviously damning question. Gretchen rolled her eyes and looked down the drive, half expecting Lachlan's SUV to come tearing up it any minute.

While she could admit Martha had done *something* . . . brave—or at least not cowardly—in killing Garrett, she had no patience for someone who'd clearly known he needed to be put down years earlier and had the courage to act only when provoked.

Gretchen glanced at Martha. She still looked shell-shocked, the gun dangling from one finger, her gaze unable to land in any one place for very long, her breath catching every couple of inhales or so. There was no time for a panic attack.

"Do you know who *did* kill Owen?" she asked.

Martha licked her lips, shook her head. "I got a note. Telling me to be out of the house that night."

"And you didn't think that was suspicious."

The corner of Martha's mouth lifted. "Of course I thought it was suspicious. Plus, Owen didn't like us going out."

"But you made it work," Gretchen said.

"It's almost scary what humans are capable of," Martha said, finally meeting Gretchen's eyes. "When they want something."

"You said you were too late, but you knew whoever had sent that note was planning on killing him, didn't you?"

"Who am I to get in the way of a good plan?" Martha asked, with a little shrug. And Gretchen thought *that*, more than anything, summed up Martha.

She remembered her conversation with Lachlan.

Looking away is not the same as actively participating.

But that doesn't make you innocent, either.

In the distance, the piercing wail of a siren sliced through the air.

"Shit," Gretchen spit out. "Let's go."

"No, I'm . . ." Martha gestured to the body with the gun. "I'll turn myself in for this."

"Nope," Gretchen said, latching on to Martha's limp arm as she sailed past, pulling her along. She manhandled Martha into the passenger seat of the Porsche. "Not quite yet, my dear."

CHAPTER
FIFTY-NINE
LAUREN

Then

Nothing happened.

Lauren kept waiting for an attack. Garrett knew she knew, and yet nothing.

She spent the night strategizing. She needed everything in order to launch a real investigation against the bastard. That lesson had come at a great cost—being reckless had gotten her transferred to Amherst, where she'd lived in purgatory for eight years. This time she had to bring evidence; she had to play by the rules.

There would be no breaking into someone's house. There would be no excessive drinking. There would be no obsessive finger-pointing.

There would be no dismissing her as a hysterical, grieving mother, either.

Her phone buzzed against her butt, and she yanked it out of the pocket.

It was from Rafi.

Any news?

It buzzed again.

Ashley's been eyeing the car keys.

Had she overreacted sending them away? Panic had gripped her that night, curled tight around her organs, cutting in like barbed wire. She'd been wrong about this before.

Lauren repocketed her phone without answering. Rafi would get tired soon, but right now it helped that he and Ashley were away, somewhere she didn't have to worry about them.

For a brief second, she thought about Sandy with a flash of fear. But Lauren had dropped Sandy out of her life a long time ago. It was doubtful she was in any danger.

The only other person Lauren really ever cared about these days was Gretchen, and she could more than handle herself.

That's why when Gretchen asked what Lauren was doing that weekend, Lauren said she was going apple picking. The joke amused her, almost, and Gretchen, who barely cared enough to ask, hadn't pushed for any follow-up details.

Gretchen had been too focused on the date she was attempting. Lauren wondered if the guy was going to end up with a serrated steak knife in his carotid artery, but she gave Gretchen props for trying to be normal at least.

With the knowledge that Gretchen was suitably distracted, Lauren drove, on autopilot almost, out to Waltham for no other reason than it had become a habit.

She parked on her favored corner. Here, her SUV would be mostly blocked by a tree, but she had a view of the front of the place, the side window, and some of the backyard.

The house was dark save for the flickering light of the television from the living room. The car was gone, and she wondered if Julia had been left alone or if Martha was with her.

Lauren let her eyes unfocus. She wasn't really here on a stakeout anyway; she just felt more on solid ground here than she did most places.

What did that say about her?

There had been a few times over the years, when the nights got too dark, that Lauren had dropped into anonymous grief-support groups. They were often held in dingy church basements, with coffee that was mostly water and cookies that were mostly stale.

They didn't all play out the same. Some people got angry, some got quiet, some got teary. Some lashed out, and others picked at their own skin in a socially passable version of self-harm.

There was a running thread through all the meetings, though.

I just want to know what happened.

That had been said so many times Lauren thought it should be the groups' motto. It was said on a whisper and a shout, tear soaked and whiskey laced.

Every time, Lauren would nod in sympathy but not agreement.

She was different.

She knew what had happened.

A man named Owen Hayes had taken and killed her son because she was going to expose him for the monster he was.

The story was so neat, so believable. Not a comfort, really, but something in the vicinity of that.

Now she was adrift.

Lauren sighed, checked her phone again. This time it was a text from Gretchen, on her date.

I will kill him and then you.

And then a row of knives. Lauren couldn't help but be amused. She very much enjoyed that the polished and pristine Dr. Gretchen White used emojis.

Before she could respond, movement caught her attention.

She extinguished the light on her phone without taking her eyes off the figure now moving toward the Hayes house.

The person paused at the side window, their hands on the sill, scanning the area. Instinctively, Lauren slumped lower in her seat, but she needn't have bothered. There was a reason this was a favored location.

In the next second, the window slid up and the figure hoisted themselves up and into the house.

There was something in the movement, the easy press of a body lifting off the ground just using their arms.

Something Lauren recognized no matter how long it had been since she'd seen it.

"No," Lauren breathed out.

But she was already out of the SUV, running toward the front of the house. Unable to think beyond getting inside in the quickest way possible.

She didn't bother with stealth.

The door was unlocked, and it slammed against the wall as she headed toward the living room. Toward the TV.

Lauren didn't even have her gun drawn.

And still, when the two shots came, some feral part of her wondered if it had been she who had pulled the trigger.

CHAPTER SIXTY

GRETCHEN

Now

Beyond her initial hesitancy, Martha Hayes was a pliant passenger.

Again, Gretchen thought about how that probably best summed up Martha's life.

She didn't ask a single question as Gretchen drove them back out onto the highway, speeding away from the direction of the sirens.

But the silence let Gretchen think, once she was satisfied they'd escaped Lachlan and Abaza. The two would then be occupied with Garrett's body for hours, likely. An APB would be put out for Gretchen's Porsche—and for her—but she had twenty minutes, probably, to fix that before it became a problem.

It took fifteen to get to a town that was built up enough to have a rental-car business.

When Gretchen told Martha to stay where she was, Martha didn't react, just kept staring out the front window.

Renting the nondescript SUV took another ten minutes, but no one had put a freeze on her credit card yet. And that would require a judge and a warrant anyway. All that took time, and all Gretchen was looking to buy was a window, just a narrow space to slip by the notice of overeager state patrol officers on the highways.

Actually escaping the law for good would look a lot different from this.

She pocketed the keys to the Porsche and then manhandled Martha for a second time into the new passenger seat. The woman hardly blinked, and Gretchen wondered if she was in shock.

"Have you ever killed anyone before?" Gretchen asked as she climbed behind the wheel and moved the seat so her feet could touch the pedals.

The question had been meant to act like a slap to the face, an attempt to startle Martha into coherency.

"What do you mean by *kill*?"

"There's not a lot of wiggle room with that word," Gretchen said, pulling out into traffic. "Even from my admittedly skewed perspective."

"I think there is," Martha said quietly. "Wiggle room."

Gretchen lifted her brows in consideration. "So have you ever killed anyone before?"

Martha nodded. "I think I have."

She dropped silent after that once more, and Gretchen didn't bother to dig any further. While all Martha's inconsistencies and traumas were incredibly intriguing to her as a psychologist, right now she cared more about all the parts of the mystery she could sense that were about to fall into place.

For the first time since Marconi had sat in her car in the alley, smeared with blood, with big eyes and one request, Gretchen saw all the pieces.

She thought about her conversation with Zachary Daniels regarding the protégé, the kid who'd killed his mentor, the Candy Man.

She thought about that room, where someone could be locked away should he prove rebellious.

She thought about Marconi walking into the house of someone she'd stalked for nine years and being sloppy enough to get caught on camera.

She thought of mothers who could recognize children after decades apart from them.

She thought about Rafael Corado's cabin, and Dori, who'd said he'd left in a rush.

And she headed north.

In the passenger seat, Martha Hayes smiled.

CHAPTER SIXTY-ONE

LAUREN

Then

"Elijah," Lauren breathed, and it came out like a prayer, an answer, a curse.

It had been years since she'd said his name, and she hated how foreign it tasted in her mouth.

The slim figure she hadn't been able to tear her eyes from turned, gun raised.

Had he meant to shoot her, Lauren would be dead.

Her hands, her arms, her body, were incapable of defending her right now.

He didn't shoot. But he didn't react to his name, either. Just watched as she knelt by Hayes and felt for a pulse. She didn't care if the monster was alive, but she cared that Elijah had killed him.

It was a stupid thing to do anyway, checking for a pulse. Half his brain was on the living room floor, and now she had blood in the beds of her fingernails.

Lauren stood, stared down at Hayes's lifeless eyes. For years, he had been her white whale, the creature under the bed, the only reason for living. And now he was dead. Two bullets, two seconds.

And everything had changed.

"Elijah," she said again, this time with more volume. It came out a demand.

He flinched. "That's not my name."

"Yes, it is," Lauren said. Not petulant but sure. "Elijah, you need to go, now."

His attention skittered toward the open door, to the camera there. She saw the realization.

Lauren would take the fall for this kill.

She'd known—even as static had lain like a fog over her mind, even as she'd raced toward the house unable to believe what her memory had been sure of from countless nights in the community rec center watching him hoist himself out of the pool. She'd known.

Lachlan and his team would find all the ways she'd abused her privileges. They would track the story back to Vermont, to her break-in of Hayes's house. To that paper she'd written during Elijah's investigation. *Arrest Hayes.* To Abaza, who would admit that, yes, she had transferred Lauren after she'd harassed Julia Hayes in a drunken stupor.

Without a doubt, Lachlan would charge her for this, and she would let him.

Which must have been exactly how Garrett had wanted this to unfold. It was just like the night of the snowstorm all over again, with Garrett playing her perfectly. A decade had passed, and Lauren was still where she'd started, dancing at the end of Garrett's strings.

He'd had a problem—Lauren suspected he was the real killer instead of Owen Hayes, and Ashley knew about those suspicions. Garrett could convince Ashley that Lauren was crazy. But he must have known Lauren had smelled blood in the water and she wouldn't stop until she found hard evidence against him.

What better way to neutralize her as a threat? She'd set herself up so beautifully. The stalking, the police resources, the obsession with Hayes that Garrett had been the one to spark in the first place.

She wondered if he had even told Elijah to make sure her car was parked on the street before he went inside. Maybe he'd even told Elijah to be seen.

Because there was only one option here. With Elijah as the killer, Lauren would take the fall for Hayes's death. And Garrett Adams would win.

Gretchen will figure it out, some distant part of her knew. But she would deal with that next. Right now, Elijah was the important thing.

"We have a couple minutes, maybe," Lauren said, adopting the no-nonsense voice she'd deployed on him millions of times.

This wasn't a reunion.

There would be no tearful hugs.

"Leave the way you came," she said, already scanning for any sign of him that she would have to erase. "Go to Rafi's cabin." She reached in her pocket for her notebook and pen. Scrawled the address. "You have a car."

"Yes," he said quickly, like someone who was used to taking orders.

She closed her eyes, let herself grieve for one second. Then she sniffed hard, put it away in a box she would have plenty of time to agonize over in prison.

"Elijah, listen to me." She reached out as if to cup his face, and he stepped away from her. A skittish animal, a dangerous one at that. Lauren dropped arms that had gone too heavy for her to hold up. "Stop only for gas. Don't get caught—"

"You think I don't know how not to get caught?" he asked. His voice was that of a man's now, and she nearly recoiled from it. From him.

She wouldn't, she wouldn't ever do that.

"You'll go to the cabin?" she asked. Rafi would be there. Ashley, too. They would have a mess to deal with. But she would die before sending him back to Garrett. "Elijah, answer me."

Again, his expression broke her heart. He was waiting for a punch or a slap or something worse. A trained puppet who could be ordered to kill.

"He'll be mad."

"No, he won't find you," Lauren promised, without really being able to promise that. If she told anyone—Gretchen, Lachlan, anyone—that Garrett was the real killer, there was a chance they could figure out Elijah was alive. And that he'd been ordered to do this. She needed to keep as much uncertainty around Hayes's death as possible, at least until she could be sure Elijah had fled to safety. "He let you leave, didn't he? He made that mistake."

"He trusts me," Elijah said, and there was pride in those words. Pride that made Lauren want to cry. "He trusts me to come back to him."

Lauren wanted to rock Elijah in her arms, like she had when he was a child. To force him back into the boy she'd known. But he wasn't that boy; he'd never be that boy again.

Because she'd failed at keeping him safe.

What would a brainwashed child soldier listen to? Whatever it was, it wouldn't be rational.

"You don't want to lead the cops back to him, Elijah," Lauren said. "You want to protect him, don't you?"

She could see the hesitation there, and so she pushed. "Go lie low for a while. At your fa—" She cut herself off. Who knew if Garrett had made Elijah believe that he was his father. She licked her lips. "At Rafael's cabin. Garrett will be safer if you're there, away from him."

They'd been in the Hayes house too long now; surely some security system had been triggered. Or a neighbor had called in the gunshots.

"Elijah," she barked.

He flinched, but then nodded. "I'll go."

Lauren swallowed. "Now, baby."

He stared at her. "Don't pretend like you know who I am."

"I do know who you are," Lauren said, a fierceness building inside her, ready to consume both of them.

"You don't even know my name," he said, and she nearly wept at the familiarity of that head tilt. That stubborn chin.

"I know who you are," she said again. Because she didn't want to argue over something as trivial as a name. "I know who you are."

His fingers spasmed around the paper that held the cabin's address. And then he was gone. Back out through the window.

Lauren was left standing over the body of the man her son had killed.

I know who you are.

She had been so sure when she'd said it. Now all she could think of was the awful toll the world would pay if she had been wrong about that as well.

CHAPTER SIXTY-TWO

GRETCHEN

Now

The cabin was a good spot to hide. If only it hadn't been in Rafael Corado's name.

Although, despite Gretchen's prodding, Cormac still hadn't taken the lead seriously.

So maybe Marconi had been desperate when she'd been crafting whatever plan she'd come up with, but Marconi was smart even at her most frantic.

Gretchen parked in a way that blocked the other car from an easy escape down the rutted dirt path that led back to the road. Then she yanked Martha out of the passenger side and headed toward the door.

A man waited for her there. His posture was relaxed, his expression friendly. If she were a tourist who'd gotten lost on the way to a hike, he would be able to send her on her way without arousing any suspicion.

When he caught sight of her face, though, everything about him tightened. He went for the hunting rifle he must have kept at easy reach.

"This is private property."

"I'm not a cop," Gretchen said, holding her hands up for him to see she didn't have her weapons out. "I don't want Elijah."

The man—who she guessed was Rafael Corado—jerked the gun at her mention of his son's name, and she wondered if she should duck back behind her car. She had no idea how trigger happy, or just sloppy, he was.

"I don't know what you're talking about," he protested, his heads steady once more.

Gretchen was about 87 percent sure she'd guessed right. That Elijah Marconi was alive, that he'd been Garrett's protégé, that the reason Marconi was taking the fall was because she would never let her son go to jail. A tiny nugget of doubt lodged itself in her throat, but she ignored it. She hadn't gotten as far in her life as she had by bowing to the 13 percent of insecurity.

"I think you do," she said, in that gentle voice Marconi could so easily deploy and Gretchen had studied. She was glad for it now. "I don't want to hurt him or you—we just need to talk."

"*We* don't need to do anything," Rafael said. "You need to get back in your car and get the hell off my property."

Gretchen sighed. She really didn't have the patience for this. "Look, you can bluff your way into handcuffs when the police get here. I'm sure they're not far behind us."

That might be a lie, but it could also be true.

"Or," she continued, "you can let us inside. If it helps, she just killed Garrett Adams."

Martha made a wounded sound at that but didn't contradict the statement.

Rafael's attention shifted to Martha, and Gretchen saw her opening. She was close enough to step forward and disarm Rafael. He clearly wasn't an expert, and she'd been trained by the BPD's best.

But that wouldn't win her any points. He might even signal for Elijah to run.

"You really want Lauren to do life for this?" Gretchen asked quietly.

Emotions she couldn't decipher flickered in and out of Rafael's expression. The tip of the rifle slumped toward the ground.

"You can't take Elijah."

A part of Gretchen purred with the pleasure of finally being right. She couldn't remember a case where she'd made so many careless, stupid, foolish mistakes. In the end, she'd figured it out, and, really, only the final scoreboard ever mattered in the end.

"I have an idea," Gretchen murmured, but before the words were even out, a shadow shifted behind Rafael and became a person.

Elijah Marconi, it had to be.

He was tall and slim, though his broad shoulders matched his father's. His hair was a dark mop of curls that he could probably tug up into a bun at the back of his head. Gretchen devoured the boy's face, searching for Marconi in it. But he was all his father.

Except his Bambi eyes.

Something shifted in Gretchen's chest at the sight of them, and she had to stop herself from rubbing her sternum.

"Are you here to arrest me?" he asked. His voice was soft, emotionless. It was as if he were asking if it was cold outside.

Gretchen licked her lips, greedy fingers twitching. She wanted to dig them into his brain, to find all the ways he was broken. Living as the reluctant protégé of a serial killer for nine formative years had to have left untold amounts of damage in there.

She forced her heartbeat to slow, dragging her eyes back to Rafael, who was watching her expression with disgust.

Sloppy once again.

"No one's taking you anywhere, Elijah." Rafael's grip tightened on the rifle.

"Maybe they should," Elijah said.

In a sudden blur of motion, Martha rushed past Rafael and Gretchen.

Rafael shouted and swung the rifle, but Gretchen held up a hand. "Wait."

Elijah didn't move. If Martha wanted to attack, he'd be a sitting duck.

Martha gripped Elijah's arms tight and then pulled him into her own, folding his lanky body down so that she could press his face into her neck. She cradled the back of his head and rocked them both, side to side, side to side, Elijah as pliant as Martha had been earlier.

She wasn't passive now, though. Gretchen could see the strength in her shoulder muscles as she held the teenager, could see the flex of her thighs beneath her thin jeans. Could see the way she'd planted her feet to bear the weight of him.

"I'm sorry," she whispered again and again and again against his temple.

Gretchen studied them. Martha would have remembered him, of course; his image was likely seared into her mind as part of her long list of crimes. But Elijah had been only a child when Martha had left town. She must be nothing more than a stranger to him, but he didn't fight the embrace.

In fact, his body language reminded Gretchen of children who were so used to punishment they learned to become numb to discomfort. Placid and obedient.

Gretchen cleared her throat as she stepped into the cabin. "As touching as this is, we need a plan. The MPD detectives have already discovered Garrett's body."

It was a guess, but an educated one. She'd heard those sirens.

Elijah snapped to attention, and she saw the boy soldier where before she'd seen the victim.

All of a sudden, she saw Marconi.

"He's dead?" Some kind of fog must have lifted within him, and his voice came out sharp and urgent.

"Yes," Gretchen said, curious at this transformation. She would have paid money for a photograph of each microexpression that crossed his face. They went too fast to get them all, but she caught guilt, anger, grief, joy. This was the moment to ask—she knew she would regret it if she didn't. "Did he ever make you kill any of the boys?"

Martha and Rafael both inhaled noisily to make their protests known, but Gretchen ignored them. She kept her eyes on Elijah. Child soldiers weren't exactly known for their squeamishness.

Elijah tipped his chin up, just as Gretchen had seen Marconi do a thousand times. She wasn't sure she liked this, seeing the hints of Marconi in this stranger. Mostly because she could feel him slipping into her calculations already. She had the urge to protect him, and she hated it.

"No," Elijah said, in that unemotional tone. "Just Owen Hayes. To make it look like Lauren Marconi had killed him."

Gretchen nearly grimaced at the tough road ahead for the kid. He clearly had a dissociative disorder from his time in captivity. "Did you help Garrett kidnap those boys?"

"Yes." No emotion, just a response. He was used to giving answers and telling the truth. She sighed.

"Did he try to make you torture them?"

Again, Martha and Rafael protested, Rafael's loud and angry. Both Gretchen and Elijah ignored them.

"Yes," Elijah said. "And then he tortured me instead when I didn't do it."

"Why didn't he kill you, then?"

That silenced Martha and Rafael. They could all now hear the wind creeping in between the cabin's logs.

"Because I never fully broke," Elijah said. "And he wanted to break me more than he wanted anything in the world."

"Why are you asking him these questions?" Rafael said, fast and angry and scared. Understandably so.

346

"I need to know if he's savable," Gretchen said, calm in the face of Rafael's fear.

He reared back at that, but Elijah held her gaze.

"And?" he asked.

Despite years of brainwashing, of trauma and torture and captivity, the only life he'd taken was someone who was his own special type of villain. "Yes."

The room seemed to sigh, and Rafael cleared his throat. "You're right, we need a plan."

"Why did you bring us here?" That was Martha. She said it like she knew the answer. Maybe she wasn't so useless, after all.

Gretchen tipped her head, her eyes locked on Martha's. "I think you know there's only one way for this to go."

CHAPTER SIXTY-THREE

Martha

Now

The woman was right.

There was only one way for this to end.

Martha would take responsibility for both deaths. Elijah would walk free.

It would be Martha's penance, paltry as it might be compared to her sins.

Have you ever killed anyone before? the woman had asked in that curious but otherwise emotionless tone she seemed to favor.

If Martha were to be technical about it, she hadn't. But she could have stopped Garrett easily. There had been sufficient evidence to go to the police from when she'd first seen Peter Stone in that hallway and known it wasn't Damien.

She had spent too much of her life asking herself why. Hours, while she'd been scrubbing her bathtub or feeding Julia or doing laundry or screwing Garrett. She'd asked herself why she couldn't be stronger.

And Martha had never once wanted to acknowledge the answer. It was simple.

She was scared. She was scared that she didn't actually have enough evidence to prove it was Garrett, scared he'd twist it to somehow make it seem like she was the guilty one, scared that Owen would walk away from charges since he'd never actually *done* anything. And then he would have killed her.

She'd been scared that if she didn't placate the monsters, they'd turn on her and rip her to shreds.

Now they were both slain, and she couldn't remember why she'd been so terrified of them in the first place.

Bullets had a way of quieting the *maybes*.

"Yes," Martha forced herself to say. It was time for her to not be scared. "I'll lie. I'll say I killed Owen, too."

Julia had been her one last-remaining concern. A part of Martha had dreamed she'd get away with killing Garrett and then go west with new identities. Lose herself in the bustle of Los Angeles, or the remoteness of Alaska. But that had been foolish. The water was already tugging her deeper and deeper still.

Some part of her must have known that already. She'd dropped Julia at her sister's. Maybe it would give the girl a chance to grow up normal without Martha as a lead weight pulling her under.

Martha tried to feel something at the loss of her. But she'd numbed herself so long ago she didn't think that was possible. All she felt was grief for this boy in front of her.

And maybe a little for herself. Because no one else would.

"Perfect." The woman clapped her hands twice. "I'll take Martha back, she'll make her confession and bring along that gun, and we can get Marconi out for an Oprah-esque tear-jerking reunion."

A figure filled the doorway, silhouetted by the setting sun. The woman cursed, and Rafael's rifle lifted.

"Yeah, sorry, Gretch," the man said, stepping into the cabin, expression apologetic. "That's not going to work."

CHAPTER
SIXTY-FOUR
GRETCHEN

Now

Lachlan fucking Gibbs.

If Gretchen had even slightly less of a grip on herself, she would walk over and light him on fire.

"Detective Gibbs," she said as sweetly as she could. "I don't think you have any business here."

He shot her an incredulous look and then directed his attention to the rest of the little group.

"Look, let's all just calm down," he said, and it was then she realized everyone in the room had a gun. She was guessing in Elijah's case, but it seemed like a safe bet. He was a kid who'd been raised by a serial killer, and he was fleeing an execution. She would judge him as careless if he didn't have a weapon. "We can sort this all out at the station."

"There's nothing to sort out," Gretchen said, placing herself in the center of their little standoff. The move wasn't to protect anyone in particular; it was to better control the situation. "Martha here has confessed to killing both Hayes and Garrett Adams. You don't need the rest of us."

"You really think this strategy is going to work with me?" he asked, eyebrows raised. "This is what you're going for?" Before she could respond, his gaze drifted over her shoulder to Elijah and Martha. "Look, there are clearly extenuating circumstances. We can work with the DA—"

Elijah moved before any of them could react.

In three short strides, he had a gun out and the muzzle pressed directly to Lachlan's forehead. "I'm not going to jail."

His voice came out dull and hollow, not the angry shout anyone would have expected. Something about the lack of emotion convinced Gretchen that Elijah would pull the trigger no matter how many of them were there to witness it.

"Lachlan," Gretchen said, trying to infuse that warning into one word.

"You killed a man in cold blood," Lachlan said to Elijah, because he was foolish and terrible and Gretchen hated that she was going to have to figure out a way to save him. Because Martha could take the fall for Hayes, but she wasn't about to take the fall for a Boston police detective's death.

Which meant Elijah would be charged or have to be on the run the rest of his life.

And Marconi would not be pleased about that.

"Gibbs," Gretchen said, sharper this time, "this isn't the hill to die on. Everyone paid for their crimes."

"Elijah didn't," Lachlan said. The two were locked in a staring contest that would have been ridiculous if the stakes weren't quite so high. "He can't just walk away from this. I'm sorry."

Gretchen saw the trigger finger on Elijah's free hand twitch, and swore silently.

"When I said 'hill to die on,' I meant literally," Gretchen drawled. "Just in case that wasn't obvious."

Lachlan didn't blink. "You can't just have ethics when they're convenient to you."

"I'm not going to jail."

Rafael was inching closer to the pair, possibly planning to yank Elijah away. He'd never be fast enough, though. Elijah had trained at the knee of a killer. Rafael had flinched when she'd simply said his son's name. He wasn't equipped to handle any of this.

She held up a hand, made a swift cutting gesture to get Rafael to stop. He did, though his body swayed forward like he hadn't actually wanted to obey.

Gretchen risked a quick glance back at Martha, who was watching the scene with the blank gaze of a woman resigned to her fate.

Satisfied that two of the erratic elements in this potential atomic bomb were stable for now, Gretchen turned back to Elijah and Lachlan.

She had known since meeting Lachlan that his black-and-white thinking would get either him or someone else killed. If Marconi had been here instead of him, they already would have sent Elijah and Rafael fleeing to Canada, and they would be loading Martha into the back of the SUV.

A case closed, a job well done.

But Lachlan Gibbs lived his life on the sole belief that when push came to shove, he would always do what he saw as morally right even if the consequences were fatal. No amount of persuasion would get him to budge.

What she needed to do was de-escalate the situation, to change the circumstances.

Which mean getting Elijah to believe there were more than two ways out of this cabin.

"Elijah." Slowly, she stepped away from him—so as not to make him think she was going for his gun—but she turned as she did so she could meet his eyes if he ever took them off Lachlan. He wasn't a natural killer, or he already would have taken the shot. He wanted to be talked out of this; he wanted to be given another option. But he *would* pull the trigger. Both Gretchen and Lachlan had the experience to know all that with one glance.

"My name is Dr. Gretchen White, and I'm a friend of your mother's," she said, without stuttering once on the word "friend" or "mother." Elijah's eyes didn't flicker, but Gretchen thought she saw some new tension in his shoulders. "Lauren Marconi. You remember her, don't you? You were seven when he took you from her."

Elijah's jaw swiveled at the mention of Garrett, but he showed no other signs of listening.

Other than the fact that he still hadn't shot Lachlan.

And for once in his life, Lachlan was keeping his mouth shut.

She thought about all the movies and TV shows she'd watched to learn how to interact with people. There'd been plenty with moments like this, fraught with emotional undercurrents she'd never be able to intuitively tap into. She'd never once let that derail her, and she wasn't about to start now.

"I hated her on sight," Gretchen said, to surprise him. And it worked. He almost turned his head at that, but he stopped himself. Smart, careful, and in control of himself. It did not bode well for getting out of here with everyone alive. "I thought she would be boring. She was like elevator music—bland, uninteresting, but so annoying you can't ignore it."

Gretchen realized now that had been part of Marconi's strategy to fly under the radar. "And then she started asking questions. Some were fucking stupid questions."

The corners of Elijah's mouth twitched at that.

"But some were really fucking brilliant," Gretchen admitted. She leaned on the vulgarity again, because she knew it was particularly startling when uttered with her upper-crust voice when she looked as polished as she did. "Just quietly really fucking brilliant, our Marconi."

Our Marconi.

Hers and Elijah's, and no one else's.

"You don't know me, so you don't know how rare that praise is," Gretchen said, with a casual gesture toward Lachlan. Elijah braced himself, but when she didn't move toward him, he relaxed. Lachlan snorted, playing along.

"Praise for someone other than yourself?" Lachlan said. "Yeah, you could call that rare."

Gretchen rolled her eyes theatrically just in case Elijah was watching, and then shifted a little as if just redistributing her weight. Again, he tensed. Again, he relaxed when he realized she wasn't going for him.

"She never talked about you," Gretchen said, and she knew it sounded harsh. It was supposed to. This wasn't a kid who would buy sappy, melodramatic lies. She knew other people would play it that way. She also knew if it had been literally anyone but her in this position, Elijah would be stepping over Lachlan's body right now. Gretchen was interesting and unexpected, and it was keeping Elijah listening.

"She never talked about you," Gretchen repeated. "Maybe because she wanted you to just be hers." She shook her head. "Probably it was because she was plotting to avenge your death for nine years, and like I said, she was too fucking smart to blow it by running her mouth."

Again, his lips twitched. Gretchen ducked her head, the motion covering up the half step she took toward them. She wondered if Lachlan was plotting to grab the gun while she distracted Elijah, and she really hoped not. All she needed was for him to do absolutely nothing. Knowing Lachlan, she couldn't bet on it.

"Marconi wanted to take the fall for you, you know," Gretchen said. "Obviously you know that. And she's tough, all five foot nothing of her. You know. You've seen her." She gestured again to him. This time, no change in posture. He was getting used to her little moves. "She's not going to let you go to jail."

Lachlan made some kind of sound in his throat—a dissent, maybe—and she thought again of matches and burned flesh.

"Rafael," Gretchen said, shifting under the pretense of turning toward the man with the rifle. Really, it took her an inch closer to Elijah. "Would Marconi ever let her son go to jail?"

"Never."

"She let me get kidnapped," Elijah countered in that dull voice. The first thing he'd said since she'd begun talking.

"Huh." Gretchen tipped her head. "Touché."

It was Rafael this time who stuttered something out, probably a defense of Marconi, but she held up her hand, making the gesture sweeping this time. He cut himself off.

"What's the plan, Elijah?" Gretchen asked. "You just going to shoot us all?"

"You don't want to send me to jail," Elijah said, lifting the shoulder of his free arm in an unaffected shrug. "So no. Only this guy."

"You can't run forever."

"Nah, bad guys don't get caught," Elijah said. Bitterness there. Warranted bitterness. His file had sat cold in the police archives while he'd been locked in a room twenty minutes outside town for nine years.

"Again, you make some good points," Gretchen admitted, and this time she definitely saw the corner of his mouth tick up. "All right, cards on the table, Elijah. I don't really care what happens to you."

His eyes actually flicked to her, lightning fast, at that. They were back on Lachlan before any of them could blink, though. "Then why are you trying to talk me out of shooting him?"

Gretchen studied Lachlan and then sighed dramatically. "Because your mom would be annoyed with me if I didn't find a better way out of this predicament." She paused, considered. "Actually, she'd be disappointed, which is worse, you know?"

"Yeah," Elijah said, like he did. A relic from a past life. *Our Marconi.*

"More important, I'd be disappointed in myself," she continued, "because I'm pretty fucking brilliant myself. And if something as easy

355

to fix as this"—again, she gestured and also shifted closer—"trips me up, then that would be pretty disgraceful, you know?"

She could tell Lachlan wanted to say something. But he was restraining himself. Now he knew what she felt like every day around him.

"What's the endgame, Elijah?" she asked. "You're not a killer."

"I killed someone."

"Doesn't make you a killer," Gretchen argued. "You haven't taken the shot yet."

Lachlan cleared his throat but didn't say anything.

Gretchen thought about a scene so similar to this it nearly hurt. But Shaughnessy had been egging her on to make the kill back then.

"You're not the monster he tried to make you into," Gretchen said, her chest tight with some kind of emotion she didn't have the right language for. "Don't let him win, Elijah."

He didn't say anything.

"Don't let him win," she repeated. She hated—despised—the tremor she heard in her own voice. But she couldn't stop. She was talking to herself as much as she was talking to him. "He wanted you to be a monster. You never broke. He wanted you to break, but you never did."

Gretchen shifted a final time so that she was shoulder to shoulder with Lachlan. Elijah had grown accustomed to her movements so that she might have been able to snatch the gun from him. But the risk wasn't necessary. The boy would hand the weapon to her.

She held out her hand. "Don't let him win."

The room had gone silent despite the number of people crowded inside, the wind an eerie soundtrack layered over the hush.

Elijah breathed out, breathed in.

And then, in a quick, natural move, he flipped the gun and held it out to Gretchen, never once taking his eyes off Lachlan.

Martha let out a little sob.

Without fanfare, Gretchen took the weapon, and then shifted Elijah behind her, meeting Lachlan's eyes. "I didn't clear the cabin. You should check the back rooms to make sure there isn't anyone else there. It's proper procedure."

Rafael went to say something, and she shook her head.

A muscle tightened in Lachlan's jaw as his eyes darted between Elijah and Gretchen. "Don't put me in this position. Please."

"I'm not putting you anywhere," Gretchen murmured. "You're doing it to yourself."

His hands stretched against the outside of his thighs, and she could tell he wanted to reach for the cuffs, detain Elijah before anything else could happen. Before she could deliberately let Elijah escape.

"I didn't clear the cabin," she repeated. "There could be someone dangerous in one of the back rooms."

"Gretchen . . ."

"If your ethics get in the way of doing what's right, how worthwhile are those ethics in the first place?"

Lachlan stretched his hands out again, stared helplessly toward the hallway leading toward the back of the cabin. When he returned his attention to Gretchen, she saw her victory in his grim expression. He knew what she was planning. Knew that the second he took his eyes off them and left the room, she'd send Rafi and Elijah out to one of the cars to flee. He was going to let it happen anyway.

She was fairly certain the Lachlan Gibbs of four days ago would have died first.

Gretchen was almost proud of him.

"This will be on you," Lachlan said.

It was a warning, not a threat. He would have to report what happened; she would take responsibility for letting Elijah escape. That meant possibly not working with the BPD any longer.

She played it out in her head. She had a feeling that if she let Elijah get taken in, he would get some amount of jail time. Hayes hadn't been the man who'd been holding him, so there wouldn't be sympathy on that front. He wouldn't get life, but he wouldn't walk away. Marconi wouldn't want to work with Gretchen then anyway. And working for the BPD without Marconi or Shaughnessy didn't seem all that appealing anymore.

"I know."

He cleared his throat, looked down, a battle clearly raging inside him.

There was no way for Martha, Rafael, or Elijah to understand what was happening, but they must have sensed it was something important. Each of them was silent and still as they all watched Lachlan grapple with what to do.

When he finally looked up again, there was grief in his eyes, and she thought it might be for himself.

She nodded once, and he nodded in return.

Then he said, his voice thick with emotion, "I'll check the back."

CHAPTER
SIXTY-FIVE
LAUREN

Now

Lauren lifted her face to the sky as she stepped outside the prison gates. It was strange how quickly freedom became precious once it was taken away.

The expensive lawyer—whom Gretchen had absolutely hired for Lauren—had explained why Lauren was being released only hours after being processed. But Lauren hadn't fully absorbed it all at the time.

She *had* carefully kept the shock out of her expression as he'd explained that Martha Hayes had come forward to confess to killing both Owen Hayes and Garrett Adams. The men's horrific predilections would be splashed over the front pages of every tabloid and newspaper in the city tomorrow, and there would be few jurists who would want to see Martha sentenced to the full extent of the law.

The coroner had reluctantly admitted that the time of death was just wide enough that it was possible Martha could have killed Hayes and then taken her daughter out to a public dinner to secure herself an alibi.

With that bit of information, it made more sense that Lauren had walked into the house suspecting something was wrong, found a body, and checked his pulse.

Lauren would be suspended from the BPD for abusing her privileges, but apparently even that shark DA had made clear that this would be something handled within the department.

None of it had made sense, of course, and so she assumed it had all been Gretchen's doing. When the lawyer had asked if she had any questions, she'd kept quiet. She'd doubted he knew much more than she did, and at the end of the day, all she'd truly cared about was if Elijah had been arrested or not. Martha taking the fall instead seemed like poetic justice served, and she wasn't about to start pulling at any of those threads.

Lauren hadn't heard from either Lachlan or Gretchen, though she assumed one of them would be waiting for her in the parking lot.

Instead, Ashley Westwood was there, leaning against a shiny, black SUV.

"So we got the bastard, huh?" Lauren asked, and Ashley grinned, her cheeks pressing up against big Gucci sunglasses.

"And an extra one to boot," Ashley said, pulling Lauren into her arms like they were the best of friends. Her familiar perfume curled around Lauren just as tightly. There was an odd familiarity to the moment, déjà vu played out through the years, their lives intertwining in the most horrific ways. She didn't even know Ashley that well, but she would always associate her with this. A hug that was more than a hug.

They were the mothers of the boys in the basement. And they always would be.

"I'm sorry for telling Garrett," Ashley said, her voice breaking. "It will be the biggest regret of my life."

Lauren wanted to shrug, say all's well that ended well. But the choice had turned her son into a killer, and she would never be able to forgive that.

When she didn't rush to reassure Ashley, the woman's mouth slanted up in a facsimile of a smile. There was only sadness there, though.

She reached into her purse and extracted a folded leather pouch. "This is my apology."

"What is it?"

Ashley glanced around, but the lot was empty except for them. "Money, a new ID." She paused, took a breath. "The location of the hotel where Elijah and Rafi are waiting for you."

Lauren wanted to grab it all and run. She stared at Ashley instead. "What?"

"They're not under suspicion or anything right now, but . . ." Ashley gave her a significant look that Lauren didn't understand. She still felt about fifty steps behind everyone else. "I'm guessing you all don't want to stay in Boston after everything."

"They're not under suspicion?" Lauren asked, clinging to the reassurance like a lifeline despite the fact that she had, in theory, already known that.

"No," Ashley said, finally seeming to get Lauren's confusion. She proceeded to give her a whispered account of what had happened in the days after Lauren had been arrested. Lauren even smiled at Ashley's description of Lachlan as an *uptight prick*, and Gretchen as an *ice-cold genius*. Although Ashley hadn't witnessed what sounded like an impressive standoff, she'd been able to hear what was happening from the back room. "We thought the police would put out an APB on Elijah the second Lachlan could call in the escape. But he didn't." She paused, looked like she wanted to say more but didn't.

"What?" Marconi pressed.

"I think he might have lied on his report or something," she said slowly, like even she wasn't sure. "To protect Elijah."

He must have if the cops hadn't immediately thrown out a net to catch Elijah. It just didn't sound like something Lachlan Gibbs would do. She wondered if Gretchen had talked him into thinking it was the *right* moral choice. "But then . . . we don't need to run if Lachlan didn't report that Elijah killed Hayes. Why the IDs? The money?"

"Reporters got wind of the story—they're swarming everywhere," Ashley said. "They're calling it a real-life version of that movie *The Room.*"

Lauren grimaced not only at the idea of the spotlight but at the very real reminder that Elijah had been raised by a serial killer for more than half of his life. The road ahead was going to be anything but easy.

Ashley winced right back and continued. "And . . . to be honest, I don't think Rafi wanted to rely on Lachlan's goodwill, if that's what it was. Right now, the cops are so distracted, Elijah's probably low on their list. Eventually they'll hunt him down, to talk to him at the very least. Rafi didn't want to risk anything coming out if they interview him, so he and Elijah got the hell out of Dodge. Or halfway out. They're waiting for you."

After everything they'd all been through, Lauren agreed it was the right call to leave Boston. Maybe they could come back one day, but the city had never been home to Rafi or Elijah anyway.

It hadn't ever been home to Lauren, either, if she was honest.

There was no decision to be made here. Lauren took the leather pouch.

It was lighter than she'd expected. "Rafi and Elijah have theirs already?"

"Yeah, they had their go bags packed," Ashley said. "A few hours later and your friend might have missed us completely."

Lauren stared at her as she realized something. "You had a go bag, too, didn't you?"

"Rafi's my only family," Ashley said with a sad shrug. "But I was just borrowing him."

"No." Lauren reached out, grabbed Ashley's hand. "Not from me, if that's what you mean."

"He loved you," Ashley pointed out.

"You know that's not how it works," Lauren said. "We weren't right for each other. This isn't going to be an eighties family sitcom reunion here."

"I know," Ashley said, though she didn't sound certain. "But . . . it should be you. Because of Elijah. Maybe one day you all will come back to Vermont. Once this all dies down."

Neither of them believed that. Lauren trusted Lachlan's word more than Rafi did, but even she could admit it wouldn't be safe to hang around, waiting for someone to remember something suspicious about Elijah, or for Martha to let what really happened slip. The best option was to put a few thousand miles in between her son and anyone who might know too much about him.

It made Lauren wonder if it really was her presence that kept Ashley from joining them. Lauren thought about the way she'd felt chained to Montpelier when she'd believed Elijah had been buried there. Ashley said Rafi was her only family, but that wasn't true.

She almost didn't want to ask, but had to. "Did they identify Joshua?"

Ashley nodded, her eyes hidden behind those sunglasses. "Do you think . . ."

Lauren nudged Ashley's shin with the toe of her boot. "What?"

"Do you think you'll ever forgive yourself?"

It was a loaded question. As a detective, Lauren knew there was nothing to forgive. It hadn't been her fault Elijah had been kidnapped; that had been on Garrett. But as a human, it was harder to internalize that fact.

"I think . . . I'm going to try," Lauren said, finally.

Ashley hugged her once more, their lives intertwining this one last time. "Me too."

———

It was a risk stopping by Lachlan's place. Lauren did it anyway.

He opened the door after one knock, stared at her, and then stepped back, inviting her in.

"I won't stay long," she promised. She wasn't even sure why she was here.

"I'm glad you came," he said, and she heard the sincerity there.

She glanced at the time. "Shouldn't you be at work?"

It was why she had shown up when she had. Then she could have told herself she'd tried to say goodbye without actually doing it.

"Ah." He ran a hand over his head in a familiar gesture. "Nah."

Lauren eyed him. "You quit," she guessed.

He laughed a little, sheepish. "Don't really have the high ground to stand on anymore."

"Because you covered for Elijah."

Lachlan didn't admit it, but his silence was enough. She thought about thanking him, but she doubted he'd done it for her, and the gratitude would just make him uncomfortable.

"You gotta keep watch on him, Laur," he said. And there was the Lachlan she knew. "I'm trusting you."

She fought down the urge to lash out. What he said was true, after all. Elijah would need help. And he would need watching. There was no way he'd emerged psychologically whole after his ordeal. "Prison would have broken him fully."

"And the monster would have won," Lachlan murmured, and she tilted her head in question. He shook his. "Something Gretchen said."

"Hey, look, you guys worked together and didn't kill each other." Lauren punched him lightly on the shoulder, trying to shift the heavy mood.

"I can see how she grows on you."

"Like fungus," Lauren said.

"Toxic fungus," Lachlan joked back. It was weak humor, but it cut some of the awkward tension between them.

She shoved her hands in the pockets of her jacket, shuffling. "I'm sorry this led to . . ."

"Nah," he said. "I thought I could fix stuff from the inside. But I think one of the few good things I've done in my whole career was let Elijah walk away."

"You did more than that," Lauren argued, then she hunched her shoulders. "But I'm glad you're getting out, too."

His eyes narrowed at that. "I shouldn't ask you where you're headed, huh?"

"You're not morally obligated to report it anymore," Lauren teased. "Probably for the best you don't, though."

He nodded. "I'm sorry I didn't believe you were innocent."

Lauren hadn't been certain which way he'd fallen. "You didn't have to admit that."

Lachlan laughed. "If you think that, maybe Gretchen was right."

"She'd love to hear you say that," Lauren said. "About what?"

"We didn't know each other all that well."

"Maybe not," Lauren admitted. "You would have known that if I had been the killer, I would never have gotten caught."

"That's what Gretchen said."

Lauren grinned. At that, she hadn't had to guess. "I know."

———

Lauren debated the last stop. Probably because it would be the hardest.

She stood outside the pizza place for five minutes, watching through the window.

They didn't say goodbye—they weren't like that. Gretchen wouldn't want her gratitude, either, though it sounded like Lauren owed it to her.

Someone bumped into her shoulder, shook her out of her thoughts.

Lauren stared at the door for another long moment.

And then she turned and walked away.

CHAPTER
SIXTY-SIX

GRETCHEN

Now

Gretchen wasn't waiting.

After every successful investigation, she treated herself to a slice of the greasy pizza and hoppy beer at her favorite hole-in-the-wall. If it was the place she'd known Marconi would look for her first, then that was just a bonus.

But Gretchen White didn't have expectations when it came to other people. She would eat her slice and then leave.

Except when she finished, she ordered another beer.

Marconi had been set to be released at 11:00 a.m. Cormac Byrne had called her personally to tell her that. As if he expected her to thank him. She deleted his number after she'd hung up.

She glanced at the time.

It was 2:00 p.m. now.

The bell above the door jangled, and Gretchen's eyes snapped up.

It was just a young college student, all flailing limbs and messy hair. "Anything else for ya?" the waitress asked.

But Gretchen had caught movement out the window. A familiar jacket, the stubby end of a ponytail.

The person walking away.

Gretchen swallowed and shook her head.

She pulled out a hundred-dollar bill, dropping it on the table.

The waitress was pure Boston and too cynical to do more than raise both brows and then quickly pocket the money.

Gretchen wasn't disappointed. She never handed out knives because that just led to having your belly slit open.

She stepped out onto the sidewalk, shrugging into her coat as she did. She tipped her face up to the sky, and remembered that date from less than a week ago. It felt like years since she'd tried chasing normal.

What would she do now?

Lachlan had surprised her in his report. While he definitely had laid the blame at her feet for letting two witnesses get away, he never actually put down on paper that he suspected Elijah of killing Hayes. That meant her censure would be less severe. Maybe she'd get the cold shoulder from the department for a month or two, but they'd come crawling back to her the second they had a crime that dealt with her specialty.

But who would she even work with? Lachlan was out. The news had surprised her and hadn't. He wasn't the type who could live with himself when he thought he'd had a lapse in morals. It was ridiculous of him to have been wasting himself on the force anyway, though. She'd practically done him a favor.

Shaughnessy was dead; Marconi was certainly going to chase after Elijah, wherever he landed. Rafael had alluded to new identities as she'd shuffled them into the rental SUV she'd driven to the cabin. But they probably wouldn't even need them because of Lachlan.

The darkness within her started to whisper. Why chase normalcy when there were so many fun things out there she had yet to try?

What was stopping her now? Not a career, not a family, not anyone to disappoint.

There would be no Bambi eyes watching her with expectation.

A sour taste sat in her mouth, but she ignored it.

This was what she'd always wanted.

"Excuse me."

Gretchen nearly snarled at the interruption only to be met with an elderly man in a pageboy hat. He held out a slip of paper to Gretchen.

"A nice young woman asked me to give this to the lady with white-blonde hair and a grumpy face," he said, with the patient amusement of the very old. "She said you might yell a bit first."

"She was wrong," Gretchen said as sweetly as possible, snatching the paper out of his hand. She jerked her head toward the pizza place. "Go get a slice on me. Tell them Gretchen sent you."

"Don't mind if I do," the man said and tipped his hat.

Gretchen took a breath and then unfolded the message.

On it was a number. A burner phone, if Gretchen had to guess. Beneath it, in Marconi's recognizable scrawl:

In case Boston gets boring.

ACKNOWLEDGMENTS

It takes a village to put out a novel, and I am so thankful for mine.

So, so many thanks to the brilliant and wonderful Megha Parekh, who is such a champion for morally complex badass women. I am so grateful for all the thought and care you've invested into my work over the years, and the way you trust me with my wild ideas.

To the rest of the team at Thomas & Mercer, I can't even begin to convey my gratitude at getting to work with so many talented and passionate people. I always brag about how amazing the team is—from the editors to the proofreaders to the cover designers and marketing gurus who get the books in front of the readers. Thank you so much.

To agent extraordinaire Abby Saul, who can essentially live in the acknowledgments of all my books. I am forever grateful to have you in my corner in ways that could never be summed up in a few sentences.

To my family and friends, who are the most supportive people on the planet. I love you.

And to my readers, please know that I count you as my village as well. The trust you put in me each time you start one of my books is something that I cherish. Thank you for being here, for letting me tell you stories. It's such an honor.

ABOUT THE AUTHOR

Photo © 2019

Brianna Labuskes is the Amazon Charts and *Washington Post* bestselling author of the psychological suspense novels *What Can't Be Seen*, *A Familiar Sight*, *Her Final Words*, *Black Rock Bay*, *Girls of Glass*, and *It Ends with Her*. She was born in Harrisburg, Pennsylvania, and graduated from Penn State University with a degree in journalism. For the past eight years, she has worked as an editor at both small-town papers and national media organizations such as Politico and Kaiser Health News, covering politics and policy. Brianna lives in Washington, DC, and enjoys traveling, hiking, kayaking, and exploring the city's best brunch options. Visit her at www.briannalabuskes.com.